THE CHOSEN ONE

THE
CHOSEN ONE

SAM BOURNE

ISIS

LARGE PRINT

Oxford

First published in Great Britain 2010
by
Harper
an imprint of HarperCollinsPublishers

Published in Large Print 2010 by ISIS Publishing Ltd.,
7 Centremead, Osney Mead, Oxford OX2 0ES
by arrangement with
HarperCollinsPublishers

British Library Cataloguing in Publication Data
Bourne, Sam, 1967–
   The chosen one.
   1. Presidents - - United States - - Fiction.
   2. Murder - - Investigation - - Washington (D.C.)
   - - Fiction.
   3. Women political consultants - - Washington
   (D.C.) - - Fiction.
   4. Conspiracies - - Fiction.
   5. Suspense fiction.
   6. Large type books.
   I. Title
   823.9'2–dc22

       ISBN 978–0–7531–8232–1 (hb)
       ISBN 978–0–7531–8233–8 (pb)

Printed and bound in Great Britain by
T. J. International Ltd., Padstow, Cornwall

For Fiona, my sister — and a true heroine

PROLOGUE

New Orleans, March 21, 23.35
He didn't choose her, she chose him. At least that's how it seemed. Though maybe that was part of her skill, the performer's art.

He hadn't stared at her, hadn't fixed her with that steady gaze he knew freaked the girls out. He didn't want to make anyone uneasy. So he pretended to be like those out-of-town guys, cool and unbothered. On a business trip, only visiting a strip club so they could say they had tasted the true New Orleans experience — letting their hair down, sampling a little sin. The city didn't mind those guys. Hell, New Orleans had made a living out of them: sleaze tourism, nicely packaged.

So he did his best to act uninterested, even glancing down at his BlackBerry, only occasionally stealing a look at the stage. Not that that was the right word. Too big. The "performing area" was little more than a jetty pushed out among the low-lit tables, a few square feet with barely enough room for a girl to peel off her bikini top, jiggle the silicone on her chest, bend over and show her g-stringed ass before blowing a few kisses to the men who had slotted a twenty under her garter belt.

1

The thrill of these places should have faded long ago, but somehow he kept coming back: this spot had been a fixture, every Wednesday night, for years. It wasn't really about the sex. It was the dark he liked, the anonymity. He would get the odd greeting and smile of recognition from behind the bar, but that was it. Men here avoided one another's gaze: if your eyes met, it was in your mutual interest to look away.

Still, he took no chances. He didn't want any strangers recognizing him, not with everything that had happened. He didn't want to chat. He needed to think.

Be calm, he told himself. Things are on track. He had dropped the bait and they had picked it up. So what if there was no word yet? He should give it time.

The amber pool of bourbon at the bottom of his glass was inviting. He stared into it, raised it to his lips and knocked it back in one sharp swallow. It burned.

He glanced back to the stage. A new girl, one he'd not seen before. Her hair was longer, her skin somehow not quite as plucked and smooth as the others'. Her breasts looked real.

He was guarding himself against giving her the Stare but it was too late. She was looking directly at him. And not the blank, dosed-up gaze of the girls who called themselves "Savannah" and "Mystery" either. She was seeing him, seeing right through to him. Had she recognized him, perhaps from the TV?

He fiddled with the BlackBerry again, the device slick from the moisture in his palm. He fought the urge to look up, only to surrender a few seconds later. When he did, she was still holding him in that steady gaze.

Not the fake leer perfected by the girls who know how to kid a bald, drunk guy that he's hot. This was something more genuine; friendly, almost.

Her spot was over and she was gone, ending with the obligatory shake of the rear. Even that seemed aimed in his direction.

To his relief, the machine vibrated in his hand, forcing him to be busy with something else. A new message. He scanned the first line. Another media request. Not what he was waiting for. He scrolled through the rest of the day's email, pretending to read.

"You know what they say: all work and no play —"

"Makes Jack a dull boy."

He interrupted her even before he had seen her face. She had pulled up a chair at the small, dark-wood table he had made his own. Even though he had never heard her speak, he knew from the first syllable that it was her.

"You don't look like a dull boy."

"And you don't look like a stripper."

"Oh, really? You don't think I've got the goods for —"

"I wasn't saying that. I was saying —"

She placed her hand on his, to silence him. The warmth he had seen in her eyes on stage was still there. Her hair hung loose, falling onto her shoulders. She could have been no more than twenty-five — nearly half his age — and yet she exuded a strange . . . what was it? Maturity. Or something like that, something you rarely saw in this sort of place. Alongside him, his hands clammy, stabbing at his email, she was a statue of calm. He signalled to the waitress to bring them a drink.

Then, in an accent that was not Southern, perhaps Midwest, maybe California: "So what kind of work do you do?"

The question brought a warm wave of relief. It meant she didn't recognize him. He felt the muscles in his back relax. "I'm kind of a consultant. I advise —"

"You know what," she said, her hand still on his, her eyes searching for the door. "It's too stuffy in here. Let's walk."

He said nothing as she led him out onto Claiborne Avenue, the traffic still heavy even at this late hour. He wondered if she could feel, just through his hand, that his pulse was racing.

Finally, they turned down a side street. It was unlit. She walked a few yards, turning left into an alley. It ran along the back of a bar, one of the few around here that had survived Katrina. He could hear a party inside, the sound of a toast delivered through a muffled loudspeaker.

She stopped and turned to face him, stretching up on her tiptoes to whisper into his ear. "I like it outside."

Long before he had absorbed and understood her words, the blood was surging towards his groin. The sensation of her voice, her breath in his ear, flooded him with desire.

He pressed her hard against the wall, reaching immediately for her skirt. She pushed her mouth against his, kissing him enthusiastically. Her teeth bit into his lower lip.

4

The skirt was up and he began working at his belt. She pulled away from his mouth, offering him her neck instead. His tongue fell on it instantly, taking in the scent of her for the first time. It was familiar — and intoxicating.

Her hands ignored his unbuckled belt and moved upward, heading for his face. She was touching him, her fingers gentle. They moved down to his neck and suddenly pressed on it hard.

"You like it rough," he murmured.

"Oh yes," she said, the index- and forefingers of her right hand now firmly on his windpipe.

He wanted to pull down her underwear, but she suddenly seemed to be further away from him, her crotch no longer tight against his. He heard himself rasping.

He tried to prise her fingers off his throat, but there was no budging them. She was remarkably strong.

"Look, I can't breathe —" he gasped. He caught a glimpse of her eyes, two bright beads in the night. No warmth now.

"I know," she said, her left hand joining her right in fully circling his throat.

There was no coughing or spluttering, just a slow wilting in her hands, as she choked the life out of him. He fell quietly, any noise drowned out by the drunken chorus of *Happy Birthday* coming from the bar.

She straightened her skirt, reached down to remove the BlackBerry from the man's jacket pocket, and headed off into the night, her scent still lingering in the Louisiana air.

CHAPTER
ONE

The previous day
Washington, DC, Monday March 20, 07.21
"Bollocks, bollocks, bollocks. Crap and bollocks."

First she'd been thinking it, now she was saying it out loud, the words carried off in the onrush of wind.

Maggie Costello twisted her wrist to get another look at her watch, the fifth time in three minutes. No getting away from it. 7.21a.m.: she was going to be late. But that was OK. It was only a one-to-one meeting with the White House Chief-of-bloody-Staff.

She pedalled furiously, feeling the strain in her calves and the heaving pressure on her lungs. No one had said cycling was going to be this hard. It was the cigarettes she blamed: she was fitter when she smoked.

So much for the fresh start. New job, new regime, she had told herself. Healthy eating; more exercise; quit the fags; no more late nights. If there was a plus to finding herself suddenly single, it was surely that she could now start each morning bright and early. And not just normal-human-being early, which 7.21a.m. certainly counted as in Maggie's book. No, she would start her day Washington early, so that a meeting at 7.30a.m. would not feel like bumping into someone in the middle of the night. To the new Maggie, 7.30 would feel like an ordinary moment in the heart of the working day.

That had been the plan at any rate. Maybe it was because she had been born and raised in Dublin, only coming to America as an adult, that she didn't fit. Whatever the explanation, Maggie was fast coming to the conclusion that she was innately out-of-sync with all these bright, shiny Washingtonians, with their polished shoes and impeccable self-discipline, because no matter how hard she tried to embrace the DC lifestyle, getting up at the crack of dawn still felt like cruel and unusual punishment.

So here she was, late again, whistling down Connecticut Avenue at a lethal speed, willing Dupont Circle to come into view but knowing that, even when it did, she would still be at least three to five minutes away from the White House and that was before she had chained up the bike, cleared security by putting her bag and BlackBerry onto the conveyor belt that fed the giant scanning machine, dashed into the ladies' bathroom, torn off her T-shirt and cycle-clips, swabbed her armpits, used the hand-dryer to restyle her hair, wrestled her still-sweating body into her much-loathed regulation Washington uniform, a barely more feminine version of a man's suit and shirt — and somehow altered her appearance from under-slept scarecrow to member of the National Security Council and trusted Foreign Policy Advisor to the President of the United States.

It was 7.37a.m. by the time she stood, panting and still red-faced, before Patricia, secretary to Magnus Longley. She had been with Longley for more than forty years, they said; rumour was, he had scooped her out of the typing pool on his very first day of work at his father's law firm. The pair of them had been around forever, he a monument in permanent Washington, she his stone base.

It had been Patricia who had summoned Maggie to this meeting, in a telephone message that had woken her blearily at 6.29a.m., only for her to fall back into a fatal doze that lasted another twenty-five minutes.

"He's waiting for you," Patricia said, peering above her glasses — attached by a string around her neck — just long enough to convey a sharp look of disapproval, for her lateness, of course; but for other more important reasons, too. That cold, lizard's blink of a glance had taken in Maggie's appearance from top to toe and found it sadly wanting. Maggie looked down and realized with some horror that her trousers, ironed so carefully last night in preparation for the next day but thrown on in haste this morning, were now unacceptably creased and marked at the ankles by a line of cycle grease. And then there was her autumn-red hair which, in a gesture of personal rebellion, she kept long and tousled in a town where women tended to keep it short and businesslike. Patricia's expression conveyed more clearly than any words that no self-respecting young lady would have gone to work dressed like that in her day. And in the White House, too!

Maggie passed her hand through her hair one more time, in a futile bid to impose some order, and stepped inside.

Magnus Longley was a veteran Mr Fix-it who had served either in the House, Senate or the White House since the Carter era. He was the requisite greybeard appointed to balance out — and allay any anxieties over — the President's youth and lack of Washington experience. "He knows where the bodies are buried," was what everyone said about him. "And he knows how to bury any new ones."

His thin, aged head was down when she came in, poring over a neatly-squared pile of papers, a pen in his hand. He scrawled a comment in the margin before looking up, revealing a face whose features remained always neat and impassive. He still had all his hair which, now white, was combed perfectly into a parting.

"Mr Longley," Maggie said, extending a hand. "I'm sorry I'm late, I was —"

"So you think the Secretary of Defense is an asshole, is that right, Miss Costello?"

Maggie, parched already from the breakneck cycle ride, felt her throat run dry. Her hand, still outstretched and ignored, came down and reached shakily for the back of the chair facing Longley's desk.

"Shall I repeat my question?" The voice was deep and strong, surprising from a man of his age, the accent creaking with old money and Park Avenue breeding. Longley was a New York aristocrat; his father had been a pal of FDR's. He spoke the way Americans talked in

1940s movies, an accent halfway across the Atlantic to England.

"I heard the question. But I don't understand it. I never called the —"

"No time for games, Miss Costello. Not in this office, not in this building. And no time for such infantile behaviour as *this* —" the word punctuated with a loud flick of the fingers against a single sheet of paper.

Maggie tried to peer at the upside-down paper, suddenly full of dread. "What is that?"

"It is an email you wrote to one of your colleagues at the State Department."

Slowly a memory began to form. Two nights ago, she had worked late. She had written to Rob, over on the South Asia desk at State. He was one of the few familiar faces around; like her a veteran of pressure groups, aid organizations and eventually UN peace missions in horrible, forgotten corners of the world.

"Shall I read the relevant paragraph, so that we're clear?"

Maggie nodded, the recollection growing ever less hazy.

Longley cleared his throat, theatrically. "'Intel on AfPak suggests close collaboration with Islamabad', et cetera, et cetera, 'none of which seems to be getting through to the assholes at the Pentagon' —"

She had a nasty inkling of what was coming . . .

"'— especially the chief asshole, Dr Anthony Asshole himself'." He placed the paper back on the desk and looked up at her, his gaze icy.

Now she remembered it all. Maggie's heart fell with a sudden swoop into the pit of her stomach.

"As you can imagine, the Defense Secretary is not too happy to be described in these terms by an official of the White House."

"But how on earth did he —"

"Because —" Magnus Longley leaned forward and across his desk, enabling Maggie to see the first signs of liver spots on his cheeks. "Because, Miss Costello, your friend at State is not quite as brilliant as you evidently think he is. He forwarded your proposal regarding intelligence co-operation with Pakistan to colleagues at the Pentagon. But he forgot to use the most important button on these goddamned machines." He gestured vaguely in the direction of his desktop computer, whose screen, Maggie noticed, was dark and very possibly coated with dust. "The delete key."

"No." The horrified response came out as a whisper.

"Oh yes. The entire thread of messages." He handed her the print-out.

She took one look, noting the list of senior Pentagon officials who had been cc'd at the top of the email — including the handpicked, ultra-loyal advisors to the Defense Secretary — and felt the blood drain from her face. She stared down at the paper again, willing it to be untrue. But there it was in black-and-white: *asshole.* How on earth could Rob have made such an elementary mistake? How could she?

"Any case for the defence you'd like to make?"

"Are you certain he knows?" she asked feebly.

He gave her the first movement of a sneer.

12

"Maybe his aides didn't pass it on, maybe it hasn't reached him." She could hear the desperation in her own voice.

Longley raised his eyebrows, as if to ask if she really wanted to pursue this line of argument. "He's the one who raised it with me. Personally, this morning. He wants you gone immediately."

"It was just one word in one email. For Christ's sake —"

"Don't take that tone with me, young lady."

"It's just office banter. It was one remark —"

"Do you even read the newspapers, Miss Costello? Or perhaps you are more of a *blog* reader?" He said the word as if he had just caught a whiff of a soiled dishcloth. "Twitter maybe?"

Maggie decided this was part of Longley's shtick, playing the old fart: he couldn't be as out of touch as he liked to pretend, not when he had stayed on top in Washington for so long. She remembered the Style section interview she had read, in which Longley had claimed the last time he had stepped inside a movie theatre was to see Deborah Kerr and Burt Lancaster in *From Here to Eternity*. "Have I missed much since then?" he had asked languidly.

Now he was sitting back in his chair, relaxed, "Because you may have picked up that our Defense Secretary is — how can we put this? — not one of the President's obvious loyalists."

"Of course I know that. Adams ran against him for the nomination."

"You *are* up-to-date. Yes. He may even run against him again."

"A primary challenge?"

"Not inconceivable. The President has assembled what is admiringly referred to as 'a team of rivals'. But as Lincoln understood, it may be a team, but they're still rivals."

"So he —"

"So he's not going to let this go. Dr Adams wants to flex his muscles, show that his reach extends beyond the Pentagon."

"Which means he wants me out."

The Chief of Staff stood up. Maggie wasn't sure if the creak she heard was the chair or Longley's knees.

"That's where we are. The final decision is not Dr Adams's, of course. It rests in this building."

What the hell did that mean? *This building*. Did Longley mean he would decide — or that whether Maggie kept her job or not would be settled by the President himself?

Longley had pulled his shoulders back, so that he could deliver his final remarks. "Miss Costello, I fear you forgot Longley's First Rule of Politics. Don't write so much as a note to the milkman in this town that you wouldn't mind seeing on the front page of the *Washington Post*. Above the fold."

"You think Adams would leak it."

"Wouldn't you? Revive stories about the Baker-Adams rift, implicitly putting himself on a par with the President? No thank you. The reason he's inside the

14

tent is so that he can piss out, not all over the Oval Office carpet."

"Does the President know about this?"

"You seem to have forgotten that Stephen Baker is the President of the United States of America. He is not a *human resources* manager." His mouth seemed to recoil from the phrase, as if uttering such an absurd, new-fangled term might stain his lips. "I don't want to be unkind, Miss Costello. But there are hundreds of people who work for the President. You are not of a rank at which your employment would be of concern to him. Unless there is a reason you think otherwise, in which case perhaps you would be so good as to disclose that to me."

So that meant the final decision rested with Longley. She was finished. Maggie balled her hands into fists as two instincts warred inside her: fight and flight. She certainly wanted to hit this sanctimonious prick, who appeared to be enjoying the situation far too much; at the same time she wanted to run home and throw herself under the duvet. Doing her best to control herself, she bit her lower lip, hard enough to get the zinc taste of blood.

Longley glanced casually at his watch, a vintage Patek Philippe, elegant, unfussy; unashamedly analog. "I have someone waiting for me, Miss Costello. No doubt we will speak again soon." She was dismissed.

Maggie passed Patricia on the way out who, she noticed, did not so much as look up, let alone make eye contact. No doubt a gesture of discretion she had learned in many long years of serving Magnus Longley, who had probably sacked enough people over the years to fill RFK Stadium.

She waited till she was in her own rabbit-hutch of an office, an eighth the square footage of the Chief of Staff's, before she would even breathe out properly.

Once she was sure the door was closed, she used her forearm to sweep everything — two tottering piles of classified documents, magazines, paper bags from the deli, chewed pens and other assorted detritus — off her desk and onto the floor. The gesture made her feel good for about three-fifths of a second. She fell into her chair.

Was this going to be the story of this year, having a magical opportunity in her hands, only to screw it up royally? Forget this year, was this going to be the story of her bloody life? And all for the sake of one supremely stupid moment of unguarded honesty. Not that Adams wasn't an asshole: he was, First Class. But it was absurdly naïve to put it in an email. How old was she? Nearly forty, for God's sake. When would she learn? For a woman who'd made her name as a skilled diplomat, a peace negotiator for Christ's sake — with all the sensitivity, discretion and sureness of touch that required — she really was an idiot. *Eejit*, she could almost hear her sister Liz teasing her in fake bog-Irish.

It wasn't as if she hadn't had a chance. When she had got back from Jerusalem — hailed as the woman who had at last made a breakthrough in the Middle East peace process — she was, everyone told her, able to write her own ticket. She had been swamped with job

16

offers, every think-tank and university had wanted her name on their headed notepaper. She could teach international relations at Harvard or write editorials in Foreign Affairs. There had even been a whisper from ABC News that, with the right training — and a suitable wardrobe — she might have the makings of on-air "talent". One executive had sent a handwritten note: "I truly believe you are the woman to make international relations sexy."

But it was none of this that had made her return to the States nearly three years ago so thrilling. Instead, and much to her amazement, things had actually worked out with Uri. She had wondered if the relationship would prove to be little more than a glorified holiday romance: they had, after all, come together during the strangest and most intense week in Jerusalem and he, out of his mind with grief after both his parents had died within days of each other, had hardly been thinking straight. She had learned long ago to be suspicious of relationships hatched on the road, especially those lent glamour and significance by the constant presence of danger and proximity of death. Love among the bombs felt delicious at the time, but it rarely lasted.

And yet when Uri had invited her to share his apartment in New York she hadn't said no. True, she couldn't quite bring herself to sign on the dotted line marked "official cohabitation": she had kept her apartment in Washington, planning to divide her time between the two places. But when it came to it, both she and Uri simply found that they wanted to spend most nights in the same city — and in the same bed.

There had seemed to be no reason for it ever to stop. But somehow, just a few weeks ago, she had found herself sitting on the steps of the Lincoln Memorial, looking out at a gleaming Washington, DC — scrubbed up and ready for the inauguration of a new president — with Uri at her side, his voice cracking, saying that they had run out of road. That he still loved her, but that this was no longer working. She had made her choice, he said. She had voted with her feet, deciding that her work mattered above all else: "The bottom line, Maggie, is that you care about Stephen Baker more than you care about me. Or about us."

And, even though the tears were falling down her cheeks, she hadn't been able to argue. What could she say? He was right: she had dedicated the last year not to making a life with him, but to helping Stephen Baker become the most powerful man in the world. That he had won the presidency — against all the odds — felt almost miraculous. She had been so swept up in the euphoria of that triumph that she had forgotten to pay attention to her own life. Somewhere, in the back of her mind, she had thought that once things got back to normal, she would concentrate on making her relationship with Uri work; she would patch things up. But suddenly it was too late: he'd made his decision and there had been nothing she could say.

So now here she was, yet again, another relationship officially screwed up and on the verge of losing the very job that had sabotaged it. This was her life all over. Give

Maggie Costello a shot at happiness or success and she'll fuck up both. She wanted to howl like a banshee, to expel all her frustration and misery: but even in her despair she knew she wouldn't do it. Washington was the buttoned-down town. No outward expressions of emotion wanted here. That was one of the reasons she was beginning to hate it, from the depths of her Irish soul. So instead, she put her head in her hands and muttered to herself, again and again: *Idiot. Idiot. Idiot.*

This bout of self-loathing was interrupted by a vibration somewhere near her thigh. She dug out her cellphone. Where the number should have appeared it just said: *Restricted.*

A voice she did not recognize spoke without saying hello. "Is this Maggie Costello?"

"Yes."

"Please come to the Residence right away. He wants to speak to you."

Confused, Maggie replied, "Who wants to speak to me?"

"The President."

CHAPTER
TWO

Washington, DC, Monday March 20, 08.07
There was no time to visit the bathroom: she had been
summoned to see him "right away". But there was no
way in the world she could go to the Residence looking
like this. Maggie swung open the door to the ladies',
praying she would run into no one that she would have
to speak to.

Shit.

Tara MacDonald, Director of Communications,
African-American mother of four and undisputed
matriarch, first of the Baker campaign and now of the
Baker White House — coiffed and confident in her
midlife prime, coming out of the stalls and checking
her make-up.

"Hi there, Maggie, how you doing, sweetheart?"

Maggie froze, reluctant to take up her position in
front of the vanity mirror. Lamely, she ducked her head
and began to wash her hands.

"I'm OK."

"You seem a little, I don't know, agitated."

Maggie turned to MacDonald with a harried attempt
at a smile. "I've just been summoned. To the Residence.

I thought I'd better . . ." she nodded towards the mirror, ". . . you know, make myself presentable."

The instant change in Tara's expression — as if her smile muscles had been suddenly severed — told Maggie she'd made a mistake.

The older woman pursed her lips. "That right? The Residence. That's quite an honour."

"I'm sure it's nothing important. Probably wants some input ahead of the UN speech."

"Sweetheart, he has a National Security Advisor for that." Tara MacDonald went back to the mirror, but Maggie could see she was not done. "Well, ain't you the insider. And there I was thinking you were just an NSC staffer."

Maggie ignored the remark, staring at the mirror, aware that she had already been here a minute — which was a minute longer than she should have been. Besides, she had heard this kind of barb before.

The face that stared back at her looked pale and strained: no surprise, really, given the excruciating little scene that had just been played out in the Chief of Staff's office. In the panicked dash to get here this morning she'd forgone her usual lick of paint: there had simply been no time to apply concealer to the dark shadows beneath her eyes or the tinted moisturizer that did its best to conceal the tiny crows' feet that now perched at the corners of her eyes along with the cigarette-lines around her mouth. Just a touch of mascara and a sweep of nude lipstick was all she'd managed, and it showed. Not much evidence at the moment of what the gossip column of the *City Paper* had recently referred to as "the delectable Maggie Costello".

After yet another attempt to restore swift order to her hair, she headed off — walking as fast as she could without triggering a security alert — through the press briefing room and then outside along the colonnade towards the White House Residence, home for little more than two months to Stephen Baker, wife Kimberley, their thirteen-year-old daughter Katie and eight-year-old son, Josh.

The Secret Service agents ushered her through without so much as a question, clearly expecting her. Through one set of doors, then another and suddenly she was in what looked like any other American household at ten past eight in the morning. There were cereal boxes on the table, school bags spilling over with gym kit on the floor, and childish chatter in the air. Except for the minor matter of armed officers posted outside the door and state-of-the-art, encrypted communications equipment in every room, it looked like a regular family home.

Stephen Baker was not at the table scouring *The New York Times* over his half-moon reading glasses as she was expecting. Instead he was standing in the middle of the kitchen, jacket off, with an apple in his hand. Standing opposite him, three yards away and staring intently, was his son Josh — clutching a baseball bat.

"OK," the President whispered. "You ready?"

The little boy nodded.

"Here it comes. Three, two, one." He tossed the apple, slowly and at just the right height for it to make contact with the little boy's bat.

Struck firmly, the fruit went flying past the President's hand and splattered into the wall behind him.

A voice came from the next room, raised to full volume. "Josh! What did I say about ball games inside?"

The President made a mock-worried expression for the benefit of his son and then, conspiratorially, put his finger to his lips. In full voice he called out, "All under control, my love," as he retrieved the apple from the floor and wiped the pulp from the wall. Then, catching the eye of the Secret Service agent who had witnessed the entire episode, he mouthed, "You too. Not a word."

Even here, without the trappings and grandeur of office, he was a striking man. Six foot three, with a full head of brown hair, he was always the first person in the room you noticed. He was lean, his features fine and sharp. But it was his eyes that grabbed you. They were a deep, penetrating green and — even when the rest of him was animated and quick — they seemed to operate at a slower pace, gazing levelly, never darting. During the TV debates, the camera seemed to seek them out, as if it were as mesmerized as the audience. When commentators wrote about Candidate Baker exuding calm and steadiness, Maggie was convinced it was not his answers or policy ideas they had in mind. It was his eyes.

And now they were looking towards her. "Hey Josh, look who's here. Your favourite Irish aunt."

"Hi Maggie."

"Hi Joshie. How's your new school?"

"S'OK. I play baseball, which is cool."

"That *is* cool." Maggie was beaming. Josh Baker was a contender for America's cutest boy and having first met him nearly two years ago she felt as if she had almost seen him grow up.

That first encounter had come on a summer Saturday in Iowa, at the State Fair in Des Moines. Stephen Baker had been there with his family — Josh, then aged six, kept nagging to ride on the bumper cars — as the candidate tried to endear himself to the ever-discerning, and crucial, people of Iowa. Baker was then the rank outsider in the Democratic field, the little-known governor of Washington State. His name recognition was zero, he had no national experience and carried no regional advantage: historically, Democrats liked governors from the South who might deliver a chunk of votes that would otherwise be hard to reach. Washington State? In a presidential primary, that counted as a disability.

Still, Rob — Maggie's old pal from her Africa days, who had ended up in the State Department and had just dealt the death-blow to her nascent career — had been insistent. "Just meet him," he had said. "You'll know right away."

Maggie had stonewalled, resisting, refusing to be swayed by the barrage of calls, emails and texts that followed. Maggie Costello? Working for a politician? The idea was ridiculous. She had ideals, for God's sake, and ideals had no place in the snakepit of modern

24

politics. The young Maggie Costello had had nothing but contempt for politicians. She'd seen what they and other power-seekers had done to godforsaken bits of Africa, the Balkans and the Middle East, first as an aid-worker, latterly as a behind-the-scenes diplomat. It sounded corny, but as far as she was concerned there was only one mission that mattered: trying to make the world a better place, especially for those on the sharp end of war, disease and poverty. The way she saw it, politicians tended, at best, to get in the way of that process; at worst to profit by others' disadvantage.

Besides, she'd argued to Rob, the election was more than a year away; Baker's candidacy was just a few months old and the Beltway wisdom had already written him off as an also-ran. They suspected he was running as a future vice president, trying to get himself noticed. The only poll she had seen gave him a score of "negligible", too small to measure. And anyway, what did she know about US presidential politics?

"It doesn't matter," Rob had insisted. "You know foreign policy. He's governor of Nowheresville: the closest he gets to foreign policy is having lunch at the International House of Pancakes. Just go, just meet him and you'll see what I mean. He's different: he's something special."

So, sighing inwardly, she had gone to the Iowa State Fair and watched Baker mingling with the hog-farmers, eventually crowning a giant pig the winner of the hotly-fought Big Boar Contest. "He's bigger than I am, he's better looking — why isn't *he* running for president?" Baker had said to delighted cheers. She waited before introducing herself. She wanted to see him in action.

It didn't take long to see he was a natural. His manner was easy, his interest in people shone through as genuine, not the synthetic sincerity of the blow-dried, bleached-teeth politicians usually deemed presidential material. Unlike most candidates, he knew there was a difference between listening and staying silent while you wait to speak again. He actually listened. And whatever quality it was that had won over her cynical friend, Rob, it seemed to be working on the usually wary folk of Des Moines — people who had grown sceptical of the procession of suitors who invaded their state every four years smiling brightly with their faces aimed towards the television cameras, making promises they never kept. Baker, on the other hand, had the crowd in his thrall: they watched him eagerly, mirroring his expressions, grinning when he grinned, reflecting back the warmth they felt from him. And unlike other candidates, who seemed to have been parachuted into such events from another planet, he genuinely seemed to be enjoying himself, making real human contact with the people around him, rather than using them as props for a photo opportunity.

Finally she stepped up to say hello.

"So you're the woman who brought peace to the Holy Land," he had said, wiping an oily hand on his apron as he paused from flipping chops on the outdoor grill beside the Iowa Pork Producers' tent. "It's a pleasure to meet you."

"Nearly," she had replied. "Nearly brought peace."

"Well, nearly's a hell of a lot further than anyone ever got before."

They snatched moments of conversation as he shook more hands, posed for camera-phone snaps or exchanged banter with a local reporter. He would break off — to admire a life-sized cow made entirely of butter or to have a bumper car ride with Josh — then pick up exactly where they had left off.

Eventually he asked her to hop in the car that would take them to his next event, an evening speech in Cedar Rapids. Kimberley and the kids would be in the back; she could ride with him up front. When she looked puzzled as to how there would be room, he smiled. "I have the most crucial job on the 'Baker for President' campaign: I'm the driver."

They talked for the entire two-hour journey, until the three Bakers in the back were fast asleep, the children's heads resting on their mother's shoulders. He listened as much as he talked. He wanted to know how she had started, asking her more about the work she had done as a volunteer in Africa, straight after graduation, than about the high-level shuttle diplomacy that had made her name in Jerusalem.

"You don't want to know this," she had said eventually, with an embarrassed wave of the hand.

"No, I really do. Here's why. You know who I'm going to be in this campaign? I'm going to be the hick. 'The logger's son from Aberdeen, Washington'."

"But that's one of your great strengths. You're the American Dream."

"Yeah, yeah. The folks like that. But I'm running against *Doctor* Anthony Adams, PhD of New York. I'm the boy from the sticks. I've got to convince Georgetown and *The New York Times* and the Council on Foreign Relations — all that crowd — that I'm not too provincial to be President."

"I thought you *wanted* to be the outsider: Mr Smith goes to Washington and all that."

"No, Maggie. I want to win."

Soon he was telling her how, once he'd got a scholarship to Harvard, he'd met people who spent the vacations in Paris or London or jetted off for weekends in the Caribbean. He, meanwhile, had to go back to Aberdeen and work shifts in the lumber yard or at the frozen fish processing plant: his father had emphysema and there was no other way to pay the bills.

"Eventually I got away. My first trip out of the country. And I went to Africa. Just like you."

He looked away from the road long enough for them to smile at each other.

"I was in Congo, Zaire as it was then. Jeez, I saw some terrible things. Just terrible. And it's still going on, if not there, then somewhere else. It's like they're taking turns: Rwanda, then Sierra Leone, then Darfur. The burning villages, the rapes, the children orphaned. Or worse." He glanced at her again. "I know you've seen some real horror yourself, Maggie."

She nodded.

"Well, it's a long time ago now." He paused for a long minute until she wondered if she was meant to say something. Then he spoke. "I believe I can win this thing, Maggie. And if I do, I want to do something that only an American president can do. I want to dedicate some of the enormous resources of this country to stopping all this killing."

She frowned.

"I'm not talking about sending our army to invade places. We tried that already. It didn't work out so well." Now it was her turn to smile. "We need to think of other ways to do it. That's why I need you." He let that sentence hang in the air while she stared at him in disbelief.

"Something tells me that you never forgot what you saw when you were twenty-one, Maggie. You never forgot it. It's what makes you work so hard, even now, all these years later. Am I right?"

Maggie looked out of the car window, picturing the position papers, conferences and endless meetings of which her life now consisted. Each day she felt she got further away from that angry twenty-one-year-old woman she had once been. But he was right. What fuelled her still was the fury she had felt then about all the violence and injustice — all the sorrow — in the world and the determination to do something about it. These days, her ideals seemed to have slipped so far into the distance, it was a struggle to glimpse them. But Stephen Baker had just reminded her that they were still there. She turned back to him and nodded.

"And that's how I am, too. I never forgot what I saw out there. And about eighteen months from now, I'm going to have a chance to do something about it.

Something big." He shifted the car down a gear. "Will you be with me, Maggie Costello?"

Now, nearly two years later, the President was reaching for a red plastic lunch box with one hand and opening the fridge with the other. "So what's it to be, junior? Apple or pear?"

"Can't I have candy?"

"No, young man, you cannot. Apple or pear?"

"Apple."

Stephen Baker wheeled around, an expression of deep seriousness on his face. "That's not so you can use it to play baseball, is it?"

The boy smiled. "No, Dad."

"Josh."

"I promise."

The President put the fruit into the box, clipped the top shut then placed it in his boy's hand. Then he bent to kiss his son on the top of his head. Maggie noticed that he shut his eyes as he did it, as if in a moment of grateful prayer. Or just to savour the smell of Josh's hair.

"OK, young man, scram."

Just then, Kimberley Baker came in, clutching a bag bulging with gym gear. Blonde and pretty as a peach in her college days, she was now usually described as "rounded" or, by the less kind, "plump". Magazines had obsessed about her weight when her husband first announced, the celebrity press zooming in on cellulite patches or a close-up of her rear end in an ill-advised trouser-suit. She had gone on daytime TV, told how she had gained weight when Katie was born and how she had tried multiple diets — "including all the nutty ones!" — to take the pounds off, but failed each time. Now, she said, she was comfortable with who she was and had decided to devote her energies to something more worthwhile than her waist size. The women in the audience had stood and cheered their approval, the host had hugged her and, within a day or two, she was declared a role model for female empowerment.

No less important, the political cognoscenti had decided that Kimberley Baker was an enormous asset to her husband. Female voters, in particular, had long been sceptical of Barbie doll, Stepford political wives; they liked what it said about Stephen Baker that his wife was a real, rather than artificially flawless, woman. That she was from Georgia, thereby connecting him with the vote-rich South, was an added bonus.

The Bakers could not say they were used to life in the White House, even if Tara MacDonald had already briefed *People* magazine that they were loving it. But Kimberley was certainly making an effort, chiefly for the children's sake. She had been worried about it from the start, anxious about an eight-year-old boy and a thirteen-year-old girl entering the most vulnerable time in their young lives in front of the gaze of the entire world. She remembered her own adolescence as one long stretch of blushing embarrassment: the notion of enduring that with a battery of cameras permanently in your face, scrutinizing your clothes and your hair and relaying those images around the globe, seemed truly unbearable. During the campaign, Stephen Baker always got a laugh when he joked that the only two people who truly wanted him to lose the election were his opponent and his wife.

Now Kimberley was fussing over both Josh and her shy, gauche, pretty teenage daughter, bundling them out of the door and into the hands of a casually-dressed, twenty-something woman who looked like an au pair. In fact, she was Zoe Galfano, one of a Secret Service detail whose sole duty was the protection of the Baker children.

"Maggie, something to drink? Coffee, hot tea, juice?"

"No thanks, Mr President. I'm fine." The phrase still snagged in her throat on its way out, but there was no getting around it. Everyone addressed him the same way, including his closest advisors and oldest friends, at least inside the White House. He had realized early on in the job that if he asked some people to call him by his first name, then those to whom he had not made the same offer would feel offended. He'd end up telling everyone, "Call me Stephen," and that was too casual. Better to keep it formal — and consistent.

He checked his watch. "I want to talk about Africa. I saw your paper. The killing's starting up again in Sudan; there's hundreds of thousands at risk in Darfur. I want you to work up an option."

Maggie's mind started revving hard. Magnus Longley was all but certain to take her job away, and yet here was the President offering the opportunity she had always dreamed of. The timing was perverse — and painful. But she felt a rush of the same optimism that had always got her into trouble — and also got things done. She took a deep breath. Perhaps, somehow, the whole Asshole Adams debacle would melt away.

"An option, for action?" she asked.

Baker was about to reply when a head popped around the doorframe. Stu Goldstein, Chief Counselor to the President: the man who had masterminded the election campaign, the man who occupied the most coveted real estate in the White House, the room next door to the Oval Office. The veteran of New York City political combat who stored a million and one facts about the politics of the United States in a phenomenal brain atop a wheezing, morbidly obese body.

"Mr President. We need to go across to the Roosevelt Room. You're signing VAW in two minutes." A small turn of the head. "Hi Maggie."

Baker took his jacket off the back of a kitchen chair and swung his arms into it. "Walk with me."

The instant he began moving she could see the Secret Service agents alter their posture, one whispering into his lapel, "Firefly is on the move." *Firefly*, the codename allocated to Baker by the Secret Service. The bloggers had been kept busy for a week, deconstructing the hidden meaning of that one.

"What kind of options are you after, Mr President?"

"I want something that will get the job done. There's an area the size of France that's become a killing field. No one can police that on the ground." As they walked, a pair of agents hovered close by, three paces behind.

"So you're talking about the air?"

He looked Maggie in the eye, fixing her in that cool, deep green. Now she understood.

"Are you suggesting we equip the African Union with US helicopters, Mr President? Enough of them to monitor the entire Darfur region from the sky?"

"It's like you always said, Maggie. The bad guys get away with it because they think no one's looking. And no one *is* looking."

She spoke slowly, thinking it through. "But if the AU had state-of-the-art Apaches, with full surveillance technology — night vision, infra-red, high-definition cameras — then we could see exactly who's doing what and when. There'd be no place to hide. We could see who was torching villages and killing civilians."

"Not 'we', Maggie. The African Union."

"And if people know they're being watched —"

"They behave."

Maggie could feel her heart racing. This was what anyone who had seen the massacres in Darfur had been praying for for years: the "eye in the sky" that might stop the killing. But the African Union had always lacked the wherewithal to make it happen: they didn't have the helicopters to monitor the ground below, and so the killers had been free to slaughter with impunity. Now here was the American President vowing to give them the tools the dead and dying had been crying out for. The spark of excitement was turning into a flame — until she remembered that she was about to lose her job.

"We only have very narrow majorities in the House and Senate, sir. Do you think —"

He smiled, the wide, bright smile of a confident man. "That's my job, Maggie. You give me some options."

By now they had arrived in the West Wing, standing in the corridor just outside the Roosevelt Room. An aide tried and failed to hand him a text, another stepped forward and reminded him who was in the front row and needed to be acknowledged. A third leaned forward and applied four precise dabs of face powder for the sake of the TV cameras. Someone asked if he was ready and he nodded.

The double doors were opened and an unseen tenor voice bellowed out the words that were simultaneously thrilling and wholly familiar.

"Ladies and gentlemen, the President of the United States!"

CHAPTER
THREE

Washington, DC, Monday March 20, 08.55

She watched as a packed Roosevelt Room rose to its feet, adults acting like schoolchildren, standing to attention at the sight of the man in charge. Everyone did that, wherever he went. She was almost used to it.

They were applauding him now, a room full of some of the most senior politicians in the country. Most were smiling wide, satisfied smiles. Sprinkled among them were a few faces she did not recognize. Women, though not dressed in the brightly-coloured, tailored suits favoured by their Washington sisters. It took Maggie a moment to work out who they were. Of course. The victims. An occasion like this was not complete without victims.

She tried to sneak in discreetly, in the tail of the entourage, but still she caught the eye of Tara MacDonald, which registered surprise and irritation, noting that Maggie had entered the room with the President.

Crisply, as the applause was still subsiding, Stephen Baker began directing those in the first row to gather behind him. Knowing the drill, they formed a semi-circle, standing as he sat at the desk. Maggie identified the key players: majority and minority leaders from the Senate, whips and committee chairs from the House, along with the two lead sponsors of the bill from both chambers. Closest to him was Bradford Williams, solemn and distinguished: the former congressman whose selection to be the first African-American vice president had been notched up as yet another one of Stephen Baker's historic breakthroughs.

"My fellow Americans," the President began, setting off the loud clatter of two hundred cameras, a pandemonium of motors and bulbs. "Today we gather to see the new Violence Against Women Act signed into law. I'm proud to sign it. I'm proud to be here with the men and women who voted for it. Above all, I'm proud to be at the side of those women whose courage in speaking out made this law happen. Without their honesty, without their bravery, America would not have acted. But today we act."

There was more applause. Maggie smiled to herself as she noticed there was not so much as a note on the table, let alone a fully-scripted speech. The President was speaking off the top of his head.

"We act for women like Donna Moreno, whose husband beat her so badly she was hospitalized for two months. We act for women like Christine Swenson, who had to fight seven years of police indifference before she could see the man who raped her convicted and jailed. They are both here in the White House today — and we welcome them. But we act for those who are not here."

Maggie glanced at the people she had joined, lined up against the far wall nearest the door, the traditional zone occupied by the senior aides to the President. It was a curious bit of choreography. On the one hand, it signalled their status as mere staff, serving at the pleasure of the President. They stood like butlers, hovering several paces away from the dining table, awaiting instructions. Everyone else was allowed to sit: even the press corps.

And yet, to be among this group was a mark of the highest possible status in Washington. It said you were close to the President, even one of the indispensables who needed to be "in the room". While the invited guests sat bolt upright, their suits pressed and their hair fixed for their big day at the White House, the staffers slumped against the wall, their ties loose, as if this were no more than another day at the office. Maggie looked at the Press Secretary, Doug Sanchez, young and good-looking enough to have caught the interest of the celeb magazines: he had his head down, barely paying attention to proceedings, scrolling instead through a message on his iPhone. Aware he was being watched, he looked up and smiled at Maggie, nodding in the direction of the President and then back at her, with a lascivious raise of the eyebrows. Translation: *I saw you and him arrive together* . . .

"For the women who have been attacked and not believed, even by the law-enforcement officers who should have protected them," the President was saying now. "For the wives who have been made prisoners in their own home. For the daughters who have had to

fear their own fathers. Each of them is a heroine and —
from today — they will have the law on their side."

More applause as President Stephen Baker reached
for the first of a set of pens fanned out on the desk
before him. He signed his name, then reached for
another pen to date the document, then several more to
initial each page.

"There," he said. "It's done."

The guests were on their feet again, the cameras
clacking noisily. The President had come around in
front of his desk to shake hands with those who had
come to witness the moment. There were double-clasps
with the congressional leaders, a hand placed on the
forearm to convey extra warmth, hugs with the leaders
of the key national women's organizations and then a
more hesitant, careful extension of the hand to the first
of the "victims" carefully selected by the White House
Office of Public Engagement.

Suddenly the cameras began to whirr more
insistently so that the room was lit by the strobe of a
hundred flashbulbs. Several journalists were on their
feet, craning to see over the photographers. Maggie
could only just glimpse the source of their interest.
Christine Swenson had placed her arms around the
President's shoulders and was resting her cheek on his
chest. Tears flowed down her face. "Thank you," she
was saying, over and over. "Thank you for believing
me."

"If that isn't leading Katie Couric tonight, I'm David
Duke." It was Tara MacDonald, hardly glancing up
from her BlackBerry.

Maggie couldn't take her eyes off Swenson, sobbing with gratitude. Only as an afterthought did she look at the President. He had placed his arm around the woman, enveloping her in a fatherly hug — even though he was at least a decade younger than she was.

Eventually the embrace broke up, the President handing Swenson a handkerchief so that she could dry her eyes.

Now he was handing a pen each to Donna, Christine and the congressional bigwigs. It was a White House tradition, one of dozens to have acquired the status of a religious rite: the President would sign a bill with multiple pens, so that he would have at least a dozen to present as souvenirs. Each one could be said to be "the very pen President Baker used to sign the . . ."

Aides were now beginning to nudge the President towards the lectern, to take questions from the press. He put out a restraining hand, signalling that he was not quite ready. He carried on speaking to the women who were huddled around him, one or two of them holding up camera-phones to get a snap of the man up close. He was standing, listening intently.

Maggie could hear the woman who had his attention.

". . . he took his belt off and began whipping my boy like he was a horse. What makes a man behave like that, Mr President? To his own son?"

The President shook his head in weary disbelief. Phil, the "body man", placed his hand on Baker's shoulder once again: the gesture that said, *we really must wind this up*. But the boss ignored him. Instead, he used his height to reach over the immediate circle of women who were surrounding him, searching for the hand of one of those who had held back. Maggie had noticed her already: unlike the others, she had been too shy to introduce herself. Ordinarily, those were the people who missed out; they never got their moment with the President. But Stephen Baker had noticed her, just as he always did.

It took Tara MacDonald to impose some discipline. She strode over to the huddle and addressed not the President but the women. "Ladies, if you could all take your seats," she said in the kind of commanding voice used to bringing hush to a church. "The President needs to take some questions."

This was an innovation, one that Baker himself had insisted upon. Traditionally, presidents made themselves available to the press only rarely, doing occasional, set-piece press conferences. The rest of the time, reporters might try to hurl a question but it would usually die in the air, victim to the President's selective deafness.

Baker promised to be different. If he did a public event, it would now end with a few minutes of light interrogation. The Washington punditocracy gave this fresh, transparent approach a life expectancy of about a fortnight: Baker would soon realize he'd made a rod for his own back and quit.

"Terry, what you got?"

"Mr President, congratulations on signing the Violence Against Women Act."

"Thanks." He flashed the wide signature smile.

"But some people are saying this might be the first and last legislative achievement of the Baker presidency. This was the one thing you and Congress could agree on. After this, isn't it going to be gridlock all the way?"

"No, Terry, and I'll tell you why."

Maggie watched as the President went into a now-familiar riff, explaining that though his majorities in the House and Senate were narrow, there were plenty of people of goodwill who wanted to make progress for the sake of the American people.

He then took another question, this time on diplomatic efforts in the Middle East. Maggie felt a surge of anxiety, a leftover from the election campaign when it had been her job to make sure he didn't stumble on the subject of foreign policy. No need for her to worry about that now.

Sanchez leaned in to say, "This will be the last question."

Baker called on MSNBC.

"Mr President, I'm sorry to come to a subject that might be awkward. Did you deceive the American people during the election campaign, by failing to reveal a key aspect of your own medical history — specifically the fact that you had once received treatment for a psychiatric disorder?"

CHAPTER
FOUR

Washington, DC, Monday March 20, 09.24
There were perhaps two seconds of frozen silence as
the question cut through the air, like a missile before
impact.

Every head in the room swung around to look at
Stephen Baker. His posture had remained the same, he
had not collapsed in a heap, nor was he shaking his fist.
But, Maggie saw, he was now gripping the lectern so
tightly his knuckles had turned white. They matched
the pallor spreading over his face as the blood drained
from it.

He began to speak. "Like every other candidate for
this office, I released a medical statement during the
campaign. From my doctor. That statement included
all the details he —" Baker paused, looking down at the
lectern as if searching for a script that wasn't there.
The pause, barely a second, seemed interminable. He
looked up again. "All the details he deemed to be
relevant. And I think now is the time to attend to the
business of the American people." With that, he turned
on his feet and headed for the door, a long snake
of aides at his heels — leaving behind a loud chorus of

"Mr President!" bellowed by every reporter with a follow-up question.

The staff scattered in every direction. Goldstein, Maggie noticed, headed straight across the corridor towards the Oval Office; MacDonald and Sanchez went in the opposite direction, to the press room. En route to her own office, one of several bunched together next to the Press Secretary's, she hesitated, standing in the doorway, looking in at those charged with handling the media: the scene was crazed, every person on a telephone, each one of them simultaneously hammering away at a computer. She could see MacDonald and Sanchez talking intensely: she lip-read Sanchez saying, "The trouble is, he looked like shit out there."

Maggie felt both out of place and useless, like a sightseer at a fire station on full alert. With a start, she remembered her meeting with Magnus Longley that morning, his threat that her job hung by a thread. Soon she might indeed be no more than a sightseer here.

She turned to leave, taking one last glance at the TV screen. The Breaking News tag along the bottom conveyed a single, devastating sentence: "Source tells MSNBC: President Baker received psychiatric treatment for depression."

No wonder Baker had turned the colour of ash. The word *psychiatric* reeked of political death. People might like to brag they were liberal and tolerant these days, but mental illness? Different story. Maybe if you were a celebrity, perched on Oprah's sofa, admitting to a few years of therapy . . . But *psychiatric treatment*: that

44

sounded like electrodes, rubber rooms and men in white coats. It was *One Flew Over the Cuckoo's Nest*.

Besides, Stephen Baker was not a movie star who could weep a few confessional tears on daytime TV and make it go away. He was the President of the United States. Americans could tolerate all manner of weaknesses in each other — especially if they were accompanied by contrition and redemption — but not in a president. They needed their president to be above all that, to be stronger than they were. Few men ever met that impossible standard. But a nation that looked to its leader to be a kind of tribal father never stopped expecting.

Voters would be rattled by this news, whoever was in the White House, Maggie knew that. But Stephen Baker had been lionized, ever since his campaign took off in the depths of the Iowa winter. Word had spread that, at last, a different kind of politician had arrived: one who really did seem to talk straight.

YouTube clips of him telling audiences what they didn't want to hear became cult viewing. He told farmers outside Sioux Falls that ethanol subsidies would have to stop: growing corn to make oil made as much sense as distilling the finest whisky — then using it to clean out the drains. There had been some hecklers, but most of the crowd of farmers were slack-jawed. No candidate had ever dared to say such a thing, not to their face anyway. How come this guy wasn't pandering to them like everyone else had?

"I hate what you say, but it took some guts to come here and say it!" shouted one woman, as wide as a truck, from the front row. Soon they were nodding and then they began applauding, more surprised by themselves than by the candidate standing before them. The three-minute video went viral.

Soon the press was writing up Baker as something more than a regular politician. He was a truth-teller, destined to lead the American people out of a dark moment in their history. The more overheated reporters became lyrical: "Cometh the hour, cometh the man . . ." What could have been an uncomfortable report in *The New Republic*, detailing some of the battles Governor Baker had fought, and the enemies he had made, in his home state of Washington concluded by quoting Jesus: "Only in his hometown . . . is a prophet without honour."

Yet now he had been accused of failing to level with the nation. And instead of knocking back the charge, he had paled at the very words.

Maggie was stepping into her office when she saw Goldstein heading away from the Oval and towards the press area. No matter that he was way above her in the Washington food chain, Maggie regarded Stu as one of the few unambiguously friendly faces around here. They had whiled away many long hours on the plane during the campaign, talking while reporters tapped away at their keyboards, staffers dozed and Baker sat back, his iPod headphones jammed into his ears to prevent anyone attempting a conversation. She figured that if anyone knew the truth of the MSNBC story, it would be Goldstein — the man who'd been with Stephen Baker from the start.

She walked down the corridor so that she could meet him halfway, then cut to the chase. "We're in the toilet, aren't we?"

"Yup. Somewhere round the U-bend and heading underground." He carried on walking. Given his bulk, he was advancing at quite a speed.

"Is it true?"

"Tell you what, why don't *you* go over to the Oval right now, poke your head round the door and say, 'Mr President, is it true that you used to see a shrink 'cause you were about to throw yourself off Memorial Bridge?'"

"They didn't say anything about suicide."

"No, Maggie, they didn't. But check Drudge in about thirty minutes. I bet that's where they get to."

"Jesus."

"Jesus is right."

"How bad's it going to be?"

"Well, as people used to say back when Dick Nixon was using this place to turn the Constitution into confetti, it's never the crime, it's always the —"

"— cover-up."

"Most folks won't mind if the President's *meshugge* — a real loony tune," he gasped, his breath too short to reach the end of his sentence. She could see crumbs embedded on his lapels. "Just so long as they knew about it before they pulled the lever."

"They'll be angry he didn't reveal it in the campaign."

"You betcha," he said bitterly.

She couldn't tell whether Goldstein was irritated that something he'd long known had leaked — or whether he was disappointed that the President had kept a secret from him.

"What's he going to do?"

"He wants to make a personal statement. Right away."

"Is that a good idea?"

"Right now, Maggie, nothing about this is good."

It came back to her then, the brief flap during the campaign over medical records. Mark Chester, Baker's much older opponent, had refused to disclose his, issuing a terse "doctor's summary" instead. Most expected Baker to seize the moment and release his records in full, waving his clean bill of health in Chester's face, each rosy-cheeked detail drawing an implicit contrast with the Republican's pale and brief account. But he had done no such thing, choosing to issue a doctor's summary of his own. Everyone gave Baker credit for that: he had shown compassion, sparing the embarrassment of the older man.

Now, standing in a corridor of the West Wing, Maggie wondered if they'd all been duped. She had never considered that Baker might have taken the chance to avoid full disclosure not to play nice with Chester — but to cover up his own embarrassments. But it was what everyone would be thinking now. MSNBC would either have to be flat-out wrong — which would rank as one of the major journalistic blunders of modern times — or Stephen Baker would have to come up with a damn good explanation for why he hadn't told the truth.

She headed back to her office, sat at the computer and tried to focus on drafting an options paper on Sudan. That was what she was here to do; that was what *he* had asked her to do in a conversation that already seemed to belong to a different era. But now she understood why people always said that the White House could only deal with one crisis at a time. You were too distracted to think of anything else.

She clicked on the TV. All channels were now on the MSNBC story. CNN was interviewing a man claiming to be an expert on depression.

The blogs were obsessed. She went to Andrew Sullivan.

This could be a defining moment for the republic. Mental illness is one of the last great taboos, a subject kept in the dark. And yet one in three Americans is affected by it. Stephen Baker should be brave, tell the truth and call for an end to prejudice.

She next went rightward, to The Corner.

Normally it takes at least a few years for a Democratic politician to start falling apart. Credit to Baker for speeding up the process. Now all he needs to do is show similar alacrity and fast-track his deficit-reduction plan.

Over at the liberal Daily Kos she detected definite anxiety:

> MSNBC is so far citing just one unnamed source. They'd better have proof.

She glanced up at the TV; still no more news. Time seemed to have slowed to a crawl. Her mind was wandering, something in recent weeks she had been working very hard to avoid. She was back on the steps of the Lincoln Memorial, replaying the conversation with Uri in her head. As the memory unspooled, she felt the melancholy creeping back inside her, like a vapour entering her lungs. To push it out and away, she reached for the Sudan file: maybe that bulging box of memoranda and cables, all classified, would help her tell the President what he needed to do. And distract her from herself.

The TV announced a news alert. The network that had broken the story now confirmed that it had documentary evidence of Stephen Baker's past treatment for depression. "MSNBC is satisfied these papers are genuine," the anchor declared with the portentous baritone Maggie guessed was usually reserved for presidential assassinations.

So it was true. Maggie sat back in her chair. Until now, she realized, she had held back her reaction, unsure what, exactly, she was meant to be reacting to. Now she no longer had that excuse.

She wanted to be like that blogger, full of compassion and apparently unfazed by the prospect

50

of a president with a history of mental illness. She knew that should be her attitude, too, just as she knew she should eat organic food. But she couldn't quite persuade herself to feel it.

Besides, she had the same attitude as the "folks" Stuart had talked about. It wasn't the crime — being depressed was surely no crime — it was the cover-up. If medical disclosure meant anything, it should have meant levelling with the electorate.

But that wasn't quite it, either. Maggie knew it would have been risky, verging on suicidal, for a candidate to start blubbering about his time on the psychiatrist's couch in the middle of a presidential election — especially when his opponent had allowed him to skip the details. She knew why he hadn't been able to come clean with the voters. But that didn't soothe the nagging sensation she felt somewhere between her brain and her gut. For a fleeting second, the sensation formed itself into a sentence: he should have come clean with *her*.

She tried to push the feeling away, clicking again on the refresh button on *The New York Times* website, not taking in a word she read. It was, she knew, ridiculous to regard this as a personal betrayal. There had been many people far more senior than her on the campaign team; Stephen Baker was under no obligation to share the stories of his past with her. He had told her no lies. It was not as if she had ever asked the question.

And yet the nagging feeling was still there. She had jacked in her job and gone to work for him nearly eighteen months ago, in those days when his staff could fit into a minivan and the pundits said he might be a realistic prospect in the presidential cycle after next. They had run up tens of thousands of air miles together. She had eaten in his home, played with his son and daughter and chatted with his wife. She had put her faith in him. And so had the country.

The Breaking News ident was flashing again on the TV. Maggie reached for the volume control. "This word just into us here at CNN: the President is to make an emergency statement."

At Sanchez's invitation, she watched it in the press room, fighting hard not to put her hands to her face and peer through splayed fingers, the way she used to watch teatime science fiction as a child.

"My fellow Americans," he began, his voice steady, his face calm and businesslike. "I am not here to deny what you heard today. I am here to tell you what happened. With the frankness and candour that I should have shown earlier.

"Long ago, in my early twenties, I hit a difficult patch in my life. I have not spoken about it before because the source of my unhappiness involved another person.

"As you know, my mother died a few months back — in the very last week of the campaign, as it happens — so perhaps now it can be told. Though even now, as I brace myself to say these words, I tremble at the thought that I might be dishonouring her memory. But you need to hear the truth.

"When I was a teenager, I suspected my mother was an alcoholic. It took me some time to reach that conclusion. When you're thirteen years old and your mother sinks some vodka into her orange juice at breakfast, you don't always notice. And if you do notice, you don't always know that that's not normal. That that's not how all moms behave. But by the time I was in college, I knew for certain.

"Once I was making my own way in the world, this knowledge began to eat away at me. Was I fated to follow in her path? To stumble the way she had stumbled? Would I too become an addict of alcohol?

"I was laid low by these thoughts. And, yes, eventually I sought professional help. The help of a psychiatrist, among other folks. I wanted to know if my destiny had already been determined, if it was written in my genes.

"Eventually I came out of what the poets call this 'slough of despond'. But it was not the doctors who lifted me from that dark place. My mother, on hearing that I had sought help, was shaken out of her own disease. You might say it was a wake-up call. She woke up, joined AA and got sober. When she died last October, she was proud to say that she had gone twenty-four years, eight months and nineteen days without a drink. It was a great achievement. I'm as proud of her for that as she was of me for getting to the brink of the presidency. But it was private. And I chose to honour that.

"Perhaps that was a mistake. But now I hope you understand. Why I needed the help in the first place and why I did not rush to tell you, the American people, all about it. I cannot know how you will react to this news. But I am taking the risk that you will respond as so many American families do when they are confronted with news that disappoints. With the generosity of spirit that made us — and makes us still — a great nation. Thank you."

Maggie stood, staring, barely daring to breathe. In the silence, she heard the sound of a single pair of hands clapping. Then another and then several more, until there was loud, sustained applause. She was sure she heard Tara MacDonald give a single whoop.

Sanchez passed her his iPhone, already open at the Sullivan blog. She only had to read the first sentence: *Stephen Baker has just reminded the American people why they chose him to be their president last fall.*

"OK, people," Tara yelled, silencing the last few claps of applause. "We're not out of the woods yet. Fox and the others are going to be yakking all night about 'the questions that still need to be answered'. We need to be ready." She shot a glare at Maggie and Sanchez standing together. "We don't need to be talking to each other, we need to be talking to the American people. I want a list handed to me no more than ten minutes from now, giving the names of surrogates ready to be in front of a camera heaping praise on President Stephen Baker for being brave, for being honest and for being a devoted son. Any questions?" She didn't wait for a reply. "Good. Now get to it."

Maggie decided to take the hint and leave, mouthing a thank you to Sanchez. Tara MacDonald was right to be cautious, but Maggie had lived in America long enough to know that the public would like what they had seen. They would not turf out a new, young president for the crime of loving his mother and worrying about the inheritance she might have passed to her son.

She was right, too. The cable networks were kind, hosting discussions about whether alcoholism was hereditary and on the usefulness of therapy. For a few blessed hours, authors of books with titles like *Please Mommy, Stop* and *Talking Makes It Better* replaced the usual political talking heads. Almost all spoke with compassion for Stephen Baker, though Rush Limbaugh had apparently taken to his microphone an hour after the President's personal statement to ask his listeners, "Do we really want a whack-job with his finger on the button?"

The consensus in the White House was that Baker had dodged a bullet. Indeed, the relief lasted all the way until the next day. Except in the Baker household. Where it was about to vanish in the cruellest way possible.

CHAPTER
FIVE

Washington, DC, Monday March 20, 19.16

Jen, those new sneakers are COOL!

Katie Baker read the messages on her new friend Jennifer's Facebook wall and was all set to add her own. But her fingers hesitated over the keyboard. Back in Olympia, she would have hammered out a dozen messages by now but here it was so different. Her mom had told her she had to be triple careful. "Remember, sweetie: no names, no pictures."

No pictures? That was so harsh! *Everyone* posted photos on their Facebook page but here — in fact, ever since November — she was told she couldn't. "You *can* put up pictures, honey," Mom had said. "Just none that show you, your brother or any of your closest friends. Nothing that identifies you."

Her brother? Like that was ever going to happen. She didn't mind keeping that annoying jerk out of her pictures. But her *friends*? Why did she have to be the one who was different?

Oh, yes. Because her father was President of the United States, that's why. Which was cool, no doubt.

She had already met several of her favourite stars and she had been in *People* magazine — though in that picture she'd had to hold hands with her brother. Yeeuch!

Someone had sent a new message which popped up on Jen's wall.

> I heard that Brandon invited you to the Zygotes show at the 9.30. Does that mean you two are like going out?!!

She began typing. *OMG, Jen! If that is true, I am so jealous! I love the Zygotes!*

She wondered if that gave away too much detail. The 9.30 hardly counted as giving away a place, did it? So the 9.30 Club was in Washington, DC. Was there anyone in the world who didn't know that thirteen-year-old Katie Baker lived in Washington, DC?

She clicked out of Jen's and back to her own Facebook page. What she saw when she got there made her frown.

Kimberley Baker was preparing supper, doing her best to keep things normal. Partly for her husband's sake, mainly for her kids. Politically, the President of the United States might have survived what had happened today but she was not so sure how Stephen Baker would cope.

The most private thing about him was now public property. When they were going out it had been the last revelation he had made to her. Only once they had been together many months did he tell her about his mother's alcoholism and the treatment he had sought. Once he had spilled everything, and she had responded with a long, tight hug, he had asked her to marry him. And now he had had to expose the secret he had guarded so zealously on national television. She knew how much he would hate that.

Still, he was a strong man; he would survive. But what about Katie and Josh? To her surprise the kids had seemed to be doing OK. They had started school, made some friends; Katie had even been to her first DC slumber party. Of course, Kimberley had questioned the motives of both Jennifer, the classmate who had been so eager to make Katie her BF, and her equally keen parents. Kimberley didn't need to open the *Washington Post* to know that the Bakers were now deemed the hottest social property in the city and any contact, even vicarious, was a major trophy.

She had wondered if this morning's revelation would see all that come crashing down. She didn't care about herself; she wouldn't mind if she never went to another Washington party. But she couldn't bear to imagine what her children might be put through. Stephen had agreed they would maintain the no-newspapers rule they had observed back west. Nor was it any kind of sacrifice to ban cable TV. And the staff were wonderful, never mentioning a thing.

But, she knew, that was not where the danger lurked. It was school, specifically the meanness of other children, that frightened her. She knew how cruel they could be. Yes, most of the pupils at the school they had chosen would be fawning over Katie and Josh, but it would only take one rebel, one troublemaker who saw there was sport to be had in teasing the daughter of the President of the United States. And what ammunition any would-be playground tormentor had just been handed. *Psychiatric treatment.*

And yet the children had said nothing about it. They had come home, picked up from the school gate by Zoe, the Secret Service agent masquerading as an au pair — albeit one who drove an armour-plated minivan with blacked-out windows — and bounded up the stairs as if nothing were out of the ordinary. In Josh's case, Kimberley Baker knew that meant all had been well. Her son couldn't hide anything, even if he wanted to.

But Katie offered no such assurance. Was her silence proof that nothing had happened, that she had survived the day without mockery — or evidence that she had suffered an indignity so great it could not be expressed?

There was a message from her friend Alexis.

Hi K, hope you're feeling OK this evening. Sorry today was so hard. You seemed to be coping really well though. You're one tough chick!

Katie Baker read it again, checking the name. It was definitely from Alexis, but it made no sense. Alexis hadn't been at school today. She'd got that bug that was going round. How would Alexis know how she'd been coping?

She typed out a reply.

59

I don't understand! Aren't you in bed with that yukky bug thing?!!

Katie clicked open another window: tour dates for the band Emily and Hannah had said were *the* hot group of the year. She was about to hit the preview to hear some of their music when she heard a light knock on the door.

Her agent, Zoe, poked her head round the door, taking care to stay outside her room. "Your mom says it's time you came down for dinner."

"'Kay. Be right there."

The door shut and Katie closed the tab open to the band's website. She was about to close down Facebook when she heard the message alert announcing Alexis' reply. She glanced back towards the door. It would only take a minute.

The First Lady looked over at her husband, now chopping garlic for a tomato sauce. He was sitting on a stool tucked up against the breakfast bar, both tie and shoes off. Whenever she regretted her husband's choice of career — which was often — Kimberley Baker fell back on this consolation. She had deployed the same line when he was Governor, too. As he had put it in at least three dozen interviews, before flashing that million-kilowatt smile, "At least I get to live above the shop."

So she tried to savour this little scene of domesticity — the four of them having an evening meal together —

60

and pretend that the National Security Advisor was not waiting just along the corridor.

Actually, it was still just the three of them. Katie had not yet come down despite Zoe's summons. Kimberley decided she'd had it with relaying messages via the Secret Service agent, and was poised to shout with the full force of her lungs for her daughter to come to the table — and to hell with the dozens of officials and staff who would hear her screeching — when the door swung open.

"Ah, good evening, young lady," said the President, his eyes still focused on his painstakingly slow work at the chopping board. He didn't see what his wife saw: their thirteen-year-old daughter standing there with every last drop of blood drained from her face.

"Katie, what is it?" Kimberley cried. "Katie!"

The girl was staring straight ahead. Her mother grabbed her by her shoulders, trying to shake a response out of her.

"What's happened? What's HAPPENED!"

Instinctively, Stephen Baker looked to the door. Had there been some kind of attack, had an intruder broken into the White House Residence? Zoe, having quietly entered the room behind her charge, read the President's expression. She shook her head. *We've seen nothing*.

When he spoke, his voice conveyed the same steady calm that voters had warmed to even before he was elected. He knelt down so that he could look his daughter in the eye. "Was it something on the computer?"

She nodded.

"One of your friends, saying something mean?"

"I thought it was. At first."

The President and his wife looked at each other.

"What did they say?"

"I don't want to tell you."

The President stood up and gestured towards Zoe. Swiftly, she left the room, returning a matter of seconds later holding an open laptop computer, its shell a blaze of tie-dye style, psychedelic swirls. Teen chic.

Kimberley took the machine from Zoe and looked at the screen. It was her daughter's Facebook page. Katie had begged to be allowed to keep it and her parents had eventually relented, reluctantly and with strict conditions. No photographs of herself or anyone else who might identify her. No real names. No contact details. And an IP address arranged through the White House comms department that would reveal only the United States as her place of residence, with no town or city specified. Only her closest friends from back home in Olympia, with perhaps a few more added this week in DC, knew that Sunshine12 was in fact the daughter of the American President.

Stephen Baker scanned the screen, searching among the multiple open windows, banner ads and thumbnail photos for what had so distressed his daughter.

And then he found it. A message from one of Katie's schoolfriends: Alexis. He'd heard the name mentioned a few times.

No, I'm not in bed. I'm not really sick. And I'm not really Alexis either, to be honest. But I am sorry about your Dad. Must have been such a shock to find out about his past medical problems. Did he ever tell you about that when he sat at the end of your bed, stroking your hair and telling you a bedtime story? Did he tell you Grandma was a pisshead and he had to go to the head doctor because he was a mental case? My apologies for spilling the beans. Ooops. Silly me. But I wonder if you would be a doll and take a message to him from me. Thanks, sweetie. Tell him I have more stories to tell. The next one comes tomorrow morning. And if that doesn't smash his pretty little head into a thousand pieces, I promise you this — the one after that will. Make no mistake: I mean to destroy him.

CHAPTER
SIX

Washington, DC, Tuesday March 21, 05.59
Maggie got the call before 6a.m.: Goldstein, sounding caffeinated.

"Put on MSNBC. Now."

She fumbled for the remote, down at the side of the bed. It wasn't there. She reached across to the blank, empty space that made up the other half of the bed and found it marooned there, stabbed at the buttons until finally the screen fired up into a too-bright light.

"It's an ad for car insurance, Stu."

"Wait. We got a heads-up."

There was the portentous sound of a station ident, a whizzy graphic and then the morning anchor, all glossy lips and improbably static hair. The image over her shoulder showed the President, the words strapped across the bottom of the screen: Breaking News.

"Papers seen by MSNBC suggest Stephen Baker received campaign contributions that came, indirectly, from the government of Iran. Details are still sketchy but such a donation would constitute a serious violation of federal law, which prohibits candidates from receiving contributions from any foreign source, still less a government hostile to the United States. Live now to . . ."

Iran? What on earth did Stephen Baker have to do with Iran? They could not be serious. Something truly bizarre was going on here. Bizarre and sinister. Two bombshells in twenty-four hours. She knew every one of her White House colleagues would be asking the same question: "What the hell is going on?"

She could hear Goldstein barking an instruction to someone outside his office.

"What the hell is this, Stu?"

"You've probably got some Irish word for it, Maggie."

"For what?"

"For when someone sets out to fuck you in the ass and stab you in the heart, all at the same time. What's that in Gaelic?"

"You think this is part of some plan?"

"Two stories, two days running, on the same network. That doesn't happen by accident, sweetheart. That means they have a leaker. A *source.*" Goldstein paused just long enough to let out a wheeze. "Someone, in other words, who's out to destroy this presidency."

"But these stories have got nothing to do with each other. They're twenty-five years apart."

"Which proves it's organized. Some well-resourced outfit, with enough money to do serious oppo."

"Stuart," Maggie said, now out of the bed and walking towards the shower. "I'm glad you called but why me? Shouldn't you be speaking to Tara and —"

"Did that thirty minutes ago. *Iran*. You're our Middle East gal, remember. Need you to think about the angles. If this does not turn out to be bullshit, then who might have done this at that end? Government or rogue? And why now? What game are they — Shit."

Goldstein's cellphone rang, the first notes of the theme from *The Godfather*, the movie loved by all political obsessives. "This is how power works, Maggie," he had said when the film was screened on a return flight from California. "Watch and learn."

He must have put the call on speaker because she could hear a voice, high-strung and rattled, at the other end. She couldn't make out all the words but she could hear the urgency.

". . . a doorstep at the Capitol, demanding a special prosecutor."

Stuart's response was instant and ferocious. "That prick. Was he on his own or with colleagues?"

The voice: "One other. Vincenzi. You know, bipartisan bullshit: one Republican, one Democrat."

"Assholes."

Maggie tried to say goodbye, but it was clear Stuart was not listening. He was absorbed in this new conversation, apparently unaware that he was still holding the receiver. All she could do was hang up. Or stay on the line and eavesdrop . . .

Stuart spoke again, a sound like a faulty air conditioner coming from his chest. "What did he say he wants? An independent counsel or a special prosecutor? What were his exact words?"

Maggie could hear a muffled sound, which she took to be the luckless official, whoever it was, squirming under the fire of Goldstein's interrogation.

Stuart was off again. "I'll tell you what difference it makes. *Special prosecutors* no longer exist. They were abolished. The only reason a person would start talking about special prosecutors is if they were either a moron — which the senator from Connecticut is not — or if they wanted to make a point."

More muffled sound.

"The point being that the words *special prosecutor* have a very particular sound in this town. The sound of Archibald Cox. Don't tell me — *sheesh*. Am I the oldest freaking person in this White House? Archibald Cox? Watergate?"

Maggie tried to catch his attention. "Stuart? Stuart!" But it was too late. She hung up.

They had now, she understood, entered a new realm of seriousness. If a Democrat was calling for an independent counsel to investigate a Democratic president, there was no way he could fight it. It was no longer "partisan": now it was above party politics. Baker would have to agree. In the space of a few weeks he had gone from St Stephen — the coverline on a British magazine story about the new president — to Richard Nixon, under investigation.

Maggie felt as if she were standing on the deck of a ship taking on water. They had all been so euphoric that unseasonably warm evening in November when Baker had won. She'd been caught up in it, accepting the ribbing from Stu and Doug Sanchez, as they mocked her earlier pessimism. "Oh ye of little faith, Costello, who said it would never happen," Sanchez had said as he embraced her, maintaining the hug a moment or two longer than necessary, his hands brushing her bottom in a way that was not quite accidental. More than ten years her junior, he had a nerve, that boy. But it was that kind of night.

She had tranquillized her doubts, allowed herself to believe that this time it would be different. Her own experience told her that politics was bound to end in failure. She had seen it when she worked for the United Nations, where even the most elementary, obvious truths — "These people are dying and need help!" — could get tangled up in turf wars, rivalries, bureaucratic indecision, vanity and, that most decisive of categories, "interests". So often she had felt — she stopped saying the words, knowing that to utter them out loud made you a hippy, a naïf who could be ignored — that something must be done. And so often it had not been.

For years she had come to believe that the last truly worthwhile work she had done was back when she started out, as an aid worker in Sudan. Handing out sacks of grain from the back of the truck: that had value. The minute she had stepped back from the frontline, lured by the promise of helping more than one person at a time, she had been less use. The titles were grander — first she had been involved in *policy*, then *strategy*, finally, at the UN and the State Department, she had been at the highest levels of *diplomacy* — but she remained stubbornly unimpressed. *Help* was what she was interested in, and she'd begun

68

to lose faith that she, or anyone in these grand jobs, could ever deliver it.

Then Stephen Baker had appeared. Reluctantly and despite herself, she had allowed the hide she had grown over her once-tender idealism to be pierced. He had done it to her, breaking through layer after layer of scepticism, until he had found the person underneath — the person she had not been since she was twenty-five.

Now, though, the ship was listing. She had got it wrong. Again. Politics would always rise up and strangle hope, like a weed choking a flower. She had been stupid to think it would be any different this time.

But another, sharper pain gnawed at her stomach. Maybe she had not only been wrong to forget that politics always intruded, always stood between good people and doing good. Maybe she had been wrong to assume that she was working for good people. For a good man.

After all, Goldstein had not denied the accusation. *If this does not turn out to be bullshit* was the best he could offer. Did that mean Baker *had* taken money from the Iranians? If he had, that made him an idiot — and worse.

By now, she was out of the shower and standing in a towel, staring at her wardrobe, wondering what you were meant to wear for a full-blown political crisis. A special prosecutor, Jesus.

The cellphone rang again, displaying "restricted". Maggie grabbed it. "Stu, you didn't need to call back."

"Excuse me?" A woman's voice. "Is this Maggie Costello?"

"Yes."

"Can you hold for Magnus Longley?"

Maggie felt her guts clench.

"Miss Costello?" The voice was dry enough to sand a table. "I'm sorry to disturb you so early but I thought it best to let you know of my decision immediately. I'm afraid Dr Adams is . . . adamant." Longley sounded pleased with his pun. "He insists that you be removed from your post. And I see no alternative but to bow to his wishes."

Maggie felt as if someone had plunged a needle into her neck, mainlining fury directly into her bloodstream.

"Does the President know about this?"

"Perhaps you haven't seen the news, but the President has rather a lot on his plate at the moment."

"I know that, but just yesterday he asked me —"

"You should come in early this morning and clear your desk. Your White House computer log-in will expire at twelve noon. And you will need to surrender your pass."

"Don't I get at least to —"

"I fear my 6.45 meeting is due to start. Goodbye, Miss Costello. And thank you for your service."

She stood there a full five seconds, the rage inchoate and rising. How could they do this to her? After all she had sacrificed? And just when she had so much to give? Not twenty-four hours ago, she had been asked by the President of the United States himself to draw up a plan to save lives — perhaps thousands or tens of thousands of lives — in Darfur. Besides, she was needed on this latest Iran problem. Stuart had said so.

And now that was all going to come to nothing because of, what? Calling a bloody pompous old git an asshole — when that was exactly what he was.

She turned around, raised her arm and was about to hurl the phone at the bedroom wall — bracing herself for the satisfaction of seeing it shatter — when it began to ring. That stopped her. Her arm raised aloft, she suddenly felt ridiculous. She looked at the display: *Restricted.*

She hit the green button. A woman's voice again, different this time. "Please hold for the President."

A second later, it was him. A voice known to millions, though in a tone heard only rarely and by those closest to him: "Maggie, I need to see you. Right away."

CHAPTER
SEVEN

Washington, DC, Tuesday March 21, 07.33
Baker had insisted they meet in the Residence; him, her and Stuart. Maggie called Goldstein immediately and explained that she'd just been fired. "I've got to surrender my pass by twelve noon, for Christ's sake!"

"OK," he said. "That means we've got a few hours."

"Is that meant to be funny?"

"No. And Maggie? Come to my office first. I need to give you a heads-up before we go in."

She was there twenty minutes later. Stuart was tearing his way through a memo, his eyes red and agitated. He looked awful.

She spoke from the doorway. "Is that the file on the Iranian?"

He didn't look up but kept his eyes fixed on the document on his desk. "Known in this country as Jim Hodges, resident in the state of Texas."

"He's a US citizen! So then we're off the hook. The whole point is —"

"But he's also Hossein Najafi, citizen of the Islamic Republic of Iran. Who just happens to be a veteran of the Army of the Guardians of the Islamic Revolution, better known as the Revolutionary Guard."

"But he gave the donation as Jim Hodges. How was anyone to know that he was really —"

"Because we're meant to check these things!" Now Goldstein was looking up, his voice raised, his eyes bugging out with rage. "We're the fucking White House. *He's* the fucking President of the United States. He sends people into wars. To die. He's meant to know who he meets, for Christ's —"

"He *met* him?"

"Yes! Some fundraiser. During the transition."

"So there'll be a photograph."

Stuart's reply came in a quieter voice. "Yes."

"And people will ask why we didn't have the basic intel to know we were letting an Iranian spy get close to the President-Elect."

"Yes." Stuart spread his hands across the table and let his head fall onto them. "And why —"

"— on earth the Iranians would want to give money to Stephen Baker."

"You could make the ad now." He picked his head up and did a mock voiceover. "'The Ayatollahs like Stephen Baker so much they gave him cash. In secret. Is Baker working for you — or them?'"

"It's a nightmare," Maggie agreed.

"But that's not why he wants to see you. Us. Not completely, anyway."

"Why, then?"

Stuart hauled himself upright and told Maggie about the message sent to Katie Baker via Facebook. He reached for a piece of paper to read the final paragraph: *And if that doesn't smash his pretty little head into a thousand pieces, I promise you this — the one after that will. Make no mistake: I mean to destroy him.*

"Jesus."

"Oh yes." Stuart checked his watch. "He wants us over there right now."

Inside the Residence, the difference in mood from the previous morning was palpable. Kimberley Baker had taken the children to school early — the White House breakfast event she was chairing on cervical cancer awareness would just have to start without her — so that they could be out of that atmosphere. She spent the journey repeating what she had said last night, over and over: reassuring Katie that Daddy was going to be fine, that the police would find and punish whoever sent that horrible message and she would make sure there would be no more of them.

The President was in the kitchen again, but this time he was pacing. Maggie had seen Stephen Baker receive all kinds of bad news during the campaign and, on all but a handful of occasions, he had remained calm, almost preternaturally so. He would keep his voice down, when others would raise theirs; he would be forgiving when any other candidate would be demanding instant revenge; he would stay seated when the rest would be leaping to their feet. But now he was pacing.

"Thank you both for coming." He nodded towards two chairs but remained standing. "Maggie, I take it you now have the full picture?"

"Yes, Mr President."

"And you know why you're here?"

"Not entirely, sir."

"The crank who wrote that message to my daughter. He warned there would be another big story 'tomorrow morning'. And there was. Which means he's no crank."

Goldstein now spoke. "Or at the very least he's a crank who knows how to hack computers. He must have identified the White House IP address, and worked backwards from there, searching teenage websites for a match. Then hacked into this girl's —"

"Alexis," the President added.

"Right. Into her account. Smart."

To her surprise, the President suddenly turned and fixed Maggie with his deep green gaze. Though this time, the steadiness was gone. He looked hunted. "You should have seen my daughter, Maggie. She looked terrified."

"It's horrible."

"I always promised Kim that whatever happened we'd keep the kids out of it."

Stuart replied. "And you have, sir."

"Until now, Stu. Until now."

Both Maggie and Goldstein remained silent, while Baker resumed his pacing. Finally, she felt she had to speak.

"Sorry, Mr President. I'm not sure I'm completely clear on what needs to be done here. On what you want us to do."

Baker looked to Stuart and nodded, giving Goldstein the cue to answer on his behalf.

"This has to be handled extremely carefully, Maggie. We need to know who this man who contacted Katie is.

If he really is the source of these stories and is determined to reveal more; we need to identify him. Fast."

"Can't the Secret Service help? He made a direct threat against you."

Once again Baker said nothing, looking to Stuart.

"The agent assigned to Katie is running a trace."

"Good," said Maggie. "So we'll see what she finds out."

Now the President spoke. "I need someone I trust involved, Maggie."

"You can trust the Secret Service."

"They will investigate the threat to my *life*."

Stuart leaned forward. "But this is not just a physical threat, is it? This is political. Someone is out to destroy this presidency. Two leaks, carefully timed for maximum impact. And threatening another."

Maggie nodded. "I know."

"Which is why we need our own person on it. Someone who cares. Someone who has the resources to do, you know, unusual work."

"What do you mean, *unusual*?"

"Come on, Maggie. We know what you did in Jerusalem. Put it this way, you weren't just drafting position papers, were you?"

"But I don't even work for you any more!" It had come out louder and angrier than she had planned. The intensity of her outburst surprised even her.

"I'm sorry about that," the President said quietly.

"Longley runs his own show, you know that, Maggie." Stuart paused, then brightened. "But it doesn't mean you can't help. If anything, it's better. You have distance. Arm's-length."

"Deniability, you mean. You can disown me." She was staring hard at him.

The President drew himself up to full height and let his eyes bore into her. "I need you, Maggie. There is so much we hoped to achieve. Together. To do that, I need to stay in this office. And that means finding this man, whoever he is."

She held his gaze for a long second or two in which she thought of the conversation they had had in this same place twenty-four hours earlier. She thought of the barely-started options paper for Darfur on her computer, of the helicopters that this president was ready to send and the lives they would save. She pictured a Darfuri village about to be torched to the ground and the militiamen on horseback poised to set it ablaze; she saw them reining in their animals and turning around, because they had heard the sound of choppers in the sky that told them they would be seen and caught. She thought of all that and the certainty that nobody other than Stephen Baker would lift a finger to help those villagers.

"All right," she said, still looking directly into the deep green of his eyes. "We find him. Then what?"

Stuart answered. "We see what he wants. We ask what —"

The President wheeled round to address his closest advisor directly. "I hope you're not suggesting I engage in dialogue with a *blackmailer* —"

"Not you. Nowhere near you. A million miles from you."

"You mean you?"

"Not even me. Or at least not a me that anyone could identify as me."

"No way."

"He said he has one more story that will —"

"Well, I'm not going to authorize any such thing. And you know better than to ask."

Stuart gestured an apology, heaved himself up out of his chair, muttering a "one, two, three" under his breath as he undertook the necessary exertion. Maggie followed his lead and headed for the door.

I'm not going to authorize any such thing. Both Maggie and Stuart knew what that meant. They had been given their orders. Deniability, the lubricant of high-level politics. The message had been clear. Do whatever you have to do. Just make sure it has nothing to do with me.

As they walked back to the West Wing, Maggie turned to Stuart. "We better start drawing up a list."

"A list of what?"

"Of everybody who wants to drive Stephen Baker from office."

CHAPTER
EIGHT

Washington, DC, Tuesday March 21, 09.16
In the office of the junior senator from the great state of South Carolina, they liked to pride themselves on the knowledge that a visitor had only to cross the threshold to feel as if he had stepped inside the Old South. The receptionist on duty was usually blonde, under thirty, wearing a floral print and always ready with a welcoming smile, a "Yes sir" or a "Yes ma'am". Nearly always a "Yes sir". Outside that door, they could offer no guarantees. You entered the swamp that was Washington, DC at your own risk. But here, once you were a guest of Senator Rick Franklin, you were south of the Mason-Dixon line.

The visitor, once he'd helped himself to the pitcher of iced water in the waiting area, would notice more than the Southern smiles. His eye would be caught first, perhaps, by the bronze plaque above the reception desk depicting the Ten Commandments, as if etched on two tablets of stone. Not for Senator Franklin the niceties of separating Church and State in a public building.

Then, if he were especially vigilant, he would spot the TV monitor tuned not to CNN or MSNBC, as would be the case in most Democrats' offices, nor even Fox News, as in most Republicans', but to the Christian Broadcasting Network. Midterm elections might be nineteen months away, but there was fundraising to be done — and it paid to give the folks the right impression.

That was the outer area. Once a visitor had pierced the perimeter, and entered the private office of the Senator himself, he would get a rather earthier glimpse of the realities of political life. In here, it was Fox or MSNBC, usually the latter. "Know thine enemy," Franklin would say.

In the last twenty-four hours, however, it had hardly felt like an enemy. The network, usually pilloried in Franklin mailings as news for arugula-munching liberals, had been making the weather on the Baker presidency; and for those on Franklin's side of the aisle it had felt like sunshine. Some of his colleagues had simply sat back and enjoyed the show. First, St Stephen of Olympia revealed as some kind of wacko, in need of treatment. The joy of it was that story still had some distance to run. What kind of treatment exactly? Were electric shocks involved? Was he ever an inpatient? Was there a "facility" that might be photographed, complete with exterior shots of a building reminiscent of the Cuckoo's Nest, that could run on a loop on Fox?

Senator Franklin could feel the saliva welling as he imagined the meat still to be picked off that particular bone.

And this morning the Iranian Connection. Iron law of scandal: gotta have a good name. "The Iranian

80

Connection" did the job perfectly. Exotic and dramatic, like a movie, but with the added threat of somewhere dark and scary. Sure the details were obscure, the experts unintelligible bald guys captioned on TV as "forensic accountants", but that only made it better. The liberal editorial boards could sweat through their tieless shirts explaining that there was "no case to answer", but that wouldn't wash with the folks. Oh no. They would see a blizzard of numbers and laws and rules — and they would conclude that, whatever the fine print might say, Mr Perfect President was no longer as pure as the driven snow.

Which is why he had got on the phone to his Democratic colleague within minutes of the story breaking. Calling for an independent counsel was the no-risk move. If the investigation found nothing, then Franklin could claim to have performed a public service, getting to the bottom of baseless rumours. If it found something, then bingo! And, in between, day after day of stories full of mind-numbing detail on campaign finance law and on the horror show that was the Iranian regime. The mere fact that these subjects were raised in the same breath as Stephen Baker would generate a quite perfect stench of scandal. Voters would be forced to conclude, as they had so many times before, "Ain't no smoke without fire."

He knew Vincenzi would be a reliable ally. Sure, he was a Dino — Democrat in Name Only — and sure, everyone knew he couldn't stand Baker, but Vincenzi's presence at his side would give Franklin the lofty, bipartisan patina the media could never resist. "This is above party politics," they had both said in their statements. The press always lapped up that shit.

As for the phrase "special prosecutor", that particular bolt of inspiration had only come to him as he headed over to the hastily arranged press availability. The nerds would say it was inaccurate, but they'd be too late. The poison arrow would already be in flight.

So Senator Franklin felt able to hum *Happy Days are Here Again* as he straightened the blotter on his desk and moved the paperweight — the one that, if you looked closely, revealed a Confederate flag preserved as if in amber inside the thick glass. Things were going according to plan.

He carried on humming even as there was a gentle rap on the door. Cindy, his Head of Legislative Affairs, coming in with a smile he hadn't seen since the night he was elected more than four years ago. It always gave him pleasure watching her move, her rear end tightly contained in a skirt that was never any lower than the knee. But now there was a spring in her step that gave him an extra pulse of enjoyment.

"I can see you come bearing glad tidings, sweetheart."

"I do, sir, I do."

They played these games, the Southern gentleman and the demure young lady, with dialogue sub-*Gone With the Wind* — but only when the political or personal weather was clement.

"Pray tell."

"I do declare, Senator," she said with a girlish flutter that, even though he'd seen it a hundred times, still sent electricity to his groin, "that the source of MSNBC's recent tales of woe has been — what's the word — *outed*."

"Outed? Already? What the hell's happened?" The game was over. Too important for games.

"Daily Kos. They've named him. Seems some liberal hacker broke into the MSNBC system and found the emails between their Washington bureau and the leaker. Then went ahead and named him on his own website. Kos picked it up."

"You sure the White House weren't behind this?"

"Can't be sure. But Kos are adamant that it was some ultra-liberal crazy outraged his beloved Baker was being slammed. Seems to add up."

"And what have they found about him?"

"The hacker?"

"No! Fuck him. The leaker."

"All they have so far is that he's late forties, white and from New Orleans."

CHAPTER
NINE

Washington, DC, Tuesday March 21, 10.55
"Get in. I'll brief you in the car."

Maggie did as she was told, impressed by the authority of this woman, who could only have been in her late twenties. Maggie had seen her in the White House Residence, dressed like an au pair, young and unshowy. Her name was Zoe Galfano and she was the lead Secret Service agent assigned to the Baker children, with particular responsibility for Katie.

"It's a classic threat message," Zoe said, as Maggie strapped on her seatbelt. "Not especially unusual in the White House. Except this was different."

"Because it was addressed to Katie?"

"That, and the fact that it's not easy to get a direct message to her. Hijacking a Facebook identity took ingenuity."

"Was it hard to trace him?"

Zoe turned to look at Maggie with a smile. "We don't know it's a him."

"Right."

"No preconceptions. That's part of the training."

"And all this internet stuff, you learn that too?"

"I did. Figured I was never going to have the edge in the muscles department." She flexed a bicep. "So I decided to focus on those areas where I could compete with the men on a level playing field."

"I hear that," Maggie muttered, looking out of the window.

"Graduated top of my class in psychology and computer studies."

They were driving out of the District and into Maryland, two other agents following two cars behind. It was strictly against protocol for White House staff to meddle in Secret Service business, but Goldstein had spotted a loophole: "As of today, you're not White House staff any more. You're a family friend. Katie Baker wants you there, so you're there."

Just before she had got into Agent Galfano's car, the identity of the alleged leaker of the MSNBC stories had begun to surface on a blog, though there had been no official confirmation from the network. And still no name. A white male from New Orleans was all they knew. Maggie's first job was to see if the creep who had terrorized Katie and the guy who'd been feeding MSNBC were one and the same.

Zoe parked up. They were on a residential street in Bethesda, quiet on this midweek morning. The agent checked the address once more and looked back up at the house. Number 1157. Out loud, she confirmed that this was the right street, right block. Four houses away, a woman in her sixties was bending down, ostrich-style, apparently to examine the bottom of a rosebush. Zoe turned to Maggie. "We're going to have to do this quietly." She spoke into the radio on her cuff. "Are you good to go, guys?"

Maggie heard nothing in reply.

"Wait for my word, Ray. I'll go first, walking pace, you two hang back a few yards. Remember, weapons are not to be visible. Repeat, *not visible*."

She turned to Maggie. "Now, Ms Costello. The suspect is likely to be armed and dangerous. Do you understand?"

Maggie nodded.

"I consider it a great risk that you're here. But Mr Goldstein insisted that you accompany me at all times, so here you are. That means you do whatever I tell you to do. Duck, run, hit the floor. Instantly. Are we clear?"

"We're clear."

She watched Zoe check out the house once more. Curtains open on the top floor, blinds, halfway between open and closed, on the ground. Garden neatly kept. No car in the driveway. Light on upstairs. She saw the agent feel for her gun, holstered just below her armpit.

Zoe raised her cuff once more. "Go."

Not waiting for an answer, she opened the car door and strode purposefully up the path, not waiting for Maggie to catch up with her. She passed the mailbox, flipping it open in a single quick movement: empty. She glanced over her shoulder to see the pair from the other car start out on the sidewalk, three yards behind her.

They were not in uniform but they were hardly disguised. If the black SUVs with tinted windows didn't give it away, the dark suits and curly wire in the ear surely did. Zoe had told Maggie that she had thought about putting in a request for different vehicles, but that would have meant form-filling and more explanation. Mr Goldstein had been clear: no widening of the circle and no time to waste.

The front door revealed nothing. No nameplate. Zoe looked back towards the other agents, one of whom was looking into the recycling bin, searching for old letters or envelopes that might yield a name. He shook his head.

Zoe rang the bell, moving her ear close to the door to pick up any footsteps. Maggie pictured the man inside, in a bathrobe, legs apart, his face blue from the computer screen, jerking himself off as he stared at the bodies of girls not much older than Katie Baker.

No preconceptions. That's what Zoe had said.

The agent knocked on the door, loudly. Maggie saw her glance at her watch, give it five seconds and then nod to Ray. Without hesitation, he shouldered the full weight of his two-hundred-and-twenty-pound frame into the door, busting its lock on the first attempt.

Zoe was first in, legs astride, weapon brandished in a double-handed grip. Ray and partner followed; then it was Maggie's turn. She hesitated, then stepped forward, the way she had once closed her eyes and jumped off the tallest rock at Loughshinny beach: don't even think about it.

"SECRET SERVICE!" Galfano bellowed. "Put your hands up!"

Something caught the agent's eye. She swivelled around, to see an archway leading to what seemed to be the kitchen. A nod towards Ray instructed him to join her and head that way. A flick of her revolver told the other agent, now in the doorway, to check out the upstairs.

She stepped forward gingerly, noting the change in the light coming from the kitchen. One pace behind, her heart banging in her chest, Maggie sensed it too. Someone was moving in there. Silently, but moving all the same.

"We are agents of the United States Secret Service!" Zoe shouted once more. "Come out with your hands up."

The first noise, a kind of grinding sound. Was that a key turning in a backdoor lock? Was he getting away?

Zoe now rushed through the archway, her finger tight on the trigger. "Freeze!"

A half-second later they saw the source of both the change in the light and the noise. The image Maggie had had in mind had been half-right. There was a computer — but no man. Just a lonely machine on the kitchen table, the flickering green lights of a router right next to it.

Zoe lowered her gun and stepped towards the machine. She could see from the blinking cursor that the computer was functioning. She turned to Maggie. "I'm sorry, Ms Costello, this seems to have been a wild goose chase. I really —"

But Maggie stopped her. "Look —"

The cursor was moving, apparently of its own accord. They watched as it zipped around the screen, finding the Word icon, clicking it open to reveal a blank document. And now words began to appear on the screen, letter by letter, typed by some unseen hand.

Welcome to my home. Sorry I'm not in. Do make yourself comfortable. Do I take it from your visit that your boss is keen to talk?

CHAPTER
TEN

Washington, DC, Tuesday March 21, 14.26
"Aren't people going to talk?"

"What? About you and me?"

"Yes. Me, in here."

"Something tells me, Maggie, that people worked out long ago there's not a chance of that happening: you're not my type." And with that, a smile spread across the large, flushed, wobbling face of Stuart Goldstein, the first smile Maggie had seen in what felt like weeks but was actually less than thirty-six hours.

At his request, she had gone straight to his office as soon as she had returned from the raid on the Maryland house. He had had to put her on the visitors list at the bloody tourists' entrance at Fifteenth and Hamilton Place; she had had to show her passport to gain admission to the White House.

"I mean it, Stu. People will be suspicious."

"Maggie, right now we have seven senators calling for an independent counsel to investigate the President for 'alleged financial links' to fucking Tehran. People in this building have got other things to worry about than your employment arrangements."

Maggie bowed her head in a "you're the boss" gesture and continued her report back: the Secret Service was conducting an urgent trace on the dumb terminal they had discovered in Bethesda. They had so far narrowed down the location of the master computer to the south-eastern United States, but could not be more specific.

They were waiting for the TV to deliver what it had promised. Fifteen minutes earlier, Goldstein had had a call from a contact inside MSNBC warning him that the network was about to air a live interview with the source of its two recent stories on Stephen Baker. The partial identification in the blogosphere had given way to a full ID, once the collective investigative might of the internet had got to work.

The source had been named as Vic Forbes of New Orleans, Louisiana. Stu had immediately put one of his best researchers onto it: he knew he was in a race against both the media and the Republicans to know everything about Forbes that could be known. And then to *define* him. Crank, attack dog, dopehead. Whatever would shatter his credibility.

"Here's what I don't understand," Maggie said, while the TV cut to a weather forecast. "The shrink thing. How come that didn't come out before?"

"I still haven't quite figured that out. Not to my own satisfaction."

"Do you think the others knew and didn't use it?"

"No way. Adams and Rodriguez were trying to kill him in the primaries. And Chester in the general. They all had oppo research digging away, night after night, climbing all over his past. And the media, working twenty-four/seven."

"What about you? Did you know?"

"Come on, Maggie. You're my favourite Irishman and all that, but I can't get into my personal relationship with him."

"So you *did* know."

Goldstein smiled enigmatically, an expression which was accompanied by a counterpoint of snorting, as the exhalation that would normally have exited from his mouth re-routed via his nose. He really was monumentally unfit. "Whether I did or did not is not the important thing here. What matters is how the fuck did this Vic Forbes find out?"

"Maybe he spoke to the shrink?"

"Difficult. He died fifteen years ago."

"There would have been records. Papers."

"Nuh-uh. None."

"Bills?"

"Put it this way, yours truly did not come down with the first shower of rain. I am used to the dirtiest dirty tricks. You don't get to be a councilman in New York unless you know how to rip a guy's heart out with your teeth. I made sure in Baker's first race that the enemy couldn't dig up any surprises."

"Because you had dug them up first."

"Exactly. Wielded the spade myself." He held up his hands, the effort of which once again altered the rhythm of his breathing. "Then I did it again for the governor's race."

"With professional help this time, I bet."

"You're damn right. I had two of Seattle's finest — ex-cops actually — investigate Stephen Baker as if they were determined to convict him of a felony. Find out everything. Go through his phone bills, house deeds, mortgage payments, bank accounts, college transcripts. They hacked into his emails and tapped his phone for all I know. Spoke to everyone, interviewed old girlfriends, made sure there were no old boyfriends. If there was a wall Stephen Baker had pissed against, they went to sniff it. Then I did it all over again before he announced for President."

"Before?"

"Oh yes. Not much point doing it afterwards, is there?"

"And did they find anything?"

"You know everything they found. So does the American people."

Maggie smiled at the realization of it. "Of course. The big 'I experimented with drugs' admission. Getting stoned rebranded as a science project. *Experimented*, my arse."

"Sure, it's bullshit. But it worked, didn't it? Once you get it out there, you get to define yourself —"

"— before they define you. What about Iran?"

"Well, that couldn't come up during the campaign 'cause it hadn't happened yet. That took some serious digging. Somehow Forbes knew what we didn't know ourselves."

"You didn't know Jim Hodges was Hossein Najafi?"

Goldstein jerked his head back, as if affronted. "Listen Maggie. Even my *booba*, may she rest in peace, knows that you don't take money from fucking I-ran! Of course we didn't know."

"Were we set up? Someone sent Hodges in here to embarrass us?"

"Maybe. Maybe the Iranians did it. Make Baker look like an asshole. Right now, though, the only thing that bothers me about Hodges is how Forbes knew about him. And about the shrink." He stared at the TV. "I want to know who this bastard *is*."

In the end, she was disappointed. Vic Forbes did not look like a monster or a pantomime villain. In truth, his face, as he stared dead-on at the camera, conducting a satellite interview from a studio in New Orleans, was forgettable. It was lean, like one of the whippets her grandfather's friends used to keep in Dublin. His nose seemed to be pinched, too thin at the bridge. He was bald, save for some slight grey at the temples, which had Maggie put his age at around fifty, though it was perfectly possible that he had looked the same way when he was thirty.

If she had guessed how this scene would have played out, she would have imagined embarrassment would at least feature in it somewhere. Maybe shame was too much to ask for in this day and age, but you'd think a man who had anonymously smeared the President would at least have the courtesy to seem uncomfortable, even if he couldn't bring himself to squirm in his chair.

But Forbes was having none of it. Maggie watched mesmerized as he batted away a series of questions as if he'd been doing this all his life.

Describing himself as a "researcher", he insisted he was aligned with "no party and no faction", a phrase that, to Maggie's ears at least, reeked of pomposity.

"I am a truth-teller, if you will," he said. "I had this information — this truth — and I felt guilty that I wasn't sharing it with the American people. It's an old-fashioned phrase, but I believe they have a right to know. They have a right to know who their president really is."

"But *how* did you get it?" the interviewer asked. "Surely the American people have a right to know that too, don't they?"

Maggie felt her own fist clench, involuntarily. *Come on.*

"Well, Natalie," he began.

Good, thought Maggie. He seemed flustered.

"The thing is . . . Look, in an ideal world . . ."

Maggie glanced at Stuart, who was as transfixed as she was, hoping that they were witnessing the unravelling of Vic Forbes on live television.

"The point I would make, Natalie, is to ask you this: would you reveal your sources, if your network had broken a story like this without my help? Of course you wouldn't." Maggie felt the air deflate out of her. "And nor would anyone ask you. That's a basic principle of journalism."

"Yes, but you're not a journalist, are you, you scumbag bastard!" Stuart hurled an empty Styrofoam cup at the TV.

The same sentence ran through Maggie's head, on a repeat loop: Who is this guy?

Stuart's phone rang. He stabbed at it, putting it on speaker. "Hey, Zoe, whaddya got?"

Maggie heard the agent's voice, stiff and correct. "It's still very early in our inquiries, Mr Goldstein."

"I know that. And I also know that electronic data of this kind is complex and searches can take several weeks —" his voice was rising, "— and that it's impossible to be certain, I know all of that, Zoe. But I need to know. WHAT. HAVE. YOU. GOT?"

The sound of shuffled papers was finally followed by an intake of breath.

"OK, Mr Goldstein. Our preliminary investigation —"

"Zoe."

"New Orleans. We think the person who sent that message to Katie Baker's Facebook page was white, male, extremely adept with computer technology and from New Orleans, Louisiana, sir."

He hung up, shooting one eye at Maggie, the other on the TV.

"So, Stu, he's the same guy, right?"

"Confirmed," Goldstein said, staring at the screen, watching Forbes perform. "How come this guy's so good? All that BS about 'the people's right to know'. Where did that come from? He looks like shit; he's sweating. But he's impressive. He's careful. He's like a goddamn politician."

Without taking his eye off the screen, he reached for the remote and hit *pause*. (A set-top box, allowing the pausing and rewinding of live TV, was now an essential tool of the trade: it meant never having to miss an enemy gaffe again.) He rewound and watched the last minute again.

"What are you looking for?" Maggie asked.

"I don't know," he murmured. "But I'll know it when I see it."

There he went again, more guff about his "duty" to lay out the facts before the American people. He couldn't play judge and jury, but people should know he was serious and the President should know he was serious.

But on this second viewing Goldstein was not listening. He was *looking*. And now he saw what he had glimpsed so fleetingly. Maggie could see it too. A movement of the eye, still looking at the camera but no longer as if trying to meet the gaze of the unseen interviewer: he was, instead, looking into the audience. More than that, he seemed to be addressing someone specific.

The President should know I'm serious.

Goldstein hit *pause* once more, freezing Vic Forbes at the moment he lifted his eyes, the signal that he was speaking to an audience of one.

The President should know I'm serious. Deadly serious.

CHAPTER
ELEVEN

Washington, DC, Tuesday March 21, 18.15
For the third time in two days, Maggie was in the White House Residence. "Maybe I should get myself sacked more often," she had said to Stuart. "It seems to be a good career move."

This was an emergency meeting, called by the President. He wasn't pacing this time; his exterior, at least, was calm and cool. He had chosen one of the wooden chairs, allowing him to stay upright even if everyone else would be forced to slump on a sofa.

Maggie looked around the room, five of them had been called here — Goldstein, her, Tara MacDonald, Doug Sanchez, and Larry Katzman, the pollster.

"Thank you for coming," Baker said, steadily. "This is not a White House meeting, which is why we're gathering in my home. You'll notice my Chief of Staff is not here. This is a discussion among my campaign team. Old friends." He attempted a smile. "Some of you work in the White House. Some of you don't."

Maggie stared at her feet.

"I need your advice," he went on. "This presidency is under sustained assault. We knew it would happen one day. But not as soon as this." He paused. "Stuart, remind us what we know."

"Thank you, Mr President." Stuart Goldstein cleared his throat and moved to the edge of the sofa he was on so that he could have a line of eye contact with everyone in the room.

He looked horribly uncomfortable. Maggie always felt for Stuart in casual situations. His body was not designed for it. He needed a suit and a hard chair, preferably on the other side of a desk. In casual clothes, or on a couch, he was lost.

"Vic Forbes, from New Orleans, Louisiana, supplied MSNBC with two stories in the course of little more than a single news cycle. Both of these stories were calculated to cause maximum damage and both required deep investigative skills. Or inside knowledge."

Maggie saw Tara MacDonald shift in her seat.

"At the same time, he has made an indirect, but personal contact with the White House."

Now both MacDonald and Sanchez sat to attention.

"Last night someone posing as a friend of Katie Baker's sent her a message via Facebook."

There was a gasp.

Stuart went on. "This message effectively claimed responsibility for both the first MSNBC story and, in advance, the second. He said it would come in the morning and it did. He also made a very direct and personal threat against the President."

There was a pause. All eyes were on Baker, who eventually spoke. "Tell them what he said, Stuart. His exact words."

Goldstein cleared his throat. Maggie noticed that he looked nervous. Was that because he was not used to addressing a large group, like this one? No. As Maggie watched, a hint of colour appeared at the top of Goldstein's cheeks, and she realized the source of his awkwardness. He was straying, however indirectly, into a wholly alien realm. Talking about Katie Baker and her friend Alexis, discussing live chat on Facebook, forced Stuart Goldstein — married to a fellow political consultant but without children — to enter the world of family life, of fathers and daughters, of vulnerable teenage girls, a world, in short, utterly remote from his own.

He began to read. "*I have more stories to tell. The next one comes tomorrow morning. And if that doesn't smash his pretty little head into a thousand pieces, I promise you this — the one after that will. Make no mistake: I mean to destroy him.*"

Tara MacDonald gasped, suddenly looking like the mother of four that she was, an angry and protective matriarch, as she shook her head and muttered, "That poor child." In an instant the fury that had been brewing inside the White House ever since the psychiatrist story first broke had a focus: loathing for this man who had not only sought to derail the Baker presidency in its infancy but had dared to prey on a child.

Stuart continued. "Secret Service traced the communication to a house in Bethesda, Maryland. They raided the property. The computer was there, but not the person. Turns out the machine was a dumb terminal. Guy was operating it remotely. Eventually he was traced to New Orleans."

"So he's the same guy? Forbes?" Sanchez, his voice urgent, as if that was all he needed to get his coat on, head out and find the man himself.

"Yep."

There was a subtle movement in seats, as people braced themselves for the meat of the discussion: what do we do now?

Stuart held up a fleshy finger. "There's one more thing. Agent Galfano did some extra probing, based on the computer IP address in New Orleans. She examined the data records of the so-called liberal blogger who so ingeniously hacked into MSNBC's emails, thereby revealing their source."

One step ahead as always, Tara MacDonald shook her head. "Don't tell me. New Orleans."

"Yep. Forbes."

Sanchez whistled in apparent admiration. "The guy outed himself."

A noise like a door opening out on a snowstorm came through the room. Anyone hearing it for the first time would have been puzzled. But these veterans of eighteen months on the road together were used to the sound of Stuart Goldstein sighing. "Seems so," he said.

Sanchez crinkled his forehead, in a way that recalled the precociously bright teenager he had obviously been all of seven or eight years ago. "Why the fuck would he do that?"

Now Maggie spoke. "So that we'd listen to him." All heads turned to her, including, she noticed, the President's. "He knew what we'd do. He knew we'd trace his message to Katie. He wanted to be certain that once

101

we'd found him, we'd know he was for real. He *wanted* us to match him up to the MSNBC source."

Stuart came in behind her. "First rule of blackmail. It's not enough to have the goods. Your target has to *know* you've got the goods."

Baker decided he had heard enough. "Thank you, Stuart. Everyone, that is the background to the decision we need to make this evening. Who wants to go first?"

Tara MacDonald didn't wait for the customary polite silence. "I wanna be clear what exactly it is we're talking about here? Are we discussing *negotiating* with a blackmailer?"

Neither Baker nor Goldstein said anything.

"Because that's a whole world of pain we're entering if we go there. I mean, do we really think something like this could ever stay secret? I don't mean whatever shit this guy's holding, I mean the fact that we *talked* to him. Do we really think that's going to stay underground? Uh-uh."

Sanchez fiddled with his watch. "Doesn't it depend a little on what we think the guy might have?"

Maggie felt the air suck out of the room. You had to admire the balls of the guy, the fearlessness of youth and all that. But there was only one person who could answer that question and you didn't want to be the one to ask him.

There was, to everyone's relief, a knock on the door. A butler, probably seventy years old. "Sir, I have an urgent note from the Press Office. For Mrs MacDonald."

Baker beckoned the man forward; he walked in stiffly and presented the piece of paper to her. She pulled on the glasses that hung around her neck on a chain and read rapidly. Then she cleared her throat. "Forbes has just released a statement. Most networks are only quoting it in part, but apparently there's a full version on Drudge. It reads as follows. 'I want to make clear that the further information I hold on Stephen Baker does not relate to the way his campaign was funded nor to the state of his health.'"

Maggie realized she was holding her breath. So was everyone else. MacDonald kept reading.

"'It's about his past. An aspect of his past that I think will shock many Americans. An aspect of his past that the President has not shared with the nation. An aspect of his past he may not even have shared with his own family.'"

Maggie felt a new mood enter the room. It was a sensation she dimly recalled from her teenage years at home in Dublin. She could picture her younger self, sitting on the couch beside her sister Liz, cringing as a vaguely sexual scene appeared on the TV; her father getting up out of his chair, fumbling to change the channel. That was the sensation she could feel spreading over her and, surely, everyone else in this room: embarrassment. Sheer, hot-faced, look-away embarrassment.

What mortifying secret might the President have kept from his own wife? No one could bring themselves to look at him.

Maggie stole a glance at Stuart: he too was avoiding Baker's gaze. But she could see that Stuart Goldstein's embarrassment was already compounded by something that shook him much more: political panic.

How much more of this could this new presidency take? Here was a committed assassin, somehow armed with weapons-grade dirt, determined to destroy Baker. He had already landed two direct hits and now, it seemed, he was preparing for a third. Surely there would be a fourth. And a fifth. The confidence of Vic Forbes — swaggering even in this written statement — suggested he would not rest until he had finished the job. And Baker was no more.

Her voice dry, Tara spoke again. "There's one last paragraph. 'I do not plan on providing the full details today. I just wanted the American people to be aware that I have them. I wanted everyone following this story, especially those following it real close, to know I have them.'"

The gall of it was stunning. Vic Forbes was using a combination of live television and the internet to present a blackmail demand to the President of the United States.

Stuart did not let the silence linger. "Like I said, this is an attempt to destroy the President. Ideas for what we should do, people."

Tara MacDonald spoke first. "I say we do a Letterman. We go to the police and then we go on TV. We expose Forbes for what he is, a cheap scumbag felon."

Larry Katzman, the pollster, piped up. "I worry about that. Initial response can be positive, but there's great volatility. Once you go public with something like this, it kind of gives people free rein —"

"They can say what the hell they like about you," added Sanchez, clearly making the effort to substitute one four-letter word for the other he had in mind. "Makes it legitimate. Remember, David Letterman could only make his move because he fessed up to whatever the blackmailer had. Got in his retaliation first."

The pollster responded, emboldened. "In other words, the critical variable is the nature of the, er, allegations, the charges . . ." His voice trailed off, as he reached for the glass of water on the coffee table in front of him.

Tara MacDonald stepped in again, perhaps, thought Maggie, as an act of compassion, protecting the dweeby pollster from twisting in the silence for a second longer. "Seems we're out of good options. If we say nothing, Forbes is gonna keep coming at us, letting off these bombs. If we try to fess up, then the bomb's gonna be going off anyway. OK, it's gonna be us pressing the detonator and that helps. But we still don't know what damage it's gonna do.

"Which leaves making contact with this prick and trying to cut some kind of deal. Which I don't even want to think about. I mean, even if we managed to pull it off, which I have to tell you I seriously doubt, do we really think it would stay quiet? Of course, it wouldn't. Because nothing in this town ever does."

Now Sanchez added his voice. "I have to say, this is bad enough." When he saw a quizzical eyebrow from

Goldstein, he gestured around the room. "This. This meeting. Just imagine this on Glenn Beck: White House operatives sat around in the Residence discussing possible negotiations with a —"

"All right, all right," Stuart interrupted. "We get the idea. A series of dead ends. But right now there are also rather too many known unknowns. We don't know what Forbes knows and we need to. Somehow, between now and tomorrow, we need to be inside Vic Forbes's head. Whatever he has —"

But he didn't get to finish his sentence. Stephen Baker, the cool, steady, unflappable Stephen Baker, the man who had barely put a foot wrong in a two-year, outsider's presidential campaign, the man who had debated much more experienced rivals without ever slipping up, the man who had never broken a sweat even when his poll numbers were in the tank and his bank accounts dry — Stephen Baker finally snapped.

He slammed his fist onto the table and raised his voice, something his team had never seen or heard before. "Vic Forbes! VIC FORBES! I don't want to hear that man's name again? Do you understand me?" He shook his head then, his voice much quieter, he murmured, almost to himself: "I want him gone."

CHAPTER
TWELVE

Washington, DC, Wednesday March 22, 06.35

She was with Liz, in the shady area at the back of their garden. They were holding hands, Liz tugging her, a five-year-old girl impatient to show her big sister what she had found. They were wading through grass that had grown taller than they were, brushing their bare arms. Any second now, they would find it. It would be here, at the bottom of the garden.

A loud siren yanked her from sleep and bolted her upright. Her heart was thumping. The siren sounded again, though now Maggie realized it was the ringer on her cellphone, left on her bedside table. She squinted at her watch: 6.35a.m.

"Hello."

"Maggie. It's Stuart. Did I wake you?"

"No. Not at all." It was a reflexive lie. No one in Washington ever admitted to being asleep, not even at 6.35a.m. In DC setting the alarm for 7a.m. counted as a lie-in.

"Sorry about that. Anyway, put the TV on."

"Is this like some kind of daily service? Because I don't remember signing up."

"Now." There was something different in Goldstein's voice. Not so much panic as a kind of manic energy.

Maggie's eyes were still closed, as if she were half-expecting to glimpse whatever it was Liz had promised to show her. She fumbled for the remote, knocking over both a glass of water and her watch in the process.

"Jesus."

"My first reaction too."

"Hold on, I haven't got it on yet." She leaned over the bed, to grope on the floor there. Her hand was met with a discarded T-shirt and a pair of sneakers, as well as an eyemask she'd once picked up on a business class flight.

At last, the remote. She aimed it at the small box in the corner and waited for it to glow into life. It was tuned to MSNBC: unable to sleep, she'd been watching a re-run of Olbermann in the middle of the night.

Still squinting, she gasped at what she saw. "Fucking hell."

"My sentiments exactly."

She couldn't say anything else, even though she knew Stuart was waiting for an instant reaction. But she simply couldn't speak. All she could do was stare at the words streaming across the bottom of the screen.

Breaking News: Vic Forbes found dead in New Orleans.

CHAPTER
THIRTEEN

The Corner, National Review Online, posted March 22, 07.39:

It's too early to speculate, details are sketchy, yadda, yadda, yadda. (The fullest account so far seems to come from AP.) Suffice it to say, we know what Democrats would be howling right now if there were a Republican in the White House. Don't we? Well, conservatives should not sink to their level. Instead, we should do no more than point out that some deaths are more convenient than others. And for Stephen Baker the death of Vic Forbes is very convenient indeed.

From the comments thread, Talking Points Memo, March 22, 08.01:

We shouldn't speak ill of the dead and I don't want to speak ill of Vic Forbes. Like everyone else in Washington, apparently, I never knew the guy, never even heard of him until this week. But I would be lying if I said that a deep wave of relief did not come over me when I heard the news just now. I'm not proud of that, but there we are. I want to be honest. Bottom Line:

Forbes was trying to destroy the elected president of this country and that was a threat not only to Baker and the Democrats — though it most certainly was that — but to the United States constitution. With his death, that clear and present danger to the republic has passed . . .

CHAPTER
FOURTEEN

Washington, DC, Wednesday March 22, 06.37
Maggie kept staring at the screen, which showed a residential street in New Orleans, a row of timber-clad houses in light blues and greens, with the one clearest in vision now behind yellow and black tape. Even from here, the words were in focus: *Police Line Do Not Cross*.

She clicked channels: same street, different angle. With a reporter doing a stand-up. She could hear Stuart breathing heavily into the phone, waiting for her to speak. She turned up the volume on the TV.

"*. . . few details at this hour, Tom. What sources are telling this network unofficially is that the circumstances in which Mr Forbes was found were —*" and here the reporter made a great show of looking down and checking his notebook, "*— bizarre.*"

"Bizarre?" echoed Maggie.

"Let me in and I'll tell you."

"You're here?"

"Cab just pulled up."

Now she needed to absorb the strangeness both of what she had just heard on the television and the notion of Stuart Goldstein in her apartment building.

111

Whatever affinity she felt for him as a colleague, she would never have described him as a friend. He hadn't been to her place, she hadn't been to his; that line had never been crossed.

"You're here," she said again, uselessly. "Can you give me five minutes?"

"Two."

Under the duvet, she was wearing only a man's T-shirt — white, large and bearing the name of an Israeli basketball team. It had belonged to Uri, though she had never worn it while they were together. But last night she had dug it out, smelling it before putting it on, even though she knew the scent of him had been washed away long ago.

As she rushed to pull on a pair of jeans and to find a sweater, grateful that Stuart would take longer than most to get into her building, into the elevator and out again, she kept one ear on the intriguing tale tumbling out of the TV.

"... we're not able to disclose all the circumstances of Mr Forbes's death at this time, Dan, and that's not only because some of our sources are speaking only on background. It's also because this is a family network and it's still early on in the day."

What were they talking about? What on earth had happened to Vic Forbes that they couldn't give the details? Last night she and the rest of the band of brothers who had got Stephen Baker elected President had sat there facing a series of brick walls. There had been no good options. Whichever path they took, Vic

112

Forbes with his bald head and his thin, bland, smiling face had stood there blocking their escape.

And now he was gone, helpfully magicked away and just in the nick of time.

She heard the knock on the door and the unmistakable sound of Stuart Goldstein's breathless panting outside. She did a last scope of the apartment, scanning for potential embarrassment. Now that she had closed the door to her bedroom, the place looked tidy enough. One of the advantages of Washington hours: you were barely home long enough to make the place a mess.

But still, and even in just that brief glimpse, she had seen something that had made her not quite embarrassed — no dirty laundry on the floor — but ever so slightly ashamed. In that short, stabbing second she experienced the apartment as if through the eyes of another.

She had seen that it was elegant, located in the much-admired art-deco grandeur of the Kennedy-Warren building, and stylishly furnished, with a sprinkling of items that hinted at her past life of constant and exotic travel. But she had also seen that it was, however subtly, empty. That it was, visible to the naked eye, the home of a person alone. And, her eye falling on the crisping leaves of a dying ficus, one without the nurturing ability even to keep a houseplant alive.

"Stuart," she said, stepping back with a sweep of the hand in the exaggerated manner of a butler ushering him inside — a small piece of theatre designed chiefly to avoid any confusion over whether there would be a kiss on the cheek or handshake. The issue had never arisen at work or during the campaign. But they had never visited each other at home before.

She headed straight for the kitchen to put on a pot of coffee, though Stuart told her not to: "I've had so much coffee, I'm *schvitzing*. He had clearly been up for several hours. When had Forbes died? How long had Stu known? She tamped down the ground beans: he might not need it, but she certainly did.

He joined her in the kitchen, impatient to get on with things, pulling out a chair tucked into the small kitchen table and lowering himself into it. The fixedness of his gaze told Maggie to do the same.

Their faces now just a few inches apart, the words raced out of him. "Forbes was found hanged in his bedroom in New Orleans."

She knew this already. "Right . . ."

Stuart lowered his voice. "He was wearing women's underwear. Stockings, garters, the whole deal. With an orange stuffed into his mouth."

"A what?"

"A segment of orange. Apparently it's used to disguise the taste of amyl nitrate. It's bitter, so you bite on an orange as a chaser."

"Is this some kind of joke?"

"Do I look like I'm joking?"

"He was wearing stockings?"

"Yes. It's still unofficial, but that's what the police are saying."

"Jesus." Maggie stood up so that she could pace.

114

"The police say it's not as uncommon as you'd think. Couples strangle each other for kicks. Guys who are alone hang themselves. Starving the oxygen to the brain gives you a rush. 'Auto-erotic asphyxiation' they call it."

"I may be a convent girl, Stuart, but I'm not a bloody nun. I know about that." The expression on his face made her rush to qualify. "I mean, I've *heard* about it. Christ." There was a pause. "And what was the orange for again?"

"Hide the taste of the amyl nitrate. Which apparently adds to the ride." He made a shrug which said, *what do I know from such things?* "One theory is that Forbes was getting off on the success of his little project. Making contact with the President, interviews on cable TV. Seems like he was aroused."

"Is that what the police are saying?"

"No. All they know is that he'd been in the news during the last forty-eight hours, as the source for a couple of stories damaging to the President. Remember, no one else knows what we know. Do you have any cereal?"

"What?"

"Breakfast cereal."

Maggie passed him a box of Cheerios. He immediately plunged a hand deep inside and fed himself a large mouthful.

Neither of them had said what she knew he and everyone else in the White House must be feeling — what, for that matter, she was feeling. Ordinarily, she would have resisted saying it. She would have known that, as a White House staffer, it was unwise even to voice such a sentiment to a colleague, lest it get out. But to hell with that. She was now Maggie Costello, independent citizen. She could say whatever she liked. "Solves a problem, though, doesn't it, Stu?"

"I was worried you'd say that."

"Worried? Why?"

"Because if you're saying that, so will plenty of other folks. In fact, they've already started."

"What do you mean?"

"Blogs. Wingnuts mainly. But that's how it always starts. On the margins, then spreads inward."

"They're claiming Baker had something to do with this?"

Goldstein reached into the pocket of his triple-extra-large jacket and pulled out his iPhone. A few stabs at the screen, followed by a swipe or two, and he was reading. "'*It was Napoleon who said he wanted generals who were neither courageous nor brilliant, but lucky. Seems as if Stephen Baker is one of life's lucky generals. Just when he was on the precipice, staring into the abyss, guess what happens? That's right: the guy who was going to push him over the edge wakes up dead in New Orleans. Love him or hate him, you've got to admit it, this Prez has someone up there who likes him. Though they do always say, you make your own luck . . .*'"

"So?"

"Come on, Maggie. 'You make your own luck'? We know where this is heading." Goldstein's phone

116

vibrated in his hand. He stared at it, then held it up so that Maggie could see the screen. "Another one."

Maggie stepped forward, leaning over to stare at the tiny screen. An email from Doug Sanchez. No message, just a grab from another political website, not quite mainstream but well-known. Its headline: "*The Baker presidency turns into* The Godfather: *key tormentor now sleeping with the fishes.*"

Goldstein let his weight fall back into the seat which, being a modest Crate & Barrel kitchen number, was fighting a losing battle to contain it. "I'd say we're twenty-four hours away from an outright accusation of murder."

Maggie said nothing. She understood perfectly: Stuart was right to anticipate this reaction to Forbes's death and right to want to get ahead of it. He did not seem to feel any of the relief that had washed over her the instant she saw the news. Instead, he seemed just as troubled as he had been when Forbes had hacked his way onto Katie Baker's Facebook page, announcing his intention to destroy the Baker presidency.

She poured herself a coffee, then returned to the table.

"We had seven senators calling for an independent counsel *before* this broke. It won't just be Rick fucking Franklin talking about a special prosecutor now, you mark my words," he said bitterly. He fed himself another fistful of Cheerios.

"I see."

"It's all about context. That's politics, Maggie. *Context.* Normally the only people who would give two shits about Vic Forbes swinging from a noose with his dick in his hand would be right-wing nutcases who think the Federal Reserve is a European plot to destroy America. But as of two days ago we're in a different context."

"Thanks to Forbes."

"Ironically, yes. Thanks to him, people who used to trust the President now don't. They think he might be crazy and in the pay of the ayatollahs. So now they'll be ready to believe he is capable —"

"— of murder."

Stuart looked at her hard. "You heard what he said last night."

Maggie hesitated. Of course she had heard what Stephen Baker had said last night, but had — she now realized — made an instant decision to push the memory of it out of her mind.

"Do I need to remind you?"

"You don't need to remind me," she said in little more than a whisper.

" 'I want him gone.' That's what he said."

"I heard it."

"Well, if you heard it, then so did everyone else in that room."

"Jesus, Stuart, you think someone in the team is going to leak this?" The very word — team — stirred a brief but bittersweet sensation of nostalgia. White House personnel were known as "the staff", but the group of veterans from the campaign had always been and were still known to each other as "the team". She might have been dumped from the former but she would always be part of the latter. Magnus Longley couldn't take that away from her.

"I see two scenarios, Maggie, and they both stink of shit. First scenario, and I admit this stinks even worse than the other, is that someone tells their best pal at the *Times* that 'you'll never guess what the President said' . . ."

"No one would do that."

"Not even deliberately. Just chatting, shooting the breeze. You know what DC is like: people talk. They can't help themselves."

"Then you shouldn't have gathered the team. Not if you don't trust them."

"If it had been up to me, we wouldn't have."

At this, Maggie couldn't help but raise an eyebrow. Stuart Goldstein usually observed the discipline of a Tudor courtier, dutifully deferential to the protocol of collective responsibility: he would defend any decision of the king as if it were his own. Maggie had never before heard him reveal a disagreement between himself and Stephen Baker, at least one which did not end in the eventual vindication of the President, offered as self-deprecatory evidence of the almost supernatural judgment of the man they all worked for. ("I told him, you don't need to visit in person. Do it by phone. But he insisted. And you know what? He was right.")

But this was different. And even though it hardly amounted to lacerating criticism, Maggie noted it as a sign that the tectonic plates were shifting somehow; that this crisis was real.

"If that happens, Maggie, if it gets out that he said those words a matter of hours before Forbes was found dead, then . . ." His voice trailed off, as if the thought was too awful even to voice out loud.

"So what's the other scenario?"

"That no one leaks. But that the President's most senior aides, his most trusted counsellors, do what you did: file away what you heard in some corner of the brain, where it never quite goes away. That some little piece of them will be thinking, 'That was funny. Baker said he wanted Forbes gone and look, hey fucking presto, Forbes was gone the very next morning.'"

"But if they don't say anything, then —"

"Then it's still a disaster!" Stuart pounded the table again. His usually cheerful, gnome-like countenance was gone, transformed by sorrow or anger, Maggie couldn't quite tell which. "Maggie, do you know how long a presidential term is? In days?" He didn't wait for an answer. "It's fourteen hundred and sixty days. Do you know how many days we've had? Sixty-one. That's all. Can you imagine if he has to stagger on for fourteen hundred fucking days without the trust of his most senior advisors? If they think what you were thinking, the moment you heard the news just now?"

Maggie stared into her coffee, reluctant to meet Stuart's gaze — chiefly because she could not deny what he had just said.

"We have to know the truth, Maggie. Everything. That's the only way we're going to be able to rebut all the lies and the conspiracy theories that are building and spreading right now." He gestured towards his

120

iPhone, as if it held a lethal virus that was growing with every second. "We need to get the facts, Maggie. The full story. Otherwise the Stephen Baker presidency is going down."

Maggie held his gaze and then, in a new tone, brisk and businesslike, she began working through the questions to be answered.

"First, you need to know if it was a suicide. Then you need to know if Forbes was alone."

"Does this look like the work of a lone gunman to you, Maggie? Think of the scale of the operation. The depth of the research. The media savviness. The unmanned computer in Maryland, relayed to New Orleans. All that would have taken time and money. Resources."

"So you need to know if he was part of a team. If he was, the threat is still there."

"Right. Who are they? Is this Republican dirty tricks? Foreign? Someone we haven't thought of?"

"And what is this nuclear secret he was about to drop?"

Goldstein pointed his finger directly at Maggie, a charades gesture she had come to love: he deployed it during their discussions-cum-tutorials, the sign that she had asked precisely the right question or made the key point. "What indeed? What exactly do they have on Stephen Baker that convinced Forbes that he could blackmail the President of the United States?"

And, Maggie thought, could have made the President of the United States consider paying up. For that, surely, was what lay behind last night's meeting:

Baker would not have summoned them all unless he had been actually considering acceding to Forbes's demands.

Her mind was whirring now, rattling through multiple questions, each one of which spawned dozens more — forming a vast, elaborate labyrinth that she could visualize. A decision-tree, the management gurus called it, depicting one question as it split off into two branches — yes and no — which themselves split off again and again. Most people would probably be terrified by the sight of such a thing, but Maggie revelled in the complexity of it. The diplomatic negotiations which had dominated her recent professional life worked the same way: you had to consider each path the parties might take, and then work out which tributaries and detours might lead off each path, always looking for the dead ends. But before any of that there was one large fork in the road.

"You've got a lot of work to do," she said.

"What do you mean 'you'? I don't like this 'you'. It's 'we', Maggie. You, me and Stephen Baker."

"Do I have to remind you again, Stuart? I was fired."

"And do I have to remind you that I already said that's an advantage? Distance. Besides, you do this for him, there's no way the President is not going to bring you back. He wants you to do that Africa thing." He took another plunge into the cereal box.

Maggie watched him munch, looking at her, waiting for an answer. She realized that she felt a twinge of disappointment at his last remark, dangling the carrot of a return to her old job. If she were going to help, it wouldn't be for that reason, for herself. It would be because she believed in Stephen Baker, believed in what he was trying to do, had believed him, in truth, from that very first car ride across the vast empty spaces of Iowa. She couldn't stand by and watch his presidency destroyed by some cheap dirty tricks campaign. Too much was at stake.

"OK," she said, finally. "You'd better go. I need to leave now."

"Where are you going?"

"Where do you think? I'm not going to get any answers here, Stu. I'm going to New Orleans."

CHAPTER
FIFTEEN

Email chatter, intercepted by the National Security Agency, Fort Meade, Maryland. Thought to be the text of a statement issued by a key leader of violent jihadism, whereabouts unknown:

I bear witness that there is no God but Allah and that Mohammed is his messenger.

The head of the infidels worldwide has a new face, but the rotten heart is still the same. They try to trick and to deceive, but our nation, the Islamic world, is old and wise and will not be deceived. Baker is still the same infidel, still the same coward, even if he tries to wag his tail instead of baring his teeth.

But not all Muslims are as wise as they should be. Some forget how America has abused the people and sacred places of islam for many decades, how with fire from the north to the south, from the east to the west, this Shaitan has slain our children. These unwise Muslims want to touch the hand of Baker, believing that he is reaching to them in the name of peace.

This has hurt our cause. Our enemies gloat that we are losing our support, that our numbers are falling. I say to the warriors of Islam, these few words: we are now in a new struggle, to keep the faith of every Muslim, to prevent naïve brothers and sisters being tricked by the smiling face and honeyed words of the deceiver Baker.

May God find a way to remove this man, so that Muslims may see the true face of America once more.

God is great and he hates confusion. May peace and God's mercy be upon you.

CHAPTER
SIXTEEN

New Orleans, Wednesday March 22, 18.15 CST
The billboards on Interstate 10 told her she was in a different country, a universe away from the buttoned-up pieties of the capital. One sign promoted a gun show, the next a burlesque club with a slogan that made Maggie smile: *Ten beautiful girls and one ugly one!*

"This your first time in N'Awlins?"

Maggie nodded, not wanting to get into conversation with the cab driver just yet: she wanted to keep looking out of the window. She needed to think.

"'At's a pity," he replied, ignoring her attempt at aloofness. "Shoulda been here before Katrina. Not the same place no more."

She surrendered: "Were you here the whole time?"

"I stayed till I saw the water rise so high my church was drownin'. I went to Atlanta. My ma refused to leave. She ended up one of those bodies you saw on the evening news. Floating."

"Oh my God, I am sorry."

"Nothing for you to be sorry for, ma'am. You ain't the government. Not your fault. You doing the right thing, coming back to N'Awlins. We need all the visitors we can get."

126

She had asked for the French Quarter, to be as close as she could get to Forbes. It also made for useful cover. She could be a tourist from Dublin too naïve to know anywhere else to stay. Or she could be a journalist.

It was a plaintive message on the machine from Nick du Caines, the dissolute New York-based correspondent of a much-loved, if ailing, British Sunday newspaper that had given her the idea. She had sat through enough of his anecdotes to know he treated his press card as if it were a magic ticket, granting admission to every ride at the fair. If Nick was to be believed, there was no one and nowhere to whom a journalist could not gain access.

If Nick was to be believed, that is. Part of his charm, if you didn't count the wreckage of his personal life and the complexion battered by three decades of "experimentation" with vodka, whisky and every kind of drug the pharmaceutical industries — legal and illegal — had managed to generate, was the grey zone he inhabited when it came to the truth. Or *la veracité*, as he would doubtless refer to it, resorting to his comedy French accent whenever he wanted to skirt round a topic that might be awkward. ("Mags, it's late, you're gorgeous, I am full of *ardeur*, so what about a little *liaison, dangereuse* or otherwise?")

She had tried calling him as soon as she left home for New Orleans. While she raced around packing a bag, she called Nick's cellphone at least three times. No point trying the office: he had sublet that to the correspondent from Danish television — "All on

127

the QT, if you don't mind, Mags: London would not be best pleased" — preferring to work from home. Though that, Maggie suspected, was a laughable euphemism: from what she could divine, Nick du Caines didn't work during the week at all, instead building himself up to a fever which crested on Friday night as, in a sweat, he spewed out thousands of words, hammering away at his keyboard until dawn on Saturday — just making the lunchtime deadline in London.

So where the august correspondent would be at this hour of a midweek morning was anybody's guess. Though you'd get good odds for the bed of a lonely, ex-pat European — the wife of the Belgian ambassador, perhaps, or that dark-eyed Kosovar who had worked for du Caines as a translator during the Balkan wars and somehow ended up in DC in his wake several years later.

No luck on the way to Reagan Airport, but there was a sign of life when she touched down at Louis Armstrong International: a busy signal. Now, just as her cab was navigating its way down streets with improbable names like Abundance, Cupid and Desire, she finally got through.

"Mags! My long-lost comrade! What the hell is happening at the White House? Seems like the place is falling apart. Just heard on the old bush telegraph about your unwanted *au revoir* from there. Sounds like you got out just in time. Bastards, though, for firing you. Or 'letting you go' as the tossers in HR would no doubt phrase it. Is there anything your Uncle Nick can do?"

128

"Well, actually —"

"Perhaps a brief tale in the paper, setting the record straight? You know, 'The New McCarthyism that lost Baker his best diplomat', that kind of thing? I love 'New McCarthyism' stories: the posh papers' version of 'political correctness gone mad'. Might fight for space this week, though, what with —"

"Nick —"

"Still, any port in a storm. Things are terrible on the paper, threatened with a bloody —"

"Nick!"

The cab driver turned round, a look of hurt on his face. Maggie pointed at the phone and mouthed an apology. Sure that she now had Nick's silence, she lowered her voice. "Nick, there's something I need."

"I can't tell you how long I've been waiting to hear those words, Mags my love. Shall I come over at eight? Or right now? I love the afternoons."

"Not that, Nick. I need some advice."

"OK."

"About being a journalist. I can't tell you much about it yet, but I promise when I can you'll get it first."

"A story?"

"Yes."

"Oh bless your little Irish heart. What is it you need to know?"

For the next ten minutes, Nick du Caines proceeded to teach the core elements of a crash course in journalism's black arts. They agreed that she would be Liz Costello of the *Irish Times*: if anyone were to be mischievous enough to check up on her via Google —

"A loathsome practice, but increasingly common these days," lamented Nick — then they would at least find something. The fact that the Costello byline would be attached to witty reports on Dublin nightlife would be a problem, but a surmountable one.

"Say you're comparing the two scenes for a long article for the magazine," Nick advised, before exciting himself with another thought. "Say you're writing it for the travel section: a post-Katrina piece, 'Return to New Orleans'. They'll be so grateful they won't care if you don't have a press card."

"And why don't I have a press card?"

"Say you were mugged. That'll make them even more desperate to make you love them."

"Won't they start asking me for details? Taking witness statements, all that crap?"

"Good point. Say it happened in DC. You're applying for a new one. In the meantime, any questions, they're to call your bureau chief in Washington, one Nicholas du Caines."

"What if they Google you?"

"They never do. Name's too difficult. And remember you never write, you *file*. It's never an article, it's a *piece*. And don't save anything onto the machine. My laptop was once crushed under a motorbike by some hairy biker: lost a three-thousand-word feature on the new Hell's Angels. Those memory sticks are fucking useless too. Save everything online, Mags. In the ether." He sighed. "New Orleans, eh? It'll be a riot."

Nick warned her that the city would be swarming with journalists after the Forbes death: "I'd be there myself if it wasn't for the fact that the foreign desk is even more broke than I am." She was to head for the hotel where all the reporters would be staying. There's always one, he explained. He promised that the second he had rung off, he would call his mate from the *Telegraph* and find out the name. Within two minutes, there was a buzz on her BlackBerry: *The Monteleone. Demand a room that doesn't look over the street. Bloody loud at night.*

The second she got out of the cab, she was hit by a scent that reminded her of a combination of Africa and Washington in August: the sub-tropical tang of damp and decay, with a hint of sweetness. She looked around, instantly hit by the lushness that seemed to tumble off every Paris-style balcony, vivid purple bougainvillea or trailing plants of dense green. The place seemed to ooze with fertility, drunken and heady.

It was still early, but Nick had told her to head for the bar all the same: thanks to the time difference, the European hacks would all be off deadline by now. Even their "damned bloody websites" would be asleep. "They're better anyway," Nick had said. "Much more forthcoming than our tight-lipped American colleagues, most of whom stay on the bloody mineral water all night."

The Carousel Bar was the kind of place that would normally make Maggie recoil: it had, God help us, a theme — the circus, complete with a spinning merry-go-round, elaborately decorated, in the centre of the room. But there were also black-and-white portraits of past guests, among them Tennessee Williams,

Truman Capote and William Faulkner, which made her feel rather more forgiving.

She spied a group of half a dozen — five men, one woman — at a corner table. Past experience told her this was the foreign press corps; and she was right. There, sipping at a vile-looking concoction, was a man who perfectly matched Nick's description of his *Telegraph* pal — sandy-haired, gawky, eager.

"Tim?" she asked, prompting the man to his feet, simultaneously putting down his drink and offering a handshake. His face bore the expression Maggie had seen ever since she turned eighteen, a look that even the most sophisticated men were not fully able to conceal, one that contained both a split-second act of assessment and the passing of a positive verdict. She felt rumpled after the flight and she was exhausted after the last two days. But the gaze of Tim from the *Telegraph*, probably ten years her junior, told her that whatever it was she had had at eighteen had not completely vanished.

"Hurricane?" he said, raising his glass with a smile. "The post-Katrina cocktail of choice, apparently."

Remembering Lesson One in Nick du Caines's journalism for beginners course, Maggie insisted she would get this round — taking orders for more Hurricanes from the rest of the table. As she did, she noticed a man at a corner table, alone. Dark-haired, thin-faced and older than the others, he had a laptop open and was speaking softly into a cellphone. Was he a journalist too?

132

By the time she came back to the table, Tim had already filled everyone in: she was Liz from the *Irish Times*, a pal of Nick's and therefore to be welcomed.

"Where we got up to, Miss Costello," explained Francesco from *Corriere della Serra* — a bald man in his late forties, who nevertheless gave off a whiff of foreign correspondent glamour, starting with his battered photographer's jacket and its countless pockets — "was the police statement today that they are 'looking for no one else' in connection with Forbes's death."

"Means they are treating it as suicide," added Tim keenly.

"And what do we think of that?" said Maggie, taking a sip of her cocktail. Sickly sweet, it made her gag: how anyone would want to drink this over a glass of Jameson's was beyond her.

"I don't see how they could do anything else," said Francesco. "There was no sign of a break-in at the apartment," he said, counting the fingers off his hand for emphasis. "There were no fingerprints except his own. And this is a known form of sexual — how do you say — *fetish*."

"The Louisiana coroner might call it death by misadventure." It was the woman, whose voice sounded Home Counties English to Maggie but who was, apparently, the New York correspondent for *Der Spiegel*. Like the others, she had got on a plane the moment Forbes's death was announced: since they'd been in New Orleans since lunchtime, they were now officially experts. "It's not a suicide if Forbes didn't want to take his own life."

"It seems," said Tim, turning to face Maggie, his voice lowering as if he was hoping to turn the group conversation into a more intimate exchange between the two of them, "as if our Mr Forbes was so thrilled at his success in wounding the President, that he wanted to celebrate, as it were."

"And we think Forbes was into the whole auto-asphyxiation thing?"

"Oh, yes. He was a gasper, all right." Tim smiled, pleased with himself.

"A gasper?"

"That's the word for it, I'm told: those who get their kicks being choked." Seeing Francesco straining to join their conversation, Tim decided to say more, to keep Maggie to himself. "We have a piece from our medical correspondent which says Forbes fits the profile completely. Middle-aged man; risk-taker; thrill-seeker; loner."

"We know all that, do we?"

"And don't forget the New Orleans factor."

"What's that?"

"N'Awlins!" He attempted a Southern drawl, without success. "The Big Easy, the Big Sleazy. He lived just off Bourbon Street, for God's sake. This is sin city, and he was right in the middle of it. He fits the bill perfectly."

"Is that what the *Telegraph* is saying tomorrow?"

"That's what *I'm* saying. Can't speak for the bloody comment pages. The editor *loathes* Baker, thinks he's some crazed socialist. He asked the foreign desk to get me to write 'The ten clues that say Forbes was murdered'. Been reading too many blogs."

"That would be a cracking story, though, wouldn't it?" Maggie said, before noticing that the woman from *Der Spiegel* was staring at her. Was she jealous? Had Maggie got between her and young Tim?

"Don't I know you from somewhere?"

"I don't think so. Not unless you spend time clubbing by the Liffey." Maggie could hear her own accent change, dialling up the Irish.

"No, you definitely look familiar." Still the cut-glass English accent, with impeccable idiom, but now the German undercurrent had become audible. "Were you in a magazine?"

"I'm not a model, if that's what you mean." Maggie saw Francesco and Tim break into appreciative smiles. She didn't like where this was going. "Actually, I get this a lot. I have one of those faces. People say I look like a lot of people."

"Must be that then."

Maggie smiled in what she hoped was a sisterly fashion, but elicited only a cool response. She glanced down at the pile of BlackBerrys and phones on the table: it would only take a couple of searches of the name Costello and this woman would soon have her rumbled.

A phone call came for Francesco and, thankfully, the moment was broken. Seizing his chance, Tim turned to her and suggested the two of them go out for a bite of dinner. "We could compare notes on the story if you like — though, obviously, only if you think that's useful."

Maggie remembered another of Nick's rules: better to hunt in packs, at least if you're a novice. She needed to tag along with someone, so it might as well be someone eager.

She got to her feet, accepting the table's collective gratitude for getting the round in — including a mouthed thank you from Francesco — and followed Tim out. As she left she looked back at the thin-faced man, to see that he was staring straight at her.

They headed down Iberville Street, hearing the jazz riffs that curled like cigarette smoke from each doorway. Eventually they reached the Acme Oyster House: she had a plate of chargrilled oysters, so fresh they made her tingle, while he gobbled up a pound of spicy boiled crawfish.

Over dinner, she listened politely as Telegraph Tim told the story of his life: Eton, Oxford, then straight to Kabul as a stringer, impressing the foreign desk, becoming a favourite of the new editor and eventually earning a transfer to Washington. His father, a retired general; his life, one of seamless privilege. Maggie nodded and laughed in the right places and did the occasional shake of the head, thereby exhibiting the full length of her hair, a move which tended to elicit an almost Pavlovian response in most heterosexual men.

After dinner they walked along Bourbon Street, continuing to trade speculation on the Forbes case as they watched frat boys lurch out of the multiple bars.

136

Was Forbes a Southerner? Was he a native of New Orleans? If not, had he come here pre- or post-Katrina?

"Can we go there?" Maggie said suddenly.

"Where?" Tim replied, looking for whatever it was that had caught Maggie's eye.

"The house. Forbes's house."

"It's sealed off, Maggie. Crime scene and all that. No media access."

"I don't mean to go in. Just to look from the outside."

Tim, who had visited earlier that day, was only too happy to play tour guide, leading Maggie a few blocks east, turning right, then heading into the crush of antique shops, restaurants and hotels on Royal Street before they finally reached the tree-lined and residential Spain Street.

The homes were decent enough, timber-clad in pastel colours, but they were small, many of them single-storey, and without the ornate, wrought-iron balustrades that made the heart of the French Quarter as alluring as a subtropical Paris. It suggested that Forbes had been anything but wealthy.

"There it is," said Tim, gesturing ahead. Ribbons of yellow-and-black police tape still barred the front porch and the three-step walk-up; there were a couple of TV satellite trucks parked outside.

Maggie gazed at it, trying to imagine the life of the man who had lived there. Who he had been and what he had wanted. Just then, she spotted some activity. A policeman was approaching and behind him what appeared to be a colleague in plain clothes. She turned

137

to Tim — "Isn't that . . .?" — but he was off chatting to one of the technicians by the TV truck, asking if there had been any developments.

Maggie took another look. It was him: the thin-faced man from the Monteleone bar, now being ushered into Vic Forbes's house, a place that was off-limits to the press. And yet he had been there, among the journalists, in what was, in effect, the media hotel. What was going on?

Tim was back at her side and Maggie said nothing. She scribbled a few lines in her notebook, then agreed that they stroll back to the Monteleone together. They re-entered the pedestrian throng of Royal Street, full of shops open to the heady spring evening. As they passed a display of scented candles and an array of gothic masks for Mardi Gras, Tim launched into a long story about the cricket club he had founded in New York, allowing Maggie to stop listening and to think.

The simplest explanation for what she had just seen was that the man was indeed a plain-clothes cop who had earlier been at the bar of the Monteleone undercover. But why? Surely he hadn't been eavesdropping on the hacks: of what possible value could that be?

They were back at the hotel now, Maggie reluctantly agreeing to return to the Carousel Bar, where the table of international journalists had reformed, albeit with a slightly different cast list. This time, though, she insisted on whisky.

Within twenty minutes, the thin-faced man was back, once again taking a table on his own, once again pulling out his laptop as if to begin journalistic work.

Maggie excused herself from the group and, with no clear plan, strode right over to the man. "Excuse me," she began, hoping she was looming over him.

"What is it?" he said. American, the accent rougher than she was expecting. Not Southern; closer to New Jersey.

"Who are you?"

"I'll tell you if you tell me." He cracked a smile, showing bad teeth.

"My name is Liz Costello. *Irish Times*."

"Lewis Rigby. I write for the *National Enquirer*. Freelance."

That was not what she was expecting. "As in the supermarket tabloid?"

"Yeah, the supermarket tabloid that broke the biggest political story of the last year, thank you very much."

"Mark Chester's love-child? That was you?"

"Not me personally. But yeah. You wanna sit down?"

Maggie pulled up a chair, forming a new strategy in light of this fresh information. "So," she said, her voice friendly and collegiate now. "You here on the Forbes story?"

He smiled, as if licking his lips at the prospect. "You bet."

"Right," Maggie said slowly. "It's just I had a tip that earlier today a reporter for 'the *Enquirer*' bribed a serving officer of the New Orleans Police Department in order to gain access to a crime scene. It didn't sound like the kind of thing the *Philadelphia Enquirer* would get up to, so it must have been you. You know that's a felony in all fifty states, with very heavy penalties."

He turned ashen.

"Yep. My source has hard evidence." The bluff was the oldest trick in the negotiator's book. Through years of talks, Maggie had discovered that even the wiliest operators would fall for it.

"Jesus Christ."

"Don't worry. I'm not going to blab. Not to the police, not to the *Enquirer*."

"You're not?"

"We've all got a job to do."

He let out a long gulp of air.

Maggie continued. "Just so long as you share whatever you've got with me."

"You gotta be kidding. There's no way the *Nat* —"

"— *National Enquirer* is going to want to face charges of corrupting a police officer. Too serious. Which is why you're going to get on the phone to your friend and ask him to arrange another visit to the house. With me as your pal."

It took him approximately five seconds to compute what he'd heard. "But no photographs, all right? Those are my exclusive. Otherwise I'm screwed."

"Deal."

His brow remained furrowed. "How can I trust you not to take it somewhere else?"

"You can't." Maggie smiled. "But you don't have much choice."

He gave a short, glum nod.

"So," Maggie said, gesturing for them to leave the bar. "When shall we do this?"

"There's only one time we *can* do this. He's only on duty tonight. We'll go there right now."

CHAPTER
SEVENTEEN

New Orleans, Wednesday March 22, 23.03 CST
The TV trucks were still there but, Rigby counselled, one was local and, at this hour, off the air while the other was Japanese: nothing to worry about. Yesterday there had been two dozen. The New Orleans Police Department had been repetitive in its consistency, drilling away at the message that they were looking for no one else in connection with the death of Victor Forbes, that the admittedly bizarre circumstances of his demise all but confirmed that it was death at his own hand, whether deliberate or not was hard to determine and might never be known.

The message had seemed to penetrate. Maggie had clicked on the TV the instant she got into her hotel room after check-in: hopping channels, she had detected a change in tone. True, Fox, and the nutjobs, were still crying murder, but the mainstream voices were calmer. "A personal tragedy for Mr Forbes seems to have brought to an end what threatened to be a political calamity for President Baker," said some precociously serious twenty-something talking head from *The New Republic*.

142

Rigby insisted on waiting across the street, standing in the shadows where he would not be seen. Eventually the policeman Maggie had seen earlier — African-American and at least six foot two — came into view. Rigby stepped out to meet him. He nodded his head towards Maggie and uttered the single, reluctant word, "colleague". The cop shrugged, as if to say "Like I give a shit".

In silence he led them under the tape and up the stairs. No furtive looks over his shoulder, he acted as if this were perfectly normal police procedure. Anyone watching would assume they were witnessing nothing more than a police officer opening up a crime scene to, say, two senior detectives.

Once inside, with the front door closed, he handed them each a pair of latex gloves, produced from a box. He put on a pair too, then turned on the lights. "You know the rules, but I'll say it again. You don't move anything, you don't take anything. You got five minutes, max."

Maggie's eyes swept over the room, trying to capture as much information as she could. Hardwood floors. Minimal furniture. Paintings on the wall: Holiday Inn prints rather than art. A coffee table bearing two large books: aerial shots of the earth and an atlas. No photos anywhere. It looked unlived in, like a corporate rental. It felt empty.

"Is this how it was, officer?" Maggie asked. "Or have you taken anything away?"

The policeman turned around, his bulk seeming to fill the room. Unsmiling, he seemed offended, not so much by the content of the question as at the very idea that he had to talk at all. "Nothing has been removed from this area, as far as I'm aware. Some items were taken from the bedroom for further forensic examination." He concluded with a glare. "No more questions."

Rigby had already moved across the ground floor and was on the first step of the spiral staircase to the bedroom, apparently grateful for the chance to take a second look around, even if it had cost him an extra few hundred dollars.

Maggie followed, peering into the kitchen/diner area, which stood at the rear of the open-plan living room. The breakfast bar's surface was spotless. She flipped open the oven: apparently unused.

By now, she was lagging behind. She could hear Rigby's footsteps through the ceiling. He was doubtless standing at the spot where Forbes had been found dead.

She clanked her way round the wrought-iron staircase, emerging onto a small landing giving onto three rooms: bathroom, bedroom and a small study.

She remembered another tip from Nick du Caines. "First place any profile-writer heads to is the bathroom," he had said during their rapid-fire tutorial. "Bloody goldmine in there. Ask to go to the loo and then check the meds cabinet. Viagra? You can then saunter out and ask your interviewee sensitive questions about impotence. Rogaine? Very nice, especially if you're doing an actor. But the motherlode is Xanax. Or Prozac. Or Lithium. That's very heaven. You put on your most caring face and ask if the rumours are true:

144

'Are you currently being treated for depression?' Jack-bloody-pot."

Maggie darted in, noted the cleanest shower curtain she'd ever seen, and opened the medicine cabinet: empty, save for one tube of toothpaste and a can of shaving foam. No brush, no razor.

Across the landing, she could see Rigby standing in the centre of the bedroom, apparently photographing every surface he hadn't caught last time.

She looked into the study. Even through the doorway she could see that it was as full as the downstairs was empty. Side on was a glass desk, dominated by a vast computer screen. It was flanked by two others, each angled into the other. As she got nearer, she saw shelves packed with what looked at first like the toys of an adolescent boy: a remote-control helicopter on one, a couple of miniature cars on another. Only after a few seconds did she see that both carried small cameras.

She looked towards the bedroom, anxious that she not waste time: the officer would declare the visit over at any moment and she needed to have seen it all. She looked under the desk to see a curtain of cables, dangling in space, connected to nothing. So those were just monitors on the desk; the police must have taken the machines.

She heard a creak, the sound of Rigby leaving the bedroom.

She passed him on the landing. "I'll just take a quick peek."

"You want to focus on the beam by the window," he said, in a show of helpfulness. "That's where it happened," he said, miming the shape of a noose. Then he headed, camera in hand, for the study.

She stepped in, bracing herself. But there was no need. This room was as soulless and empty as the one downstairs. A bed, a side table, an old-fashioned armoire. No photographs anywhere.

Knowing the futility of the move in advance, she pulled open the drawer of the bedside table: empty. If there had ever been anything in this place that might have shed light on Vic Forbes, the police had clearly removed it. What Maggie had assumed was going to be a crucial first step — not a breakthrough, but a start — was turning out to be a dead end.

A raised voice from half-way up the staircase. The cop: "We need to clear this premises in the next ninety seconds."

It was then that she heard it.

The first sound came so soon after the policeman had spoken that she assumed that it must somehow be connected to him: perhaps an alarm he had triggered, or a Taser being warmed up.

But when the second buzz came, she could tell that it was much closer. It was inside this room.

No longer moving gingerly, she yanked open the armoire. A row of suits: mostly grey, some dark blue. She rifled through them, each one revealing precisely nothing. (And not, she noticed, a dress or garter belt to be seen. Police must have taken those too.)

She wheeled around, looking first at the bed, then staring up at the beam where Rigby had told her Forbes had been found dangling. Nothing.

She squatted, checking the floor of the closet, her hand patting furiously in the dark, feeling for anything that might explain that noise. Straightening up, and on tiptoes, she checked the top shelf, again using crude touch to do the searching. Nothing.

Then it came once more, a low buzz, lasting no more than two seconds.

She patted her own pocket, feeling for her phone. She pulled it out, but she knew that was pointless: her phone was set to sound, not to vibrate.

"Come on." Rigby was at the door. "We're leaving."

The cupboard door was still open, standing as a barrier between them, preventing him from seeing her hands. And it was her hands that realized what had been slow to reach her conscious brain. They began groping at the pockets of the suits, one after another until, at last, inside a jacket whose scent was different from the others, they found what they were looking for.

Turning to face the man from the *Enquirer*, she shone what she hoped was her warmest, most engaging smile — even as she closed the cupboard door with one hand while the other took the small device and, without daring to look at it, slid it into her own pocket.

CHAPTER
EIGHTEEN

Washington, DC, Wednesday March 22, 22.15
"So now it's your decision."

"I know."

"You've spoken to colleagues. They say you'll have the full weight of the Republican party in Congress behind you."

"They *say* that. You know how much verbal agreements are worth in this town."

"I do, sir. They're not worth the paper they're written on."

That one word had done it, as she surely knew it would. *Sir.* Said like that, in that sweet, eyelash-fluttering way of hers. He felt his loins stirring. This little routine he had with Cindy always turned him on, but she was playing it more expertly than ever tonight, the demure-yet-pert Southern belle with a hint of sauce beneath that courtly exterior. She only had to call him "sir" in that educated Charleston accent, and he was transported back to the nineteenth century: he was master of the house and she was bending over to submit to his will . . .

He looked at his watch: ten fifteen. He would have to act fast. But still he wanted to go through the arguments one last time. "If this is to work, Cindy, then the Forbes stuff is critical. It's just the lunatics right now, but we have to make the base *believe*. Tell me again. What's Rush been saying?"

"He's saying the American people have the right to raise questions. No more than that."

"Beck?"

"Good. He interviewed an expert on murder cases that were faked to look like suicide."

"So you think this could stick? If I'm to make this move, our folks have to be dead certain that Stephen Baker had Vic Forbes killed."

Obligingly, Cindy turned around, giving him a chance to see her from behind, and bent over to retrieve a piece of paper from her briefcase — taking rather longer to do so than was strictly necessary.

"We don't have many allies down there, not after —" She paused, reluctant to say the word that had inflicted such damage on Republicans. "After Katrina. Governor Tett is ours, obviously, but he's surrounded by Democrats. Especially in New Orleans itself."

"Journalists?"

"The good news is that the *National Enquirer* is sniffing around."

"That *is* good news."

"If there's something to find, they'll find it."

He looked out of the window, contemplating the long sweep of twinkling lights that was the American capital. He watched the slow red winking at the top of the Washington monument.

"You do realize how serious this is, don't you, Cindy?"

"I do."

"This is the big one. It's the bunker-buster. If we get it right, Baker will be finished."

"And you, sir, will only just be started." She fluttered her eyelashes again, signalling a return to character. "Strike me hard if I'm wrong."

That was it, the surge of lust was now too great to resist. Senator Rick Franklin glanced down at the portrait on his desk, the one that showed him and his four children smiling warmly at the lens, while his wife of eighteen years gazed adoringly up at him: the full Nancy Reagan, as that particular pose was known in the political communications industry. He turned the picture face down, so that it lay flat against the wood, right next to the discreet statuette he had received when he was anointed a "Hero of the American Family" by the Christian Coalition.

He looked at his watch. If they were quick, there was time.

"Now, Cindy, I am about to follow the rules of this house and administer the punishment that you deserve. First, is the outer door of the office locked in the usual fashion?"

"It is, sir."

"Second, are you wearing that underwear that you know tempts your master?"

"The one sir calls 'the eyepatch'?"

"That's right."

"Yes, sir. I'm ashamed to say I am."

They were practised enough, the Senator and his aide, that they could run through the whole ritual — all the way to climax (his) — in a matter of minutes.

Once it was done, he felt ready to make the move that he knew would define his career and might well alter the course of American history. He zipped up his fly, buckled his belt and nodded that Cindy, now straightening her stockings, should stay.

He dialled the number Cindy had put in front of him, the first move in a sequence that he had never had to follow before; heard the operator answer and realized, with a rush of adrenalin, the import of what he was about to do.

"This is Senator Rick Franklin. I need to speak to the President of the United States."

CHAPTER
NINETEEN

New Orleans, Wednesday March 22, 23.45 CST
The device she had found had been burning a hole in Maggie's pocket for the best part of an hour. Lewis Rigby had insisted they bury the hatchet with a drink. No hard feelings and all that.

Throughout their conversation, though her eyes didn't waver, Maggie did not listen to a word the grubby little hack was saying. Instead all her brainpower was channelled into her fingertips, as she turned the object she had snatched from Forbes's suit pocket over and over in her own.

It was round and flat, a disc; and yet it had buzzed. It was too thin to be a cellphone, even a novelty one. There were no buttons, nor one of those clam-shell flaps that might conceal them. A moment of panic seized her, one she hoped Rigby did not glimpse as she pretended to be fascinated by the story of how exactly he had come to tap the cellphone of the former mayor of Atlanta just in time to hear him call the Hot Guys chat line.

What if she had been half-right? What if the buzzing sound had indeed come from the wardrobe, and from the suits, but she had reached into the wrong pocket?

What if she had had the chance to grab Vic Forbes's cellphone, only to come away with a flipping bar coaster or whatever this piece of crap was?

They finally got back to the Monteleone where she made her excuses, though not before running into a crestfallen Tim, who gently asked whether her headache had cleared.

"My what?"

"Your headache."

Christ, she'd completely forgotten. That had been her explanation for leaving the bar, hoping Tim wouldn't notice that Rigby was waiting for her just outside. "Oh, yes. Right as rain. Thanks for asking."

"So perhaps you'll join me for that nightcap we missed out on?"

She checked her watch: gone midnight. "You know I've had a long day, Tim. Flight down and all that. Would you hate me if I had an early night?"

Of course he wouldn't, he insisted, his words brimming with the caring solicitude of an English gentleman, even as his eyes wondered if, since she was taking to her bed, she might want some company.

Once upstairs, having shaken him off and closed the door behind her, she plunged into her pocket and pulled the thing out. Fucking hell, if it wasn't actually a poxy coaster after all. From the bloody "Midnight Lounge, S Claiborne Street".

She threw it on the bed, convinced that she had screwed up royally. What the hell was she doing here? She was an analyst of international relations, a diplomat for Christ's sake, and here she was, fannying around pretending to be a journalist, playing at being Sherlock bleeding Holmes. And she was crap at it. Somewhere in that house — in that *cupboard* — was Forbes's BlackBerry, bursting with the information that would answer every one of the questions that would save Baker, and she had missed it, passing over the magic lamp and reaching for the wooden spoon instead. She could curse —

There it was again. The buzz. The coaster was buzzing.

She picked it up and stared at it. At last she smiled. So that was what this was. She hadn't seen one of these things in years. Not really the style of the kind of places she dined in these days. Not very Washington.

But maybe joints like the Midnight Lounge in New Orleans still went in for handing customers a pager while they waited for a table. Get a drink at the bar; when the pager buzzes, you can be seated. She wondered how the police could have missed it: but perhaps it would only have started going off again late in the evening, as the Midnight Lounge reopened for business.

And if it was still buzzing now, its batteries still alive, did that not suggest Forbes had picked it up recently, maybe even *very* recently?

She glanced at the bed, with its enticing offer of rest after an exhausting day that was already eighteen long hours old, and then back to the coaster.

She was damned if she knew how she would explain her miraculous resurgence of energy if she ran into Telegraph Tim, but she'd just hope to bloody well avoid

154

him. Mind made up, she went downstairs, stepped outside and hailed a cab. "Midnight Lounge on South Claiborne Street please. As quick as you can."

In her haste, she didn't notice the man watching from the other side of the street. The same man who had seen her arrive from the airport, step out with that British journalist and then return with another person entirely — male, Caucasian, one hundred eighty pounds, five feet eleven — to the Forbes residence. Nor did she notice this man flag down a second cab, so that he could follow her into the New Orleans night.

CHAPTER
TWENTY

As Stuart Goldstein made his way to the Residence —
a hop, skip and a jump for most White House
employees, but not Stuart, whose last memory of
hopping, skipping and jumping coincided with the Ford
administration — he concluded that Stephen Baker was
not like other men.

Of course, he knew that already. He had always
known that, since they met in New Orleans nearly
twenty years ago at a conference for rising stars in the
Democratic firmament. Back then Baker had been the
man to watch in the Pacific North-west, building up a
defence practice in Seattle that had the town's
granola-eaters wetting their knickers in excitement at
its fearlessness in acting for even the most under of
underdogs.

Goldstein had taken instantly to Baker. Handsome,
fluent, smart, he also had that rarest quality in a
politician: courage. He had picked fights with powerful
forces in the state, those whose asses most ambitious
twenty-somethings would be bending double to kiss.
And somehow he had done it without making them
hate him. The guy had been just a few years out of law

156

school and already they regarded him as a worthy adversary. The big corporate boards, the lobby firms and logging interests all loved his profile: the son of a lumberman who had worked his way through college, pulling himself up by his all-American bootstraps. When it came to young Stephen Baker, they had only one question: how do we get him to come work for us?

But back then, in their first lunch a few months later at the Metropolitan Grill in Seattle, when the two had clicked intellectually, politically and tactically, Stu Goldstein had come away with a vague sense of dissatisfaction. It was a feeling that, in the early years, used to nag away at him: there was something missing, some layer he was not breaking through.

Even after they had endured their first failed campaign together, and then their first success — with all those endless hours on the road, just the two of them, in Baker's beat-up old stationwagon, Baker driving because Goldstein had never learned how — it was no different. Stu's wife might joke that Baker spent more time with her husband than she did. And it was true. Probably also true that no one knew Stephen Baker better than he did. But still, he would say. There was some part of him he didn't really know.

Until recently, it had stopped bothering him. He gave up thinking about it around the time they took the Governor's Mansion. Baker was, he decided, simply not like other men. You could get to know most guys over a beer; two for the complicated ones. But Baker was carved from different timber. That was why you could spend eighteen hours a day with him on the road, sharing motel rooms during that attorney-general's race, and still not truly know him. And that was why he would one day be President of the United States.

So it was hardly a surprise that he had no idea what to expect from the late-night conversation they were about to have. He had had the call summoning him to the Residence, but that had come from the operator: no clue to gauge the mood.

Would Baker be as anxious as he had been — and as he had been unable to conceal — last night, when he had wished Vic Forbes gone? Would he be pacing, would he demand to know what the hell Goldstein was going to do to save his skin, would he want detailed updates on what Maggie Costello had found in New Orleans? Would he be fretting about the rising level of noise from the wilder shores of talk radio and cable TV, hinting there was something fishy about the strangely convenient demise of Vic Forbes?

Or would he have found some relief in the simple fact that Forbes had indeed now "gone"? Would he feel, as Stu himself had felt at various points during the day, that if Forbes truly had taken his plutonium-coated secret to the grave with him, then there was no political challenge, no amount of political heat, they could not withstand and eventually repel?

As it turned out, the President's reaction seemed to fall into the latter category. He spoke about the First Lady's spirits rather than his own. He said Kimberley was, frankly, grateful that the lowlife who had dared prey on Katie would never bother them again.

"And you? What do you think about it?"

"I think, Stuart, that a problem which was already consuming far too much White House time — for which, I hasten to add, I blame myself not you — need distract us no more."

"It's a relief, right?"

"Yeah, it's a relief." He allowed himself a smile. Not the full wattage beam that was known around the world, but a more intimate version, one that lit up only the room rather than the greater metropolitan area. "Those stories were giving me a headache. And there didn't seem to be any easy solution."

"Except the one that landed in our lap."

"Not sure I would put it like that, Stuart."

"No. Of course not."

There was a pause. In the silence, Goldstein reminded himself that whatever history they shared, Baker was now in another realm, one that prevented him talking like a buddy, even if he wanted to. But he couldn't leave without asking the question.

"Mr President, is there anything at all that I should know about Vic Forbes and his death?"

"What do you mean, Stuart?"

"I mean, is there anything at all I ought to be aware of about these events. Something that would, um, enable me to manage this process . . .?" He was flannelling, because he didn't want to say it outright.

"Stuart, you've known me a long time. In my entire political career, every path that I've taken, you've known about. You've taken most of them — hell, you've taken *all* of them — with me."

"For me to do my job —"

"Stuart, you know all there is to know."

The tone was final. The President picked up the papers at his side, a gesture that signalled the meeting was over. Goldstein began the mammoth effort required to eject himself from the sofa.

"Before you go, Stu: this morning I found myself remembering a golden Goldstein rule."

"What's that, sir?"

"Never forget the base."

"If I said it, it must be true."

"We need to mobilize them. We have enemies out there, girding themselves for battle. The Iran thing is going to be very hard for us. We need our friends saddled up."

"What do you have in mind?"

"An outreach effort. Below the radar at this stage. But finding a way for them to keep talking to us and for us to keep talking to them."

"For example?"

"Nothing showy, nothing that will look defensive. Just getting obvious people to talk to their constituencies. Get Heller in front of the Jews, get Williams on a few black radio stations."

"The Vice President's got his hands full with the Helsinki process, but if —"

"I know. Just something to be aware of. Like I said, nothing over the top. But best to be ready. Thanks, Stu."

He had just reached the door when the phone rang. The private line.

Baker looked at his watch and gave Goldstein a raised eyebrow. Who could be calling who would be put through this late? Some foreign leader, asking for urgent help? He picked up the phone, silently indicating that Stuart should stay.

"Yes. Good evening, Senator."

Goldstein made a face. *Who?*

Baker mouthed back a single word: Franklin.

Franklin? What the hell was that prick doing phoning here, and at this time? Goldstein watched his boss listening intently. Then he saw a change in him he had never witnessed before. The telephone conversation ended with Baker saying, "Senator, I appreciate the courtesy of the call. Good night." But Stuart was hardly paying attention to the words. He was transfixed by the sight of the President of the United States turning the colour of death.

CHAPTER
TWENTY-ONE

New Orleans, Thursday March 23, 00.06 CST
The cab threaded its way first through the streets close to the hotel, where blues licks still drifted through the air wreathing themselves around the wobbling groups of mini-skirted girls, drunk in their stilettos. But then it left the French Quarter behind and the streets slowly became wider and more desolate. Soon they were passing boarded-up shops and whole blocks that seemed abandoned.

Maggie leaned forward to speak to the cab driver, an African-American whose hair was tipped with grey. "Where are we going?"

"Just where you told me to go."

"Is it far?"

"'Bout ten minutes. Maybe less. You don't want to go?"

"No, I want to go. I just thought it was closer, that's all."

"Not many tourists come round here. I'm taking you the scenic route. This is the Ninth Ward."

"I see." Everyone in America knew of the Lower Ninth Ward of New Orleans, the part of the city where Katrina had packed her hardest punch. Maggie had seen the footage on the news a hundred times, but still it was a shock to see a house that had clearly been swept clean off its pilings wedged against a tree some three yards away. It was a shock to see it was still there — and that so much of the area looked as if the hurricane had just struck.

Even in the dark she could read the warning daubed in white paint on the door of one ruined home — U Loot U Die — and the other houses still marked by crosses, spray-painted in orange, the legacy, the driver explained, of rescue workers who hastily marked those buildings they had already searched for survivors — or corpses. Harder to make out in the dark, but no less striking, were the gaping gashes visible in roof after roof: the holes people had chopped as they tried to escape the rising flood waters that had chased them up into the attic and continued to rise, even there.

Eventually there were a few lights at the side of the road: a gas station, a Denny's, a liquor store, outside of which four men sat on the sidewalk drinking from bottles clad in brown paper bags. And then, what looked like a warehouse or a giant shed, a single-storey building of grey corrugated steel decorated by a vertical sign: The Midnight Lounge. The illuminated black-and-white graphic of a curvy, thick-lipped stripper might have conveyed glamour once. Now it just looked forlorn and tatty.

Maggie paid the driver, nodded to a bouncer the size of a fridge on the door, as if she came to places like this all the time, and walked in.

163

Save for a few feeble table candles, the place was cast in a deep gloom, one that matched the rancid smell in the air. She had to walk past a cloakroom and a bar in order for the dimensions of the room to reveal themselves. Now she saw what it was: a stage area, dully lit in low purple, facing a clutch of small tables, all of which lay under a blanket of darkness. A strip joint, designed to spare the blushes of the audience and — judging by the performer bending into an improbable angle at that moment — to spare nothing of those on stage.

"You here alone?"

She looked up to see a waitress wearing a strip of material that few would recognize as a skirt and the skimpiest of bras, inside which were two unmoving globes of not-quite-flesh. She could see Maggie staring.

"You here on business, darling? How about we get you nice and relaxed with a private dance, just us two girls, now what d'ya say?"

Maggie had her response ready. "I need to talk to your manager right away. A personal matter." Nervous, but doing her best to be friendly.

The expression on the human blow-up doll dropped instantly; now she looked as bored and surly as a checkout girl at an all-night supermarket. She inclined her head towards a table near the bar and slunk off, heading for richer pickings in the corner, where a bearded man, the sweat visible on his pate, was staring at the stage open-mouthed, as if he'd been hypnotized into a deep trance.

164

It was impossible to see who was at the manager's table until she was just a few feet away. A woman, short blondish hair, Maggie's age, dressed — to Maggie's relief — in actual clothes. Black cigarette pants, a spangly top.

"Can I help you?"

"Can we speak in private?"

"This *is* private." The voice, like the words, was firm but not quite harsh.

Maggie stayed in character for the part she had sketched for herself during the cab-ride over. She leaned in closer, then lowered her voice. "I need to speak about something personal. Very personal."

"It's going to have to be right here."

"OK. Can I sit down?"

The woman gestured her into the seat opposite. A black leatherette portfolio wallet filled the space between them on the small circular table. On top were papers that looked like inventories, invoices and the like — as if the Midnight Lounge was a regular American small business. Which, Maggie supposed, it was.

"I know you have your rules about privacy and all," Maggie began, her voice wavering just as she intended it to. "But I need something from you. I need to know if my husband was here last night."

"I'm sorry, we have a strict pol—"

"I knew you would say that, but this is different." Maggie hoped her eyes were full of imploring desperation and, to her surprise, she saw something that was, if not quite warm, then at least not cold, in the eyes scrutinizing her.

"I know you have a business to run, but this is about my *life*."

"I'd love to help, but we couldn't function if our guests didn't feel their confidentiality would be resp—"

"You see," Maggie whispered, playing her trump card, "I'm pregnant."

The face of the woman opposite softened, only for a fleeting second, but visibly.

"And I need to know what kind of man I am married to." She looked down, examining her own hand. "I took the ring off my finger this morning. You see, I need to know if this man is capable of being a father to my child. Or if I need to protect myself."

"What do you mean?"

"I don't want to insult what you do here."

"Why don't you go right ahead?"

The tone was sardonic but the woman's face told Maggie she should press on.

"He said he had stopped all this: coming to strip clubs, seeing hookers. He promised me months ago. I told him I needed that if we were to be a family."

"But you think he's been coming round here?"

Maggie nodded mutely, trying to look as distressed as possible, though it required an effort on her part. She had learned long ago that some men simply couldn't stay away from places like these. That was just how they were.

"I tell you, honey, if a woman didn't hate men before working at this joint . . . I'd say you were better off

166

without him. But you didn't come here for relationship advice."

Maggie gave a weak smile.

"Like I say, I'd really like to help. But we don't exactly take names at the door."

"You have CCTV though."

"Yeah, but —"

"Why not let me just see the tapes for last night? You've got a camera over the door; I saw it on my way in. That's all I need. Put me in a room and let me look. Please . . ."

"There must be, like, a million rules against that."

"I won't make any noise, I promise. But then at least I'll know if I'm being taken for a sucker or not." She laid her hand on her stomach. "Just let me look."

The blonde woman shook her head, with a small, world-weary smile. "There's not a man in this town who would let you go anywhere near those tapes. I must be an idiot."

Maggie let out a sigh of relief and extended her hand across the table in thanks. The manager clasped it, holding it for a long second or two, her eyes not shifting from Maggie's. Finally she stood up and, as Maggie did the same, she saw the woman take in the full sight of her, her gaze lingering, she thought, around her bottom.

"I gotta say, guilty or innocent, your husband must be a major league asshole. Why would he drink Sprite here when he could be having vintage champagne at home?"

Maggie said nothing, following the manager down a flight of stairs, past the restrooms and through a door marked "Authorized Staff Only". Inside was a corridor with three glass-panelled doors, all apparently opening onto offices.

They stopped at the third, the only one that seemed to be unlocked and whose light was on. One side was cluttered with old equipment, including what seemed to be a long-deceased fax machine, its cord coiled up like a defunct tail, while the other was dominated by four TV screens. Barely watching them, preferring to concentrate on the *Puzzler* magazine in front of him, was a man Maggie identified as the companion bouncer to the fridge she had seen upstairs. Perhaps he was the freezer.

"Frank, this lady is a friend of mine," the manager said, setting no more than one foot in the room. "She wants to see the tapes from last night. Give her whatever she needs. And get her a glass of water. She's pregnant."

With that, she turned and gave Maggie one last look. "I have a twelve-year-old daughter at home. She hasn't seen her father in ten years. You're smarter than I was. Best of luck."

Still bored, Frank pulled out a second swivel chair from under the work-bench that served as his desk, and nodded for Maggie to sit in it.

"You know what time you're looking for?"

Since she had assumed she was never going to get this far, she had not given a moment's thought to the question. She tried to remember what Telegraph Tim had said earlier. There had been so many details, she had begun tuning out after a while. But he had told her, she was sure of it.

"Did you hear what I said?"

"I'm sorry. I need time to think."

He went back to his puzzles.

Twelve-thirty. The estimated time of death; Tim had mentioned it twice. But when Forbes's evening began, there was no way of knowing. He could have been here hours earlier. Would she really have to get Frank to spool through four or five hours of CCTV footage, looking for, what, a glimpse of a man Maggie had never met, whom she had seen only on television?

Television. That was it. She had watched Forbes give that live interview on TV while she sat in Stu's office, before the meeting in the Residence. It had been just before eight. That would have been 9p.m. local time. And then, nearly an hour later, they had been interrupted with the statement Forbes had just released. That made it 10p.m. in New Orleans.

"Frank, is there only one entrance and exit to this building?"

Slowly, as if wrenching himself away from his Sudoku puzzle, the security guard brought his eyes to rest on Maggie. "For staff or guests?"

"Guests."

"Hmm-hmm," he said, by way of affirmation.

Anticipating her next question, he added, "Besides, there ain't no camera on the other one."

"So this one it is," said Maggie, grateful to have one less decision to make. She rubbed her temples: haggling with the European Union at three in the morning over the right language for a cap-and-trade clause in a climate change treaty suddenly looked like a walk in the park.

As Frank punched the buttons that would bring up last night's recordings, Maggie's BlackBerry chimed. A message from Stuart.

Call me urgently. Situation grave.

"Anything here, ma'am?"

She forced herself to come back to the moment. She had to concentrate.

Until now she had only been half-watching the faces going in and out. She'd ignored groups, especially those made up of the young. She had been looking for bald, middle-aged men which, given the Midnight Lounge's clientele, did not narrow it down much.

She looked at the time-code clock at the top left of the screen. It was just past eleven. A procession of heavy men, thin men, black men, white men, men who looked furtive, men who looked flushed, men who looked like fumbling boys, men who looked like wifebeaters — Christ, no wonder the manager had grown to hate the entire sex. And Maggie had only been staring at an hour's worth of the Lounge's customer base, and that was at 2x, twice normal speed.

Half-way through the second hour, at what would have been eleven-thirty in real time, something caught Maggie's eye.

It was not a man but a woman. Tall, her dark hair cut in a chic geometric bob, she instantly stood out from the rest: classier than the handful of other women the

170

CCTV had picked up that night, who either wore the forlorn expression of the luckless wife bullied into playing along with her husband's threesome fantasy, or radiated the drunken, tottering jollity of the hen night.

Not that Maggie could see her face; she kept her head down. But she walked elegantly. And with something else too. Purpose.

And now she could see why. Walking a pace behind her, as if tugged by an unseen rope, was a man in a flat golfer's cap — pulled down low to conceal his face — and a dark grey suit. He looked sharply left and right as he came out, slipping a tip into the hand of the bouncer on the door as he did so. He looked left and right again, this second sweep exposing his face to the CCTV camera. There was no sound, so there was no way of knowing if he was actually panting. But his eyes were almost bugging out with what Maggie could see, even from this grainy angle, was desire.

It was only then, once she had determined that this was a man leaving the Midnight Lounge with a beautiful woman he had picked up, that she thought to identify him. But there was no doubt about it.

She asked to freeze the frame, so that she could take a good, long look at the man who had stared so knowingly from the television set last night. For there, caught on tape and on heat, was none other than Vic Forbes.

CHAPTER
TWENTY-TWO

Trying to sound as nonchalant as she could, she asked the guard next to her about the man on the screen. "Do you recognize this man?"

"That your husband?"

"Do you recognize him?"

"I'm not sure what I'm meant to say here, ma'am."

"You heard what your boss told you. You're to help me out."

"I don't know what would help you out, ma'am. For me to say I do recognize him or to say I don't."

"How about you tell me the truth?"

"He looks kinda familiar, yes."

"You know who that is?" For a moment, she hesitated: was it possible this guard had seen Forbes on TV?

"Well, I couldn't tell you his name, if that's what you mean, ma'am."

"You couldn't?"

"That's not how it works here. We're not meant to know anyone's name. We never ask. That's the whole point. It's not Cheers."

"But you've seen him before?"

172

"He's been here a coupla times."

"A couple?"

"OK. Bit more than a couple."

"Is he a regular?"

"I'm sorry, ma'am. This must be real hard for you."

"So he's a regular, yes?"

The guard nodded.

"And what about her?" Maggie nodded towards the frozen image on the screen. The woman was only half in shot, at the extreme right of the picture.

The guard rewound and played the sequence back at half-speed: the head down, the sharp bob of hair, the elegant figure. "Hard to tell," he said finally. He rewound the tape and stared at her intently. But the woman kept her head down, refusing to reveal her face.

"Oh, OK. I can see who that is now."

"She come here often too?"

"She works here."

"Here? You mean I could go talk to her?"

"You'd have to ask the boss 'bout that. Mind you, she ain't here today."

Maggie frowned, puzzled.

"She's a dancer. Started a couple of days ago, I think. But she didn't turn up for work today."

"And do you remember her name?"

"You're kidding, right?"

"No."

"Like I said, it's not Cheers."

"I thought that was just for the guests."

"OK," he said, allowing himself a small, patronizing smile, as if explaining to a naïve child the ways of the world. "The girls have names. But they're bullshit names. Mystery, Summer, all that shit."

"So what was this one called?"

"I can't remember that, ma'am. I'm sorry. Remember, I ain't inside seeing the show. I'm on the door."

"Were you on the door last night?"

Before he had a chance to answer, the door swung open. It was the manager. She smiled at Maggie. "You got what you wanted?"

"I wouldn't say it was what I wanted."

The woman shifted her features into a pose of earnest concern. "No, of course."

Frank, eager to seem helpful, gestured for his boss to come closer and to look at the screen. "The lady wants to know who this is. I said she was new."

The manager leaned in for a closer look at the monitor and Maggie hurriedly suggested Frank rewind: she wanted to go back to the image of the woman alone, before Forbes entered the frame. The security guard might not be a cable TV viewer, with instant recall of the face of Vic Forbes, but she couldn't be so sure of the manager.

The outline of the woman now dominated the screen, the shape of her haircut the clearest feature. After a second or two, the club manager spoke. "Frank's right. She's new. Started this week."

"Who is she?"

"She dances under the name of Georgia, if that helps you."

"You don't know her real name?"

"I never ask."

"And she only started this week?"

"Right. She came in day before yesterday, I think. Offered to start right away."

"Just like that."

"Well, it wasn't a hard decision, if you know what I mean."

"What do you mean?"

The manager looked back up at the screen, a half-smile on her face. "You think your husband left the club with this girl?"

Maggie nodded, dipping her head: the anguish of the betrayed wife.

"Well, you don't want to hear any more about it then, do you?"

Maggie stared at her. "You said it wasn't a hard decision. What did you mean?"

"I shouldn't have said anything. I'm sorry."

"What did you mean?"

"I just meant that she was —" She hesitated, unsure how to put it. "*Unusual*. In this place, I mean."

Maggie kept her eyes on the manager, leaving the silence hanging. Eventually the woman spoke again. "Look, most of the girls in here *look* like strippers. Their nails are fake, their boobs are fake, their hair's fake. The college boys like those girls plenty, but the more upscale guests are looking for something real. Kind of the whole natural beauty thing. They'll pay for that. They'll come back for it again and again."

"So you hired her straight away."

"Yes. She was gorgeous, no doubt about it." She looked at Maggie, who was furrowing her brow in a show of wounded wifely love. "I'm sorry."

Maggie collected herself. "And where is she now?"

"I don't know."

"Don't worry. I'm not going to go after her."

"I wouldn't blame you if you did. But, I'm telling you the truth: I don't know."

"Did she not show up for work?"

"Not since last night," the manager said. Then, making the connection, she nodded towards the CCTV image on the screen: "Not since then."

"Have you tried to contact her?"

"I called her this evening. Her phone just rang."

Maggie looked down at her hands, digesting what she had heard.

The woman spoke again. "Listen, sweetheart, you don't want to hang around a sleaze-pit like this. Why don't you and your baby go home, have a long soak in the tub, and put all this behind you. Chain the door and get the locks changed tomorrow. How's that sound?"

Maggie managed a watery smile. "Thanks."

"I'm sorry you had to find out like this, honey. But better to find out now than later. Take it from me, that ain't no fun. Not for you, not for your child."

Maggie collected her things, digging into her bag for a tissue which she used to wipe away fake tears, thanked Frank and let the manager show her out. Upstairs, she surveyed for the last time the tables cloaked in darkness and the stage in a purple haze.

Performing was a dull-eyed bottle-blonde, who held her hands over her head in readiness for a manoeuvre that would have her literally bending over backwards with her private parts thrust forward.

Maggie headed for the door. Following the lead set by "Georgia", she kept her head down throughout so that no CCTV camera would catch her.

Once outside, she exhaled deeply, refreshed to be out in the cold and away from the stale, soiled air of the Midnight Lounge. She fought the urge to phone Stuart. Not yet; this was still not nailed down. She looked across the street, seeing a man in an idling car. He glanced directly at her, then away. Not a cab, then. Suddenly, desperately, she wanted to get out of here.

While the bouncer on the door called her a taxi, she began to pace, itching for a cigarette.

Surely what she had just seen could mean only one thing. The time stamped on the CCTV recording had been unambiguous: 23.05. Last night, Vic Forbes had been in a TV studio, then sat somewhere — perhaps at home, maybe at an internet café, perhaps on a street corner armed only with a BlackBerry — and issued his "statement" threatening to reveal a shocking aspect of Stephen Baker's past. And then he had come to his regular perch at the Midnight Lounge where he had picked up a girl. And not just some stripper, but an unusually beautiful woman. Who just happened to have started work at this place — where Forbes was a known regular — one day earlier and who had now disappeared off the face of the earth.

They had left together and, an hour or so later, he was dangling from a rope, trussed up like a drag queen with a Vitamin C habit.

There was only one way that could have happened, wasn't there? Or was it still conceivable that Vic Forbes had somehow come to his death alone?

All right, Maggie told herself. *Think*. Forbes went back to his apartment with Georgia, they'd fooled around a bit, said good night and then he — not yet sated — had got out his Rocky Horror kit for a bit of solo gasping, which then went horribly wrong.

Theoretically possible. But that was surely the less likely scenario. What was it the nuns had taught them in those moral philosophy lessons? Occam's Razor: always go with the simplest explanation, the one that made the fewest assumptions.

And that version pointed only one way.

The gorgeous Georgia had started working at the Lounge on the very day Vic Forbes had begun his public and private blackmail assault on the President.

Maggie pictured Frank, the security guard, nodding when she asked if Forbes had been a regular. Had he been there a couple of times? *Bit more than a couple.*

Whoever had been watching Forbes knew he'd be at the Lounge. Probably knew his tastes, too. So they sent in Georgia.

Forbes — unable to believe his luck — had taken the bait. He'd headed home, she did the job, then dressed his body to look like an auto-erotic suicide.

Was there another way? What if it was a real pick-up? She pictured Forbes at his front door, fumbling for his key, then tumbling inside with Georgia, ravenous for sex. He tells her of his fetish for dressing up and his penchant for breathlessness. She goes along with it, but something goes wrong. Worried she'll be blamed, she flees . . .

Again, possible. But what were the chances that a woman, who had just started working at the Midnight Lounge when Forbes got active, would go home with him on the very night he was about to strike his deadliest blow against the President, and then disappear immediately after his death — what were the chances that all that was a coincidence?

Besides, Maggie remembered Telegraph Tim saying that the only fingerprints they'd found at the house had belonged to Forbes. If she had just been an unhappy hooker, in the wrong place at the wrong time, she'd have left her prints everywhere.

No, there was only one plausible explanation for why Georgia had disappeared — and it was the same explanation for why she had appeared at the Midnight Lounge in the first place. It was a classic honeytrap — though with a lethal sting.

The police were wrong. Tim and all the other reporters were wrong.

Forbes had not killed himself, by accident or design.

Victor Forbes had been murdered.

CHAPTER
TWENTY-THREE

From *The Page*, Thursday March 23, 00.03:

> Impeachment!
> Republicans to table articles of impeachment through House Judiciary Committee in the am accusing President Baker of "high crimes and misdemeanors." Opening step in a process aimed at making Baker the first president of the 21st century to be removed from office. Massive and developing story . . .

Twenty-two minutes later, from Politico.com's Playbook column:

> I'm hearing that Senator Rick Franklin placed a call to the White House in the last hour or so, notifying the President personally of his intention to proceed with impeachment. Call was a courtesy born "out of respect for the office of President." My source tells me that Stephen Baker "pleaded with Franklin" not to do it, arguing in an emotional phone call that it was against all the rules of "natural justice" to move against him so early in his presidency. It's certainly a record, that's for sure. Both <u>Andrew Johnson</u> in the 19th century and <u>Bill</u>

Clinton in the 20th had their feet under the table for a good few years before they faced the mechanism that remains the Constitution's nuclear weapon: impeachment. Baker has been there just 62 days.

It's too late at night for me to file more than a few speculative thoughts about this, so here goes with two. First, this has only come about because of the death of Vic Forbes. Sure, that name won't appear on the charge sheet when it comes before the House Judiciary Committee in the morning. Franklin and his pals in the House will make the Iranian Connection the heart of the legal case against the President. They will say that the selling of influence to an enemy power constitutes the relevant violation of Article II, Section 4 of the Constitution, which states: "The President, Vice President and all civil Officers of the United States, shall be removed from Office on Impeachment for, and Conviction of, Treason, Bribery, or other High crimes and misdemeanors." But that's the legal case. Make no mistake, the politics has the name Forbes all over it.

His death changed the political calculus in Washington. The rumors, the suspicion at the undeniably convenient timing of Forbes's passing, all that has created bad atmospherics for Stephen Baker, a climate of suspicion where senior Republicans think they can accuse him of anything.

And, if Franklin is serious, he must reckon he can peel off enough conservative Democrats to make this thing pass. Let's face it, there's no shortage of Baker-skeptics among the Democrats who never liked the President — and all his idealistic talk of America showing an outstretched hand rather than a clenched fist to the world — anyway. If I were in the White House tonight, I'd be keeping a close eye on Dr Anthony Adams over at Defense.

Second, this will all move very fast. The Democratic majority is so slender, Republicans need only a couple of conservative Democrats to waver and the Judiciary Committee could agree to submit articles of impeachment for a vote of the entire House as soon as the start of next week. The clock is ticking on the Baker presidency. If there is even a shred of credible evidence that Forbes was indeed the victim of foul play, rather than a suicide, then the Baker presidency's future will surely be measured in days . . .

CHAPTER
TWENTY-FOUR

Maggie was in the cab on the way back to the hotel, her breathing coming faster now, her mind racing through the implications. Only one question mattered, though the answer made her blood run cold.

Who would want Forbes dead?

In response, a single sentence kept repeating itself, a sentence she had repeatedly tried to banish.

I want him gone.

It was the most obvious explanation, the one that any cold-eyed observer would reach for. *Cui bono?* Wasn't that the first question the analyst was meant to ask: who benefits? And who benefited more from the death of Victor Forbes than Stephen Baker?

For the fifth time in two minutes, she hit redial on Stuart's number. Still busy. *Situation grave*, he had said. What the hell was happening over there?

They were driving past an empty plot. It looked like scrubland now but, given its location, it had almost certainly been a fully-inhabited residential block before the levees broke. There was a sign attached to the chickenwire fence, announcing a reconstruction project, with a photograph showing the gleaming faux-colonial

183

houses that would arise on this spot. But it only made Maggie think how difficult it was going to be, breathing life into a city that had all but drowned.

Her BlackBerry, now set on silent, vibrated. She seized on it, thumbing the button frantically. "Stuart? Is that you?"

But there was only silence. The vibration had announced not a call but a message.

Stuart: *Can't get hold of you. Things insane here. Franklin and the Republicans launching impeachment proceedings against us in the morning. You have to get us something fast. Anything. Maggie, we're depending on you. HE'S depending on you.*

She felt her throat dry. Impeachment. It seemed that Forbes was going to achieve in death what he had set out to do at the end of his life — and bring down Stephen Baker.

The veins in her neck began to throb. How dare they? At long last, a truly decent, good man emerges from the swamp of politics, and what is their reaction? To tear him down, using the dirtiest, cheapest tricks imaginable. No wonder they couldn't stand a giant like Stephen Baker. He exposed the rest of them for what they were: dwarves.

Her job was clear. She had to find something that would exonerate the President, proving that he had committed no crime. She needed to establish beyond all doubt that Forbes had taken his own life. That was her duty. Her duty to Stephen Baker. *He's depending on you.*

184

And what had she done? The very opposite. She had found evidence that Franklin would seize on, suggesting the conspiracy crackpots were right. Forbes had been murdered.

Calm down. That fact alone did not necessarily implicate the President. Baker had allies, including those who would have seen Forbes as a threat to their own interests. What if one of them had decided to do Baker a favour — and take Forbes out?

Then she remembered the story Goldstein had pulled up at her kitchen table. "*The Baker presidency turns into* The Godfather". The stories had proliferated wildly since then, each one nudging ever closer to accusing Baker of murder.

Could that be it? Might someone have despatched Forbes not to help Baker but to *damage* him, by making him look like a mafia boss whose enemies mysteriously ended up dead? After all, what she had discovered at the Midnight Lounge wouldn't stay secret forever. If she were right that Forbes had been murdered, it would only be a matter of time before that information became public knowledge. Even if the Republicans did not make an outright accusation of murder, they could use the suspicion of it to insist that the President of the United States had to be removed from office.

Two minutes after she got back to the hotel, just as she was standing in the corridor and unlocking the door to her room, the phone vibrated. Stuart.

"Stu, what the hell's going on?"

"Rick Franklin making his play for history."

"It can't happen, can it?"

"Can't rule it out."

"But he hasn't got the votes. I mean, we're the majority party."

"*Meant* to be the majority party. By a whisker. And that whisker is made up of Blue Dog assholes who will vote with the Republicans if they feel that's where the wind is blowing."

"And is that where the wind is blowing?"

"That depends."

"On what?"

"On you partly, Maggie. You gotta find something to help our boy here."

Maggie swallowed. She could hear the heart-busting stress down the phone and she was about to add another huge surge of it. "Well, I've found something. But I'm not sure it helps." There was a strange crackle on the line. "What's that noise?"

"Gherkins," Stuart said, crunching audibly and repulsively. "I haven't eaten properly in forty-eight hours. I keep a jar in the office for emergencies." He belched. "So hit me, Maggie. I can take it."

"Forbes was at a strip club the night he died. He left there about an hour before the time of death. Left with a woman."

"Jesus."

"It's not cast-iron proof but I think it adds up."

"Do the police know?"

"I don't think so. I don't think anyone even knows he was there."

"Could it be a coincidence? Picks up a hooker, then offs himself? Or maybe he goes back with her, they fool around, it goes wrong and she panics. Worries that she'll get blamed."

"I wondered about that, Stu. But there were no fingerprints at his house except his. It seems, I don't know, *professional*. The woman was a dancer at the club, but she'd only started the day before Forbes died. Exactly the time Forbes started spilling the beans. And she hasn't been seen since."

"OK." She could hear the sound of him thinking. Chewing and thinking. Finally: "The thing is, and this is about the only good news we have around here, New Orleans Police Department are winding up the investigation. Apparently the coroner says there's no evidence to alter his verdict of accidental death by asphyxiation. And if there are no fingerprints at the scene —"

"They could have killed him somewhere else, near the strip club. Then taken him back to the house, dressed him up, left him hanging. So long as they wore gloves, Forbes's prints would be all over the house and they wouldn't leave a trace. I know it sounds far-fetched, but it would make sense."

"Look, Maggie, I think the police just want to let this matter rest. Seems like some people down there are trying to be helpful."

"Who's being helpful?"

"It's a Democratic town, Maggie. Of course the wingnuts are already blaming us for that as well. Obstruction of justice, all that crap."

"Stuart, at Forbes's house, all the computer stuff had gone."

"The police. Bound to have removed it."

"I know. And they'll have his phone and his BlackBerry."

"Yep."

"We know Forbes did everything by computer. The Facebook thing. The pretend hack of MSNBC emails. What I'm saying is, whatever it is I'm meant to be finding out — what exactly Forbes knew — it's going to be on those machines. If we could —"

"Can't be done, Maggie. Our only route would be Secret Service. They could put in a request to impound. But what's that gonna look like? White House poking its nose into a criminal investigation."

"But you could say he posed a security threat to the President's daughter."

"*Posed*. Past tense."

"All right. The Secret Service could say they were worried he had accomplices."

"To what?"

"To his planned assault against Katie Baker."

"Yeah, but remember, Maggie, nobody knows about that. As far as anyone knows, Forbes was just the guy who popped up on cable posing as the brave truth-teller who was going to introduce the American people to the real Stephen Baker. They don't know he was threatening a thirteen-year-old girl."

"Well, why don't you —"

"What, make that public? And thereby invite the press to notice that we hadn't immediately gone to the police, despite his threats of blackmail, because we were worried he might actually have something?"

"And then everyone would want to know why we were so frightened."

"Exactly. Which, incidentally, they want to know anyway. Forbes was on TV, remember, promising another big instalment of the story. People are going to be digging already. Probably got private detectives crawling all over New Orleans right now."

Maggie thought of Lewis Rigby. She had never asked for ID, she hadn't Googled him. She had accepted his word that he was a reporter for the *Enquirer*. "Back to the computers, Stu. Are you saying that if it gets out that the Secret Service were looking through his machines —"

"Except it won't be Secret Service in the headline. It will be the White House. Which is all we need right now. We might as well put Stephen Baker in a Dick Nixon mask and be done with it."

"OK."

"Besides."

"Besides, what?"

"Zoe — you know, the agent who took you to Maryland, on the raid? She reckons Forbes did it all in the air or something."

"In the air? What does that mean?"

"Like I know. He didn't store it on a machine, just on the internet."

"Oh, I get it." Maggie remembered Nick's hairy biker story, as well as the stiff lecture she had once received from Liz, after her sister had found her on a visit back home, poised to pull out clumps of her own hair. Maggie had lost a crucial paper she had been working on for the UN's Middle East envoy. She'd written it on her computer back in New York, then backed it up on a memory stick. She had even remembered to take the stick with her, keeping it safely in her pocket the entire flight home. Trouble was, her mother had insisted on throwing every item of Maggie's clothing in the washing machine — including the pair of jeans with the memory stick still in the pocket. Every word on it was washed away in a blur of corrupted data. That was when Liz had walked into the bedroom they once shared, to find Maggie on her hands and knees, shaking the contents of her bag out onto the floor, just in case there was a hard copy of her precious paper buried inside, even though she knew that none had ever existed.

"Mags, can I make a suggestion?" she had said with calm smugness.

"Not unless it involves you fucking right off," Maggie had said to the sister who had picked her up from Dublin Airport not much more than an hour earlier, after six months without seeing each other.

"What do you do with your photographs?"

"What?"

"Where do you store them?"

"In a bloody box, I don't know!"

"Because —"

"If this is not connected with helping me get my document back I don't want to talk about it."

"Do you store your pictures on Flickr or a site like it?"

"What the fuck is Flickr?"

"Well, what I was going to say is, that's what you should do with your documents. Don't store them on the machine. Store them online. You get a password, you can work on them wherever you like, so long as you have internet access. And if you give your password to someone else, then you can both work on —"

It was then Maggie had thrown a shoe at her sister's head. So she had never heard what exactly you could do if you shared your password, but she had got the rough idea.

She could hear Stuart still munching. It must have been his sixth straight gherkin. "Bottom line, Maggie: I'm not sure there's anything on those computers worth finding. Which means you need to find another way into this. I don't know what that is, but you're going to have to find it. If Forbes was murdered, you have to find out who did it. Every minute we can't come up with an answer to that, someone else fills in the blank with Stephen Baker."

"There's the woman who picked Forbes up."

"What, the stripper?" The sound of mastication was appalling, even down the phone. "No point. If you're right, that she was some kind of professional, then she's not exactly going to have left her business card behind, is she?"

It was true. She had flitted into the Midnight Lounge, under the bullshit name of Georgia with, no doubt, the bullshit papers to match, and flitted right out again. If she had been smart enough to wipe her prints from Forbes's house, it was unlikely Maggie was going to be able to find her.

"Also," Stu continued while building up to a swallow. "If she was a hired gun then it's not the gun we're interested in, is it? It's who did the hiring. That's what we need to find out. *Urgently*."

"I know." She wished he would stop telling her how much pressure she was under: she knew. Her mind had been churning with this and this alone for nearly nineteen unbroken hours.

"And don't forget, Maggie. We also need to know what bag of shit Forbes was about to tip over our heads."

"Right."

"And who else knows what's inside that bag."

"Got it."

"Maggie?" He sounded different, as if signalling a change in direction.

"Yes, Stu?"

His voice was softer now, the voice of the early hours of the morning. "We've kind of given our lives up for this guy, haven't we?"

"Sorry?"

"You and me. I have a wife and all, but I spend more time with CNN than I do with Nancy. And let's face it, you're married to the job."

Maggie felt a sting of something like shame. Hadn't Uri said exactly the same thing, that her devotion to the job had made their relationship impossible? They had fought and fought over that. Perhaps Uri was right, perhaps she had sacrificed their relationship for the sake of Stephen Baker. Which only made the current situation more unbearable. If the Baker presidency collapsed, it would all have been for nothing.

Stuart spoke again. "We can't let this thing go down. Not like this. Not so early. He's hardly had a chance to do any of the things we dreamed of, that *you* dreamed of. We haven't saved the world yet, Maggie."

Despite herself, Maggie smiled. *Saving the world.* She knew Stuart was teasing her, as he always had: the passionate idealistic woman among all those pragmatic, political men. But she also knew that even Stuart — cynical, poll-watching Stuart — only worked as hard as he did because he believed it too. That was the magic of Stephen Baker: he made idealism possible. When he spoke, changing the world was no longer some naïve adolescent dream, but something achievable and within reach. That was why he had been the first politician she had ever truly trusted. She would do anything — anything — in her power to stop those out to destroy him.

Injecting confidence into her voice, she said, "We're not going to let it go down. We're going to survive this. Just like we survived everything else. Remember, when Chester —"

"This is different, Maggie. We both know it. In the morning, I'm going to start counting the votes. See if Franklin has enough of our guys — even potentially — to win this thing."

"And if he does?"

"I was thinking of telling the President he should resign."

"Jesus Christ, Stuart."

"Don't go nuts, Maggie. Think about what it would mean to fight on. Wading through all this shit. And what do the history books say then? That Baker was removed from office after less than two months. Better to leave with some dignity."

"Like Nixon you mean?"

"Bad example. But then I think about us. You and me. We can't let him do that, can we? If he goes, what's left of us? Actually, you've got plenty. You're smart and you're beautiful."

Maggie didn't know what to say. She felt her eyes pricking, with real tears this time. She had talked about every point of the globe with Stuart Goldstein, every possible permutation of politics, domestic and foreign, yet he had never spoken like this before.

"But me, Maggie. There wouldn't be much left of me, would there? For twenty years, I've been Stuart Goldstein, the guy behind Stephen Baker. Without Baker, there's no Goldstein. Who else is gonna hire a big fat Jewish guy who eats gherkins out the jar? Baker was the only one who never cared about all that stuff."

She could hardly bear to listen. "Stuart, don't. We're going to come through —"

"So what I'm trying to work out is, if I'm being selfish for wanting to fight this. If I'm doing it for my sake, not his. Maybe the best thing for him is if we let him walk away."

"Enough, Stu. Enough late-night maudlin talk. I can get that in Ireland." She wanted him to laugh but he didn't.

"You're right. I know. I know. I'm just so tired, that's all. We've worked so hard . . ." His voice tailed off, exhausted, on the edge of defeat.

Maggie felt her heart swell. She had to do this for both of them: for all of them. "Go home, Stu: go home and get some rest. I'll call you in the morning. Things will look better then, trust me."

"Good night, Maggie."

She cut the connection and closed her eyes. What had she got herself into?

CHAPTER
TWENTY-FIVE

Washington, DC, Thursday March 23, 07.55

"I love the smell of fresh bagels in the morning."

Senator Rick Franklin and his Head of Legislative Affairs, Cindy Hughes, had just stepped out of the elevator onto the fifth floor of the building on L Street which, to the naked eye, looked like a regulation 1970s-built office block in Washington, DC. Functional and dull.

To those in the know, however, it was — for this hour every Thursday morning, at least — the epicentre of American conservatism. Or, as those on the inside would put it, "the movement".

This was the Thursday Session, when the conference room of a single right-wing think-tank would host the activists, lobbyists, congressional staffers, movers and shakers who together represented Washington's key "movement" conservatives. At the back of the room, jugs of coffee and trays of fresh bagels alongside bowls of cream cheese. If you were fifteen minutes early, you'd load up a plate and take a seat. Any later than that and you'd be standing at the back or at the sides or spilling into the corridor. The Thursday Session was the American right's hottest ticket.

When Franklin appeared something happened that he at least had never seen before: a spontaneous round of applause which soon turned into a standing ovation. He had been used to the red carpet treatment at the Thursday Session for at least a month, ever since he had won himself folk-hero status by heckling the President's first speech to Congress. The media had hated it of course; the press back home were embarrassed: "Frankly, Mr Franklin, you're a disgrace!" ran one column in *The Greenville News*. But it had made Rick Franklin, once little noticed outside South Carolina, a star.

This, though, was different: a reception for a *leader*. He thought back to Cindy's remark of last night, just before he spread her across his knee and before he telephoned the President to notify him of his imminent impeachment. *And you, sir, will only just be started.* Already his push to remove Baker had anointed him as *de facto leader* of the opposition. If he were to succeed, then in three short years' time, surely he would be frontrunner for . . .

He waved aside the offers of an empty seat: he was far too humble for such gestures of deference. Instead, and humbly, he stood close to the door. His body language was politician's semaphore for "I'm here to listen".

Matt Nylind, the activist who had turned this meeting into the dominant force it had become, called for order. Franklin took a good look at him. Classic behind-the-scenes operative; looked like an overgrown college student. One tail of his shirt was already edging its escape over the waistband of his trousers; his glasses were smeared. Just the fact that he wore glasses: no politician would wear glasses. Who was the last? Truman? But these guys — the dweebs who crunched the numbers, drafted the Republicans' policies and found the flaws in the Democrats', who blogged twenty-four hours a day and never stopped working to advance the cause, inch by inch — these guys could look awful. No one cared. No one ever saw them. Maybe Nylind would occasionally do a turn on Fox. But basically they were creatures of the dark. Better that way: if voters ever got a glimpse of them in daylight, they'd head screaming for the hills. No, the current division of labour made the best sense. Men like Franklin — with their gleaming white teeth, full heads of hair and pretty wives — would be front of house while the elves stayed hidden in the grotto, working their magic.

Franklin looked at them and felt a surge of gratitude. If it weren't for these guys, with their BlackBerrys and their obsessive reading of indigestible pamphlets from the Cato Institute, his job would be so much harder. And he loved his job. He glanced at Cindy, standing next to him, her face a picture of studious concentration, and thought how much he loved the perks too.

Nylind was making his introductory remarks: ". . . some big news overnight, but before we get to that I want to run through other items on our agenda. First, governors' races in Virginia and New Jersey. Baker stole both of those last fall but we're trending two points

behind on the generics. And that was before last night."
There was some bullish laughter and a smattering of
more applause in Franklin's direction, which he duly
acknowledged by inclining his head minutely. Humbly.

Nylind resumed. "OK, the legislative agenda. The
banking bill. Polling is horrible for us on this right now.
Suggestions for how we can turn it around?"

Immediately a voice piped up, though Franklin
couldn't see whose it was. "We gotta death-tax it," the
voice was saying. "When the Democrats called it an
'estate tax' it was popular. Once we called it a 'death
tax', we killed it. We need to do the same with this bill."

"Who is that?" Franklin whispered to Cindy,
enjoying the scent of her that came to him as he bent
closer to her.

"Michael Strauss. He's the head of the American
Bankers Association. Lobbyist for the entire financial
services sector. Normally sends a deputy. Must be
something cooking."

Nylind was asking for new names for the banking
bill. A woman close to the front suggested the
"anti-wealth bill". Nylind nodded, but without
enthusiasm. "Let's remind ourselves of its core
elements. This bill will cap bonuses from now till these
banks have paid back the federal government every last
cent they owe. Which could take decades. It will be the
biggest cap on wealth and individual freedom since
Leonid Brezhnev."

"Why don't we call it the Brezhnev bill?" asked the
woman, undeterred.

Nylind muttered, more to himself than the room. "Yeah, 'cause that will play really well with eighteen to twenty-fours." Then, his volume duly adjusted: "Let's get to the matter of the moment. Republicans on the Hill have set a remarkable lead, showing an aggressive response to the Iranian Connection with a move to impeach the President."

More applause, which seemed to make Nylind impatient. Such displays were fine for the TV cameras, but here, in his meeting, they just wasted time. "Clearly that's gonna depend on headcount, pulling in moderate Democrats. Which in turn means shifting public opinion to our side of the issue. I suggest the climate will depend less on the technicalities of donations from Iran and more on the general mood created by the Forbes episode. Where do people think we've got to on that?"

This was what Franklin had come to hear.

A man standing directly opposite, also too jammed to get a seat, spoke up, identifying himself as a producer of one of the nation's best-known talk radio shows. "There's still plenty of flesh on that turkey," he began, with an accent Franklin placed in Alabama. "Like the psycho piece. More to say on that, I reckon. And what was this bomb Forbes was gonna drop? Folks are mighty interested in that, I can tell you."

Nylind interrupted. "The White House are trying to say that's all old news now that Forbes is dead. Drawing a line and all that BS."

"BS is right. House Judiciary's gonna keep the Iran story alive. And we're going to keep hammering away at it on the show. Exactly how much money changed hands? When did it stop?"

"*If* it stopped!" Someone in the middle of the room, too quick for Franklin to identify.

Now, towards the back, a woman stood up. Franklin recognized her; he'd seen her on *Hannity*. Sweet-looking, if a little bland; longish hair, maybe some surgery. Attractive, but vanilla cupcake. Kind of like his Cindy, but without the sauce. An image of his assistant in her eyepatch underwear flashed through his mind. He told himself to concentrate.

"Are we too prim here to talk about the other dimension of the Forbes case?" Now Franklin remembered. She was a former prosecutor turned TV talking head.

"The other dimension?" Nylind was smiling, enjoying himself. He always was a hog-in-shit at these Thursday Sessions, Franklin reflected, but he looked extra ecstatic at this moment.

"Yes, Matthew." Her tone was that of an impatient schoolmistress, circa *Little House on the Prairie*. And they said conservatives didn't have a sense of humour. "We all know what I'm referring to. The very *convenient* demise of Mr Forbes. At precisely the right moment for the President."

Nylind surveyed the room. "Once again, let me remind our media colleagues here that the Thursday Sessions are always and forever off-the-record. If you're here, it's because you're a player not a commentator. Remember the rule. You leak, you leave.

201

"Good. So we all heard what the lady said. Do we want to go there?"

"Some of us already have." A few titters.

"But does it make strategic sense?" Nylind, perennial college boy, was playing the designated adult.

"There is a risk to it." The talk radio guy again. "It can make us look wacko. Even if we're right. Can look a bit, you know, 9/11 truther."

"There's another problem." All heads turned towards the back of the room, where the chief aide to Congressman Rice of Louisiana was seated. "There'll be a coroner's report today, declaring Forbes's death a suicide." The room hushed, the quiet that always comes when meetings used to the hot air of opinions suddenly get a cool gust of fact.

He continued. "I got off the phone from the New Orleans Police Department just before I came here. They're going to announce this morning that their investigation is formally concluding."

Loud tuts and several shaking heads.

"It seems awful quick." The woman, former lawyer.

Nylind jumped in, ahead of the staffer from the Louisiana delegation. "Let's not forget, gentlemen —" this in spite of the fact that between a quarter and a third of those in the room were women, albeit women whose political DNA prevented them from crying foul at sexism "— that there are a lot of Democrats in Louisiana. Since Katrina, most of the state officials, in fact. That goes for the mayor of N'Awlins. Who appoints the police chief."

202

The lawyer spoke up again. "I don't think that should shut us up. Just because a few party hacks are closing this thing down to help their buddy Stephen Baker. If anything, it makes it worse."

"Just remember what I said," said the talk radio producer. "The guys who say the CIA took down the Twin Towers. Controlled explosions and all that. They make a lot of sense when they're talking to themselves in rooms like this." A few murmurs of agreement, but no enthusiasm.

He ploughed on. "I'm not saying it's off-limits. Hell, we'll probably do it on the show this afternoon." Laughter. "But that's radio. And sure it helps the impeachment effort. Right kind of mood music, no doubt. But it can't be a strategy for the Movement."

A few hands rose, but Nylind moved to wrap things up. He wanted to talk about the chairmanship of the Federal Reserve, sensing a vulnerability in Baker's nomination.

Franklin looked at Cindy and signalled that they should leave.

In the cab back, he stared out of the window, eyeing the blue sky and the wisps of cloud. He wanted to ask the driver to turn off the god-awful foreign music he was playing — sounded Arab or something — but Cindy held him back. The last thing they needed was some row about racial insensitivity.

"You know what I'm thinking, Cindy?"

"What's that, Senator?"

"I'm thinking that it's interesting that the Democrats down there in N'Awlins are closing ranks like this, shutting down the investigation. That means there's something they don't want the likes of you and me finding out. Like my mammy used to say, if you see a woman get out a broom, chances are there's a pile of shit somewhere that needs cleaning up."

"Well put, Senator."

"It also means that this is the moment of maximum vulnerability for the White House. You know what they say: if you can't kick a man when he's down, when can you kick him?"

"I like the sound of that, sir."

"Yup," Franklin said, gazing at the succession of grand neo-classical buildings that lined the road to Capitol Hill, as if Washington truly were the new Rome. "I think it's time to put some serious pressure on Baker — and those who work for him."

CHAPTER
TWENTY-SIX

New Orleans, Thursday March 23, 09.12 CST
"Good morning, Maggie. You are cordially invited to a funeral."

"Excuse me?"

"A funeral!"

"A funeral? Whose?"

"Are you all right, Maggie? You seem a bit —"

"Sorry. Didn't get much sleep last night."

Telegraph Tim looked wounded, shooting an involuntary glance across the breakfast room of the Monteleone Hotel at Francesco of *Corriere della Serra*: had the older man — Italian and experienced — succeeded with the lovely Miss Costello where he had failed?

Maggie read his face and sought to relieve his pain. "You know, that headache. Couldn't sleep." The truth was, she had collapsed into bed shortly after two and, shattered by a day that had begun in Washington nearly twenty hours earlier, had slept deeply. "So what's this funeral then?"

As she contemplated the scrambled eggs and cooked tomatoes of the breakfast buffet, Tim excitedly explained the morning's developments.

Forbes appeared to have left no wife or children or family of any kind that could be tracked down. In most cities, that would be a bleak and lonely state of affairs. But not New Orleans. This city still had the Paupers' Burial Society, a relic of the antebellum days of plantation owners doing good works. The white-suited tobacco growers may have been slave owners, but there was a little corner of their hearts where resided some good. Tim appeared to be quoting from the story he had already written for the newspaper.

"They left a pot of money to be spent burying the poor. The fund is still there, still paying out."

"But Vic Forbes wasn't a pauper." She had to stop herself saying she had seen his apartment.

"That's the beauty of it. It's not just for the poor. It's for anyone who dies alone within the city limits of New Orleans. If police can find no next of kin, the Paupers' Burial Society step in."

Maggie smiled. "Must be a pretty liberal bunch, given the way Forbes wound up."

"Apparently they don't care. Anyway, it wasn't their decision."

"No?" Maggie said, choosing between grapefruit juice and orange.

"No," said Tim, hovering behind her. He explained that while most cities would have wanted the Forbes episode to fade away as quickly as possible, the mayor and tourist board of New Orleans had, after Katrina, a what-the-hell attitude: they had nothing to lose. They reckoned there was a marketing opportunity to be had. With so many journalists in town, why not lay on a

206

show? Prove to the outside world that the city hadn't drowned, that it was still a place with party in its soul.

An hour later, Tim was bouncing from one foot to the other in his delight. He couldn't believe his luck. This was what any editor in London wanted from a story out of New Orleans. "Liz," he said to Maggie, "truly, we have been blessed on this one. Sex, death, men in tights — and now this!"

Standing on the kerb, he swept his hand at the procession now getting underway on the street. Leading the way was a trio — clarinet, banjo and tuba — playing what began as a slow, mournful spiritual: *Nearer My God to Thee*. Behind them was a larger group, dressed the same way: black trousers and red shirts, bearing trombones, trumpets and saxophones, one man with a snare drum on a strap around his neck. These musicians were not yet playing, but moving in a stately fashion. The walk was slow, not quite a regular march, more a sort of graceful shuffling in time to the music coming from the front. Finally, behind them, came the hearse.

When they got close to the media huddle, a woman with a clipboard — a PR for the tourist board, Maggie guessed — had a quiet word and the march drew to a halt, though the music kept playing.

Now more men, all but one of them black, gathered around the hearse. After a minute of pulling and shoving, they emerged holding the silver casket. There were at least a dozen of them, clutching the rails on both sides of the coffin that served as handles. Why so many, Maggie wondered, used to no more than six pallbearers at any funeral she had been to. A moment later she understood.

The refrain kept playing, but the volume was rising. Instead of the clarinet carrying the tune alone, now there was loud brass support, another trumpet or sax joining every few bars. And, as if lifted by the music, those around the coffin made a sudden, swift move that produced a few gasps among the press pack, all but one of whom were white.

The pallbearers raised the coffin aloft, so that it was high above their heads. But they didn't hold it still; instead they made it sway. Then they brought it down again, to waist level where, once again, they began shifting it from side to side, as if they were rocking a cradle. Whispering the explanation that had been passed along from the PR girl, a TV reporter standing behind explained to the woman next to him that this was another tradition of the jazz funeral: let the deceased dance one last time.

The procession headed down Bourbon Street, towards the cemetery. The TV guys hastily decoupled their cameras from their tripods and hoisted them onto their shoulders, while the reporters scrambled to catch up. Maggie, back in character as Liz Costello of the *Irish Times*, did the same, joining the growing crowd behind the coffin.

These people too were half-strolling, half-dancing to the music, some twirling parasols in the air, others holding a handkerchief aloft. An improbably wide white woman with little sense of rhythm beamed at Maggie. "This is the second line!"

"What's that?" Maggie said, straining to be heard above the music, which was now thumpingly loud.

"The second line!" the woman said, her smile unbroken. "It was in my guide book. You dance along with the funeral. It's a New Orleans tradition!" And with that, she held up a white tissue and did a twirl.

By the time they reached the burial ground, Maggie had drifted from the journalists. She put her notebook away and watched as the long snake of people now turned into a thick crowd at the gates of the cemetery. The music began to wind down as a priest called for hush.

He said a few words of welcome, dwelling on New Orleans and its customs. As if remembering himself, he then added a quick mention of Vic Forbes before suggesting that they all head to the graveside.

The crowd was thinner now, dominated by the men in red and black — those, Maggie suspected, who were being paid to be there. She hung back, not wanting to claim a proximity she didn't have, close enough to hear, far enough away not to be visible.

The priest offered a series of platitudes, further evidence that he, like everyone else there, had never so much as met Vic Forbes. The words seemed to waft into the air and die on the breeze.

Maggie looked around, only belatedly realizing that someone was standing next to her. A man with white, thinning hair, sixty or so, in a grey suit — camouflaged to blend in perfectly into a cemetery. Against the grey of the tombstones, he was almost invisible. Like her, he had no notebook. And, like her, he wasn't dressed like a tourist: he was in a dark, formal suit. Could this man be the one true mourner for Vic Forbes?

She gave him a solemn look, eyebrows raised, the look people give each other at funerals. "Hello," she whispered. Then, trying her luck, "Did you know him well?"

His gaze remained firmly ahead, watching the priest, but he spoke immediately, not answering the question, but asking one of his own. "What line of work you in?"

An instinct told her not to claim to be a journalist, not now. "I'm in the foreign service."

Now he looked at her.

"Did you know him from the Company?"

Intuition took care of her answer. "That's right."

"You here as the official representative?"

This was one trick Maggie had learned in a thousand negotiations. However fast your mind was whirring, however hard you were scrambling to assimilate new information, you had to give no outward sign of it. Best to react as if there was nothing to react to. So she looked impassive as she processed what she had just heard. *The Company . . . the official representative.* Maggie looked at her own clothes, looked at his, and a realization began to dawn. "I'm here to pay the Company's respects, yes."

The man exhaled, as if he had just peeled off the first of several protective layers.

"Figured you must be. Bob didn't have many friends, if you know what I mean." *Friends* was offered

210

with an emphasis that suggested the word referred to women. "That's good. Didn't know if you still did that, but that's good."

Maggie nodded stiffly, trying to play the role this man had assigned to her. Official representative. Her mind, though, raced with a single word. *Bob.*

"Long time ago now, of course. But he was good at his job. Even in some tight spots. Honduras, Salvador, Nicaragua."

Maggie turned her face towards him, a three-quarter turn meant to convey warmth. The penny had now dropped fully into the slot. "That was important work. The nation owes you a debt. Both of you."

"Oh, he could be an asshole too, don't get me wrong. Funny that he ended up in New Orleans. Probably lived up the street from me. Had no idea."

"You weren't friends then?"

"Hadn't clapped eyes on him in nearly twenty years. Then I see him all over the tube this week, badmouthing the President." He waited for Maggie to nod. "I was thinking I should get back in touch — for old times' sake. Next thing I know, he's dead."

"Yes."

They both paused, watching the priest throw a handful of earth on the coffin. Maggie had to fight the urge to bombard this man with questions: she had to do whatever an official representative of "the Company" would do. And that, she decided, meant playing it ice-cool.

The funeral party was turning away from the grave now and Maggie sensed her chance was about to slip away. She would have to push her luck. "I confess we did not quite know what to make of this . . . latest outburst."

"Like I said, he could be an asshole. That was the thing with Bob Jackson. Marched to his own drum."

Bob Jackson. Were they dealing with someone who had lived a double life? Was Vic Forbes his true identity, or a fake? Expressionless, she filed that away to be wrestled with later. She pushed again. "What about his death? The police here say it was suicide."

He smiled, as if he'd been told an old, but good joke. "I know. But after the guy had been threatening the President like that, you gotta wonder, haven't you?"

Maggie kept her face impassive. The band was now playing a raucous version of *When the Saints go Marchin' In*. She turned as if to head back, praying that he would not take that as his cue to say goodbye. But he was a man of sixtyish alone in the middle of the day, with memories of the glory years working for "the Company" who had found someone — a woman, decades younger than him — who was willing to listen. Somehow she suspected he was not about to leave.

He walked alongside her, keeping time with her funeral stroll. She said nothing, waiting for him to fill the silence. Men, especially eager men, almost always obliged.

"Look, I would not rule it out. Jackson was not always the most popular guy around. Loner. Kind of obsessive. He might have made some enemies, even before this Baker thing."

Maggie raised an encouraging eyebrow. *Go on.*

212

"But here's what makes me doubt it. Anyone who knew anything about Bob Jackson would have known that he would do what he was trained to do. What we were all trained to do."

The trumpets and trombones were making it hard to hear. "I don't follow."

"The blanket. No point taking out a guy like Jackson. Or any of us. Not if you're worried about what we know. He'd have prepared his blanket."

"Of course," Maggie said, even as she thought furiously, *What the hell is a blanket?* They were now back by the cemetery gates, about to be swallowed up by the crowd that had waited to make the return journey. Maggie could see Telegraph Tim interviewing one of the horn players. Any moment now, he could come over, breaking her cover. She shifted on her feet, hoping to show him only her back.

There was so much she needed this man to explain. Should she ask for his name and number, so that she could arrange a meeting? She could say the Company still had some unanswered questions about "Vic Forbes", and ask if he would be willing to help. But she hesitated. The man was experienced and well-trained. He would demand a business card; he would phone Langley to check her out. She was lucky to have got this far. It would be madness to push any further.

No. She would have to get what she needed now. The two of them had stopped walking, so that for the first time she was looking him directly in the eye. It struck her how similar to Forbes — or Jackson — he looked.

The same banal features, the same blandness of expression: faces designed to disappear.

"Jackson was a pro, no doubt about that," Maggie said finally, the official representative paying tribute. "He'd have prepared his blanket, just as you would. He'd have known what to do with it too."

That was it, cast out like one of her father's fishing lines and with about as much chance of success. Inside she was wincing at the clumsiness of it.

"Yep, he sure would," the man said.

She was about to press him further when she felt a hand on her shoulder and turned to see Tim behind her, looking proprietorial. She made a face that she hoped said *not right now*. He looked disappointed, maybe even a little offended, but to her relief he moved away.

But when she turned back, the man who had been at her side for the last ten minutes had vanished, lost in the crowd.

She had to call Stuart right away. With this information they could get to work; this could be just the breakthrough they needed. Hurriedly, she thumbed the buttons on her phone, trying his direct line at the office. Straight to voicemail. Next she tried the mobile. *I'm sorry but this phone is no longer in service. I'm sorry but this phone is no longer in service. I'm sorry . . .*

Goddamn it! Now she dialled the White House switchboard. "Stuart Goldstein, please," she said, as a group of "mourners" jostled her at the cemetery gates.

The operator's voice was hesitant. "May I ask who is calling?"

"My name is Maggie Costello, I'm on the National Security — I mean, I used to be on the —"

"Ms Costello, I've been told to direct your call to Mr Sanchez. Please hold."

There was an interminable delay, filled by piped classical music. Maggie could feel her palms grow moist. Finally she heard the voice of Doug Sanchez, though with none of the pep she was used to.

"Hi Maggie. I don't know where you are but you may want to sit down. I have some very bad news, I'm afraid. Stuart is dead."

CHAPTER
TWENTY-SEVEN

Diplomatic cable:

From the Interests Section of the Islamic Republic of Iran, housed within the Embassy of the Islamic Republic of Pakistan, Washington DC
To the Head of the Army of the Guardians of the Islamic Revolution, Tehran

TOP SECRET. ENCRYPTION SETTING: MAXIMUM.

Situation for SB deteriorating. Following our previous conversation, I can report that SB is now without the advice of his chief aide. We may not have the problem of the outstretched hand for much longer. Suggest that normal service will be resumed soon. Ends.

CHAPTER
TWENTY-EIGHT

New Orleans, Thursday March 23, 11.23 CST
His voice wavering, Doug Sanchez explained that two joggers had found Stuart's body at six o'clock that morning in Rock Creek Park. Initial examination suggested he had died after swallowing thirty tablets of Dextropropoxyphene — a painkiller whose packaging warned against use by those with a history of "depression with suicidal tendency" — and then slashing his left wrist. The police were about to issue a statement saying they were not looking for anyone else in connection with his death. The President had already spoken to Stuart's wife. Doug was about to face the press for an off-camera briefing.

Maggie was too stunned to speak. She had worried about Stuart's life expectancy almost from the first day she had known him. She thought his very existence — carrying that enormous weight, burdening himself with the most intense stress — represented a kind of challenge to science, as if he were pushing the boundaries of the possible. She often imagined him standing at the back of a high school gym at some campaign rally, chomping on a corn dog and keeling over with a massive coronary. But suicide? The very idea of Stu Goldstein, who gobbled up life the way he gobbled up food, killing himself would have seemed absurd.

Until last night. That last conversation they had had unnerved her. She had never heard Stuart sound so exhausted, so utterly defeated before. She heard his voice in her head, softer than usual. *There wouldn't be much left of me, would there?* And then: *Without Baker, there's no Goldstein.*

Get some rest. That was the best she'd been able to come up with. What sort of a friend was she? Why hadn't she recognized that he was a man on the edge? She felt the strong need for a drink.

Sanchez was still speaking. "Listen, Maggie, I've got to go do this briefing. But here's what's happening. The President has told me what you and Stuart were working on. About Forbes. He's asked me to —" He hesitated, apparently embarrassed. "He's asked me to continue Stuart's work. From now on, you and I are to liaise." Ordinarily there would have been a flirtatious frisson attached to that sentence. But not now.

Sanchez went on: "Except where there are things for you to discuss directly with him, apparently." He sounded put out. "In fact he told me to transfer you over to him once we'd spoken. OK? We'll talk later."

"OK." The news was still sinking in. She felt nauseous . . .

"And Maggie, listen. I'm sorry I had to be the one, you know, to —"

There was a click and the sound of more hold music. Telegraph Tim and the other reporters were looking

218

over at her now. They appeared curious, maybe even a little annoyed by her deliberate separation from the pack: why was she ignoring them? Who was she talking to so earnestly on the phone? Had she found out something they hadn't? When she waved for them to go on without her there were a couple of hard stares, but they went, which was a relief. She found a quiet spot by a tree. The cemetery was almost empty now, save for one or two stragglers, including a white man in a dark suit standing by the gates, also talking into his cellphone.

"Please hold for the President," came the faraway voice on her BlackBerry.

"Thanks."

Another click and then: "Maggie, I'm very glad we've reached you." It was the same voice she had heard when Baker talked to his children in the kitchen at the Residence, or to her during the early days of the campaign. Warm, gentle, full of empathy. The voice of a strong, protective father.

"Yes, Mr President."

"This is a terrible blow for all of us. I know how close you were to Stuart."

"You were too, sir."

"Yes. I was." He paused, as if fighting to keep the lid on his emotions. "But I think we both know what Stuart would have wanted. He would have wanted us to fight this thing, Maggie. Especially now."

"I'm not sure that was the mood he was in, Mr President."

"He was not himself yesterday, I know that. But Stuart was not a quitter. He was a fighter." His tone changed. "I just can't believe . . ." The sentence trailed away. "Suicide: not Stu —"

"You're not saying that . . . someone might have done this?" It came out as barely more than a whisper.

"I'll tell you what I think, Maggie. I think this presidency is under assault. I think we are facing nothing less than an attempted *coup d'état*. And we have to fight that with all we've got. It's not about me or my presidency any more, Maggie. This is about the Constitution of the United States. If they can remove an elected president, then they can do anything."

"Who's 'they', sir?"

She heard him sigh. "We don't know that yet, do we? And even to talk about it sounds nuts. But we need to find out who they are. I'm relying on you, Maggie. Keep digging at the Forbes thing. We need information, fast."

"I understand."

"We're going to do what we can at this end. I've taken four straight days of this shit, on the defensive. We're going back on offence right now. We're going to start working the phones, telling those Democrats on Judiciary to grow a pair and start defending their president."

"I'm glad to hear it, sir."

"Now what have you got?"

Maggie tried to focus, to put Stuart out of her mind, to act as if she were briefing the President on an outbreak of violence in the West Bank. She braced

220

herself, extracting a crumb of confidence from the little information she had so far unearthed. "Sir, it's unconfirmed but I strongly suspect that Vic Forbes was in fact Bob Jackson, a former agent of the CIA."

A sharp intake of breath at the other end of the phone. "Jesus Christ. Where did this come from?"

"I've just been at the funeral. I met a former colleague of his who repeatedly referred to 'the Company'. He was much older than Forbes, but he said they worked together in Honduras, Salvador and Nicaragua. He said they were both retired."

There was a silence, two or three beats. "You know what Stuart would say, don't you? 'At least with Kennedy, they waited a few years. Gave the guy a chance.'"

"You don't think —"

"Well, what does it look like, Maggie? An ex-CIA agent? That's who they use, for God's sake. That's who they always use."

"Who?"

"I can hear Stuart saying it. 'The Watergate break-in? Who were the Plumbers, Stephen? Who were the dirty tricks squad? They were ex-CIA. Howard Hunt, those guys.' Jesus."

"So you think Forbes was working for —"

"I don't know."

"Well, there can only be two possibilities. Either the CIA had hired Forbes to blackmail you — or he was working for someone else."

The President spoke more softly now. "We're missing Stuart already, aren't we, Maggie? I relied on him so much."

"I know, sir."

"He would say that Hunt and the others — the Plumbers — they were ex-CIA but they weren't working for the CIA."

"Which leaves the key question: who was Forbes working for?"

"That's what you need to find out, Maggie. Tell me again, when was Forbes in the Agency?"

"He was Jackson then. Bob Jackson. Started decades ago. He would have been in his twenties. He was forty-seven when he died."

"I'll put Sanchez on it. See if he can get that confirmed. The Secretary of State is waiting for me. Talk to Sanchez. And stay safe, Maggie. We need you strong, we need you healthy. I'm relying on you: we all are."

"Thank you, Mr President. I'll do everything I can." She said the words, accepted the burden, but they rang hollow. What could she do, on her own? She wasn't a detective. She wasn't a spy or an investigator. She was just Maggie Costello, failed diplomat, failed White House staffer, failed friend, failed . . . everything.

Her hands were trembling. She was standing at the gates of a cemetery, rain was in the air and Stuart Goldstein was dead. She felt a desperate, urgent need to be away from here. To be back home, in a hot bath, with a whiskey in her hand and none of this happening.

She headed for the roadside and, as she climbed into a passing cab, she reached for her BlackBerry. Without thinking, led only by instinct and by need, she entered the area of her phone's alphabetized contacts where she only rarely dared tread: U. For Uri.

The phone rang three times. She knew that, if it went to voicemail, she would hang up. But, as so often in the past, he surprised her. He picked up. Without missing a beat, he said: "Hi. How's my favourite ex-White House official?"

She paused, not wanting her voice to betray her.

"Maggie? You OK?"

She nodded, knowing the uselessness of the gesture. She swallowed, determined to get a grip.

"Maggie? What is it?"

"Stuart's dead."

"Oh, God. I'm so sorry. What happened?"

"I don't know." She could feel her nose twitching now, the sign that tears were about to follow. "They say it's suicide. But I just can't believe it."

"I know how close you were, Maggie. You always said he had such a big heart."

At that, she let out a full sob. These last few days had, she realized, left her like a coiled spring; she had been wound so tight.

"Where are you, Maggie?"

"I can't say," she said, which only made her want to cry more. "In a cab."

"Do you want me to come down to see you?"

She wanted to say that was what she wanted more than anything in the world — but it was impossible. "I just needed to hear your voice."

"OK, so I'll talk," he said. Just hearing his accent, still alien even after all the time he had spent in the

States, triggered something in her — despite everything that had passed between them.

"You know what," he said. "I was thinking of you today. I was looking at some footage of Baker at the Iowa State Fair —" The change in his tone suggested he was shifting the subject away from Stuart to safer ground, giving her something else to focus on. He was like that, Uri: sensitive to her moods. Too sensitive sometimes: he knew her too well.

She tried to pull herself together, engage in the conversation. "Was I in the pictures?"

"No," he said, the word dipping down in the sing-song voice you'd use to tell a child that the world doesn't revolve around him. "No, none of you. But it did remind me of you. That's where you first met him, wasn't it?"

"You make it sound like a love affair," she sniffed. " 'First met him'."

"Well, there were always three of us in that marriage, Maggie," he said gently, the smile still in his voice. "You, me and the future President of the United States."

"Where are you?"

"I'm in an editing suite in Manhattan, listening to a million hours of interviews all on the same subject."

"You doing the Baker film?"

"Didn't I tell you? When did we last speak? It happened last month. PBS want ninety minutes. The full life story. Baker the man."

She did her best to sound enthusiastic. "Wow. That's really good, Uri. Big job."

224

"Thanks, Maggie."

"You'd better hurry, though."

"It's not looking good, is it? I don't get it. The guy was Mr Invincible and now he's fighting for his life."

That was too close to the bone. She felt the tears rising again. "It's good to hear your voice, Uri." It came out as a gulp.

"Yours too. You sure you're OK?"

She wanted to tell the truth, she wanted to let it all out, to hear what sense he could make of Stu's apparent suicide, of what she had just heard in the cemetery, to piece it together, like co-conspirators, just as they had when they first met, back in Jerusalem. Those days had been terrifying — and violent — and yet she looked back on them now as among the happiest times in her life. Despite herself, and when she hadn't really been looking, she had fallen in love.

"I wish I could talk about it. But I'm on assignment. You know, usual rules apply." With an iron will she staunched the tears.

"Mother's the word."

"*Mum's* the word."

"Oh, yeah? And how's your colloquial Hebrew getting on?"

Despite everything, she smiled, imagining the dark curls of hair on his head, remembering the smell of him next to her. And that nearly undid her resolve. "I'd better go, Uri. There's another call coming in."

"OK."

"Thanks, Uri."

"Anytime. And if you want to talk, you know where I am. Day or night."

She pressed the red button, ending the call. A moment later, as if to keep her honest, the phone rang. Sanchez.

"We need to meet, Maggie. Urgently. Come back to Washington. Not here. I'll text you the time and place. There's something I need to give you. As quick as you can."

She hung up, her heart pounding, thinking. *Now what?*

And thousands of miles away a man she had never met was listening to every word.

CHAPTER
TWENTY-NINE

Undisclosed location, Thursday March 23, 18.00 GMT
"Are we on a secure line?"

"Yes, sir. Maximum encryption."

"Good." He leaned forward, resting his elbows on the table, bracing himself for the start. The technology was state of the art, but he still resisted this form of communication. Call him old-fashioned, but he preferred to look a man in the eye. Or several men, in this case.

The technical people had reassured him that there was no chance this call could be monitored by any intelligence agency, domestic or foreign, or indeed by any non-state actor. He knew, rationally, that he should accept that. But he envied his predecessors. They had operated at a time when all this would have been done in person. They would have sat opposite each other, face to face. Not in a windowless room, deep underground, staring only at a bank of monitors. Bad enough if it was just one person he needed to speak to. But a conference call?

Still, there was no alternative. The discussion was urgent and this was the way it would be done.

"Gentlemen, we've all been following recent events."

There was a murmur of agreement.

"I know there is some concern about — how shall I put it? — the law of unintended consequences."

A voice chipped in, on the line from Germany. "I worry that the cure might be worse than the disease."

He cut him off, eager to maintain his authority. "I understand these misgivings. But I would urge colleagues not to underestimate the man we have chosen."

"I agree." Another voice, this time from New York. "He is not to be underestimated. But my colleague in Germany is right. Removing Victor Forbes has created at least as many problems as it has solved."

Once again he felt the need to re-establish command. Had his predecessor ever been challenged like this? Perhaps he should have asked him during the transition. "Gentlemen, as I said before, I understand the anxiety. My strong view is that we removed a problem that posed an absolute and immediate threat. If it had been allowed to stand, our entire project would have been jeopardized. We acted swiftly and efficiently.

"Now, admittedly, that move has left us with other challenges. But none of these, on its own, endangers us. They are manageable."

"What about Goldstein?" Germany again.

"As the chair of this group, I acted on live intelligence. The risk that he could have rendered our project void was too great."

"All right," said the voice from New York. He wondered if these two, Germany and Manhattan, were operating in some kind of tag team. Had they liaised with each other before the conference call? Should he be worried?

"I'm happy to accept the decisions that have been taken. But it's time to secure our asset, as it were," New York continued. "Otherwise, we risk defeating the whole object."

"Understood," he said, eager to seize on that declaration of support, however tepid. "That will be the next phase of our work."

There was a murmur of agreement.

"One last thing, gentlemen. It seems as if there is someone looking more closely at the Forbes case than we might have hoped. A woman. I wanted everyone to be clear that we are aware of her — and that we will ensure she causes us no trouble."

"Make sure we do." A first intervention from London.

"You have my word," the chairman said. "She will be removed from the picture if necessary."

CHAPTER
THIRTY

Washington, DC, Thursday March 23, 19.41
Doug Sanchez's instructions had been clear. The information he had to give her could not be conveyed over the phone or by email or by fax. They had to meet face to face. She was to take the next plane to DC and then head straight to Union Station and stand facing the Amtrak departures board. In happier times she might have laughed at the intrigue of it all, political operatives pretending they were secret agents. But that talk of the Kennedy assassination and the CIA had come from the President himself. It was clear Stephen Baker genuinely felt he could no longer trust anyone.

There was a sudden flurry of movement, as passengers who had previously been waiting suddenly took off in a hurry. She looked up at the departures board to see that it had at last revealed the track number for the Acela Express to New York, leaving in ten minutes. In the throng of people, she felt herself jostled. She looked to her left and there was Doug Sanchez, handsome in raincoat and scarf, looking straight up at the board.

He kept his gaze upward, prompting her to do her own bit of playacting. She pulled out her BlackBerry, smiling and saying hello as if it had just vibrated with a new call.

"Maggie, listen. This is radioactive. It is a federal crime to leak the identity of a CIA agent."

"Even a dead one."

"In the eyes of the law, I'm not sure. In the eyes of Fox News, definitely."

"So I was right. Forbes is ex-CIA."

His gaze was still fixed on the board. "Took a whole bunch of crap to confirm it, but yes. The trouble is, none of our people are in there yet. Fucking Senate. It's all holdovers from the last crowd."

"So who helped you?" Maggie asked, still grinning into her phone and looking in the opposite direction.

"The number three there is a holdover from the crowd *before* the last crowd. One of ours."

"And?"

"He did more than was required. I asked for a simple yes or no. Was Forbes an agent or wasn't he? But then he sent me his personnel file."

"Jesus."

"Not all of it. A summary."

"What's it say?"

"That you were right. Jackson is the same age as Forbes. He retired three years ago. Served everywhere, Saudi, Pakistan. Central America in the eighties."

"Why'd he quit?"

"Doesn't say. Just says 'discharged'. That could mean anything. Could be straight retirement."

"OK. What else?"

"There's a full résumé. I didn't even read it properly. We need deniability on this. Like I say, I didn't ask for the whole nine yards." He paused. "I've been wondering if this is some kind of set-up. Send it to us, see what we do with it."

"So there has to be no trail on this, I get it."

"Nothing. Remember the legendary 'Josh diary'?" White House staffers lived in fear of that story: the young aide whose personal diary had been subpoenaed in some long-forgotten presidential investigation, allowing a grand jury and teams of lawyers to pore over the exact details of when he'd broken up with his girlfriend and why. All of which leaked of course. An independent counsel — or a special prosecutor — would demand everything: telephone, fax and email records would be just the start of it. They had to ensure there was no record of Sanchez passing this information to her.

"So how do we do this?"

"I'm going to drop the stack of newspapers under my arm —"

"Max!" Maggie gave a false laugh, as if her friend on the phone had said something hilarious.

"I'll drop them, you'll bend down to help me out, you'll give me everything back —"

"Except —"

"Except the brown envelope. Ready?"

"OK."

He counted to three, then dropped the papers. A whole pile went from under his arm: the *Washington Post*, two blue document wallets, a pile of A4 computer printouts. Instantly, Maggie bent down so that she was opposite Doug as he apologized profusely.

"I'm such an idiot," he said. "Thank you so much."

"I'll call you right back," Maggie promised her imaginary friend. "There you go," she said to Doug, smiling brightly. She handed him back a wad of paper, keeping hold of the brown envelope.

"Thanks," Doug said, making eye contact for the first time. She saw that he was genuinely rattled; a redness around his eyes testifying to nights deprived of sleep. Maybe he too had been poleaxed by Stu's death. She began to like him more.

Under his breath, he said, "Don't let us down, M. We need you. He needs you." And then he turned and walked away.

CHAPTER
THIRTY-ONE

Washington, DC, Thursday March 23, 20.14
She rode the Metro home, itching to look in her bag. But she didn't dare risk it. What if someone looked over her shoulder? What if she dropped it and someone picked it up? Come to think of it, what if — today of all days — she was mugged? She remembered those stories of government officials leaving laptops on trains or in the backs of cabs, prompting the loss of secrets vital to national security. She squeezed the bag between her thigh and her arm, twining the strap around her hand for good measure. If some low life felt like stealing a purse, he'd have to pick on someone else.

She walked the short distance from Cleveland Park station to her apartment, fighting the urge to look over her shoulder every other step. Her hand trembled as she put the key in the lock. Once it had slid in, the door didn't swing open easily as it would usually; it seemed stiff. Maggie gave it a shove with her shoulder and it opened.

She reached for the light switch. Her eye swept across the open-plan studio space, taking in the hall she stood in, the kitchen to her left and the rest of the living area. Had the cleaner come? She hadn't asked her to.

And yet there was a scent of something in the air, as if the place had been scrubbed. She closed the door behind her and shot the bolt.

She unzipped her bag, where she saw her purse, her phone, a lipstick — no sign of the envelope! Instantly, she began pulling items out of the bag, one after another until — thank Christ up above, there it was. Paranoia was infectious.

She opened up a kitchen cabinet, took down a bottle of Jameson's. Drop or two of water, a sip standing up, then she moved over to the couch and let herself fall into it. Blood pumping, she picked up the envelope.

Inside was a two-page document, stapled together, the crest of the Central Intelligence Agency discreetly placed in the right-hand corner. In the top left, a small mugshot that, after a few moments, she recognized as a young Vic Forbes. In the centre in bold type, it simply stated the subject's name: Robert A. Jackson.

The resemblance between the young Jackson and the Forbes who had been on television earlier that week was barely discernible. He had hair then, brown and straight but covering all his head; a moustache too. Large glasses of the kind everyone wore in the early 1980s but which looked comic now.

She began reading, taking each line slowly. It began with the year of his birth, then a summary of his education: high school in Washington, then college at Penn State. Spanish major. Three years in the Marines, then recruited to the Agency. Deployed almost immediately to Central and Latin America. First assignment, Economic Attaché, US Embassy in

Tegucigalpa, two years. Later to San Salvador, this time as a Trade Attaché, eighteen months. Finally to Managua.

She looked at the dates. Jackson would have been there when those places were at their hottest: he was in Nicaragua during the precise period when Oliver North and his pals were funnelling weapons to the Contras and lying to Congress about it. Maybe Jackson, with his fluent Spanish, was the funnel.

He would have been young. In his early twenties, running around war zones, drinking tequila with paramilitaries, handing over rucksacks stuffed with CIA dollars. In her twenties she had been bumping up and down dirt roads from Eritrea to Kinshasa, hitching lifts from guerrillas in flatbed trucks. She wondered if the young Jackson had felt the same thrill she had, the unique charge that comes from being in a place where every day is a matter of life and death.

And then what for Bob Jackson? A long stint back at Langley, stretching through the late 1980s and into the next decade. Probably pacing the corridors, looking for a role. When the Wall came down, and all the proxy skirmishes of the Cold War were wrapped up, warriors like Bob Jackson were suddenly left twiddling their thumbs. Maggie looked at the photograph, imagining how he must have felt.

There was mention of a temporary assignment in Spain, which she saw would have coincided with the bombing of the Madrid railway, and a couple of other spells in Asia, also presumably related to what his political masters would have called the War on Terror.

She was still getting no sense of him at all.

On the next sheet were the personal details which revealed only how little there was to reveal.

Marital status: single.

Children: none.

Significant associations: negligible activity of which the Agency is aware.

So he had been a loner who had died utterly alone. She remembered again the hungry desire on his face caught on the CCTV camera at the Midnight Lounge and, for the first time, felt a twinge of sympathy. Maybe what she had seen in Forbes's eyes had not just been simple lust, but a different need. For the warmth of another person.

Maggie pictured him, turning up week after week, Wednesday after Wednesday, sitting at the same small table in the dark, gawping at the jiggling, surgerized bodies — and then heading into the night, back to that spartan house on Spain Street, where he would spend the night in the comfort of his own right hand. Maybe that was why he had looked so excited on that grainy TV image. At last he was with somebody.

She exhaled loudly and took another glug of whiskey. Christ, she still had her coat on. She should get up, have a shower, maybe eat. She got up and turned to head for the bathroom. As she did, she saw the winking light on her answering machine, which Liz had called "retro chic" on her last visit. Reaching over, she pressed "play".

One message from a married friend asking why she hadn't come to brunch. She had clean forgotten.

Another from the dry cleaners saying her jacket was ready. Then the third:

"Could have sent you a text, or an email or a bloody Tweet," it began, the accent unmistakable. "I could have scrawled on your Facebook wall, or tried to Instant Message you, or whatever it's called, but something told me you'd want to hear a human voice on your return from the Lost City of Atlantis. Mags, it's Nick here, sweetheart, keen to know how my brightest pupil performed in her Journalism for Beginners practical. With flying fucking colours if Tim from the Telegraph is to be believed, though it sounds as if you skipped out without a goodbye. Very rude of you. I do hope you have not betrayed our unspoken bond of fidelity, Ms Costello. As luck would have it, I'm in DC for a few days. Call me if you fancy a bowl of Ethiopian sludge in Adams Morgan. Or failing that a drink at the Eighteenth Street Lounge."

Her response surprised her. So often she would give Nick the brush-off. She was too busy or she was seeing Uri. But tonight she wanted to see him. It wasn't simply that she needed company, though she did. The last visitor to her apartment had been Stuart: he had been sitting in her kitchen just yesterday, stuffing his ludicrous face with Cheerios, keeping the angst at bay. The memory brought a wave of grief, followed by a surge of panic. She was alone, and she needed help. This thing was too big for her, there were too many angles. Sanchez was bright, but he had not a fraction of Stuart's nous or experience; nor his humanity. Besides, he was clearly nervous about even being seen with her, let alone speaking by phone or email.

Her head was swimming: too many hours alone. On flights, in cabs, she had gone over it all, over and over again. She needed to know whether Jackson's blackmail effort had been sanctioned by his former employers at the CIA or some other faction within the US government. Or was the President right, had Jackson been a mercenary, a dirty tricks specialist contracted to do a job, just as Nixon had hired old Company men to bug and burgle the Democratic enemy? And what bearing did any of that have on what was still a, if not the, key question: who might have wanted him out of the way?

Not that she could be open with Nick du Caines. He always insisted that he was discreet. "Soul of discretion, Mags, I swear! You say it here," he would say, pointing at his ear, "and it goes direct to the vault. Triple locked. Titanium bolts." And then he would mime the act of closing a heavy door. But she could not risk it. Nick might have the best of intentions, but if he was drunk, or coked-up, and he was trying to get some Dutch intern at the World Bank into bed, who knew what he might say?

They met at the Eighteenth Street Lounge, a place where the corners were dark enough, and the couches sufficiently battered, to play to Nick's Hemingway fantasies: the seedy, world-weary ex-war correspondent. He leapt up when he saw her come through the unmarked door, embracing her and letting his hands run up and down her back. Trying it on before she'd even got her coat off. Throughout she kept her hand on her bag, inside which was the envelope Sanchez had handed to her at the station. She wanted to be within touching distance of that document at all times.

He'd ordered a Scotch for her already. "Your favourite malt," he promised.

They talked first about Stuart, Nick nodding in all the right places. Then they talked about New Orleans, Nick urging her to tell mocking stories about Telegraph Tim and to describe her skilful integration into the press pack, taking it all as a compliment to his teaching skills.

"Now, Mags, are you able to tell me what any of this is about, so that the beloved and historic newspaper that I work for might at least have something resembling a story?"

"Still losing money?"

"Millions. And the beancounters will soon be wondering why they need a US bureau when they could just as easily rely on 'bloggers'." He fairly spat out the word, impersonating as he did so the cringing, mealy-mouthed voice of a Dickensian bookkeeper, which is how he always depicted the accountants who he claimed ran his newspaper.

"It's nothing you can use yet, but actually I can tell you something."

Light spread across Nick du Caines's face, his eyes widening in an expression of childlike joy. "She loves me!" he bellowed, at an embarrassing volume. "Hallelujah, Miss Costello. The words I've yearned to

hear from your lips more keenly than any others —
save, of course, for 'Nick, will you undo my —'"

She gave him a look.

"Sorry. I'm all ears."

"At this stage I have no more than a suspicion.
I know everyone's been thinking the same thing, but I
really do think Forbes may have been killed."

"Fuck."

"No actual proof yet."

"OK."

"Something tells me it was done professionally."

He sat up straight: if he'd been a dog, his ears would
have pricked up.

"What I want you to look into, as inconspicuously as
you can, is whether there is any evidence, any evidence
at all, of involvement by the," she dropped her voice to
the barest whisper, "CIA."

"Fuck me sideways."

"Not a word, Nick."

He took a swig of his drink. When he looked at her
again, his expression was deadly serious. "You wouldn't be
asking this unless you already had some evidence. I can't
proceed unless I see that. Or at least know what it is."

Maggie smiled, remembering that Nick du Caines
hadn't won a hatful of awards for investigative reporting
by accident. Lascivious old lush, he might be, but he
was still a journalist to the nicotine-stained tips of his
fingers. "I can't show you anything: you know that. All
you can know is that I have reason to suggest you look
in that direction. Anything you find, you need to share

with me first. Publish it before it's ready and there'll be no more from me."

"That's not such a massive threat, Mags. Not if you've got the CIA bumping off a US citizen who just so happened to have criticized the President. That's quite a big story all by itself."

"Not if it's only the tip of the iceberg."

"What are you saying?"

"I'm saying, be patient. Wait till you see the whole picture."

"I like what I'm seeing right now," he said, licking his lips before raising his glass to them.

She let Nick walk her home — swiftly, through years of experience, swivelling her head to offer her cheek when he moved in for the goodnight kiss. As always, his slobber was worse than his bite. He was a lech, but no more. He reached for her hand, kissed it and walked off into the night.

Once in her apartment, she opened her bag and pulled out Jackson's file. Something had been niggling at her all night, something that had struck a faint, muffled chord in her head earlier that she had not been able to identify.

She turned back to the first page and read it again, slowly. Her head was foggy with whisky and the bar. What the hell was it?

She looked at the first few facts, which she had skimmed over. The date of birth, the school, the college.

The school.

242

Again, she felt it, or rather heard it, a feeble echo in her head. The name was familiar, but she had no idea where from.

James Madison High School, Washington.

She found her BlackBerry and Googled it. It produced a list of dozens of James Madison High Schools, some in DC, some just outside, some with a guest speaker who had visited from Washington, DC.

Hold on, what if . . .

She changed the search, making one small adjustment.

But she was too impatient to wait for the little device to load up with results of its search. She went to the pile of books stacked on the floor by the bookcase: the new ones, for which there had been no room on the already jammed shelves. She rifled through them, throwing aside the new tomes on the Middle East, the future of the UN and "whither US foreign policy in the 21st century?".

At last. *Running Man: Stephen Baker, His Insatiable Quest for Power and What it Means for America*. By Max Simon PhD.

It was a hatchet job, gobbled up by the Fox constituency — with a sales spike reported in the Deep South — which had been torn apart in the *New York Times Book Review* and by a legion of liberal bloggers. She had picked it up at an airport the day before election day, telling herself it would bring good luck. (She couldn't even remember the convoluted superstitious logic behind that one: probably something about showing respect to the enemy.)

She had never got around to reading it; after the Baker landslide it suddenly didn't seem quite so relevant. But she'd given it a glance and remembered that it did at least pretend to be a proper biography with a cursory chapter on Baker's childhood. Now she was flicking the pages furiously.

She saw a paragraph about Baker's birth, with some obviously bogus detail about the mother clasping the hand of her newborn son. She turned to the next page.

In those days Cliff Baker lived a nomadic life, pitching up wherever work could be found . . .

More padding which she skipped. Here it was.

. . . logging meant Washington State and for the teenage Stephen that prompted yet another move, starting at a new high school in his sophomore year. He enrolled, for what would be his last two years of education before attending Harvard, at the James Madison High School in Aberdeen, Washington.

That was it. Jackson hadn't been educated in Washington, DC — as the casual reader of his CIA résumé would have assumed — but in Washington *State*. She all but ran back to the couch to retrieve the BlackBerry that had now completed its search. Sure enough, it confirmed there was only one James Madison High School in the state of Washington.

Maggie could hear the sound of her own breathing. Finally she had found a connection between the President and the man she had seen buried in a lonely grave in New Orleans earlier that day. These two men — one who had risen to the highest possible pinnacle,

244

the other who had sought to bring him down — had something in common. They had a shared past.

Stephen Baker and Vic Forbes had been at school together.

CHAPTER
THIRTY-TWO

From Swampland, posted 20.13 Thursday March 20:

Call me naïve and idealistic, but if something good is to come out of the <u>death of Stuart Goldstein</u> let it be this: let the paranoid right in America shut the hell up. When the President's tormentor, Vic Forbes, was found dead — and when every possible sign pointed to suicide — the Right immediately cried foul play. Or rather they didn't cry; they whispered it, as invidious gossip and innuendo, hinting at it in the <u>blogosphere</u> and on <u>Fox</u>. The likes of Rick Franklin did nothing to stop such talk; on the contrary, they exploited it, allowing it to "alter the atmospherics", to change the climate of opinion against Stephen Baker so that they could bring forward their spurious charges of impeachment against the President. Put simply, senior Republicans used conspiracy theories about Forbes to incubate the conditions in which they could hatch their plot to topple a legitimately elected president.

Well, let's hope they have the decency to at least fall silent now. They have tried to paint the Baker White House as the Corleone family, murderously rubbing out its enemies. The result is that a good man — a man whose life was dedicated to public service — has been driven to his death. Stu Goldstein loved politics and could play hardball with the best of them. He loved the game. But what's been happening in Washington these last few days is not a game. This is politics as blood sport.

So let there now be a pause, a ceasefire, while those responsible for guiding our republic take a breath. Let both sides pause and reflect. And let this be Stuart Goldstein's legacy . . .

From the comments thread at Fox Forum:

Re: Stu Goldstein found dead. Lamestream media are saying conservatives should stop accusing the Baker folks of being involved in Vic Forbes's death, as if we're somehow responsible for Goldstein's suicide. When I heard Goldstein had killed himself, my first reaction was, "Sounds like a guilty conscience . . ."

From Twitter, Thursday March 23:

\# stuartgoldstein Maybe Baker bumped him off just like Forbes: because he knew too much . . .

\# stuartgoldstein What if Franklin took out Goldstein, because he knew he was the I guy in White House who could defeat impeachment?

\# stuartgoldstein I reckon Baker had Goldstein killed so that people would now suspect Republicans of murder . . .

CHAPTER
THIRTY-THREE

Washington State, Friday March 24, 11.11 PST
Maggie was too late for the red-eye to Seattle so she left on the dawn flight the next morning. Perhaps thirty-five minutes after landing she was in a white rental car, she couldn't tell you what make, driving south-west along 1-5, the fatigue almost overwhelming her. It was cumulative now, day after day without proper sleep. Besides, she couldn't stop thinking about Stuart. The initial shock and sadness had given way to new feelings: anger — and fear.

The President's words on the phone the previous day came back to her: *Stuart was not a quitter. He was a fighter. I just refuse to believe* . . .

She had been all too ready to believe it, a fact that now made her slightly ashamed. She had accepted without question that Stuart Goldstein had cracked under pressure, heading to the park in the early hours to slash his wrists.

But now she wondered at the convenience of it. Baker was in desperate trouble and Stu his most trusted and capable lieutenant. If the President was right — that they were facing nothing less than an attempted *coup d'état* — then it was not out of the question that the enemy, whoever they might be, might see fit to kill Goldstein. After all, someone had murdered Forbes.

But that made no sense: Forbes's death was surely designed to help Stephen Baker. Goldstein's death could only hurt him.

On the other hand, the effect of the Forbes killing — apparently so fortuitously solving a Baker problem — had been to damage Baker, enabling his opponents to hint that he was some kind of gangster. What if that had been the objective all along? In which case, couldn't Forbes's killers and Goldstein's be one and the same, bent on taking down a troublesome new president?

The notion that Stu Goldstein — vast, lumbering, cunning and often gross, but also gentle, kind and motivated only by the idealist's desire to make the world better — could have been murdered filled Maggie with fury. She was haunted by the image of someone stalking Stu, grabbing him from behind, striking terror into a man who, thanks to his bulk and a life of brainwork unrelieved by exercise, would have been utterly defenceless. She could imagine him screaming as his wrists were cut, his blood jetting out. And then his inert body dumped in Rock Creek Park.

Maggie shook her head to stop the images coming. Who could have done such a thing to a man like Stuart Goldstein? Incomprehension turned to fear. If these men had seen an advantage in killing Stuart, wouldn't she be the very next target? If their motive was the thwarting of Baker's efforts to defend himself, then surely there was every reason to remove her. She and Stuart were the presidential defence team. She wondered if her conversations and texts with Stuart had been secure. They had been using the White House's encrypted communications system. But if Stu had been murdered, it had been done professionally; and people like that would have their ways of listening, watching, following . . .

She checked her rear-view mirror. There was a truck behind her. But behind that? She couldn't tell. She relaxed her grip on the steering wheel. Her hands were trembling.

Not much further to go now. Soon she would arrive in Aberdeen. Washington State was as far away from Washington, DC as you could be, on the other side of the country, the other side of the continent. The drive had been long, the landscape monotonous but, she told herself, that was all to the good. It gave her a chance to think.

She turned on the radio, trying to negotiate its buttons with her free hand. She wanted music as a distraction, but made the mistake of hitting the AM band and came across Rush Limbaugh instead.

"Here's what kills me about the liberal news media, folks. This is what kills me." He paused, leaving two or three seconds for effect. *"They have such a Short. Attention. Span. That's right. They don't pay attention. They forget to take their Ritalin or something, I don't know. Let me give you an example. Cast your mind back just a few days ago. It was wall-to-wall Vic Forbes."* He paused again, then fell into a sing-song delivery for the next phrase. *"Wall to wall! You could not move for Vic Forbes. Fortyeight hours, he was all anyone wanted to talk about. Forbes*

on the President's 'psychiatric' episode. Forbes on the Iranian Connection. Then Forbes promises the big one." Another pause. "The BIG ONE, ladies and gentlemen. And what happens? He's found dead and the liberal media forget what they'd been talking about twelve hours earlier. Clean forgot!" Now he went high-pitched and effeminate, the prissy voice of the East Coast liberal. "'Whoops! Where was I? I forgot!' And of course, now it's tributes on MSNBC and in the New York Times to that great liberal, Stuart Goldstein: the heavyweight champion of interest group, Democrat identity politics. That's who he was, my friends. And heavyweight is the right word. The guy was heavier than I am! And that's saying something."

He allowed himself a little laugh, one that made Maggie want to rip the radio out of the dashboard and hurl it out the window. But he was still talking.

"You see, even I'm at it now. Changing the subject. Let's not get distracted. That's how they are, folks. And that's how the liberal elite want you to be too. Forgetful. They want you to forget that Mr Forbes was about to tell us something. Well, we don't forget on this show. Not here, no sirree. Let's go to a call. Bloomington, Indiana, you're on . . ."

She listened to the caller for a while, who introduced himself as a "dittohead", then went on to condemn Stephen Baker's upcoming visit to China. She hit FM, found an alternative rock station and cranked the volume knob to full, hoping somehow to channel the new rage coursing through her. How dare he?

She checked the mirror once more. Still the same truck. She strained to see the driver, but the angle was too steep.

At least the landscape outside, while unchanging, was easy on the eye. Mile after mile of tall pine trees, scraping the sky like sharp pencils. She had passed mirror-clear lakes, forests dusted with Christmas-card snow and all of it bathed in a piercing blue light. Were it not for the noise of the logging trucks thundering past her on the interstate, laden with tree-trunks stacked like cigarettes, she would have kept the window down, so that she could gulp in the cold, fresh air.

She had flown to Seattle without calling Sanchez. She knew she was meant to "liaise" with him, but she wasn't going to start deferring to a twenty-seven-year-old guy whose place of work prior to the White House was the corner table at Starbucks, Dupont Circle branch. Besides, their encounter at Union Station suggested contact was now officially difficult if not forbidden. She understood why. If she emailed or texted or phoned, it would show up on records. And he had outed Bob Jackson, CIA agent, to her. Of course, rationally, that shouldn't matter: Jackson was already dead and there was no danger posed by revealing his affiliation to the CIA. But the connection between rationality and politics, Maggie had learned some time ago, was very slender indeed.

There was his safety to think of, too. If they really did face an enemy ready to kill, it helped no one to put Doug Sanchez in the firing line.

What was more, if she were honest, she didn't want him trying to talk her out of it. What did she have? Little more than a hunch. That's what Stuart would have said. She could hear him saying it: "You're going backwards, Costello. We need to know what Forbes or Jackson or whatever the fuck his name is knew. You're not writing his biography. 'Tell me about your childhood', and all that crap. You're meant to be finding out what he had and where he hid it."

That voice was nagging away at her even as she clocked up her hundredth mile from Seattle's airport, even after the pine forests gave way to the lake and finally the sign saying "Welcome to Aberdeen". A thin strip of new signage, in the same colours and typeface, had been added just below: "Onetime Home of President Stephen Baker".

As she looked around the place — shabby and peeling in the way of all small towns that have lost the role that once shaped them — she wondered if she had made a bad mistake. She was a continent away from Washington, DC — where the President she believed in was fighting for his political life. Was she really going to help him by snooping around a place that was on the other side of America and might as well have been the other side of the world?

She had punched the zipcode for the high school into the satnav and now it led her straight into the car park. She checked her watch. Thanks to the three-hour time difference and her early flight, it was still only early afternoon. The place should still be functioning.

She looked over her shoulder: no sign of that truck — or of any other vehicle she recognized.

There was a framed photograph of Stephen Baker in the hallway and, next to it, an eighth-grade art project: "Dear Mr President", in which students of James Madison expressed, through a drawing or a poem, their hopes for their most famous alumnus. When she saw the earnest pictures of handshakes, one hand white, one hand black, or of a bruised and bandaged globe, she was taken back to her own school days, and the art room of the convent. The world had been bruised by nuclear weapons back then, rather than global warming; but there were always wars, and the misery they caused. Not much had changed. Looking at the pictures reminded her of her earlier self, the earnestness that had inspired her to take up her chosen career, trying to bandage the world. And now these children were being inspired by their new president. A lump rose in her throat, reminding her why she was here.

"Can I help?"

Maggie spun around to see a smiling woman with long straight hair. In an instant calculation, she guessed that she was Maggie's age, but that motherhood, and life in Aberdeen, Washington, had added ten years.

"Oh yes, I'm looking for the Principal's office."

"I'm the Principal's secretary."

"Good. I wonder if I might —"

"He's busy with students right now. What's your question?" The smile remained fixed.

"It's about a former pupil at the school."

"Are you a journalist? All media inquiries go through —"

"No," Maggie said, with what she hoped was a warm grin. "I'm not a journalist and it's not about him."

The secretary stood and said nothing. She was not going to make this easy.

"My name is Ashley Muir," Maggie said, extending a hand. "I'm with Alpha, the insurance company. I'm here because one of our policyholders has, sadly, passed away. He left insufficient instructions as to beneficiaries and I —"

"Do you have ID?"

"I have my business card." Maggie opened her bag and pulled out the card she had been handed by Ashley Muir, Head of Government Relations for Alpha, at an awful Sunday brunch in Chevy Chase. He had called too, a couple of times, suggesting they go out on a date. She had said no but she was grateful to him now for giving her the only business card in her desk drawer that combined insurance and a female first name.

The secretary studied it for a moment. "This says something about the government."

"One of my duties is to look after policyholders who also happen to be federal employees." Maintain eye contact, Maggie told herself. Don't look down or away: classic signal of an untruth. Reading other people's body language was one of the skills you had to acquire in backroom diplomacy; but she was finding that deploying it on your own behalf was rather more difficult.

"So what is it you want?"

"I'm starting at the beginning, you see," Maggie said, moving towards the office, hoping it would send a subliminal cue to the woman to take her there. "Which is why it would be an enormous help if I could see the school record of the policyholder in question."

"Hmm," the secretary said, as she did indeed lead Maggie into the office. "Well, we don't keep the records here."

Maggie could feel her spirits sag. Wouldn't that be typical: to trek the entire width of the American continent only to be told the papers were kept in — where? — some storage facility in Maryland, no doubt.

"In fact," the secretary's smile was now back, "I didn't have any idea they were kept at all until last year." She paused, as if anxious that Maggie might not follow. "With the election and all."

Maggie nodded, happy to play the pupil.

"Then suddenly everyone wanted to see Stephen Baker's school file: *Vanity Fair*, ABC News, Inside Edition. All of them. Had to call the files from that class up from the basement. But it was all there, yearbook entry, the whole deal."

"So the files are here, in the office, now?"

"Oh, no. Once we'd got Stephen Baker's file, we put the rest back into storage."

"I see." This was painful.

"Oh, it was a wonderful thing to see. He was only here for a year or so, of course. But it was a nice picture. And his grade score. Through the roof!" She laughed.

"Yes, he seems like a very smart man."

"Well, people voted for him round here, I can tell you."

Maggie felt a little warmer towards this woman at hearing that. "So about this file?"

"Well, you'd need to fill out a form and we'd have to process the request, then I'd have to get Terry — our janitorial manager — to go down to the basement and retrieve it. So if you were able to come back, say next Thursday, then I —"

Instead of a frustrated grimace, Maggie managed to give her an apologetic smile. "The problem, I'm afraid, is that I'm based in Washington, DC. I can't be here for a full week."

"We could mail it to you. If you just leave your address, I'm sure —"

"Sadly, there is a degree of urgency. The courts will need notification of intestacy, before we can proceed to the probate process." She saw the baffled expression on the secretary's face and pressed ahead, dredging her memory for any jargon she could remember that would sound suitably intimidating. "This will require an immediate declaration of kinship, heredity and outstanding claims on the estate. It's a legal process and the courts could issue a subpoena against any person or individual who obstructs that process. Which would mean this school. Or indeed you." She felt cruel doing this to the poor woman, but there was too much at stake to play nice.

The smile had gone now.

"There is one more thing I should explain. The policyholder left behind a considerable sum of money.

257

There is scope in the terms of the policy for a facility fee." Maggie said these last two words slowly, so that they might sink in, then repeated them: "A facility fee to be paid to anyone who assists in the disbursement of funds." She leaned forward, ensuring that eye contact remained locked. "That too could of course include you."

"I'm not sure I follow, Miss Muir."

"The point is that we believe the policyholder died without a will. We think he left a lot of money with no one to give it to. My duty is to be absolutely sure that he did not leave any family or dependants behind and — once I'm sure of that — well, then the sum has to be distributed somehow, doesn't it?" She laughed and the secretary's eyes widened.

"In previous situations like this, schools have been recipients for such monies. And of course there would be compensation for your time and effort in helping us conduct our inquiries."

"So what would you need exactly?"

"All I would need is for you to take me to wherever those files are kept, so that I can take a quick look at the one belonging to our client and then I will be on my way."

"That's all?"

"That's all. I'm in the business of friends and family. That's what I'm looking for: friends and family."

The smell of bullshit was filling her own nostrils, but somehow Maggie sensed it was working.

The light was fluorescent, the smell stale. Upon rows and rows of metal shelves, mounted on Meccano-style

258

uprights, were hundreds of cardboard boxes. Each one was labelled in the thick but fading ink of a marker pen. She began reading off the years. 2001–2, 2000–1 . . .

The secretary had just asked the difficult question Maggie had been hoping to avoid — whose file is it you're looking for? — when she was called away to deal with a fourteen-year-old boy with a nosebleed. She nudged Maggie through a pair of double-doors, then unlocked another dark green door before rushing upstairs with a pack of tissues, calling back over her shoulder, "I'll be back shortly!"

Maggie was left alone, accompanied only by the gurgling of hot water pipes. She didn't have much time. With her head angled, she read quickly along the sides of these old brown boxes. 1979–80, 1978–79, 1977–78 . . .

Turning the corner, she found at last the right year. She pulled the box down and, with no table to rest on, set it on the ground and knelt beside it, coughing as the dust of the floor rose to her throat.

Inside were two parallel rails on which hung a series of dark green files. She did a quick flick through the Bs: the Baker file was gone, no doubt removed during last year's campaign, when journalists kept asking for it. A few Cs, a large number of Ds, a handful of Es; on and on until, at last, there it was.

Jackson, Robert Andrew

There was a home address, which Maggie swiftly scribbled in a notebook. There was a mother, Catherine Jackson, but by the word "father" only a blank.

Copies of his school report, including praise for his leadership of the debate team. High scores for history and for Spanish, decent in maths. Not what she needed. She turned the pages fast, hoping something would pop out, something that —

What was that?

A sound, close by. Metallic, but not the banging of a pipe. It came from further away and yet it was definitely down here, in the bowels of this building. It sounded somehow *deliberate*. Man-made.

She scoured the file, speed-reading. There was another reference to the debate team, written by a Mr Schilling. The date was three years after the first one: Jackson would have been seventeen.

. . . Robert's contribution to the debate team has not been quite as enthusiastic as it was previously. I suspect the loss of the captaincy of the team made him a little sore. If he is to pursue a political career, he needs to learn that every career includes its defeats!

A political career. Maggie kept going. A letter to Mrs Jackson from the Principal, suggesting a meeting at the school to resolve the "disciplinary matter we discussed on the phone". A reference accompanying an application to Harvard. A rejection letter from Harvard.

Finally, at the back of the file, a photocopied page from the high school yearbook. In the photograph Jackson wore the same expression Maggie had seen on his CIA file: smiling and hopeful, but with a hint of something else, too. Arrogance, determination or youthful ambition — it was hard to tell.

Keeping the file on the floor, she replaced the box on the shelf and was just reaching for the lid when she heard the same metallic sound again, this time nearer. Inside the room.

Over her right shoulder she saw nothing but more rows of boxes. Over the other were the heavy pipes of the school heating system. Suddenly aware that she was alone in a closed, dark underground room, she felt a desperate need to get out.

The sound came again and it was getting closer.

She bent down to pick up the file, pausing to shepherd a few loose sheets back between the covers, and when she came back up, she could tell the light had changed. The area where she had stood was no longer in shadow.

She turned around. There, framed in the light between two rows of shelves, just a few feet away from her, was the outline of a man. Fixed, still — and staring at her.

CHAPTER
THIRTY-FOUR

Washington, DC, Friday March 24, 12.00

"Are we on a secure line?"

"Always, Governor."

"You're not telling me you consider the United States Congress secure, are you?"

"I am not, sir, no. We have our own encryption equipment in this office."

"That's smart, Senator."

"I thank you."

"You sure you not from Louisiana?" A loud thunder of laughter down the phone, the way politicians used to laugh half a century ago: the sound of a big, Southern man who could fill a room with his own charisma. This, Senator Rick Franklin guessed, is how Huey Long would have laughed. Conventional wisdom said they didn't make them like that any more, but Governor Orville Tett begged to differ.

"I also want to thank you for getting in touch, Governor. I'm most grate—"

"We can cut the formal bullshit. We're busy men and we're on the same side, ain't we?"

"We are."

262

"So: seems like you're the main man on this Baker stuff. You're leading the troops into battle."

"I'm humbled by that description, but yes. I started this fight and I mean to finish it."

"Well, good for you. That's the kind of fighting spirit we need in our party. Too many pussies up there in DC who were ready, once Baker won last fall, to shut up shop and hang out the gone fishin' sign. That's why I want to help."

"Glad to hear that, sir."

"Here's the thing. You know that cesspit down in N'Awlins is run by Democrats. So, surprise surprise, they've canned the investigation into Forbes's death. That particular truth a bit too inconvenient for those liberals!" Another gale of laughter came roaring down the phone.

"I hear you, Governor Tett."

"Despite everything the Lord has rained down on that Sodom of the South, there are still a few good, God-fearing men down there in New Orleans. And one of them's been watching things very closely. Kind of my eyes and ears down there. Found out something mighty interesting too."

Franklin flashed a thumbs-up at Cindy, sitting opposite him, watching MSNBC on mute. He could hear a rustle of papers on the huge lump of oak he imagined served as the Governor's desk.

"Let me just get my reading glasses here a moment. OK, here we go." He made a murmuring sound, as if skim-reading, enjoying the suspense a tad too much, Franklin decided.

"He noticed a woman down there, snooping around. Claimed to be press, but was doing her own thing. My man kept a close eye on her. Even followed her to some kind of sex club."

Franklin felt his shoulders tense with embarrassment: Governor Tett had gained national fame during his first term when he had been covertly filmed in a variety of strip joints. The killer sequence — shown by Jon Stewart every night for a week — had Tett rewarding a particularly buxom performer by slipping a twenty not into her garter belt, as convention demanded, but directly into her underwear, twanging it forward and, it appeared on tape, taking a peek inside as he did so. Everyone had written the Governor off, assuming he would be impeached or turfed out by the voters, whichever came first. But Tett had gone on the Christian Broadcasting Network, sobbed about his shame, called to his saviour to rescue him and begged for forgiveness. After that direct appeal to evangelical voters — instantly dubbed "the Tett offensive" — his poll numbers went up. He'd been re-elected last year, against the national trend which saw Baker win his landslide.

"Turns out this woman's not press at all," Tett went on. "She called herself Liz Costello of the *Irish Times*. But that ain't her real name. She is, in fact, *Maggie Costello*." He stopped, like a comedian who's delivered his punchline.

Franklin waited for a moment, then realized Tett was not going to go on. "I'm sorry, Governor. The name's ringing a bell but —"

264

"I thought all you Washington insiders knew each other!"

"I'm not a Washington insider, Governor Tett. I'm a —"

"Aw, come on. I'm just jerking your chain. Maggie Costello was, until this week, a foreign policy advisor to one Stephen Baker. President of these United States."

"Oh, that's good."

"You didn't think I'd disappoint you, did you?"

"That's very good," Franklin replied, resolving to keep this information to himself until the moment was ripe. "When did she get down there?"

"I don't know that yet, but I'm checking that for you. Question you gotta ask yourself is: was she the dustbuster?"

"Dustbuster?"

"Clean-up artist! Did Baker send her in after Forbes was taken out, you know, to cover their tracks?"

"I see."

"Or maybe Baker put her in there to find out what the hell happened to Forbes — because he didn't know! It all depends on whether we think Baker had Forbes killed or not."

"Yes."

"And we don't know that, do we?"

Something in Tett's tone made Franklin uncomfortable.

The Governor wasn't done. "I mean, the only man who knows the real truth of that is the man who ordered the killing of Vic Forbes. Am I right?"

Franklin didn't answer the question, which he suspected carried more than a hint of accusation. "Of course, Governor, it may turn out that Forbes did take his own life after all."

"Yes, Senator Franklin, it might. But it might be too late to matter by then. Too late for Baker, I mean. And whoever gets that head on the trophy wall, he's going to look pretty good in three years' time, ain't he?"

"Well, I'm not thinking about that, Governor."

"You should, Senator. You should. And when you do, you remember your good friends down here in the great state of Louisiana, won't you?"

"I will certainly not forget this kindness, Governor Tett. One last question: where is Miss Costello now?"

"We have that covered, Senator. Remember, I have sympathetic counterparts across the entirety of this great country of ours. Governors with eyes and ears everywhere, each one of them with state troopers at their service, just like me. That's a lot of ground we got covered."

"That's good to hear."

"Put it this way, Senator. Wherever Miss Costello goes, there'll be someone watching. Always."

CHAPTER
THIRTY-FIVE

Aberdeen, Washington, Friday March 24, 15.24 PST

"I see you've already made yourself at home here."

Maggie heard herself panting. "You gave me quite a start."

"Did I? I am sorry." The voice was old, but steady. In the basement gloom, Maggie could still not make out a face.

"My name is Ashley Muir, from Alpha Insurance," she brazened. She thought about extending a hand, but fear got the better of her.

"Yes. So Mrs Stephenson said."

Maggie's breath came in heavy, pounding gulps.

"I have to tell you, I don't like people coming down here. Not without me."

She looked over at the door. Desperation made her cut the politeness. "Who are you?"

"My name is Ray Schilling. I am the principal of this school."

A wave of relief broke over her. "Oh, good. I am glad to hear that." She smiled an absurdly wide smile. "Can we perhaps talk in your office?"

"So you can understand my wariness, Ms Muir."

"Completely," Maggie said, enjoying the warmth of a mug of coffee in her hand.

"We didn't have many journalists last summer — Stephen Baker was a student here for such a short while. But those that did come: devious people, Ms Muir. Devious."

"Devious," Maggie agreed.

"So when I heard this story about insurance claims and whatnot, well, I thought 'Here we go again'."

"Of course you did."

"Not that you'd have found anything there, even if you had been looking for it." The Principal, white-haired with a long, narrow face, gave a self-congratulatory nod.

"Why's that?"

"I removed that file myself as soon as Stephen — excuse me — as soon as the President entered the race."

"Removed it?"

"Only to a place of safekeeping, Ms Muir. I wanted to be able to look reporters in the eye and tell them that the file was not here."

"That showed great foresight, Mr Schilling."

"Thank you. And now it isn't here at all."

"Where is it?"

"Did you know that they begin collecting material for a presidential library from the moment the oath is taken?" He spoke slowly, a function, Maggie had initially assumed, of his age. Now, she realized, it was

268

simply the speech of a man who had spent a lifetime addressing young people.

"I didn't know that, no."

"So that's where it is. Safe and sound."

"Good for you."

"Not that it will provide much for scholars to chew on."

"No?"

"No. Very thin. Must be because he was here for such a short time, you see. Unusually thin, all the same."

"As it happens, I was not looking for Mr Baker's file."

"Someone has died, I understand."

She had been hoping to avoid the name, but there seemed to be no choice if she was to play this scene through to the end. "That's right. Robert Jackson."

The Principal's face, already pale, seemed to turn a shade whiter. He sat back in his seat. "Robert Jackson," he repeated softly.

"Yes, I'm afraid so. He would have been here thirty-odd years ago."

"Nothing odd about it. Exactly thirty. I should know. I taught both of them."

"Both of them?"

"Baker and Jackson."

"Of course!" Maggie smiled. "You're the Mr Schilling on the report. You ran the debate team."

"You saw that?" Now he smiled, too. "Such a long time ago. I was very new here then. A young man, not much older than the students themselves."

"And now you're the Principal."

"Fifteen years in this job. Time for me to quit soon. But what a thrill, to see one of our students do so well. One day this will be Stephen Baker High."

Maybe, Maggie thought. *But only if he stays in office longer than two months.* "So you remember him when he was here?"

"I remember all the students I teach." He paused, then leaned forward.

Maggie recognized the manner. There were a few Mr Schillings in her neighbourhood of Dublin, as there probably were in every middling town: the educated man among provincials. She imagined him among the lumbermen and fishermen of Aberdeen with his lonely subscription to *The Economist* and his fondness for the BBC World Service. No wonder he remembered the day Stephen Baker had walked into his life, brightening the gloom.

"Stephen was always something special. No one forgot him. You couldn't."

"He certainly is very charismatic," Maggie said, as levelly as she could manage. She wanted to seem as detached from Baker as Ashley Muir, insurance investigator and voter, would be. "And the policyholder that I'm looking into," she made a fuss with a file in her bag, "Robert A. Jackson. Was he memorable in any way?"

"Well, I remember him, if that's what you mean. But, in truth that probably has more to do with Stephen Baker than it does with him. Anyway, I'm sure this is perfectly irrelevant for your purposes. An insurance claim, was it?"

Maggie scrambled to get him back on track. "I'm trying to build up as full a picture of the policyholder as I can. There's a large sum of money involved, no apparent beneficiaries. I need to find out if there's something we're not seeing."

"What might that be?"

"A surviving relative, maybe children from a marriage that didn't work out. I've decided to start at the beginning and take it from there. In my experience, the unlikeliest information can prove useful. You said he stayed in your memory because of Stephen Baker?"

"As I remember it, Jackson was not a bad debater. He could be sharp and precise. But he was so — there's no nice way to say this — overshadowed."

"Overshadowed?"

"He used to be the captain of the debate team at James Madison High. He got far in several competitions. Even reached a final in Olympia — though he lost that."

"And then?"

"And then Stephen Baker arrived in the final year. Funnily enough, they had a lot in common. Both so interested in politics, in history. I remember they got on quite well. Stephen used to tease him, called him by his middle name: Andrew. Like the president."

"Stephen Baker and Robert Jackson were friends?"

"I would say so, yes. Same class, same interests. They began debating together, a tag-team if you will. Against others in the school, then other schools. They were very effective."

"So what went wrong?"

"Well, I made this point to the reporters who came here to interview me about Stephen — about the President. He had true star quality, even then. A tremendous magnetism. Wherever he went in the school, people would follow. Especially the girls. Even the teachers were not immune."

"So what happened?"

"It's a minor thing, but in the light of what you've told me about poor Robert, I feel rather guilty. After just a short time at the school it was clear that Baker was special and it struck me that with him as captain, our debate team might finally have a chance of success."

"So you replaced Jackson with Baker."

"Yes."

"Did it work?"

Schilling smiled. "Big time, as the students would say now. James Madison won the statewide cup. Took on all those elite schools in Seattle and Redmond and Olympia and won. You have to know what that meant to a small town like Aberdeen. Things were already pretty depressed back then, logging was contracting, plenty of fathers at the school were out of work. And then, there was this . . . star."

"So you talent-spotted a future president of the United States."

"That's what I tell the reporters who come here. That's the public story. But Robert took it very badly. It broke his friendship with Stephen Baker instantly."

"And that's been on your conscience?"

"Oh, gosh no! High school friendships are a dime a dozen, Ms Muir, as I'm sure you know. No, it wasn't that. What mattered was the effect it had on Robert. It did seem to change him. He retreated into himself. He had never been adept socially but now he became very introverted. He resigned from the debate team — didn't want to be on it if he were no longer captain." He looked into Maggie's eyes, as if gauging whether he could trust her. "He became very bitter. It's a very strong word to use about an eighteen-year-old boy, but I sensed that he became *hateful*."

"Did he do something?"

"No, though these days you'd keep a close eye on him. After Columbine, no one takes any chances."

"Good God."

"Sorry, that was the wrong thing to say. He committed no acts of violence. But I had got to know him well and I saw that his resentment of Stephen Baker became unhealthy. When Baker applied to Harvard, so did Jackson. Baker, as you know, sailed in. They were throwing scholarships at him."

"And Jackson was rejected."

"Yes. Yes, he was." He paused. "Are you a mother yourself, Ms Muir?"

Immediately a picture of Liz and three-year-old Calum popped into Maggie's head. "No, Mr Schilling. I'm afraid I'm not."

"Well, people don't realize how fragile kids are at that age. These are the formative years. A young man can be shaped by what happens to him at that age."

"And what happened to Robert Jackson?"

"I would say he developed an unhealthy interest in Stephen Baker. An obsession, you'd call it. Baker became a kind of mirror to Robert, and whatever he saw in that mirror was never good enough. Robert wasn't as smart, he wasn't as handsome, he wasn't as popular. And it wasn't just a phase, either. I ran into Robert a year or two afterwards, and he still seemed to be in the grip of this fixation."

"How do you mean?"

"It was strange really. But Robert had a file with him. One of those high school files, with a rubber band across the front? He showed it to me."

"And what was inside?"

"Clippings about Stephen. Items from the local paper, neatly cut out and filed in date order. Too neat. It made me shudder."

"Did they still know each other then?"

"Well, Stephen's father still worked here, in the timber trade. He couldn't afford to retire. So Aberdeen is where Stephen came back to during the vacations."

Maggie tried to collect her thoughts. "And you say you feared Robert Jackson would do something . . . something he might regret?"

"You've just reminded me of something I said to my wife at the time. Gosh, thirty years ago and it's just come back to me."

"What did you say?"

"I said that an obsession like this only ends in destruction. Jackson will either destroy Stephen Baker — or he will destroy himself."

CHAPTER
THIRTY-SIX

Clinton, Maryland, Friday March 24, 13.23
It was windy and noisy and the ideal place not to do an interview. But Nick du Caines's source had insisted on it.

They were in a piece of scrubland, standing in front of a tall wire fence. To reach it he had had to pull off the freeway and into a rest-stop, park up, then walk through a thicket of nettles and overgrown weeds until he found what passed for a small clearing. The loud hum of traffic was constant.

They'd met here the first time, too. Not because Daniel Judd was particularly wary of meeting in a public place, but simply because this was his place of work and any time away from it he regarded as a waste.

Nick zipped up a leather jacket with an AC/DC emblem etched into the back, braced himself against the chill and took his place alongside Judd, who continued to stare straight ahead.

"I've brought you a coffee," Nick said. "Probably stone cold by now, but it's the thought that counts."

"Just put it on the ground. Between my feet. Thanks."

Nick knew better than to interrupt Judd when he was working. On the other side of the wire fence, about two hundred yards away, a crew in overalls were fussing around two stationary aircraft. Another man was driving a small electric buggy. To anyone driving past, it would have looked like nothing more than a regular working day at the small private airport known as Washington Executive Airfield.

Judd raised a pair of binoculars to his eyes, then mumbled a number into a tiny digital recorder: "N581GD." Without breaking his gaze, he reached for the long-lens SLR camera that hung on a second strap around his neck and took a good dozen pictures of one of the two planes, the motorwind whirring uninterruptedly.

Only then did he turn to Nick. "How you doing?"

"Aren't you going to have your coffee?"

"You said it was stone cold."

"Didn't do a brilliant sell on that one, did I?"

Judd said nothing. Du Caines was used to this treatment and had learned not to see it as unfriendly. The guy might have the social skills of a tree stump but Nick respected few people more.

Judd was an "airplane spotter", one of these people who stood near runways watching planes take off and land and take off again. Such people were a variant of the trainspotters Nick and his friends had teased mercilessly back in school, anoraks who could get genuinely excited by pencilling a serial number into a notebook. But it turned out they were right to get excited — and, by God, Nick was glad they had. For it was these geeks — and geeks like them around the world — who had noticed the strange pattern of private jet flights that began in regular American airports but ended in the likes of Karachi, Amman or Damascus. They had put the pieces together and discovered the phenomenon of "extra-ordinary rendition": the secret flights by which suspected terrorists were spirited away in the dead of night from the streets of Milan or Stockholm to Egypt or Jordan, nations whose intelligence agencies were ready to do whatever it took to "persuade" these suspects to talk.

It was Judd and his pals who had noted down the number of a plane that had landed first in Shannon, Ireland then reappeared in Sweden before reaching its final destination in Amman. The spotters had then visited the Federal Aviation Administration's website and clicked on the registry of aircraft licensed to US owners. There they could find not only a full archive of logs and flight plans for every registered aeroplane, but also the identity of the owners of each aircraft. All at the click of a mouse.

The plane that had touched down in Shannon en route to Amman had been the property of a small aviation company based in Massachusetts. A few clicks later and Judd had the names of the company's executives. But these businessmen proved to be curiously shy. Instead of giving an address, each one had supplied only a post office box number. That piqued Judd's interest, not least because these PO boxes were all in northern Virginia. Which just so happened to house, in Langley, the headquarters of the Central Intelligence Agency.

After that, Judd had enough to be certain. Over a drink in Adams Morgan, seated in the dark at a corner table, he had provided the dates, flight plans and registration numbers that enabled Nick du Caines to reveal to the world the plane he and his Sunday newspaper called the "Guantánamo Bay Express". He had won three awards for that one — and gave his ailing employers yet another stay of execution.

"You got that look on your face, Nick."

"What look?"

"The look that says you wanna cause trouble."

"Ah, that will be you looking in the mirror."

Judd gave a flicker of a smile and went back to gazing at the airfield.

Nick decided not to plunge in straight away. "So what's going on here? Anything?"

"Might be. Too early to tell."

"Government?"

"Like I say, Mr du Caines, too early to tell."

"Right you are. Back off. Understood."

Another long silence. Judd raised the binoculars to his eyes. Still peering through them, he said, "You didn't come out here into the middle of nowhere on a ball-freezing day to look at my pretty face, now did you?"

"I did not."

"So, what is it you want to ask?"

"That's just it. I'm not sure."

"That's not a good start."

"OK. New Orleans. What do you know about New Orleans?"

"You can do better than that, Nick."

"Would you be able to see if a CIA team flew into New Orleans?"

"This about that guy who was spilling the shit on the President?"

"Christ, you don't miss much, do you?"

"Why else would a Brit journalist be interested in New Orleans?"

"OK. Yes, it's about that. I have reason to believe — or rather *suspect* — that Vic Forbes did not die entirely of natural causes."

"Looked pretty unnatural to me."

"Yes. Indeed. But I think he may have been helped, if you see what I mean."

"So why CIA?"

"I can't say."

For the first time Judd turned away from his view through the chicken wire and looked Nick du Caines in the face. "I thought it was meant to be *me* who refused to tell *you* things."

"I know, I know. But this is one of those cases where I really can't name a source."

"I didn't ask you to name your source. I asked you why you thought it was the CIA."

"Because to answer that would risk revealing my source. And I can't do that." When Judd said nothing, du Caines added, "I would do the same for you."

"So why do you think they used an airplane?"

"The truth is, I have no reason to believe that at all. But you're the only person I know who's ever found out a *thing* about what the CIA gets up to so I'm starting with you."

"Fishing expedition."

"Total. I'm thinking that if by some chance they *did* use a plane, then that's something we can find out. *You* can find out."

"You said, 'they'."

"Sorry?"

" 'If by some chance *they* did use a plane.' Why *they*?"

Nick frowned as if he'd just been confronted with a tricky question in a pub quiz. "Yes, I did say that. I suppose I just assumed . . . All the CIA stuff I've read — Laos in the seventies, central America in the eighties, Afghanistan, Iraq — it's always teams. Isn't that how they do it? Same with the rendition thing. How many did they use for that job in Italy?"

"Thirteen."

"And that was just to pick up one guy. And it wasn't wet work. Which Forbes was."

"OK, I'll look. But it's a long shot."

"I know."

"Chances are, they drove there. Or flew separately, on commercial."

"But you'll look? I owe you one, Dan."

With that, Nick du Caines returned to the battered Nissan that served as his car: not old enough to be retro, just plain old.

But, like all those who see themselves as observers, eyeing the world through binoculars or an SLR lens, neither Judd nor du Caines imagined that, at that very moment, they were themselves being observed through a long lens.

The watchers being watched.

CHAPTER
THIRTY-SEVEN

Aberdeen, Washington, Friday March 24, 18.23 PST
Maggie concluded the meeting with a few of the bureaucratic questions — accompanied by much earnest note taking — that she thought Ashley Muir, life insurance agent, might ask.

"What about his parents? Are they alive or deceased?"

"Both dead," Principal Schilling answered. "Robert's father died even before he came to the school. Perhaps that's another thing I should have noticed: the absence of a father figure. I would approach a boy like him very differently now."

"And what about Robert's mother?"

"She died long ago. More than twenty years, I think."

"Besides the debating, was there anything else that might have made Jackson stand out as a student?"

"He was bright. You've got to remember that: before Stephen Baker appeared, Jackson was in the top bracket of the school. Not a star, but accomplished. He was interested in world affairs, in politics. He was a good linguist; almost fluent in Spanish."

Maggie was scribbling in her notebook.

"I guess," the Principal offered, "that Robert was what today's students would call a 'geek'."

"A geek?" Maggie smiled.

"It's funny, how much you remember when you put your mind to it. He was fascinated by computers. No one had computers in their homes back then, of course, but Robert was very knowledgeable. I seem to remember he started a school computer club. Though that petered out after, you know, the change in the debate team."

Maggie wrote it all down, along with the social security number and now-defunct home address Mr Schilling gave her.

"You've been very generous with your time."

"I hope it's helped. And Ms Muir? If you find out what happened to Robert Jackson, be sure to let me know."

By the time Maggie had pushed through the swing doors and stepped outside, twilight was setting in. She looked at her watch: six-forty local time, twenty to ten on the East Coast. The day had begun with a five-hour flight, a two-hour drive: the thought of driving back to Seattle now — her original plan — suddenly lost its appeal. She was exhausted. Safer to find a motel in Aberdeen and make tracks in the morning.

She was walking towards her hire car when she froze.

There, standing in the gloom right beside her car was the outline of a person: man or woman Maggie couldn't tell. The figure was standing, quite still, facing towards her, as if waiting for this moment. Was this how it had happened to Stuart: a man in the shadows, standing quite calmly, waiting for the moment to strike? Maggie felt her fist clench, an involuntary and useless gesture — one that made her realize she was unarmed and therefore utterly powerless.

Then a voice, carrying over the empty asphalt of the parking lot: "Am I glad to see you!"

A woman. As Maggie stepped nearer, she could see that she was older, early sixties at a guess. She felt her shoulders drop in relief. Either a veteran teacher or a grandmother of one of the pupils, Maggie guessed. Grey-haired, bespectacled and in a terminally unfashionable coat. A less frightening person it was hard to imagine.

"Gosh, I am so relieved, I can't tell you. My battery's dead — again! — and I desperately need someone to give me some help."

Something in the woman's voice gave Maggie an instant ache, taking her back to evenings just like this one: after school, dark and cold, being met by her mother. It didn't happen often: she and Liz usually walked or got the bus. But on those rare afternoons when it did, when she would see her mother's smiling face there by the gate, it would fill her with warmth. And with something else, too — a sensation she now longed for so deeply it caught her by surprise. There was no immediate word for it, but it belonged somewhere between safety and love. She had, she realized, moved so far away from that house she grew up in.

"Of course I'll help. Mind you, I'm not sure I have any jump leads. This is a rental."

"Oh, don't worry about that, dear. My son gave me everything. I have it all in the trunk. All I need is another car that works!"

Maggie watched, impressed, as the woman went around the back of her silver Saturn, opened the boot and emerged carrying two cables, red and black. She then lifted the hood on her own car, talking throughout.

"If I've made that mistake once, I've made it a thousand times. The same thing, again and again. I park the car, I collect my handbag and then —"

"Don't tell me," said Maggie, hovering close by, watching with admiration as the older woman placed the crocodile clips on the plus and minus nodes of her car battery. "You left the lights on."

"Oh no, dear," the lady said, looking slightly affronted. "I learned that lesson a long time ago. No, this was a different mistake. I left my key in the ignition."

"And that gives you a flat battery?"

"It does, yes. It runs the radio or something, I don't know. My son is the mechanic in the family. He knows about these things." She suddenly turned away from the engine, looking mildly alarmed. "You won't tell him, will you? About this?"

Maggie smiled, remembering the way her mother had acted when she had started learning to use a computer for the first time. She had forgotten one of her key lessons — closing down all the programs before switching the machine off — and had turned to Maggie with the same expression. "You won't tell Liz, will you?"

"No, I won't tell him. I don't know who he is. I'm from out of town."

"Are you really, dear? You're not a parent at this school, then?"

"Just visiting."

"What a shame. You could have met my Mike. He's a parent at this school." She paused. "Single parent now." She paused, as if absorbing that fact. "Now, let's get your car moved alongside mine and then get that hood open."

Maggie clicked the car door open, sat in the driver's seat, fired it up, then drove it in a near circle, so that it ended up facing the Saturn, nose-to-nose. Then she turned the engine off and began looking for the latch for the hood. Feeling in the dark under the steering wheel column eventually revealed a small lever. She pulled it, heard the click and then watched, impressed again, as the woman didn't wait for help but hoisted the hood up to full height by herself.

"OK, don't turn the engine back on just yet! Wait for me to give you the word."

As Maggie waited, she thought again of what she had heard from Mr Schilling. "An obsession like this only ends in destruction," he had said. Even three decades ago, when Robert Jackson was a teenager, Schilling had become convinced that something dangerous and fateful was brewing in him. *Jackson will either destroy Stephen Baker — or he will destroy himself.*

She pictured them here, in this car park, outside this school, on evenings like this one — Baker smiling to the girls as he slung his rucksack over his shoulder and headed home, tall and lean, his strides long and effortless. And, perhaps just over there by the side entrance, watching, would have stood the shorter, plainer Robert Jackson, denied even one of Baker's conspicuous gifts. Maggie could see him in the dusk, the teenage rage simmering inside him.

"OK! Let's give this a go!"

Coming back to herself, Maggie turned the key, lightly pumped the gas pedal and heard the car spark into action. Without moving, she watched the grey-haired lady in her tweedy coat move to her own car and slip into the driver's seat. A second or two later came the sound of her engine revving back to life.

A moment later both were out of their cars, standing in front of the humming engines now connected, like two hospital patients, by red and black cables.

"We did it," Maggie said, a wide smile on her face.

"Not bad for a couple of broads, eh?" said the woman, squeezing Maggie's arm for good measure.

"Not bad at all."

"I'm so grateful to you. Now I can pick up my grandson from football practice." She looked at her watch. "Oh, mercy me. I should have been there ten minutes ago. I'm going to have to rush off. Is there any way I can thank you?"

Maggie realized the answer was no. She could give no real name or address even though, just this once, she would have quite liked to. All she could do was extend a hand and, with a twinge of regret, say: "I'm glad I could help. Now go pick up your grandson. And remember to keep the engine running!"

She watched the Saturn turn smoothly out of the lot and head into the night. Something about the sight of it made up Maggie's mind: she would not make the long drive to Seattle. She would find a cheap and cheerful place to stay here in Aberdeen, shower, fall into bed and sleep. She was, she realized, completely drained.

She headed to the highway that had brought her here, looking for signs for the centre of town. She glided through a succession of green lights and was on her way. Traffic was thin, just a few lights brightening the dark. She wondered if this was going to be one of those American places that had no real centre — just a sprawl. Maybe she should just keep driving, waiting for the first motel that popped up.

There were some up ahead and on the left. In readiness for the exit, she eased down on the brake, but her speed didn't alter. She pressed down harder and this time the car jerked when it should have slowed down. Bloody rentals.

When the exit came into view, she moved into the right lane, gently squeezing the brake.

The car did not slow down.

Instead it was continuing at full speed. Maggie pressed down again. Still nothing. The car kept rushing forward, utterly beyond her control. She slammed her foot on the brake. Nothing!

By now the exit lane was curving off the main highway. She looked in her wing mirror: a car in the next lane. There was no way she could pull away without crashing into it. She would have to take the exit.

The road curved round suddenly. She gripped the steering wheel as tightly as she could, swerving around a road meant to be taken at half this speed. She could feel the bumps under her wheels as she careened into the side strips. The reflector signs, each marked with an arrow, were coming too fast.

Finally the road straightened out but still she was going too fast. She could see that up ahead was a red light at a crossroads, bright and noisy with traffic. Already there were two other cars waiting at the light — and she was heading at full, motorway speed towards them. She stamped impotently once more on the pedal, her knuckles white on the steering wheel. In a matter of seconds, she would either slam into the stationary cars or be smashed from the side by oncoming traffic.

She knew she had only one option but the fear of it almost paralysed her. It was only the onrushing proximity of the car in front, its red brake lights looming and, finally, the sight of two heads low down on the back seat — children — that finally prompted action.

Gritting her teeth, she swerved off the road and into the indistinct blackness beyond. As she turned the wheel, she had no idea what lay there. Hedges, trees or a grass verge? A ditch? Or a sheer drop? She had no way of knowing and now no choice but to drive into it at close to seventy miles per hour.

The headlights picked it out perhaps a split second before she felt the hard crunch of metal: a steel barrier that crumpled under the force of the car. Now a thicket of trees and a tangle of branches came at her, the car bumping and thudding at what felt a thunderous speed. Her head hit the roof of the car, ramming through the thin vinyl veneer into the hard metal underneath.

Instinct took over as she reached for the clasp holding her safety belt and, with one hand still on the wheel, unpopped it. Then, seeing what loomed ahead, she opened the car door and hurled herself out, even as she could see the ground passing rapidly beneath her.

Perhaps a half-second before she hit the ground, while she was still in the air, her heart throbbing with a nauseous urgency, she saw two things, one clearer than the other.

Less clear was the thick tree that her car had just rammed into, crumpling the entire front end. Clearer, and in her mind's eye, was the face of the woman who had persuaded her to open the hood of her car, a woman whose eyes had been kindly enough to remind Maggie Costello of her own mother.

And after that she saw nothing.

CHAPTER
THIRTY-EIGHT

Virginia, Friday March 24, 18.25
He hadn't expected to hear back so fast. Back in the old days, when it was just a few guys with notebooks and pencils, it took the best part of a week to piece together even a basic flight plan. But now there was email, and online forums and all the rest of it, things moved quickly.

The British guy, du Caines, hadn't given him much but Daniel Judd had got the general idea. As soon as Nick had called, he knew it was going to be something big. Big enough to interest readers of a Brit newspaper; big enough for Nick to hike out to the middle of nowhere to see him.

He had read that right — once the CIA was involved, it automatically became huge — just as he had been right to say that du Caines was on a fishing expedition. The journalist had nothing but a hunch. But after the rendition stuff, Judd was prepared to believe that bunch of motherfuckers were capable of anything. More importantly, he had learned a lot in the last few years about how the CIA operated. They had a modus operandi in the air and — now — so did those, like Judd, who followed them on the ground.

He logged into his email account, typing an alias formed out of his own middle name, his wife's maiden name and a bogus middle initial — Z — that he hoped would throw any snoopers off the scent. Of course, if the CIA really wanted to hack into his email they could, but there was no reason to make it easy.

He sent a message to his contact in Louisiana. Baton Rouge unfortunately; he'd come across no spotters in New Orleans. He worded it carefully. Even if he took precautions — encryption software, regularly changing his ISP, that middle Z — there were no guarantees that his fellow enthusiasts were as careful. On the contrary, in the era of federal wiretapping, he worked on the assumption that there was always someone looking over his shoulder. His wife and his brother-in-law had mocked him for years, reckoning he was some paranoid, libertarian nut who'd soon be hiding in the hills living off sachets of dried food. But once all that shit came out about FISA and government eavesdropping, it wasn't him who came out looking the fool, now, was it?

Euphemism, that was the key. No word that would be flagged automatically by the authorities and their word-hunt programs.

Hope you're well, big guy. Question for you. If our friends at the Company were planning to take a little working vacation in the Big Easy, what would be their best initial destination? Am assuming Louis Armstrong International too crowded etc. What would you advise?

He'd got a reply within four minutes.

No one but tourists uses Louis. They'd go for a place they Knew.

Neat. Just that capital K was enough. He called up the Federal Aviation Administration database, waiting for the right page to load before typing the word KNEW. Instantly the four letters were recognized as the call sign for Lakefront airport, located, he discovered, just "four nautical miles north-east of the central business district of New Orleans".

He went to the airport's website to find a photo of a rather lovely structure, complete with original art-deco terminal and a sculpture out front: Fountain of the Winds.

He read the spec: general aviation, with special provision for charter and private flights. That would be ideal for a black op, Judd decided. There was even a history of occasional military use: plausible that some of the CIA guys had used it before.

He glanced down at the dates Nick had given him, then keyed in the details he needed to call up the flight plans for aircraft that had used Lakefront in that period. He narrowed it down by selecting "In" rather than "In and Out". Whether the CIA had flown a plane out of Lakefront after Forbes's death could wait. Right now he needed to see if they had flown in.

As he expected, a long, long list of N-numbers appeared. One by one, using nothing more elaborate than the basic search function on his internet browser, he checked to see if any of those numbers also appeared on the list of thirty-three planes he and his fellow spotters, along with various peace activists and reporters like du Caines, had determined constituted the fleet leased by the CIA for its covert work, dominated by, but not confined to, extraordinary renditions.

Not one.

He would have to go the long way round. He decided to call his buddy Martin, whose greatest asset was that he was not burdened by even the meagre domestic obligations that sat on Judd's shoulders. Martin had no kids, no wife and, so far as he could tell, no friends save for Judd himself.

As always, Martin answered on the first ring. Judd walked him through the problem and they agreed to split the list. Judd would check the midnight Sunday to noon Wednesday flights into Lakefront — looking for any numbers that carried the telltale hallmarks — and Martin would do the same for the second half of the week, from noon Wednesday to Sunday midnight. "First one to find it gets free beer for a night."

"Done."

That had been close to 6p.m. It was now shortly after eleven, long after his wife had gone to bed — slamming the door, asking why he didn't just stick his dick into the computer's disk drive, he obviously loved it so much — that he felt the first nibble on the end of the line.

Every other N-number traced back to a regular commercial air operator: licensed, well-known, all-colour website, the full deal. But here was one, N4808P, owned by Premier Air Executive Services, an operator based in Maryland, whose site gave only the sparest of details — and named no executives.

Judd headed to the registry of company records. The entry for Premier Air offered three listed officers. A further search on these three men yielded a pattern Judd had seen several times before. Their social security numbers — all fully retrievable online — had been issued when they were over the age of fifty. He wouldn't have known about such things before, but the rendition saga had taught Judd that when a social security number is given to someone in their fifties, that someone is creating a new and fake identity.

But the company records contained one more curious fact about the provenance of Premier Air Executive Services, one that surprised him and which, he guessed, would particularly interest Nick du Caines. He reached for his phone.

CHAPTER
THIRTY-NINE

Aberdeen, Washington, Saturday March 25, 10.05 PST
Maggie could hear a low hum, which she assumed was in her head. She had been dreaming so vividly, she had not only seen Uri's face close to hers, she had felt the touch of his hand as he stroked her hair. But even then, as she smiled at his caresses, the hum had bothered her. It didn't fit. And so she had made herself wake up, so that she could drive the noise away.

When she opened her eyes, she saw only a white wall. There were no lines she could make out, in fact nothing that could make her certain it was a wall rather than just empty space. Or maybe a cloud. The hum was still there, though.

She moved her head and felt a surge of pain at the base of her skull. She must have let out a noise — though it sounded as if it came from down the hall — because within a few moments a nurse had scurried into the room, filling up the white space that had once been a blank wall.

"Well, good morning."

Maggie heard the same down-the-hall voice answer, "Good morning." It sounded slurred and blurred.

"Do you know where you are?"

Maggie tried to shake her head, sending more shooting pain up from her neck. She heard a yelp come out of her mouth.

"OK. We should start at the beginning. What is your name?"

With vast effort, Maggie croaked, "Maggie Costello."

The nurse — fair-haired and large-armed — checked her notes. "Good. That's what we have too. Another few questions, I'm afraid. Who is the president of the United States?"

Before the answer came the feeling, a sudden onrush of memories and the emotions they aroused. She saw the den in the White House Residence, Sanchez, MacDonald, Stuart Goldstein. *Stuart.* She felt a stab of grief, the lead weight of realization that something awful had not been imagined or dreamed but was real. Only then did she see the face of Stephen Baker: still handsome but now etched with pain . . .

"Don't worry, he's still very new. His name is Stephen Baker. How many states are there in the United States?"

"Where am I?"

"I'll come to that. I just need to ask you these questions the instant you wake up. That's our protocol. How many —"

"Fifty."

"And what day of the week comes after —"

"Stephen Baker is the president of the United States. He won last November with three hundred and thirty-nine electoral college votes, defeating Mark Chester in the general having beaten Dr Anthony

Adams in the primary. The days of the week are Sunday, Monday, Tuesday, Wednesday, Thursday, Friday and Saturday. In France they are, dimanche, lundi, mardi, mercredi, vendredi, jeudi et samedi. Now will you tell me where the hell I am, please?"

The nurse, whose eyes had widened, now let her face relax. She put her clipboard on the bed. "You're at the Grays Harbor Community Hospital, Ms Costello. In Aberdeen, Washington. Now, I promise this is not another quiz question. Do you know why you are here?"

Maggie tried letting her head fall back into the pillow, but even that small movement made her wince. Once again, it was a feeling that came to her first, the tight grip on the steering wheel, her mouth dry with panic, the sight of those red lights getting nearer and nearer . . .

"I was in a car accident. Something happened."

"That's right. Last night." She looked at her watch. "Nearly sixteen hours ago. And you are very lucky to be alive, Ms Costello. The police officer who found you says the front of your car looked like it'd been through a trash compactor."

"A policeman found me?"

"Yes, they'll be coming later. They have some questions for you, too, I'm afraid."

Maggie felt herself grimace.

"For now, you just need to get some rest. Are there people you'd like us to contact?"

At that Maggie felt a different kind of pain, but no less sharp. "Um," she began, as a single face formed in her mind, a face she felt she had just seen.

"A partner perhaps? A family member?"

"Not just yet, thank you."

"But there may be people concerned —"

Maggie asked for some time to think and, then, for her phone. The nurse left the room only to return a second or two later, this time with a look — part baffled, part melancholy — that only added to Maggie's confusion.

"Are you sure you had your phone with you, Ms Costello?"

"It's Maggie," she said, still slurred. "And yes. It's always on me. It would have been in my jacket. Or bag."

"We have an overnight bag. Also two earrings, one bottle of Allure perfume, one lip balm —" She was scanning an inventory of some kind. "No phone."

A suspicion began to grow, like a spreading stain.

"What is that list you're looking at?" Now she was hearing the strangeness of her own voice. *What ish that lisht . . .*

"It's the police inventory. They have to do it for all NCA's."

Even raising an eyebrow in inquiry hurt, but the nurse got the message.

"Non-conscious admissions."

"Oh. Do you have a small black notebook on that list?"

The nurse scanned it up and down, then turned it over, then back again.

"No."

Maggie felt a shudder pass across her skin. "A laptop? Wallet?"

The woman shook her head apologetically.

"I need to make a telephone call. An urgent one."

"There'll be plenty of time for that."

"No. Now."

The nurse stepped forward and reached for Maggie's hand. What she thought was a moment of tenderness was then revealed as something else. The main vein on her right hand was punctured by a cannula, a small tube attached in turn to a long, clear line. The nurse checked it, then produced a cuff to measure Maggie's blood pressure, pressed an unseen button that made her right arm feel as if it had become instantly inflated, and popped a thermometer under her tongue. All in what seemed like a single moment.

"I'm in bad shape, aren't I?" Maggie said, indecipherable through the thermometer.

"You fell from a fast-moving car, so that would be a yes. You have a couple of broken ribs, but your legs and arms are intact. And we'll keep checking that head of yours. Though, from what I heard earlier, you'd be on the Grays' quiz team ahead of me. Try to get some rest."

At last Maggie allowed the thought she had repressed to break surface. She could hear the voice that she had instantly found soothing.

Oh, don't worry about that, dear.

The woman in the car park had seemed kind and genuine and Maggie had swallowed it all, obeying the instruction to stay in the driving seat while she fiddled with the engine — hidden by the hood and safely unseen. She had moved fast; a professional who knew exactly what she was doing.

A thoroughly efficient job, so deft that the woman, or her accomplice, must have followed Maggie onto the highway, watched her career towards what they surely assumed was her death and then rushed to the car, opened it, stolen the key items and fled — all before the police or paramedics had got within a hundred yards of her.

That they had taken her phone, her computer and her notebook confirmed it. The President had been right. The moment those three letters — CIA — had been mentioned, he had been seized by what she had then regarded as excessive alarm. Talking of the plot against Kennedy, jumping to the conclusion that Stuart had not taken his own life — no matter how glum and melancholy he had been — telling her to watch herself, just in case. As so often, Stephen Baker grasped the reality of the situation faster and more fully than anyone.

He had been very clear: they faced a ruthless and determined adversary. Now she knew that they — whoever *they* were — were ruthless enough to kill.

A sudden flashback to last night: the car in front, getting closer, the brake lights bleeding bright red, the sight of those two heads in the back seat, two kids . . .

They were ready to kill more than just her. They had chosen a method — tampering with the brakes — that would almost certainly have led to the deaths of others.

She felt her body flood with rage. These people had murdered Stuart and had been ready to murder her, even if that meant killing two innocent children. She hated them with a loathing she could barely contain. She wanted to save Stephen Baker and his presidency, of course, now more than ever, given that it was under such cold-blooded assault. But she wanted something else, too: she wanted the people behind all this to pay for what they had done. She wanted revenge.

She could feel a trembling in her hands; it made the tube vibrate. Probably her body reacting to the sudden infusion of adrenalin her own fury had generated. Calm down, she told herself. Calm down.

As a diversionary tactic, she tried to think through exactly what information was in the hands of those who had tried to kill her. She tried to do it methodically, starting with her phone. The recent calls list was a disaster: it would immediately implicate the White House. It would reveal calls to Stuart's direct line and to Sanchez. Also to a couple of cab companies in New Orleans and in DC, and to Nick du Caines. Maybe Uri.

The laptop didn't contain much: she'd done next to nothing by email. But her notebook would have everything Schilling, the school principal, had told her. Whoever was holding it now would have all the information on Jackson/Forbes and the simmering, fraternal feud between him and the young Stephen Baker. If she was in a race against these people, she had just lost.

Or perhaps they already knew everything she had discovered, had known it for years. That brought her no relief. It just meant that they now knew that she knew. Maybe that was why she had become a target. She knew too much.

She looked around the room, the white walls suddenly revealed as a pale magnolia. A tentative wave of nausea began to rise in her throat. Why had the nurse not given her any water?

Now she was seized by a new alarm. How could she be sure this was a hospital? What if the CIA had simply spirited her away from the roadside and brought her to some closed hideaway, dressed up to look like a hospital when in reality it was anything but? This could be just a regular bedroom in one of their safe houses, with a few flickering machines brought in for effect . . .

She turned onto her side and, ignoring the pain now spreading across her chest, reached for the side table where there sat a chunky, beige phone. She grabbed for it, her hand flailing vainly. Still on her side, she pushed herself further towards the edge of the bed, the tenderness of her arms now revealed to her in sharp, searing sensations. She extended her arm once more and this time made contact.

The receiver was hers and she used the cord to reel in the rest of the phone. As she tugged at the spiral flex, she could hear the purr of a dial tone, a sound which offered some provisional reassurance. The base unit was now next to her on the bed, alongside her head. Too close to read it easily, she could see three printed lines identifying the institution and giving assorted numbers.

The four words that counted were Grays Harbor Community Hospital.

So the nurse had not lied. Either that or this was a ruse too elaborate to be plausible. Occam's Razor, Maggie. Occam's Razor.

The dial tone was still in her ear. She pressed nine and immediately a computerized voice cut in:

We're sorry, but you have no credit for calls on this line. To get credit, please contact your operator. You can pay by MasterCard, American Express . . .

Shit. Her wallet had been stolen, with everything inside it: cards, driver's licence, everything. No phone, no computer, no money. And of course she couldn't remember her credit card number. In modern America, she was as helpless as a toddler.

With great effort, she pressed zero on the phone's keypad.

"Operator, how may I direct your call?"

"I need to make a collect call, please."

"Excuse me?"

She was still slurring. She tried again, this time giving the number: 1-202-456-1414.

The White House operator must have been expecting her call. "Miss Costello, is that you? I have instructions to put you straight through to the President."

There was a delay, the perkiness of the hold music more absurd than ever. Finally a decisive click on the line.

"Maggie? Where are you?"

"It's a long story. Are you sure I'm not interrupting you?"

"Just a meeting with the Joint Chiefs. There's trouble on the Pakistan border. You sound terrible. Has something happened?"

"I think you were right, Mr President. About Stuart. Someone sabotaged my brakes last night. I think they were trying to kill me."

"Good God. Where are you now?"

"Grays Harbor Hospital. Your home state."

"We've got to get you out of there. I'll call the Governor. We can get you flown back to Washington, then —"

"No, sir. With respect —" *wiv reshpect* "— I don't think that's a good idea. That will tie you to me, confirm that what I'm doing is for you."

"To hell with that, Maggie. It's too late for —"

"Besides, sir. I came here for a reason. There's a lead I need to follow."

"In Aberdeen? What the hell has Aberdeen got to do with any of this?"

"Robert Jackson, sir. You were at school with him."

Maggie listened hard to the moment of silence that followed. Had Baker known that all along, the moment she had called him from the cemetery in New Orleans? If he had, why had he not said anything then? What was he hiding?

Finally he spoke. "Robert Jackson? Robert *Andrew* Jackson? From James Madison High: that was him?"

"You didn't recognize him when you saw him on TV?"

"They barely looked like the same person. You sure?"

"I'm sure, sir." *Shure, shir.*

"I used to call him Andrew at school. That's how I came to think of him. Andrew Jackson, like the president. I just didn't make the connection. What on earth's this all about, Maggie?"

"I wish I knew, Mr President. But I intend to find out."

"They're calling me back in, Maggie. What do you need?"

"They stole my wallet and my phone."

"OK, Sanchez will send you everything."

"Thank you, sir. But make sure he leaves no trail. Stuart wouldn't want you accused of running a slush fund, paying someone like me to poke around into Jackson's past. Tell him to be careful."

"Maggie, it's you who has to be careful. I can't afford to lose another person I trust. There are too few of you left."

"Thank you, Mr President."

She must have dozed off straight after the phone call, worn out by the effort of it, because nearly an hour had passed when she woke up. A handwritten telephone message had been left by her bedside from a Mr Doug of Dupont Circle. She smiled at Sanchez's attempt at discretion.

The door creaked open. Maggie looked up, struggling to focus. She could see that a woman had entered, middle-aged but in the dark it was hard to make out her features.

"What an unexpected surprise to see you again," she said. "There you are, dear."

Dear.

Maggie created a fist, a futile gesture for a woman with two broken ribs and a tube in her arm, but it was a reflex, the result of the bolt of fear and rage that had just coursed through her.

Now the woman was coming nearer, approaching the bed. She had a syringe in her hand. Maggie recoiled.

"No need to be scared, Maggie dear. No need to be scared at all. I have something that will make all the pain go away."

CHAPTER
FORTY

Diplomatic cable:

From the Head of the Army of the Guardians of the
Islamic Revolution, Tehran
To the Interests Section of the Islamic Republic of Iran,
housed within the Embassy of the Islamic Republic of
Pakistan, Washington DC

TOP SECRET. ENCRYPTION SETTING:
MAXIMUM.

You are to be congratulated. SB dangles by a silken
thread. But the Supreme Leader is concerned about the
matter of credit. Whatever is written in the West, it is
imperative that believers understand the Islamic
Republic to have played the critical role. Please advise
what action you will take to ensure the wider Muslim
world understands that, when the moment comes, the
head of the snake did not simply fall off: it was severed!
Ends.

Editorial from *The Guardian* newspaper, London,
Saturday March 25:

For the past week, the world has watched events in Washington with something like incredulity. Sixty-four days have passed since Stephen Baker swore the oath of office as President of the United States. When he did so, it was not just Americans who hoped they were about to make a fresh start. The world dared to hope too.

Yet a series of allegations, apparently timed to go off in sequence like a set of terrorist bombs, has left Mr Baker more vulnerable than would have seemed imaginable on that icy January morning of his inauguration. Extraordinarily, impeachment proceedings have begun against a president who has barely got his feet under the Oval Office table.

This newspaper deplores that effort. Republicans determined to topple Mr Baker should pause, reflecting that they will not simply be removing the head of their own government. Bombastic though this may sound, they will be depriving the world of its de facto leader. For that is what the role of US president in the twenty-first century entails.

Now is not the time. Not when the world faces so many grave problems, from bitter wars to a changing climate. And Mr Baker — who seems to understand those problems better than most — is not the right target. We are heartened by the news that one conservative Democrat on the House of Representatives judiciary committee has signalled that he will stay loyal to his president. We call on the remaining two waverers — those whose votes, were they to switch to the Republicans, would formally advance impeachment proceedings against Mr Baker — to do the right thing. It is not just America that needs them to act wisely. The entire world is watching.

CHAPTER
FORTY-ONE

Aberdeen, Washington, Saturday March 25, 11.25 PST
"There really is nothing to be frightened of at all, dear."

Maggie reached for the cup of coffee, still hot, that had been left at her bedside. The woman was looming over her. If only Maggie could grab hold of it, she could throw the steaming liquid in her face. She stretched . . .

And at that moment she saw the woman's face clearly. Grey-haired, yes, but not, after all, the apparently kindly lady who had sabotaged her car at the school.

"I'm sorry," Maggie panted. "I thought you were someone else."

"It's easy to get confused, dear. I was in the ambulance bay when they brought you in. You'd had quite a scrape. Now what about these painkillers?"

"Painkillers?"

"Yes, dear. The doctor says you should take them." She checked her watch. "Around now. I can either do it intravenously," she held up the needle, "or with tablets. What would you prefer?"

Maggie nodded towards the tablets. She took the tiny paper cup from the nurse and put the pills on her tongue, then knocked back a swig of water.

311

"Well done, dear."

The instant the nurse's back was turned, Maggie popped the two tablets out of the side of her cheek where she had lodged them, and tucked them under her pillow. She waited for the door to creak shut.

Right, that was it. Whoever it was who had tried to kill her once would doubtless be back to try again. She would not stay here a moment longer, a sitting duck. Lying here she could be injected, poisoned or smothered: it would be so easy.

She looked first at her hand, at the needle embedded in the largest vein. Grimacing from the pain, she removed it slowly, grabbing a tissue from the box by her bed to staunch the blood.

Next she levered herself forward away from the pillow, so that she was supporting her back with her own strength. She pulled back the duvet. For the first time she saw that she was wearing a standard hospital robe, the words Grays Harbor stencilled across it in the style of a prison uniform.

Now, with a massive exertion, she swung first one leg and then the other off the edge of the bed and slid her bottom forward till her feet touched the ground. Gingerly, she transferred her weight onto them and to her relief, realized that she could walk. Clearly she had sustained the most serious injuries in her top half.

She made it across the room to the chair where her overnight bag sat like an old friend. She unzipped it, finding trousers and a shirt inside. It took nearly ten minutes to dress herself.

She was about to leave when she remembered the note from Sanchez, still by the bed. She shuffled over and retrieved it, then moved towards the door, and froze. There, a full-length mirror projected back an image that stopped her short. Her right cheek shone with a red bruise and there were dark, deep lines around and underneath her eyes. She looked like an inmate of a women's refuge.

Cracking open the door, she tried to swing her bag casually over her shoulder — a movement that made her want to how! with pain — and began to make her escape. With all the strength she could muster, she walked past the nurses' station — no shuffling allowed now — determined not to look back.

She had gone perhaps five paces when she heard a voice behind her. "Miss? Excuse me?"

She was just a few feet from the double doors leading away from here.

"Miss?"

Over her shoulder, as nonchalantly as she could manage, she called out: "She seems much better! Thanks." She pushed the doors open and left.

The signs offered little help. Geriatrics upstairs, obstetrics downstairs, X-rays along the corridor. And then, separately, something else: student halls of residence.

She hobbled in that direction, wincing at the pain as she headed down two flights of stairs. Before long she was away from the wards and in a series of corridors containing a series of identical doors.

Finally she found what she was looking for: an exit sign. Her hunch had been vindicated. The medical students had their own separate entrance — one that, Maggie hoped, would not be monitored by whoever was watching her.

The fresh air was a shock to her, colder than she was expecting. It seemed to slap her in the face, the wind whipping her with a sudden, sharp sense of how alone she now was. Battered and penniless in the middle of nowhere, she had no way of contacting the outside world, and no one, anyway, she could contact. Her closest ally was dead, almost certainly murdered. She had no real friends, no boyfriend and no family on the entire continent.

So she would just have to rely on herself. It wouldn't be the first time.

The walk to the main road was long and agonizing. She dreaded how easily, out in the open, she would be spotted by her pursuers. At last she flagged down a cab and slumped into the back seat.

"Where can I take you?" The driver asked.

"Heron Street." She tried to smile, then saw the driver look her over in the rear-view mirror.

"You OK?"

"I'm getting there."

She pulled out the message from Doug and looked at it properly for the first time.

There is a safe way to do this. Go to Heron Street. And remember, we always believed in Western unity.

The road was wide, more a highway than a street, and as the driver passed Sidney's Casino, a building with all the glamour of a large garden shed, and several open-air car dealerships, their forecourts crammed with discounted Dodges and Chevys, she felt her brow furrow. Why would Sanchez send her here?

And then she saw it, the tall flagpole-style sign for Safeway. She smiled at the simplicity of it and asked the driver to wait, forming a guess for the last piece of Sanchez's attempt at a puzzle.

She only had to look around the supermarket for thirty seconds to see it. A counter, close to the checkout lines, below the instantly recognizable bright yellow-and-black sign: Western Union.

And remember, we always believed in Western unity.

She gave her name to the young, much-pierced girl behind the glass window who promptly asked for ID. Maggie began to explain, that was the whole point, everything she had had been stolen: passport, driver's —

"Hold on, there's a note on my system here? Says I'm meant to check your face against this?" The same upspeak Maggie would have heard back home, on O'Connell Street.

The girl produced an A4 envelope which bore the crest of the State of Washington. She tore it open and out fell a credit-card-sized rectangle of clear plastic: a driver's licence, with Maggie's face on it.

"Looks like you," the girl said.

Good old Sanchez.

"So that's your ID, which means I can give you this." The girl disappeared, returning with a wad of clean, crisp bank notes. She counted off five thousand dollars and sent Maggie on her way.

The cab took her next to Jacknut Apparel, the clothes store where she was about fifteen years above the target age and where she bought a T-shirt that would have been too much even for her teenage self: scrawled across her front, graffiti-style, were the words "evolution, revolution, retribution" on a garment so tight it was hell-bent on drawing attention to her chest. In Washington, women went to great lengths to find clothes that would make their breasts if not exactly disappear, then at least become irrelevant. In DC, gender-neutral was a compliment. Not here, it seemed.

She paid off the cab and slowly made her way two blocks down to a hair salon. She wondered about a radical cut, maybe even the cropped, peroxide number worn by the manager at the Midnight Lounge, but decided it was likely to attract too much attention. So she went half way, asking the stylist to turn her russet-brown, shoulder-length cut into a mid-length bob with blonde highlights. She didn't love it, but she looked different and that was all that counted. Glancing at the mirror, with new clothes and hair, she decided she still looked bashed-up — but at least nothing like a White House official, whether current or recently fired.

She had a few more things to get. At the top of her list was a bulk order of extra-strength painkillers, a BlackBerry, a new laptop — with built-in, ready to go internet access — some basic cosmetics, a full-sized bottle of Jameson's and a place to stay.

She decided on the Olympic Motel, which looked suitably down-at-heel and anonymous. She unlocked the door to her room to be hit by an aroma that combined cigarette smoke and disinfectant. It would do perfectly. The bed invited her to sleep for the rest of the day. But she knew she had to get to work right away.

She held the BlackBerry, shiny and new, and dialled the one number, other than the White House, she remembered by heart.

"Uri, it's me. Maggie."

"Maggie! I tried calling you. Over and over. What happened to you?"

"Long story."

"You always say that."

"But it's really true this time."

"You sound . . . different. Are you OK?"

"I was in an accident, but —"

"What! What happened? Are you —" He sounded genuinely alarmed.

"I'm fine, really." She strove to keep her voice steady. "I'm going to be OK. I just need your help."

"Do you need me to come there, because —"

"No. I need to ask you about . . . intelligence."

They had rarely spoken about it, and he had always refused to provide more than the sketchiest details, but they both knew that Uri Guttman had performed his military service in Israel in the intelligence corps and that he had risen to a pretty senior, if unspecified, rank.

So now, swiftly, she gave him a very thin outline of what had happened to her. She had been investigating an issue — she could not say what — which centred on

317

a former agent of the CIA. She had traced him to Aberdeen, had spoken to his former high school principal, had helped a nice old lady with her car battery and then found her brakes were shot and had had to jump from a speeding car.

"Jesus, Maggie. You never learn, do you?"

"What does that mean?"

"About staying out of trouble."

"I didn't ask to —"

"The whole point of the Baker job was that you were meant to quit being in shitholes dealing with shitty people who want to kill each other, and you were going to have a nice desk in Washington and —"

"That was the plan, yes. But we didn't bank on the President fighting for his political life after two months, did we?"

"You and danger, Maggie. It's like some chemical attraction or something."

"I thought you wanted to help me."

"OK. Another time. What do you want to know?"

"At the funeral in New Orleans, the retired man from, er, the Company said a whole lot of stuff I didn't understand."

"But you pretended you did."

"Right."

"Like?"

"Like blankets."

"Say again?"

"He said there would have been no point killing the man we're talking about because, 'He'd have prepared his blanket.'"

"That's what he said? 'He'd have prepared his blanket.'"

"Yes. Those words."

"Exactly?"

"Yes. I wrote it down afterwards." Shit. That was also in the notebook.

"OK, we have something different in Hebrew but it sounds like a similar idea."

"Similar idea to what?"

"We call it *karit raka*. It means a soft pillow. Like it guarantees you a soft landing if you get in trouble."

"My brain's not working at full strength, Uri."

"Well, normally you only use the *karit* in an emergency, like when you've sent out a distress signal. Inside your pillow, which might be back at base, will be a package of information that might help your organization find you and get you out of trouble."

"OK."

"But you could also use a *karit* another way. Your guy said 'there would be no point' killing the man because of his blanket, right?"

"Right."

"So that suggests he was using it as a different kind of insurance policy. I've heard of this too." He paused, as if thinking it through. "Let's say I know something sensitive."

"OK."

"And I think there would be people willing to kill me to keep whatever I know secret. It might even be the organization I work for now, or worked for in the past. I may know things they don't want to get out."

"Yes." Maggie was thinking of Forbes/Jackson and the CIA.

"Then I might make up a *karit* — a pillow or blanket or whatever — that would sit somewhere, a bundle of information that would be released automatically the moment I died."

"And the potential killers would know you had done it, so that would deter them from killing you. Because once you're dead, whatever they were trying to keep hidden would come out anyway."

"Precisely. That makes me feel good, Maggie. Maybe your head didn't get so banged after all."

"A bundle of information, you say. Like where? In a vault or something?"

"It used to be that way. Now most guys in this line of work do it virtually. Online or something. Or so I hear."

"So you *hear*, Uri?" Maggie said with the same smile in her voice she always deployed when she tried to squeeze a past secret from him. She was trying to think through all the questions now rushing into her mind.

"But it obviously didn't work. The guy I'm talking about died. It didn't stop his killers killing him."

"Either he hadn't prepared his blanket, and the bad guys knew that. Or he had, but they felt sure they could get to it before it was made public or whatever. Or they knew what was in it and weren't frightened. Or it's still out there. And they're desperate to find it."

Desperate sounded about right: desperate enough to send a car with no brakes onto the highway, where it could have killed God knows how many innocent people.

320

She said nothing, working through the permutations. It was Uri who spoke next: "Sounds like they think you're ahead of them, Maggie."

"Hmm."

"Maggie?"

"Let me ask you something, Uri. If it were you. If you had a blanket, if you had a karot —"

"A *karit* —"

"You know what I mean. Where would —"

"I was never quite at the *karit* level. But my father was, in his day. And you know what he used to say? Not just about this, about all intel things. Again and again, the same quote. From some Brit. 'If you want to keep a secret, announce it on the floor of the House of Commons.'"

"I don't follow."

"Hide it in plain sight. The one place no one thinks to look. If Churchill wanted to give the code for the D-Day landings, he'd do it in a speech to Parliament. What German would think to look there?"

"You think Company men like Forb— , like the subject of my inquiry —"

"Don't worry, Maggie. I guessed already."

"Bastard."

"Don't forget your question."

"I'm wondering whether someone who worked, you know, for the Company, would do the same thing: hiding in plain sight."

"The one thing I learned about intel was how similar these guys are. The spy books have that right: a spook from London and a spook from East Berlin have more in common with each other than either of them do with their own wives."

"Hide in plain sight. That's good. Thanks, Uri. For everything."

He was telling her she didn't have to thank him, that her only job was to concentrate on getting well, but she wasn't listening to his voice. She was listening intently instead to other sounds coming through the phone. She had heard a door closing, the bustle of another person in the room and then a change in the register of Uri's voice. That confirmed it: a new girlfriend, turning her own key in the door to the apartment Maggie had once regarded as home.

Now, her own voice altered, she wound things up. "Listen, that's great!" she said, the tone false and perky, grating to her own ears. "I owe you one."

"Maggie, listen, if —"

"Gotta go! We'll talk soon." She decided to expel from her mind immediately the sound she had just heard, the sound of domesticity and intimacy between Uri and a woman who was not her.

Hide in plain sight. Concentrate on that.

She could see how that would work for Winston Churchill. He was famous, everything he did was in plain sight. But what did that mean for Vic Forbes/ Robert Jackson? What counted as plain sight for a man who had spent most of his life hiding in the shadows?

She cracked open the new computer, waited for all the software to load up and then Googled the name Robert Jackson. She found an academic in Kansas and a councilman in Palo Alto, but no sign of the CIA agent. At least that meant no one else, including the legions of anonymous sleuths of the internet, was likely to have discovered his real identity — no one, that is, except the people who had driven her off the road and now had her notebook.

Next she tried Vic Forbes, bringing up reams of stories from the world's press, including a long feature on *Newsweek*'s website: *The short life and strange death of Vic Forbes — the anatomy of an attempt to shakedown the President.*

She scanned the piece at a ferocious rate, impatient to see if the magazine had discovered that Forbes had also made a personal attempt to blackmail Stephen Baker. It had not: it was using "shakedown" less than literally. Most of the article was speculation, wondering if Forbes had backers among Baker's enemies, noting that in his Tuesday tour of the network studios Forbes had run into, and then had an apparently "intense and engaged" conversation with Matt Nylind, impresario of the legendary Thursday Session, in which DC's conservatives wargamed the week ahead. That was among a handful of interesting nuggets the piece had turned up but there was no hint of the material she had discovered. Most described him only as a New Orleans-based researcher.

She went back to the search pages, seeing a long string of video results. Clips of Forbes's multiple TV interviews, alongside a couple of news reports on his death. She clicked on the first available interview, conducted the day he had been "unmasked" as the source of MSNBC's bombshell stories on Baker.

The sound was tinny on her machine and the video slow, but Maggie listened intently to every word.

"Like I say, I have no hidden agenda. My only interest is transparency. The American people should know everything about the man who now rules them. They have that right."

Was there some coded message Forbes was conveying, if only she was smart enough to hear it? Was she meant to note down the first letter of each sentence? Or perhaps the last? And of all the interviews he'd given, which was the crucial one?

A wave of aching tiredness fell over her. She slowly lay down on the bed, feeling the pain in her ribs afresh. It felt good, though, to rest her head on the pillow and close her eyes.

Hide in plain sight.

The whole point of a blanket, if she had understood Uri correctly, was that the information it contained could be retrieved easily — by others — after one's death. If it were too deeply hidden, it would serve as no kind of deterrent. What had been buried would simply remain hidden.

Forbes had to be sure his information would break cover. And that meant there had to be some kind of timing mechanism, like a safety deposit box programmed to pop open a certain number of hours or days after his death.

Now her mind was running fast. Such a device would work only if it somehow knew its owner had died. How could that happen?

It could be a parcel, held with a lawyer, who would know to release it in the event of his client's death. But that didn't seem likely. Everything Forbes had done, he had done alone: would he have entrusted such a valuable secret, such a powerful secret, to a fellow human being?

Besides, what had been the motif of his assault on President Baker? Technology. He had hacked into Katie Baker's Facebook account, sending messages via a dumb terminal. He had even contrived to hack into MSNBC's system, using a fake online identity.

What had the school principal said about young Jackson? *He was what you would call nowadays a geek*, fascinated by computers at a time when everyone else thought the limits of the virtual universe were marked by a game of Space Invaders.

Of course Forbes would have hidden his blanket online. And there the timing mechanism would be simple, even Maggie could see that. You'd just create some site that you made sure to visit every day or every week. If, for whatever reason, you didn't log in, the site would know. A technical wiz like Forbes would surely have no problem programming a site to do something crazy after it had been left untouched for a specified amount of time, like emailing his blanket out to those who would know exactly what it meant and what to do with it — a list of addresses Forbes had keyed in before his death, as his posthumous insurance policy.

Maggie felt a surge of energy run through her. She was sure she was right. But one stubborn question remained.

Where the hell was it?

Muttering the words "hide in plain sight, hide in plain sight" to herself, she typed in the most obvious place she could think of.

Vicforbes.com

Nothing. Nothing for .net or .org either. Same with victor-forbes and robertjackson, robertandrewjackson, andrewjackson and bobjackson.

How the hell was she meant to crack this? It was just her and a laptop in this stinking bloody motel room. What was she meant to do?

And then it came. The one person who would know the answer.

CHAPTER
FORTY-TWO

Aberdeen, Washington, Saturday March 25, 16.41 PST
She looked at the clock. The eight-hour time difference meant it was already past midnight in Dublin. She hesitated.

In the old days, she'd have happily called her sister Liz at three in the morning: she would either have just come in or been about to go out. But the arrival of her baby son Calum three years ago had put Liz's clubbing days behind her. The drug she craved now — and which she would go to extraordinary lengths to score — was sleep. Calling her at this hour of the morning was what you'd call a high-risk operation.

She dialled the number from memory.

"Liz? It's Maggie."

"Uggh?"

Maggie whispered, as if she were right there at her sister's bedside. "It's me."

"Maggie? It's the middle of the night."

"I know. I'm really sorry —"

"It's the middle of the fucking *night*, Maggie. Where are you? Has something happened?"

"I'm in Washington. But not that Washington. It's a long story."

Maggie could hear a rustle, the sound, she guessed, of Liz sitting up in bed.

"Are you drunk? You sound like you've got your head in a bucket." *Book-it*. The sheer strength of her sister's accent made Maggie miss home immediately and intensely.

"No, not drunk. I was in an accident."

Instantly, Liz's tone changed: suddenly she was a whirlwind of sisterly concern, offering help, insisting that she take the next plane, wanting to know what the doctors had said, marvelling at the fact — as Maggie had recounted it — that they had discharged her so quickly. It was simultaneously touching and stressful.

"I don't need anything, Liz, I promise. Nothing like that."

"Do you swear, Maggie? Because, seriously, I can get to wherever you are and be with you by tomorrow."

"Actually there are two things you can do for me."

"Say it."

"Don't breathe a fookin' word to our ma." She was hamming up the Irish to lessen the gravity of the request, the very act of which only confirmed the gravity of the request. "I mean it. She'll only freak out and I don't want her to know a thing. OK?"

"OK. What's the other thing?"

"Liz!"

"I promise."

"Good. The other thing is professional. I need your brainpower."

Liz croaked out a laugh. "You mean you're not calling for a recipe for courgette mash. It's nice that someone remembers the real me."

"Too many coffee mornings?"

"And playdates! There are only so many things you can say about pull-up nappies."

"Poor you."

"Though they are great. Pull-ups, I mean."

"Liz?"

"Sorry. Go on."

Maggie explained, tentatively and indirectly, what she was looking for.

"What kind of man was he, Maggie? What did he do?"

"He was retired. But he had been in intelligence. American intelligence."

"When?"

"Eighties and nineties."

There was a pause. Good: Liz was thinking. Then she heard her sister clear her throat, as if fully waking herself up, ready for action. "Now. Have we ever had the darkweb conversation?"

"I don't think so."

"OK. When you look something up online, how do you do it?"

"Google."

"And when you do that, you think you're searching the whole internet, right?"

"Right."

"That's what everyone thinks. But they're wrong. In fact, you're searching, like, point nought three per cent of the total number of pages on the web."

"I don't understand."

"You know that thing they always used to say at school, about humans only using ten per cent of our brains? Well, most of us are using just three hundredths of one per cent of the entire web."

"So where's the rest?"

"That's what I'm talking about: the darkweb. Or the deep web. The places that are hidden. What most people see and use is the tip, but there's this massive iceberg underneath."

"And what's in it?"

"A whole lot of it is junk, websites that have stopped working, addresses that have fallen into disuse, defunct internet companies. You gotta imagine it like this vast underwater landscape, full of old shipwrecks and derelict buildings that have fallen into the sea."

Maggie, lying on the bed in the name of convalescence, made a silent grimace as she shifted position, sending a new ache through her ribs and across her shoulders. She didn't want to break her sister's flow. Liz had been the same as a teenager: she could turn positively lyrical when exalting whatever theme had become her passion.

"But it's not just old stuff, Mags. Sometimes it's legitimate, maybe a database that's blocked to search for copyright reasons, because it contains commercially sensitive information. And sometimes it's vile. Like dirty address spaces that get taken over by crime syndicates. The Russians are big on that. They run spam or child porn from these disused sites. The darkweb is not a nice place."

"And is there —"

"Right. I forgot. The other stuff you find — kind of lying on the seabed — are addresses that were set up right at the beginning, when the internet was just starting, and then abandoned. And you remember who started the internet, right?"

"The US military."

"Yep."

Maggie pulled the covers tight and hugged herself against a sudden chill. "And is there any way to probe all this stuff?"

"I know how you can start."

Maggie listened, taking detailed notes, as Liz gave her a step-by-step guide. She would follow the instructions and they would speak again in the morning, Dublin time. Liz estimated that she had four hours and forty-five minutes' sleep left to her before Calum woke up. "Every one of those minutes is precious, Maggie. Don't call me before six. "Night — and good luck."

Maggie hauled herself upright and, with the sheet of paper at her side and the computer on her lap, followed Liz's first instruction and Googled "Freenet".

Two clicks later she was at a site that looked like any one of those places you occasionally had to visit to download or update computer software: grey and basic. Once she read the welcome paragraph, however, she got the first inkling that she was about to enter a different realm.

It declared that Freenet was free software allowing people to browse anonymously, to publish "freesites" that would be accessible only via Freenet and, tellingly,

Maggie thought, to "chat on forums, without fear of censorship". Liz had warned her that for every free-thinking libertarian or Iranian dissident she might encounter here, there would be half a dozen users drawn to a place where those whose sexual tastes ran to the illegal could gather unimpeded.

She read on: *Freenet is decentralized to make it less vulnerable to attack, and if used in "darkweb" mode, where users only connect to their friends, is very difficult to detect.*

Maggie followed the prompts, downloading and installing the Freenet software then answering the questions it asked her. "How much security do you need?" There was a guide, ranging from "NORMAL: I live in a relatively free country" to "MAXIMUM: I intend to access information that could get me arrested, imprisoned or worse."

Maggie swallowed, then opted for maximum. Even though she was sitting in a motel bed, her back supported by three pillows, she felt as if, at that moment, she had plunged into a pool of deep, dark water, the depth of which could not be fathomed.

She came to an index, much starker and more basic than anything you'd find on the regular web. It listed freesites, those that would remain utterly hidden to anyone above the surface.

Before long she had found "Arson Around with Auntie", a beginner's guide aimed at animal rights activists, teaching them how to firebomb laboratories. Close behind, and no surprise, was the Anarchists' Cookbook, the book spoken about in whispers even when Maggie was a student. More of a shock was "The Terrorist's Handbook: A practical guide to explosives and other things of interest to terrorists".

Maggie rapidly concluded that the darkweb she had just entered was bound to be home to fifty-seven varieties of radical, but also to those charged with hunting them down. Both fringe militants and intelligence agents would jump at the chance to drop into the dodgiest websites without leaving any footprints. She felt as if she had stumbled into a labyrinth that was the natural habitat of both cat and mouse. Everything she knew about Vic Forbes told her he would have felt right at home.

She did a search for Vic Forbes and was rewarded with an instant result. She was taken to a URL that didn't look like any she had seen before. She clicked on it, closing her eyes in a moment of superstitious prayer.

The page took a while to load up, the screen showing nothing more than blank whiteness as the "loading data" message promised more. And then, three or four seconds later, it was there. Maggie recoiled, astonished by what she saw. Not that it was such an arresting image. Just the mere fact of what it represented. For there, in front of her, was confirmation that Vic Forbes had contemplated and prepared for his own death — by hiding his most precious secret in the deepest recesses of the internet's underworld.

She looked again at the website address, so simple and so obvious. She had only to think of her own email which, when she was in the White House at least, ended

.gov. All she had had to do was type in victorforbes.gov and there it was.

Doubtless, he had been one of those pioneers who had been in on the internet from the start, able to create a personal domain when next to nobody knew what such a thing was. Perhaps he had left it abandoned, lying on the virtual seabed as Liz had said. Maybe he had picked it up just recently, decades later, pressing it into service as his blanket. But here it was, Forbes's own personal website. That it was his was unmistakable. The front page consisted of nothing more than a single, full-face photograph of him. Not the Vic Forbes who had been on television in the hours before his death, nor the young, moustached Robert Jackson in the foothills of his career and full of hope, his photo still there on the first page of his CIA dossier. This was Forbes seven or eight years ago, just turned forty: that was Maggie's guess.

It was not posed the way the CIA picture was posed — with that high-school yearbook gaze into the middle distance and just to the left of the lens. Instead Forbes was staring at the camera, face-on and unsmiling. The visual grammar was that of a passport photo, even a police mugshot. But the way it filled the entire screen made it more sinister, as if Forbes was Big Brother watching Winston Smith through the telescreen. Instantly Maggie knew that Forbes had taken the picture himself. Everything about this portrait, starting with the eyes, screamed solitude.

She clicked on it, expecting it to link her through to other pages, but nothing happened. There were no other links around the side or at the bottom. Indeed, there was no text at all.

She clicked again, then again, as if that might coax it into life. There was something missing. Yet, that this was the hiding place, the locker into which Forbes — foreseeing his own murder — had stashed his blanket, she was more certain than ever.

There was only one way to break in — and, though it would hurt, she was ready to do it.

CHAPTER
FORTY-THREE

Aberdeen, Washington, Saturday March 25, 19.00 PST
For the eleventh time in eight minutes, she looked at the clock. 7p.m. on a Saturday night in Aberdeen, three o'clock on Sunday morning in Dublin. She had promised her sister faithfully that she would leave her in peace. And she had already disturbed her once.

Maggie put aside the empty pizza carton, still decorated by congealed and processed cheese, that had represented her dial-up supper, delivered to the motel-room door. She badly wanted to call Nick du Caines — he might well know how to get out of this hole — but that was one of the thousands of numbers she had lost along with her phone.

She clicked on the TV, lighting upon C-Span's replay in full of the President's weekend radio address, which in a nod to the twenty-first century was now on camera too.

She found the remote and increased the volume.

"For too long, these weapons have cast a shadow over our world," Baker was saying. "I am of the generation that grew up looking at a clock that stood, permanently, at five minutes to midnight. We were always on the brink of catastrophe. And as long as nuclear bombs exist, we still are."

Despite her bruises and her aching ribs, she couldn't repress a smile of disbelief and admiration that verged on wonder. She had drafted a policy statement about this during the campaign, assuming it would never get anywhere. How could it? After all, they lived in the real world. The world of politics.

But here he was, the President of the United States — under fire as never before, fighting a triple scandal and facing an army of enemies determined to eject him from the White House in the fastest-ever time — building towards the climax of a speech that she never thought she would hear.

"That's why I'm glad to tell you that I have just come off the phone with my Russian counterpart and he and I have agreed to meet in the coming weeks to take the first steps towards ridding the world of these weapons altogether. I will be sending a proposal to Congress . . ."

She looked over at her computer, still displaying the webpage of Vic Forbes. That man had set out to destroy the presidency of Stephen Baker. Forbes had started this entire chain of events that had left the man she believed in — and everything he, and she, stood for — hanging by the frailest of threads. There, on that screen, was the landmine he had buried deep and out of view — and it was still ticking.

She loved her sister, she really did. But some things were more important than Liz's unbroken sleep. She dialled the number.

The phone rang twice. Then a croak remarkable for its coherence — and hostility: "This better be good."

"Liz, I'm really sorry —"

"No, I mean this better be good. As in, 'my-life-is-about-to-end-Liz-and-these-are-my-dying-words' good."

"OK, it's not quite that good."

"Maggie, you stupid bloody cow, it's gone three in the morning!"

"I know, but —"

"You know? So you can't even blame the accident! I'd have forgiven you if you were confused from the accident!"

"Oh right. Well, maybe I am a bit confused —"

"Too sodding late." Maggie could hear the sound of a duvet, furiously thrown aside. "I'd only got back to sleep about ten bloody minutes ago. Jesus, Maggie, I could strangle you."

"I'm really sorry, Liz. But I am desperate." She wouldn't mention Baker, and the need — for the sake of the world — to keep him in office. She would make it personal, an appeal to sisterly compassion. "Can I remind you that somebody did try to kill me last night? I think there's something they're trying to find out. My only chance is if I can work it out first. If I do that —"

"You see, this is what I don't get about you, Maggie. You seem to think that if you just know whatever it is you're not meant to know, then you'll be OK. Whereas the exact bloody opposite is the truth. You're only in this fucking mess because you know too much!"

"I don't think that's true."

"It bloody is! I don't know anything and no one's after me, are they? Bloody Mrs O'Neill on Limerick Street, she doesn't know fuck all and she's sound asleep right now. You see how it works? If you stay a million miles away from all this crap, then nothing happens. Simple."

"It's not quite as simple as that —"

"No, I can well believe that." Liz's voice dipped, whether to avoid waking Calum or because she was going into one of her quiet — and therefore more terrifying — rages, Maggie could not yet tell. "I can see it's way more complicated than that. This is about you needing adrenalin in your life, isn't it — to convince you your life is worthwhile?"

"What are you talking about?"

"I'm talking about you, Maggie. I'm talking about this insane way you live. Always travelling to the back end of arsehole, always dodging bullets. Why do you do it, Mags?"

"I have a feeling you're about to tell me, Liz."

"No, I really want to hear it from you. Go on. Tell me."

"Liz, I'm exhausted. I'm in a shitty motel in the middle of nowhere. I'm on my own. I hurt everywhere. I just need some help and I've turned to my sister. Is that too much to ask?"

"I remember all the bullshit answers, Maggie. 'Saving the world', all that crap. 'Making life better for children in war zones', all that Miss World shite. But I don't believe a word of it. Maybe once, when you started. But now it's something else."

Maggie could feel two competing emotions thudding through her veins, as if racing to reach her brain — or her heart — first. She had her money on anger, though sadness was not lagging far behind.

"Go on, Dr Liz. Enlighten me."

"You're trying to make up for it, Maggie."

"For what?"

"For," and now Maggie heard the first silent note of hesitation in what had, until then, been an unstoppable flow, "for what you don't have. For the husband you don't have, for the boyfriends you don't have, for the —"

"And what else, Liz? What else am I fucking compensating for? What else don't I have?"

But they both knew.

"That's why I reckon you phone me in the middle of the bloody night, Maggie. You want to wreck what I have because you're jealous."

"That is NOT TRUE!" The sound of her shout echoed around the motel room, making the walls ring. "Of course I'd love to have what you have — a great husband, a lovely boy. But for reasons I can't sodding well be bothered to go into, I don't have that option right now. I do what I do because I'm good at it. OK? I don't know how or why, but that's the way it is. All right? That's the way I am. I tried it the other way — writing memos and going to meetings and wearing a fucking suit and doing what you're meant to do — but I'm no good at it. Not the way I'm good at this."

There was silence down the phone, both of them as shocked as each other by what they had just heard.

Maggie cracked first, feeling the urge to lighten the atmosphere. "So though it's been really interesting hearing the views of your therapist, do you think you could ask him to put Liz Costello on the phone? There's something I need to ask her."

"How long since you spoke to Uri?"

"Liz! I'm serious. I wouldn't be calling unless I needed your help. Now will you help me or not?"

There was another long pause. Maggie could hear Liz breathing. Slowly she heard the rhythm change, the breaths coming softer now. Then she heard the pop of a bedside light being switched on.

"What do you need?"

Maggie explained the dead end she had hit: the Freenet software had worked, bringing her to the victorforbes.gov site, but it was a brick wall. She prayed that her sister would fall into her usual patter when resolving one of Maggie's computer crises — "Go to the menu bar, find settings, then tools, click on . . ." — firing off a series of arcane instructions that would instantly and mysteriously unlock the riddle.

Instead Liz responded with a grunted "hmm". In anyone else, you could put that down to sibling fury that had not yet subsided or else to the ungodly hour. But Maggie knew — having grown up in a house where the fiercest rows could pass as quickly as a summer storm — that it meant only that Liz had been confronted by a technical conundrum.

A series of noises down the phone confirmed that Liz had fired up her computer. "If this wakes up Calum, I promise you, I won't speak to you till our ma's funeral."

341

"Liz! Don't talk like that."

"All right, I'm in. Give me the URL again."

"What are you doing?"

"I've gone to the dark side. Freenet. What was that bloke's name, Victor something?"

A few keystrokes later and Liz was muttering again. "Creepy-looking guy. So remind me, what are we doing here?"

Maggie explained that she was convinced that Forbes, an internet pioneer, had somehow stashed his blanket online with this defunct and subterranean website the likeliest hiding place.

"But there's nothing here, Mags. Just that picture. It's your classic single-page site. Just a flag in the soil. You know, Forbes reserving that domain for himself."

"Are you sure? This really is my best shot."

"That's the thing about the darkweb. It's mainly full of crap. It's like that place in the Pacific Ocean where all the plastic garbage ends up. This is probably just some site your man set up and forgot about."

"When was all that internet pioneering stuff going on?"

"Early eighties. And the only people doing it were the American military, some academics and a few beardy-weirdy hippies."

"But this picture is more recent than that."

"OK, let's say you're right and this is not just some early-days experiment. It's still just a picture. There's nothing else."

"He was in the CIA, Liz. Couldn't he have —"

"Oh, that is so cool. Actually that is *too* cool."

"What?"

"Oh, that is genius."

"What is? Liz?"

"I've read about this, but didn't think anyone did it. But if anyone did it, it would definitely have been him."

"What are you talking about?"

Maggie could hear a furious hammering of keystrokes down the phone.

"When was this guy in the CIA again?"

"From the eighties till a few years ago."

"Perfect. I so bet I'm right. Liz Costello, you may never have cracked breastfeeding but you have cracked this motherfucker."

Liz's excitement was infectious. For the first time in days, Maggie felt herself smile properly. The exertion of her facial muscles hurt, sending a streak of pain to the back of her skull, but she didn't care.

"Steganography, Maggie. Steganography." She was speaking fast and getting faster. "Easily the coolest encryption ever thought of. Instead of a code that everyone knows is a code — so they immediately start trying to break it — you conceal your information in such a way that no one even suspects there's a message there. Only you and the recipient know. Security through obscurity."

"Liz, you've completely lost me."

"That program didn't work. Don't worry, there's tons more."

"What are you talking about?"

"You're the one who got the bloody A-levels in Latin and Greek. Have you forgotten?"

"Every word."

"Steganography. Means concealed writing. It's when a message seems to be something else entirely. So you think it's a shopping list, but the real message is written between the lines — in invisible ink."

"But there's nothing written here at all. It's a picture."

"No one said it always had to be words. It can be anything. Some Persian tyrant once shaved the head of his most trusted slave, tattooed a message on his scalp, then waited for the hair to grow back and cover it up. Then he sent the slave off to his ally with instructions that, once he got there, he should shave off his hair and show them his head. Job done."

"So there are words hidden in this picture?"

"That's what I reckon."

"How the hell could he have done that?"

"You don't want to know, Maggie."

"Try me."

"Basically every pixel in a digital picture is made up of colour values, formed by strings of ones and zeroes. If you change one of those ones to a zero it will be invisible to the naked eye. The picture will still look the same. But all those little ones or zeroes you've changed can contain some extra information, besides the colours for the picture. You just need a program to piece it all together."

Liz had been right: Maggie didn't want to know. "So you reckon that's what Forbes did to this picture?"

"Yep. In the massive data of this picture, there'll be a little parcel of hidden data. Just a few tweaks will have been enough. It's not hard. Apparently al-Qaeda use it. You send a holiday snap; guys at the other end run it through a basic program and, bingo, you've got your instructions telling you to blow up the Statue of Liberty."

Maggie winced. This was not the kind of thing to talk about on a phone line, not these days.

"So is that what you're doing, running it through a program?"

"I am."

"Can I see?"

"No." There was a pause. "Actually yes. I'll remote access you."

"You'll what?"

"I'll take over your computer and run it from here. Then you can see what I'm seeing."

"You can do that?"

"Easily."

"Can anybody do that?"

"Only if you give them all the info you're about to give me."

Methodically, Liz ordered Maggie around her computer telling her to open up System Preferences one moment, then to choose an option from the pull-down Tools menu the next — one baffling step after another. As far as Maggie was concerned, the entire process might as well have been black magic. And she couldn't shake the nagging feeling that if Liz Costello, young mum in Dublin, could take control of her computer this easily so could those lurking in the dark who meant her only harm.

"There," said Liz at last, invisibly moving the cursor around Maggie's screen as if it were possessed by a demon. It was hovering over the photograph of Vic Forbes. "I'm on. And I think we may be in luck. You said he wanted this picture to be decoded, right?"

"Yes, eventually."

"That's why he's gone for Mozaiq. Keep it mainstream."

Maggie tried not to snort.

"OK, here goes." Liz made a tum-tee-tum sound, the noise a tekkie makes when they're waiting for a computer to perform a function. Eventually she said, "Oh. It's encrypted."

A box, familiar even to Maggie, had appeared in the middle of the screen, like a plaster across the bridge of Forbes's nose. It demanded a password.

"Let me do this, Liz."

Maggie breathed deep, closed her eyes and then allowed herself a second smile. This was Forbes's blanket, the insurance policy he had designed to render futile any attempt to silence him, the mechanism that would ensure his deadliest information would surface whether he was dead or alive. Without hesitation, she typed in the twelve letters that, she felt certain, would unlock the code.

S-T-E-P-H-E-N-B-A-K-E-R

CHAPTER
FORTY-FOUR

Washington, DC, Sunday March 26, 08.41

"That you, Senator?"

"It is."

"Honour to be speaking with you, sir. Sorry to be calling you at home on the weekend. Caught you before heading off to church?"

"You have." Rick Franklin took advantage of the recline mechanism on his chair, surveyed the view he enjoyed from this sixth-floor apartment in the Watergate and marvelled at the absurdity of Washington etiquette. Elected office always ensured formal deference, even from those who so clearly wielded greater power. So the two-bit chief executive of a nothing town would be hailed as Mr Mayor by the anchor of *Good Morning America*, even though on every measure of influence the genuflector outranked the genuflectee.

It wasn't quite like that with Matt Nylind and Rick Franklin. Franklin was not only a senator, but one who had made the political weather for the last, turbulent week. Still, Nylind's Thursday Session made him a genuine force in this town. In the business of political influence they were at least equals. Yet here was Nylind, touching the forelock.

"I have quite a few items, Senator, if that's OK with you."

"Fire away."

"Banking bill. Coming up soon. Democrats are foaming at the mouth on that one. Reckon they've got the numbers."

"In the House?"

"Uh-huh."

"To reach two hundred and eighteen?"

"So they say."

"What about Delaney?"

"Yeah, even 'Delay' Delaney."

"But he's from Delaware."

"Primary challenge."

"Right," said Franklin, wondering if there was any question he could ask to which Nylind would not know the immediate answer. "So this means —"

"— that we need to switch to the Senate."

"You mean, wreck the bill there so that it voids whatever comes out of the House."

"Wouldn't put it quite like that, sir. Prefer to say that a strong pro-growth Prosperity for America bill needs to come out of the body that looks to America's long-term interests. That's what the American people expect."

It was part of Nylind's genius, this. He never crafted so much as a tactic, let alone a policy, without framing the language in which it would be sold. Thanks to him, a Democratic proposal to levy the wealthiest Americans

348

in order to fund expanded healthcare coverage became known as "the sick tax" — and promptly fell to defeat. "Define the terms, define the battlefield." That's what Nylind had said then and since, with the rest of the Republican party and the wider conservative movement — from the editorial board of the *Weekly Standard* to the production offices of Rush Limbaugh and Glenn Beck — hanging on his every word.

"I hear you," Franklin said. "But, as I know you know, I am not the ranking Republican on the Senate banking committee. Shouldn't you be talking to Gerritsen?"

"How can I put this, Senator? Whatever the formal hierarchy might be, the movement regards you as the lead man on this. Our representative, if you like."

If Nylind was aiming to flatter, he had succeeded. Franklin couldn't dispute the premise: Ted Gerritsen was one of the last remaining liberal Republicans in the Senate if not the planet. An old Maine "moderate", beloved by official Washington and the press corps, he was from the era when the Republican base was the country club, not the mega-church. He couldn't get enough of Stephen Baker — who had carried Gerritsen's state the previous November — and there had been a rumour that he was in line for one of Baker's "spirit of bipartisanship" cabinet posts. Maybe Commerce or Trade Rep. Either way, it was no surprise that Nylind regarded him as utterly unreliable.

"I'd need some back-up," Franklin said after leaving the statutory two-second pause required in Washington in order to be deemed "thoughtful", a crucial piece of reputational armour.

"You got it."

"Serious back-up. My staff have never led on a bill this size before."

"We got it all. Economists, lawyers, number-crunchers. Heck, we've even got a bill drafted!"

"Oh, yeah? Where'd that come from?"

"Well, as you know, sir, there are a lot of people in this town who have a direct interest in ensuring that Congress gets this issue right. They see the wisdom in sharing resources."

Translation, thought Franklin: *banking industry lobbyists have drafted the bill*. He remembered that man who spoke at the last Thursday Session.

"OK. Well, let's fix a meeting. Cindy from my office and whoever you recommend from yours."

"Good to know, Senator. Good to know. Next item: some of us feel we might be losing momentum on the impeachment project."

"How do you mean?"

"We still don't have our Democrats on House Judiciary."

"That's not my fault!" Franklin shot back, instantly regretting the defensiveness of his tone, as if he were a pupil summoned to the principal's office to account for himself. In a bid to assert his authority, he took his voice down half an octave. "That has to be a matter for the House leadership. That surely is their responsibility."

"Agreed, sir. But for that to happen, they need more."

"More? You saw the *Post* story today," he said, referring to an investigative piece on the Iranian Connection which had appeared on the front of the *Washington Post* that morning, setting out — in wonderfully mind-numbing detail — the chain of funds, offshore accounts and shell companies in the Caymans through which cash might, conceivably, have been funnelled from Tehran to the Baker for President campaign.

Franklin had immediately had Cindy email it to everyone who mattered, including Nylind. It was perfect. The abundance of numbers, dates and tedious minutiae made the charges look credible and serious, even if no one could be bothered to read the small print.

"Sure, but I'm not talking about that," said Nylind. "I meant more on Forbes."

"But we don't have any hard evidence on that, Matt. You and I would both dearly love to have something concrete implicating the President in Forbes's death. But until we do, allegations about Forbes cannot be part of the case for impeachment. Right now the 'high crimes and misdemeanours' referred to in the articles of impeachment relate only to the Iranian Connection. That's all we got."

"Technically, that's true, Senator. But only technically. Forbes is the mood music. He's the *soundtrack* for the impeachment."

"You mean, how he died?"

"And what beans he was about to spill. Both."

"The trouble is," said Franklin, adopting the superior tone of the man in the know, "it seems someone may be at work cleaning up all that mess. A dustbuster."

"That's what I hear too, Senator."

"That's what you *hear*?"

"There's not much that goes on that I don't know about. And let's face it, sir, you wouldn't be talking to me now if that wasn't true."

Franklin felt uneasy. How was this possible? He had told no one, bar Cindy, about that Costello woman. He was holding on to that particular nugget, confidentially provided on a private and secure phone line by Governor Orville Tett, so that it could be deployed at the moment of maximum effectiveness. Yet here was Nylind hinting that he knew about it already.

Now Franklin felt an additional tremor of panic. *There's not much that goes on that I don't know about.* Was this some kind of threat? Did Nylind know about him and Cindy? Did "the movement" know about every action, every dumb indiscretion, every sexual encounter, that occurred even within its own ranks? At this moment, hearing Nylind's even, unflappable breathing down the phone, he was terrified that the answer was yes.

"So let's be candid with each other. What exactly is it you're hearing?"

"I have very few details."

Irritated now, resentful that this, this *activist* was as well informed as he was, if not better, Franklin did not so much raise his voice as enhance it, adding some heft as he demanded, "Why don't you tell me what details you *do* have?"

"I'm not playing games with you, sir. We really don't know much."

"I understand that. Now, I repeat. What is the *little* you do know?"

"There seems to be some kind of lone, intelligence-gathering operation. By a woman formerly on the National Security team at the White House."

Shit. So he really did know.

"Our worry is that she might be standing between us and our storyline."

"Our storyline?"

"Yes, sir. On Forbes. If she's cleaning up all the mess, that hurts us with the impeachment push. We need that stuff, sir, and she's getting in our way."

The "sir" thing was needling Franklin more than ever now. He had a strong urge to get Cindy in here. Best way to drain off some of the aggression he was feeling. Like sugar into alcohol, he found his anger could turn seamlessly into lust — and it certainly beat an hour of circuit-training in the Capitol Hill gym.

"So what is it you're asking me to do, Matt?" *Matt.* Put him in his place.

"I suppose I'm suggesting you keep on doing what you're doing — but more so. Whatever resources you and other colleagues have deployed so far, we need to step it up a gear. We need to get ahead of this thing. Take radical action if necessary."

He should only know, Franklin thought to himself. But all he said was, "OK. Was there something else?"

"Oh yes, some good news. Christian Coalition are planning a new push, ahead of the next fundraising cycle. Their theme is the True American Family. They want to highlight a few beacons of family values. Some from sport — that great golf guy — some from music, and one or two from politics. I suggested you and your wife and your three sons were a perfect example of the True American Family. They are very excited about this."

"Wow," said Franklin, tepidly, thinking only of Cindy in her eyepatch underwear, bent over his desk. "That's great."

"This will give you a major fundraising advantage, sir."

"I know it."

"You see, Senator, the Movement not only taketh. It giveth too."

"I appreciate it, Matt. I really do."

Franklin hung up and rubbed at his temples. Everything about the phone call suggested progress. He was to be entrusted with a key ideological task on the banking bill; he was seen as the lead player in the Forbes business and now he was to be held up as a poster boy for family values. It all spelled career gold. Iowa and New Hampshire were not much more than three years away.

And yet, something nagged at him. It was not just Nylind's apparent omniscience, it was his manner — as if he were the general and Franklin a subordinate, expected to take instruction. What else to make of the attempt at withholding information, the unstated hint that this was beyond Franklin's level? Above his paygrade, as they said in these parts. Maybe that was how it always was between the operatives and the horseflesh, but Nylind was worse than most at disguising the fact.

Franklin gazed at his power wall, the collection of framed photographs to his right. A few showed visiting foreign leaders whose names he could barely remember, there to suggest a national security expertise he did not have. Another of him with the US commander in Iraq, included for the same reason and to underscore his patriotism. And, in the centre, a smiling handshake with the last Republican president. He loved that photograph.

He needed to get to work right away. But first there was that itch to deal with.

He reached for his phone, found the last text message he had received and hit reply.

Master requires his little lady, forthwith and without delay.

CHAPTER
FORTY-FIVE

Aberdeen, Washington, Sunday March 26, 08.55 PST
"Turns out we're a pretty good team, Mags," Liz had said, as they wrapped up what had been an hour's phone call in the middle of the Dublin night.

"Even if you think I'm wasting my life because I don't have a husband and kids."

"I didn't say that." There was a pause. "Did I? Blame it on lack of sleep."

The password had worked immediately. No variations required, just the name of the President. Once she had keyed that in, the image at victorforbes.gov had suddenly appeared to turn into a square of dark, dull grey. Almost black. At first Liz had worried that she had failed to follow a protocol programmed by Forbes, that perhaps she had set off a booby trap he had laid that closed down the site to trespassers. But then she quickly checked a site on steganography and read that the apparent fade to black was a familiar trick. She had only to turn up the brightness on Maggie's screen — a move so low-tech even Maggie understood it — and a new image revealed itself.

Though it was not really an image at all. Just six large numbers at the centre of the screen, separated by two slashes.

356

A date; American format. The month, slash, the day, slash, the year.

Working back, Liz discovered that Forbes had done some extra engineering on his apparently defunct website. It was programmed to a kind of timer: if the site remained unvisited for more than three days, then it would slowly emerge from Freenet, shedding its darkweb restrictions, and emerge onto the regular web.

"Why three days?" Maggie had asked. "Why not straight away?"

"Because three days means you really are dead. You might have a heart attack and be away from your computer for forty-eight hours, but it doesn't mean you're dead. Three days gives you some buffer."

As it happened, four days had passed since Forbes's corpse had been found and that time-sensitive algorithm had now kicked in: the website's underlying code had changed in such a way that soon the site would turn up on a search conducted not only by those using Freenet but anyone who typed the name Victor Forbes into Google. At that point, Liz explained, the encoded image would start yielding its secrets too. Hour by hour, the pixels in the Forbes self-portrait would start altering, so that the hidden image — the date — would reveal itself even if no one had had any idea it was there.

"Smart guy, your Victor Forbes," Liz had said.

"He's not mine."

"Whatever. But he found a way to make sure that, if someone bumped him off, his little secret would rise up off the seabed and burst into the daylight."

Maggie smiled. "You sure you don't want to get back to writing again, Liz?"

"You saying my choice to be a full-time mother is not valid?"

For a second, Maggie feared that she and her sister were about to plunge into yet another of their perennial sibling squabbles. Then Liz gave a small chuckle, announced that Calum was stirring and said goodbye.

Maggie sat there, staring at the screen. March 15, just over a quarter century ago, when both Robert Jackson and Stephen Baker would have been graduating college. Suddenly, she was certain that whatever Forbes had been trying to tell her from the grave must relate to the shared past of these two young men who had started out as friends and ended as lethal enemies.

More research to be done, and quickly. But starting where? Local papers from the time . . . Her fingers moving across the keyboard in a blur, she typed the words "Aberdeen Public Library" into the search engine and, to her intense relief, the website told her a "community outreach" effort meant that the library was now open for a few brief hours on Sunday mornings. What was more, the library did indeed keep the archive of *The Daily World*, the magnificently-named newspaper of Aberdeen, no doubt established in the era when a small town in the American West truly believed there was no limit to its potential.

She showered, aching at the effort of it, then packed her bags and requested a change of room, asking that someone come and move her bags later on in the day and tell her the new room number when she returned. This was a trick the Israelis and Palestinians used to deploy when engaged in secret negotiations. If you knew you were under surveillance, there was no point making it easy for those doing the watching. If you have to be a target, be a moving one.

By 10a.m. she was standing outside the fine, arched entrance of the public library on East Market Street like a customer at the January sales, waiting for opening time. Once the door was unlocked, she headed straight for the newspaper archive.

"No longer bound copies, I'm afraid," explained the librarian — early thirties, male, overweight and with a sibilant "s". "They are on microfiche."

"Microfiche? I didn't know that still existed."

He gave Maggie a withering look, one that conveyed both resentment of her East Coast condescension and disdain for her ignorance of archival methods.

"Do you need me to show you how to use the reader or," and here he allowed himself a bitchy smile, "maybe you remember using these at college? It must have all been microfilm back then, right?"

Swallowing a sharp response, Maggie smiled serenely and asked for a demonstration, explaining that she only needed to see the paper for two or three specific days in a specific year: the editions of March 15, March 16 and March 17. The librarian raised an eyebrow, but said nothing more. He showed her to a second-floor room, empty and municipal, then reappeared fifteen minutes later with little boxes that brought back to Maggie memories of her father's old cine movies, each containing a spool of film. The librarian loaded the first one into the machine and then left her to it.

Maggie adjusted to the newspaper design of an earlier generation and started scanning the front page for anything relevant. A lead story on a budget crisis at the state capital, Olympia; a report on a resignation from the Aberdeen school board. Inside, car accidents, a high school basketball player set for a scholarship to Duke and a recipe column.

She was not deterred. Logic had warned her that the paper of March 15 might be a dead end. Whatever had happened on that day might well not be reported until the next day or the day after. She spooled forward to March 16 and cued up the front, the black-and-white image wobbling between the lines on the oversized screen. The lead this time was a statement by the Governor, something about agricultural subsidies. There was reaction from a union spokesman and another story forecasting healthy profits for logging. She turned to page two.

Now she read more slowly, her eye taking in each line, searching for the words Forbes, Jackson or Baker. She peered at every photograph, leaping when she saw a page four headline "Destined for greatness" above a group shot of smiling young people. They were around the right age: Washington State students set to embark on the then-novelty of a junior year abroad. There was a Locke, a Chan, a Rosenbaum and a Massey. Not a Baker or Jackson in sight.

She looked at the next page: six. Nothing there either. Mainly ads on seven, letters on eight, more ads on nine and then an advice column, financial tips and, eventually, sport. Maggie felt her energies wilt, the dull throb in her ribs returning. The paper for March 17 proved just as empty.

She spooled back, reviewing what she had seen, now at half the pace. Still nothing. Then she did the same for the March 16 edition. Page one, news: nothing there. Two, taken up by an ad containing cut-out coupons for the Safeway supermarket and a story about sales of new cars. Three, a follow-up on yesterday's report on budget negotiations in Olympia and a half-hearted attempt at international news with three in-brief items from around the world including one, Maggie noticed, reporting the death of a soldier in Belfast.

Four, that picture of smiling young Washingtonians heading to Europe. She stared at the faces. Was one of them Forbes, under yet another name? Was Baker there? But no matter how hard she stared, she could not conjure them up.

Next was page six, a preview of a vintage car rally coming at the weekend. Then the ads on page seven.

She went back. Had she nudged the controls on the machine too fast? What had happened to page five?

She lined up page four and inched the wheel along. Up came page six. She did it again, even more slowly. There was no mistaking it. Four was followed by six. There was no page five.

After she had tracked him down, the librarian did nothing to conceal his irritation at being interrupted about such a banal matter. As he accompanied her back up the stairs, he asked a series of questions that assumed she was at fault, bungling the operation of what was a pretty elementary machine.

"You see," Maggie demonstrated, partly relieved to see that the problem had not magically corrected itself — a habit that, in her experience, afflicted all machines whenever she summoned assistance. "Four. Then six. No five."

"Maybe it was just a page of ads and so was not transferred onto microfilm?"

"I thought of that," Maggie replied, immediately spooling to the several pages comprised solely of ads which had nevertheless made the transfer onto microfilm.

"Well, that is odd, I grant you," he said finally, his voice softening. "I've never seen that before. I'll need to report that right away. This is library property. You're sure you didn't do anything to it?"

Again, Maggie had to bite back a sharp reply. "Completely sure. Are there any other copies of that day's newspaper around, do you think? What about at the office of *The Daily World* itself?"

"They gave their entire hard-copy archive to us eight or nine years ago."

"So hard copies exist somewhere?"

"They did. But we couldn't afford to store them. So we put them on microfilm."

"The originals were destroyed?"

"'Fraid so." His disappointment seemed sincere. "It happened to dozens of American papers. Their whole archives — just incinerated. Some papers were saved, by collectors. But not this one."

"So you're telling me that page five of *The Daily World* for that date has vanished? It doesn't exist anywhere?"

"Not quite. *The World* digitized some of its archive. So if you know what you're looking for, you can search their database. You just —"

"The whole point is I don't know what I'm looking for."

He gave her a look, as if she had just confirmed his earlier, low assessment of her.

"What I mean is, I'll know it when I find it. It relates to this town or this area on that day."

"But you don't know what 'it' is, right?"

"That's right."

The librarian drew up his shoulders and adopted the demeanour of an official. She saw him looking at the bruise on her forehead. "Are you sure you need to deal with this today? Maybe you could take a break and come back tomorrow . . ."

Maggie took a deep breath. Of course, she looked like a wreck; worse, even: mad. She had an idea. "Forgive me for being so demanding. And thank you for your help. It's possible I've made a mistake with the year. Do you think I could trouble you for microfilm copies of the same paper and the same dates — but for the following year?"

He eyed her warily, as if dealing with an animal he hoped he had pacified but which could turn wild at any moment.

She smiled, a move that usually worked wonders but which seemed to have little impact on this man. When it became clear she was not going to give up, he sighed and said, "March 15, 16 and 17, right? For the following year?"

"If you would."

This time she checked the page numbers first. All three sets were complete, no pages missing. She started with the newspaper for March 15, exactly a year after the date Victor Forbes had gone to such trouble to secure for posterity.

The front page once again offered nothing of obvious relevance, a story about a new defence contract that would benefit Boeing, one of the state's big employers, with knock-on effects for suppliers in Aberdeen. More mundane, local tedium on the subsequent pages.

Maybe she was chasing down the wrong alley here. Maybe the event Forbes had in mind was some national or international happening, some political landmark, far away from Aberdeen and the little Jackson — Baker soap opera. Perhaps she needed to be searching not the Aberdeen *Daily World*, but the *New York Times* or *Washington Post*.

She would check one last time, working from the last page back to the front. Sports, agony column — no emotional confession of jealousy from an R Jackson: she checked — letters, financial, ads, puff piece about a local hotel reopening . . .

Maggie had not read the story properly first time round, just taking in the headline and scanning the text for names. But this time she caught the caption.

Staff at the Meredith Hotel prepare for today's grand reopening, one year to the day since the blaze that nearly destroyed the establishment.

CHAPTER
FORTY-SIX

Transcript of *Meet the Press* on NBC for Sunday March 26:

Host: Topic A — the imperilled presidency of Stephen Baker. A week of extraordinary revelations and now the clock ticking on impeachment. Where does that leave the President? Let's ask our roundtable. Tom, let's start with you: can Baker survive this thing?

Tom Glover, Politico.com: The only two people who know the answer to that are those two conservative Democrats on the House Judiciary Committee, David.

Host: And it is just two now, since the third member of that group —

Tom Glover: That's right, since he made clear he won't vote for impeachment, it's down to just those two. You know, the majority is so wafer thin in the House — just a few votes separating the parties — that it only needs a tiny defection for the President to be in big trouble.

Host: So what's going through their minds, Michelle?

Michelle Schwartz, *Wall Street Journal*: Well, this weekend, I guess they'll be listening to people in their home districts, David. What do they make of Stephen Baker? Do they still like him? Do they still trust him?

Host: And what are you hearing?

Michelle Schwartz: I'm hearing that he remains in deep trouble. People felt blindsided by the medical revelations —

Tom Glover: Yeah, but Michelle, I think that ended up as a net positive for the President. People warmed to his candor, his very clear sincerity and his message that mental health —

Michelle Schwartz: Maybe if that had been the only thing: that one revelation and the President makes a great speech. We all know Stephen Baker is a *brilliant* speaker.

Host: You say that like it's a bad thing, Michelle. [Laughter.]

Michelle Schwartz: My point is, fine if it had ended there. But then we get the Iranian Connection which —

Tom Glover: Which is still just conjecture at this stage. No one's proven anything except an Iranian citizen — this man Hossein Najafi — made it to a White House reception. You know Stephen Baker is not the first president to have gatecrashers at his parties.

Host: Well, let's see what we do know about this story. The *Washington Post* has run an extensive piece of reporting on the Iranian Connection, let's flash some of that up here. Here's the quote:

Experts in forensic accountancy say it's possible that the donation made by Mr Najafi, though paid out of a US bank registered in Delaware, may have been sourced from the Cayman Islands and, prior to that, originated in a bank in Tehran used by the Army of the Guardians of the

Islamic Revolution, better known as the Revolutionary Guards.

Tom Glover: Lot of ifs in that, David.

Host: So that's the quote. What do you make of it, Michelle?

Michelle Schwartz: As so often, it's about context. I think
we should be honest and mention the third leg of this
particular stool — and that is the death of Vic Forbes.
If —

Tom Glover: Oh, come on —

Michelle Schwartz: If it wasn't for the persistent questions
that arise from that —

[Crosstalk. Inaudible]

Tom Glover: . . . about Stuart Goldstein? I mean if we're
going to start mentioning mysterious deaths. What, are we
gonna sit around on Meet the Press wondering which
Republican took out Goldstein? And unlike Forbes, that
man was a proven servant of the American people. I mean,
this is undignified —

Michelle Schwartz: I wasn't saying —

Tom Glover: — and it's unseemly.

Host: All right, predictions for the week ahead. Michelle?

Michelle Schwartz: I don't want to offend Tom again, but I
think it all depends on what more comes out about the late
Mr Forbes. If there is something, combined with the Iranian
Connection, then I think that will spell the end for the
President.

Host: Tom?

Tom Glover: Well, I hate to agree with my colleague here but
I think she's right. It *shouldn't* hinge on the Forbes episode,
but I fear it does. If another shoe drops on that —

something which changes our view of how he died or what he was about to say — then that could change the calculus.

Host: All right, thanks to you both. Good to have you with us. Coming up after the break . . .

CHAPTER
FORTY-SEVEN

Aberdeen, Washington, Sunday March 26, 11.29 PST
Maggie tried first to do it the official way, to see if there was a paper trail left by institutions and follow that. But she hit a series of predictable dead ends, made all the more final by the fact that it was a Sunday and every important office was closed. She called the Aberdeen Fire Department and asked if they kept records of their work — what she had in mind was the basic logbook, listing the call-outs of any given night — going back nearly thirty years. Four phone calls led eventually to a duty officer who said they did keep such records, though he wasn't sure how far back they went. Besides, they couldn't just show sensitive information to a member of the public: it would require the written consent of the Chief. She would have to submit a form . . .

Next she tried the police department who gave the same answer less politely.

So she went to the Meredith Hotel, giving the concierge — an Asian-American man close to sixty — the same smile that had so conspicuously failed to melt the librarian.

"I know this sounds like a very odd question," she began, doing her best to learn from her mistake at the library and not sound insane. "But I wonder if you could tell me who is the longest-serving employee at this hotel?"

"Excuse me?"

"Who has worked at this hotel the longest?"

Without warning, he stepped out from behind his small, stand-up desk and headed through the hotel's revolving door, raised his arm, and summoned a cab he had spotted the way an osprey can spy a fish below the surface of the ocean from one hundred and thirty feet.

Having ushered the waiting guest towards the taxi, helped with loading the bags and pocketed a one-dollar tip with a grateful smile, he returned to Maggie and her odd question. For what was a small hotel in a middling town, he seemed rather a grand concierge.

"Longest serving? That would be me, Miss."

Good. Just as she had hoped. "I'm researching the history of this area and I wonder if you could help me with something. I understand there was a fire here many years ago."

"Before my time, Miss."

"I thought you said you —"

"I've worked here fifteen years. But that was —"

"More than twenty-five years ago."

"Right."

"And there's no one else here who has memories of that night?"

"Like I say, no one here has worked longer than me."

"What about the owners?"

"Changed hands eight years ago. This hotel is part of a chain owned out of Pennsylvania now."

Maggie's face must have displayed her disappointment because he seemed hurt, eager to please again. "What do you need to know?"

"Anything you can tell me."

He leaned on his desk. "I heard it was a very big fire. Destroyed the interior of the hotel. They had to rebuild and redecorate. Hotel was closed for a year."

All of which had been covered in the anniversary story in the paper.

"And no clue how it started?"

"They say that was a mystery. Though one of the older cleaners — she's dead now — she said it was cigarettes, set the curtains on fire. On the third floor."

"But nobody died."

"Where do you hear that?"

Maggie pulled from her pocket the photocopied *Daily World* cutting about the reopening she had taken from the library. With a quick glance, she checked it again now. Nowhere did it mention any fatalities. She had assumed everyone had survived. She looked back at the concierge. "Do I have that wrong?"

"I think you do, Miss. The anniversary was a couple weeks back, right?"

"Yes. It was." She smiled again. "I'm impressed you know the date, just like that."

"Well, it's difficult to forget. They come here every year."

"Who comes?"

"The family. March 15, every year. They lay a wreath outside the hotel. Very polite, always ask permission."

"The family?"

"Of the person who died. In the fire."

"And they did this last week?"

"Yep. Same as always."

"What's the name of the family?"

"Oh, I don't know, Miss. They never say."

"And do you still have the wreath?"

"I threw it out just yesterday."

Damn. She wondered about slipping him a twenty, asking him to go look out back, but decided against it. Bound to arouse suspicions. She thanked him for his time, handed him a five-dollar bill and left. Five minutes later she was in the loading bay behind the hotel, with its giant trash cans and handful of parking spaces. Bracing herself for the stink, she flipped open the lid of the first dumpster. Just glass bottles. There was a blue one full of paper and then, next to it a large black one, with its lid ajar.

She heaved the black dumpster open and was assailed by the stench. It was full of black bin bags, but several had burst, with food scraps and rotting peelings leaking out. Breathing through her mouth, she gingerly pushed a bag to one side and leaned further into the bin. She heard the sound of footsteps behind her. She wheeled around, her heart thudding, imagining how easy it would be for anyone who wanted to simply to shove her inside. There was a man a few yards behind her — but he was just a hotel guest, unlocking his car and preparing to drive away.

She went back to her task, tearing at each bag, watching as old fish guts, rock-hard slices of bread and a wad of bloodstained tissues spilled out.

She had all but given up when she glimpsed the dark green edge of it. Using the lip of the bin as a fulcrum, her body see-sawed into the dumpster and she hooked it out. The wreath was in a sorry state, the flowers dead and brown, the greenery wilted. But there was a small, white card still attached to it, though it was damp and buckled and stinking. Chucking the wreath back into the garbage, she examined the card. It bore a single word, handwritten in ink that had run but was still legible.

Pamela.

CHAPTER
FORTY-EIGHT

Aberdeen, Washington, Sunday March 26, 11.51
She had been hoping for more, a last name at least. She wondered if she was travelling ever further down the wrong path, piling error upon error, taking one false turn after another. What if Forbes's date referred to something else entirely, nothing to do with Aberdeen? Even if it did relate to something that had happened in this town, how could she be sure it was the fire he had had in mind? It was possible that none of this had any bearing whatsoever on the death of Victor Forbes. She caught a reflection of herself as she left the hotel — the new hair, the bruise, the face still pained from the wounds she had sustained less than two days ago — and wondered what the hell she was doing.

For a moment she imagined hailing a cab to the airport and running away. She could buy a ticket to anywhere. Maybe she could turn up at Liz's flat, ask to sleep on the sofa, get to know her nephew. There would always be a bed for her at her parents'. But then Maggie reminded herself that the sweet lady who had sabotaged her car on Friday night had been ready to kill without discrimination; then she remembered what Liz had said, how no one was trying to kill *her* because *she* knew nothing. She had already drawn her sister in too deep — plumbing the depths of the Hades that lurked beneath the internet — it wouldn't be fair to expose her to anything worse.

New York? The idea filled her with instant warmth. Instantly, too quick for her to stop it, an image floated into her head — she was standing in Uri's apartment, the pair of them smiling at each other the way they smiled before a kiss.

But now rational thought caught up, trapping the image that had escaped and throttling it with reality. That apartment was no longer her territory. Hadn't she heard another woman padding along those hardwood floors? Wasn't there now another woman stepping out of the shower and shaking her hair dry before that strange, blemished Tunisian mirror, another woman sleeping on those sheets?

She could, of course, go back to Washington with her tail between her legs. But Washington was not kind to losers. And the President was there, the President who was relying on her: she would be consigning him to failure too.

No, there was no running away. She owed it to Stephen Baker, to Stuart and to herself to find out what — and who — was behind this, wrecking the Baker presidency and several lives in the process. She could not rest till she had.

She pulled out her BlackBerry and made a bet with herself. If there was any man who, on principle, would ensure his number was in the local phone book, it would be him. She called directory assistance and asked for the home number of Principal Ray Schilling.

She wondered if he would be surprised to hear from Ashley Muir, still alive and well. What if he too had been in on the plot to send her car skidding into oblivion on Friday night? If he had been, he had done a good job hiding it.

After a few pleasantries, and an apology for disturbing him at home on the weekend, she went straight in. "Mr Schilling, something you said stayed with me. 'I remember all the students I teach.' That's what you said."

"Quite true. I did say it. And I do."

"Could I test you?"

"Go ahead."

"Pamela."

Did she imagine it, or was there an intake of breath at the other end of the phone?

"You'll need to give me more than that, Ms Muir. I wouldn't ask the boys to shoot at the hoop with one arm tied behind their back."

"I'm afraid I don't have a last name. Best I can give you is that she was a contemporary of Robert Jackson and Stephen Baker."

"Same class as them, you say?"

"Yes."

"No, I don't think so. Let me try to picture the class. That's how I do it, I visualize the class as I taught them." He began muttering names, as if taking a register.

Maggie, standing in the doorway of Swanson's grocery store, closed her eyes in silent prayer.

Schilling murmured for a moment or two longer, then said, "No. As I thought, no Pamela in that class."

Maggie sighed. "What about the year below them, a year younger?"

"So that would have been the class of, when was it? Oh yes, I remember that class. No stars in that one, I'm afraid. Very weak debate team."

"And a Pamela? I'm sorry, Mr Schilling: this is very important."

"Let me think." More muttering and then he said, "Do you mean Pamela Everett?"

"I'm not sure. Who was she?"

"Well, she did stand out. Not the way Baker and Jackson stood out. But she was extremely pretty. The students called her Miss America." He paused. "Terribly sad."

"Why sad?" Maggie's pulse began to race.

"She died just a couple of years after graduation. Just tragic."

"And how did she die?"

"An illness. I forget the details. Very quick apparently."

Maggie could feel the pain in her skull return as her brow involuntarily furrowed. "An illness? Are you absolutely sure about that?"

"Yes of course."

"Did you see her?"

"No," Mr Schilling said, slightly taken aback by the question. "She had left the school by then. Besides, it all happened very suddenly. But the parents asked me to read a lesson at her funeral. St Paul's epistle to the Corinthians."

Maggie was thinking fast. "Do you think I might speak with them?"

"They left Aberdeen very soon after Pamela died. They wanted to get as far away from here as possible."

"Do you have any idea where they went?"

"I'm afraid I don't."

She was about to ring off, but there was something about the way Ray Schilling was breathing into the phone that suggested he was hesitating. Maggie kept silent, not wanting to scare him off. Eventually, and warily, he spoke.

"Ms Muir, I have not been completely frank with you. I *do* know where the Everetts are and it will not be difficult for me to find their address: I can access the school computer system from home. But I need you to be very clear about my terms."

"Of course." Terms? Was he going to ask for money?

"We have kept the Everetts' address on file all these years on the strict understanding that we share it with no one. The school has never broken that undertaking. Not once."

"I see."

"Now you'll have noticed that I have asked you no questions about your work. I have not wanted to pry. And I won't now. But when you came to me on Friday, you told me that a large sum of money is involved here. I am working on the assumption that you would not be asking me questions about Pamela Everett if the late

Robert Jackson had not — for whatever reason — remembered her in his will."

Maggie said nothing, hoping he would take her silence as confirmation.

"I could not in conscience stand in the way of some financial comfort coming the way of the Everetts. Lord knows they have had their share of misfortune."

"You are a good man, Mr Schilling."

"I trust you, Ms Muir. Now I hope you have your snowshoes with you. If you think Aberdeen is the middle of nowhere, wait till you hear where the Everetts live."

CHAPTER
FORTY-NINE

Undisclosed location, Sunday March 26, 16.00 GMT
"My thanks to all of you for making time for this conference call: I know that the weekends are precious."

A murmur of agreement, conveyed through the desktop speaker. These were men like him, with no time or talent for small talk.

"I wanted to brief you on the latest developments in the case we discussed last time. I am glad to tell you that we have sent in some very experienced . . ." he hesitated, unsure of the appropriately delicate term for such work, "*personnel* and I am assured that there will be results very soon."

"How soon?" Germany again. Of course.

"Well, put it this way. If you read your newspapers thoroughly over the next twenty-four hours, I don't think you'll be disappointed."

"That's good to hear." Manhattan. Perhaps he had broken up that particular US-German alliance: he hoped so.

"Can we say we are back on track?" A new voice: the accent, Middle Eastern, was initially difficult to make out. "I read something in the press this weekend that suggested we still had cause for concern."

"We are not out of the woods yet, that's true. As we all know, politics is an unpredictable business." He smiled his silkiest smile, though he knew it was wasted on a phone call.

"Except that's what we're all here for, isn't it?" said Germany, his tone edgy once more. "To make politics as predictable as possible. Am I right?"

CHAPTER
FIFTY

Coeur d'Alene, Idaho, Sunday March 26, 20.55 PST
In normal circumstances, Coeur d'Alene, Idaho would have been a perfectly lovely place to visit. Not that Maggie could remember what normal circumstances were. But a weekend here, in this snow-covered ski resort of a town, with its alpine chalets and cosy, crackling fires, would have been a treat. With the right person.

It had taken two tiny planes to get here, first the short hop from Aberdeen to Seattle then a connection for the longer flight to Coeur d'Alene — Maggie willingly dipping into the Sanchez slush fund to pay cash for a whisky miniature on each leg, the better to suppress the fact that her battered, aching body was now folded into a glorified baked beans can bobbing through icy skies powered by no more than a propeller.

She thought about the upcoming encounter with the Everetts. Should she stick with the story Mr Schilling had imagined for her? That she was an insurance agent needing to check out a claim that might lead to a windfall? Too cruel. So she came up with something else. Not brilliant, but it would have to do.

The cab now turned off the main thoroughfare through the town, with its cafés and charming bookshop, past several residential roads, and finally onto a lane that wound its way up a mountainside. So far up the mountain that she felt compelled to ask the driver to check his satnav was working properly. He gave her a look that told her she was not in New York any more.

She checked her watch. Nearly 9p.m. It was crazy to do this in the evening — who wanted to open the door of their remote home to a stranger emerging out of the darkness? — but urgency drove her on.

The headlights were set on full-beam now; the street lighting had long gone and the last car they had seen had passed nearly ten minutes ago. Maggie looked over her shoulder: some distant lights still twinkled.

"You a journalist?" the driver said suddenly, breaking the silence.

That took her by surprise. "What makes you say that?"

"Only, we don't get much call to come up round here. 'Cept to see the compound. And that's usually media."

"The compound?"

"That's right. The Aryan Nations compound. They're not far from here."

Maggie dimly recalled reading about the sect of white supremacists who had tried to set up a racially pure colony in the Idaho snow. "I'd forgotten that. How near?"

The driver pointed towards the top right of his windscreen. "Couple of hills that way."

"But round here, it's not . . ."

"Oh no. I'm not saying anything negative about the folks who live up here. They're not all like that, no way."

Maggie could hear a "but" in his voice.

"Except?"

He twisted his head over his shoulder. "All I'm saying is, people who come all the way up here — it ain't for the nightlife. They're trying to get away from something. Or someone."

Maggie nodded.

"With the Aryan Nations, it's black people. With some of the others, in these little shacks —" they had passed one or two barely-discernible outlines of buildings a long way off the road, surrounded by acres of nothing, "— it's the Feds. You know, the guys who think the federal government is coming to take their guns away? And some folks just need to run away."

Like Anne and Randall Everett, thought Maggie.

They drove for another ten minutes, climbing ever steeper, until the satnav told them their destination was approaching on the right.

Maggie asked the driver to pull up twenty yards away and to stay: she would pay him once they were back among what now seemed like the bright urban lights of Coeur d'Alene.

"How long you gonna be?"

"That's the trouble. It might be thirty seconds, it might be an hour or more. But keep the meter running."

He grumbled, but finally agreed and she stepped out into the bracing air. It was not just cold but fresh enough to make the skin tingle, the way it does after a plunge into iced water. Standing there listening, she became aware of a sound she had probably not heard in years: complete, impeccable silence.

The darkness was total, too. There was no fraying at the edges, no dull, electric orange of city lights hovering above the horizon. The only light to break this darkness came from the stars and the lamp above the entrance of what she dearly hoped was the Everett residence.

This house was much closer to the road than the others. There was a modest fence, but no hint of the quasi-military compounds she had seen on the way up. Indeed, as she got nearer, she could see that the house itself would not have looked out of place in most American suburbs. It was timber-fronted, with a two-step walk-up, a porch with two neatly arranged outdoor chairs covered in tarps, waiting for the winter to end, and a wind-chime, jangling in the chill air.

The porch light was encouraging, but it was hard to tell if there was any light within. Heavy curtains were drawn across both the upstairs windows. It was late, no doubt about it. Folks out here — in Idaho, for heaven's sake — were bound to be early to bed. And the Everetts would be in their sixties by now . . .

Maggie did what she always did when faced by a moment of fear: closed her eyes for a moment, then took a step forward. She knocked on the door.

There was a creak and then the sound of an interior door opening, followed by a brief cone of light, visible

386

in the pane of glass above the door, pushing forward into the hallway. And now another light came on. Maggie waited for a voice to call out asking her to identify herself. But it did not come. Instead, without fear or hesitation, the door opened.

That the woman was the mother of Pamela Everett, Maggie could tell instantly. All Principal Schilling had told her was that Pamela was strikingly pretty, nicknamed Miss America. This woman had the fine features, the clean lines, of a long-ago beauty queen.

"Hello," Maggie smiled, hating herself for what she was about to do. "My name is Ashley Muir and I'm so sorry to disturb you so late at night. But I've come a long way to fulfil the wish of a dying man. A dead man, now. My late husband. This is something I promised him I would do. I know it's crazy, but can I ask if you are Mrs Anne Everett?"

The woman looked aghast, as if even the uttering of her name out loud violated a sacred taboo. But, Maggie noticed, she did not slam the door. Nor did she call for her husband.

Maggie pressed on. "My husband died a few months ago. In one of our last conversations he told me about his first love. Your daughter, Pamela."

Now the woman's face turned white, and it was as if she had aged by twenty years. "How did you find me?"

"My husband did that. Worked that computer for months, I don't know how he did it. But he was determined, Mrs Everett."

The woman remained frozen to the spot, still holding the door, unable to speak.

"Do you think, Mrs Everett, we could speak inside? I promise this won't take long."

Still unspeaking, staring at her as if at an apparition, Anne Everett widened the door to let her in. Maggie stepped inside hesitantly, wanting her body to convey what she felt: that she was treading carefully here, not wanting to bring more pain to this house of loss.

There were reminders everywhere: a large photograph of Pamela Everett in the costume of high school graduation, several smaller photos of a girl at the seaside, on a rocking horse, blowing out birthday candles on the hallway table. For the second time in a week, Maggie looked at a woman she had never met and thought of her mother.

"Could we sit down?"

Still in silence, Mrs Everett ushered Maggie into a sitting room organized around a single chair facing a TV set; next to it, a side table bearing a tray with a half-eaten supper of cold meat and boiled potatoes.

Maggie sat on a couch whose smooth lines suggested it was rarely used. Anne Everett perched on the edge of her chair.

"My late husband was in the class below your daughter. He told me she'd have never even noticed him. But he had a crush on her. His first." Maggie smiled, the rueful smile of a widow. "He said he had hardly thought about her for years, until he got his own diagnosis. And then he remembered what he heard about Pamela Everett. The 'beautiful Pamela', he called her. And how she had died from a sudden illness. And it hurt him, Mrs Everett. It hurt him to think that maybe people would think your daughter had been forgotten. Because she hadn't been forgotten. He had remembered her. And it was so important to him that you knew that. Because, and this is what he said, if people remember us, then it means a little part of us lives on."

Maggie had told herself it was a white lie, but that did not reduce the shame she felt for what she had done. When she saw the tear falling slowly down the cheek of Anne Everett it made her loathe herself all the more. She had crossed the line, she realized. Nothing — not Stuart, not Baker's presidency, not Forbes, not her own safety — could justify this. She began to stand up, mumbling the beginnings of an apology.

"Please don't go!" The woman spoke with such urgency that her voice pushed Maggie back onto the cold, stiff couch.

Anne Everett wiped the tear from her eye and, to Maggie's great surprise, revealed the beginnings of a smile. "Young lady, I have waited twenty-six years for this day."

Involuntarily, Maggie's face turned into a mask of surprise.

"Oh yes. Twenty-six years and nine days, I have waited for someone to come and say what you just said. That my daughter *lived*. That her life meant something."

"Why did you doubt it?"

"Doubt it? I was never allowed to believe it."

"I don't follow."

"Of course you don't. How could you? How could anyone? No one ever knew. Except me. And Randall." She was animated now, leaping up from the chair. "Are you a whisky drinker, Mrs Muir? I am," she said, without waiting for Maggie's answer. From under the side table, she produced a bottle, now down to its last third, and a used glass. She poured herself a healthy measure and downed half of it.

"My daughter's only 'illness' was to have a beautiful face. That was her illness. She wasn't *sick*. Pamela never had a day's sickness in her life. She was healthy as an ox, like her mother. Same bones, same genes."

She looked to the wall, to the picture of Pamela in a ball gown, at the James Madison High prom.

"We *said* that she had gotten sick. That was the deal."

"The deal?"

"That's what he made us say. After the fire."

Maggie felt herself shudder. "What fire?" But she knew the answer already.

"Twenty-six years ago, on March 15, there was a fire at the Meredith Hotel in Aberdeen, Washington. Huge blaze. They said that everyone survived. That they got all the guests out of the rooms, standing outside in the street in their pyjamas and all." She paused, a shadow falling over her face again. "But it wasn't true."

"Pamela was in that hotel?"

Slowly, as if her head weighed heavily on her neck, Mrs Everett nodded. "We don't know who with. Some boy, on spring break. Using her for sex. She was cursed with a body that men hungered for." She looked down at her hands, clasped together. "We didn't know she had been in the hotel. We thought she was having a sleepover with her girlfriends."

She smiled a bitter smile at her own naïveté.

"It was early the next morning. We weren't even aware she was missing. We hadn't called the police. We were just waiting for her to come home, like she always did on a Sunday after a Saturday night. And then there he was, at the door."

"Who was there?"

"The man. From the hotel, I thought — at first, anyway. He explained there had been an accident, a fire. Pamela had been killed." The last word came out in a croak. "I'm sorry."

"You take your time."

Anne Everett poured the rest of the bottle into a glass and swallowed it whole. "You see," she said, looking up at Maggie, "I've carried this for so long. Randall never would let me tell. But it's eaten me alive, this secret. He took it to his grave, but it killed him too."

Maggie nodded, knowing she needed to say nothing.

"The man said Pamela was dead. And there would never be anything we could do to bring her back. All that would be left was her reputation. She could either be remembered as a 'goodtime girl' — those were the words that man used — who had died in someone's bed, or as prom queen Pamela Everett of James Madison High. It was up to us.

"All we had to do was tell people, starting that day, that Pam was not feeling well, that she'd come down with something. That she couldn't see anyone. Then, a week or so later, we should say it was more serious. That she was being transferred to Tacoma. Still no visitors allowed. Then, a week after that, there would be an announcement of her death. He would take care of everything. We wouldn't have to do anything, except stay home and tell people our daughter was sick.

"And in return he would pay us a lot of money, more than Randall would make in a year. Hell, in five years. To show he was serious, he had one of those attaché cases with him. The kind men used to carry back then. And inside it was cash. A lot of cash. I don't think I'd ever seen that much money in my life. And he promised there would be more.

"Well, Randall threw him out, of course. Said it was blood money. How dare he? Lots of noise. But the man left the case there. Just sitting in that room in Aberdeen where Pamela should have been.

"The hours went by and we were sobbing about our daughter, our little baby. But we were also looking at that money. All that money. Might have been fifty thousand dollars in that bag."

Now she hunched over, making small, noiseless sobs. Maggie crossed the vast space between them and placed a hand on her shoulder. Instantly, like an animal reflex, Mrs Everett grabbed it and held it tight. Raising her head, her eyes rheumy with tears, she let out a howl of anguish. "I said we should take the money! God curse me for it, I accepted it. I did it."

392

"I understand," Maggie said, shaken.

"I believed what he said, you see. He said we could get away; we *should* get away. Aberdeen would only ever be a 'place of death' for us. And we could use the money to set up some kind of memorial for Pamela. Perhaps a scholarship. Some way of keeping her memory alive. So we said yes. We called the number on the card. Randall made the call.

"Of course we never did set up that memorial. We were too ashamed. Everyone there at the funeral, believing Pamela had suffered through a terrible illness. Imagine that, lying about your own child's death. We deserved to be cast out. So that's what we did. We cast ourselves out. As far away as possible. Middle of nowhere. So that we wouldn't have to see anybody ever again. But you can't run away from your own shame. It stays with you."

Maggie spoke softly. "The money? Did the man ever pay it?"

Anne Everett looked up, as if jolted from a daydream. "Oh yes, all of it. It kept coming into the bank account, a few thousand more, piling up month after month. I can't bring myself to spend a penny of it, of course. Nor could Randall. It's filthy."

"And who did it come from?"

"Like I said, we never knew. We were too grief-stricken to ask. Too stupid too, probably. We talked about it, of course. Wondering and guessing. Until Randall stopped talking, a few years ago. His mouth just clammed up, I guess. That's shame for you."

Maggie had a question burning to get onto her tongue until it could be held back no longer. "And what about this . . . boy she was with that night? Did you ever —"

Anne Everett shook her head furiously. "Never did, never wanted to. We would have killed him with our bare hands if we'd have found out who he was."

"Do you have your suspicions?"

"Well, it's funny you should ask that."

"Why's that?"

"Put it this way, this last year or two, I'd been wondering when somebody would knock on that door and ask about Pamela. No one ever did, but I thought they might. I thought a journalist might come here."

"Why a journalist?"

"Because of the boy my Pamela loved when she was at high school, the boy she adored until the day she died."

"What boy?"

"Haven't you guessed? I thought you'd have guessed by now." She looked into the bottom of her glass as if it were a deep well. "Pamela was in love with Stephen Baker."

CHAPTER
FIFTY-ONE

From the Daily Dish blog, posted at 18.46, Sunday March 26:

Did you see the <u>faces of the crowds</u> that gathered on the Mall today? The sheer diversity of those faces? It was awe-inspiring — the reason why those of us who chose to be American citizens can feel glad, despite everything that has happened in the last insane few days, that we joined this remarkable country.

With the minimum of advance publicity — yours truly only heard that it was happening about an hour or two before it started — we gathered this afternoon on the steps of the Capitol to send a message to Congress: Hands off our President.

This was the Baker Nation, the young, hopeful America that elected our young, hopeful president just months ago. They resent the notion that a <u>cabal of Republican head-bangers</u>, together with a couple of <u>craven Democratic enablers</u>, might drive from office the man who represents a chance for our country at last to be the nation it was meant to be.

The TV estimates the crowd at ten thousand. I would say, looking at it, that it appears larger than that. Even if you accept the lower figure, it is a remarkable achievement. There was next to no preparation or organization. This was the closest we might get to an organic, spontaneous demonstration of popular outrage. Call it leaderless resistance, American-style.

Whatever you call it, let's hope Stephen Baker — still grieving the loss of his closest aide and long-time buddy, Stuart Goldstein — could see it from his window at the White House. Let's hope he saw it and drew strength from it. You are not alone, Mr President . . .

CHAPTER
FIFTY-TWO

Coeur d'Alene, Idaho, Sunday March 26, 22.03 PST
The words had sent a charge of electricity through her. *Pamela was in love with Stephen Baker.* Those words and the wistful smile that curled Anne Everett's lips at the thought of what might have been.

Instantly Maggie had assumed the obvious: that Vic Forbes knew what had happened to Pamela Everett and believed that Baker had somehow been involved in her death. That was why that date — and that date alone — represented Forbes's blanket. It was his insurance policy, it was the unexploded bomb he threatened to detonate against Baker, the one that would surely have destroyed his rival forever. Except the lithe beauty at the Midnight Lounge had got to him first, leaving him dangling in drag from the rafters of his own house.

But none of that could explain a stranger appearing at the Everetts' door ready to hand over serious money to protect the reputation of a lad barely out of his teens. Pamela had been a couple of years younger than Baker, Schilling had said, but even that would have made Baker no more than twenty at the time of the fire, twenty-one at most. Why would anyone go to such lengths to protect him?

Anne Everett was watching Maggie's face, studying her reaction. She had anticipated it even before Maggie had had the chance to form the thought in her head. "If you're thinking it was him, you're wrong," she said firmly. "Pamela was in bed with someone at the Meredith Hotel that night, but it wasn't Stephen."

Maggie frowned. "How can you be so sure?"

Anne Everett got to her feet. "Come with me."

She led Maggie up a narrow staircase, switching on a light at the landing. It was a naked bulb, hanging on a simple wire. So much for the fortune the Everetts had been paid to keep quiet about the death of their daughter.

Anne Everett opened a door that instantly released a cloud of spare-room must. A wave of childhood memory crashed over Maggie, dragging her back to the attic of her granny's house. She shivered as she looked around the room. Posters of Prince and Jimmy Connors on the wall, a teddy bear on the bed. A shelf of books and VHS tapes — including the Jane Fonda workout — several more packed with CDs.

"But didn't you move here after . . .?" Maggie said, unable to finish the sentence.

"Yes, we did. Randall didn't want me to do this. He said the whole point of coming here was to move on. But . . . Do you have children, Ashley?"

"I don't. No."

"Well, I think most mothers would understand." She stared at the floor, then at the empty bed. "You can't always move on. Not everyone can do it."

They stood in silence for a while, then Pamela's mother crouched on the floor by the bed, lifted the valance and tugged at the drawer that was revealed beneath. Inside was a blanket, neatly folded. She looked up at Maggie. "Randall didn't know about this place. Only me."

Beneath the blanket was a large, black-bound scrap-book. She pulled it out, then perched on the end of the bed and opened it. She patted the space next to her, encouraging Maggie to sit down. "Look," she said.

Glued into the scrapbook was a yellowing two-page spread from the *Madisonian*, the newspaper of James Madison High. At the centre was that same prom picture of Pamela Everett, except this time it was surrounded by snippets of tribute, paid by former classmates. "You were an angel, sent down from heaven. Now you are back among the stars."

She turned the page, to what Maggie recognized as a cutting from the *Daily World*. "Blaze at downtown hotel," read the headline.

Gently, Maggie inched the scrapbook closer so that she could read the story. It described a late-night fire at the Meredith Hotel, how a drill had brought all the guests out into the streets in their nightclothes as the "inferno gutted several storeys of the hotel, leading ceilings to collapse and walls to fall in." It reported "uncertainty at the time of writing" over casualties. Accompanying the story was a large, if poorly printed, black-and-white photograph of the hotel front ablaze.

Maggie looked to the top right of the cutting. March 16. Page five. *The missing page.*

She could feel her head throbbing. Who had done it? Who had removed it from the microfilm? Was it Forbes, so that he would enjoy a monopoly on the evidence? Or did he know about Mrs Everett and her secret hiding place? Was this yellowing page, stuck into an album stashed away in the faithfully reconstructed bedroom of a longdead prom queen — indeed, hidden under a blanket — his blanket?

"This is what I wanted to show you," Mrs Everett said quietly. She turned a couple more pages of the scrapbook.

Another complete page from *The Daily World*.

"There he is," Anne Everett said with that same wistful smile.

Sure enough, there stood a young, eager and handsome Stephen Baker shaking the hand of some older, distinguished man in oversized glasses. Below was an extended caption:

Washington's senior US Senator, Paul Corbyn, greets the state's first winner of a Rhodes scholarship since Corbyn himself nearly forty years earlier. The lucky young man is Stephen Baker, graduate of James Madison High School and, this summer, Harvard University. The photograph was taken in Sen Corbyn's Washington, DC office on March 15.

Anne Everett said nothing as Maggie read it again. Then she looked back at the date at the top of the page: March 18. If only she had checked the archive for that date, she'd have seen it. "This photo proves it wasn't him," Maggie said softly.

"That's right," Mrs Everett agreed, giving a tight little nod. "He was on the other side of the country that day. In Washington, DC. Last year, during the election campaign, I often wondered whether someone would knock on my door. Making accusations. That's why I'm glad I kept this. Everyone had such high hopes for Stephen Baker. Not just in America. All round the world. Hopes for the future. But not me. My hopes are all in the past, Ashley. But I often think how different things would have been if Stephen Baker had taken Pamela out that night — instead of that, that *bastard*," she spat out the word with the venom of a woman who never swears. "Then my Pamela would be alive today. I am sure of it."

CHAPTER
FIFTY-THREE

New York, Sunday March 26, 23.01
Late nights suited him. Best time to work: no email, no phone calls, no distractions. Not even a view out of the window; just darkness.

This way his vision could be dominated by the screen on the desk. Amazing what could be done on the computer these days. Pretty much everything.

There was a glass by the side of the keyboard, amber with whisky. But he had barely touched it. The ice had melted long ago, diluting the spirit to a paler, less enticing shade. He liked that it was there, proof that he was absorbed in his work.

Which he was. He hadn't heard from Maggie for a while, but that only served to motivate him further: she was clearly in a bit of trouble here, and so he was duty bound to do whatever he could to help. Besides, with Maggie it was never just duty.

He moved the mouse across the screen and clicked open the fifty-one-second video that had, at last, caused the penny to drop. It was a crucial piece of footage; he could not quite believe he had not discovered it till now. As soon as Maggie was back in DC, he would show it to her and all would at last be clear. But why wait till then? He reached for his phone and punched in Maggie's number and it rang and rang and then went to voicemail. Yet again. Sighing, he shoved the phone back into his trouser pocket.

He returned to the screen and watched the video through yet again, this time noticing something new. He sat up. Was that a noise he hadn't heard before: a metallic clang, muffled but definitely there? He spooled back and replayed the same sequence. No sound this time. Must have been outside.

He needed to think how best to organize this material, for maximum impact. What would work best? Despite the full panoply of state-of-the-art software at his fingertips, including perhaps half a dozen first-class word-processing programs, he reached for the pad and pen and began jotting notes.

There it was again. Not the same noise, more of a creak this time and, if anything, louder.

"Hello?"

Nothing.

"Anyone there?"

He checked the clock at the top right of the screen. Past eleven.

He went back to the sheet of notepaper, scribbling in handwriting that no one but he could ever decipher the logical sequence as he now understood it. He imagined relaying it to Maggie, watching as a smile spread across her face, a smile of recognition as she understood the pattern he now understood. That smile could make a man fall in love with Maggie Costello.

Reaching a knot in the clear logical line he was trying to unspool on paper, he sucked on his pen, feeling the plastic flake off into his mouth. Anticipating a choke, he reached for the watery glass of whisky, glancing at the darkness of the window as he did so.

The sight of a man's face peering in made him jump. Idiotically, he wondered how someone could be outside his window — here in a fifth-floor apartment.

It took him a half-second to understand the truth. That the face staring, dead-eyed, at him was in fact a reflection of a man standing inside — and just behind him.

By then it was too late. The man's hands were on his shoulders, pinning him to his chair, and then on his neck. He tried to gasp but it was no good: the grip was too tight.

His own reaction surprised him. He writhed and clawed at his attacker but the strength in this man's hands was insuperable; there was, he could tell instantly, a professionalism to this attack that guaranteed it would succeed. Suddenly, and with horrible certainty, he knew he was going to die.

All of this was measured in seconds. And throughout, the only face he could see was Maggie's. Even in these desperate circumstances he registered this as a curious fact. He had not realized how much she meant to him. But suddenly all that mattered was knowing that if they were ready to kill him, they would be ready to kill her — and that thought gave him determination. Letting his hands fall as if in submission to his fate, he dug into his pocket and then, summoning the strength for a big push, gave a sharp lurch to his right to shake the man off. He knew it would not save his life, but it might at least delay his death by a moment or two.

As his attacker stumbled backwards, he gulped down oxygen. All his concentration was on his left hand. Adept at using the phone when he wasn't looking at it, he jabbed at the buttons. The strangling hands were back on his neck now, attempting to get a grip as he writhed, while his own left hand remained deep in his pocket, searching for the green key that would start the call. With a superhuman effort he stopped himself from crying out straight away, knowing he needed to wait a few seconds for the machine to pick up and the message to play.

Now. He would do it now.

With his right arm he tried to lash out — backwards — at his assailant and, once again, the man had to take one hand off his victim's neck to fend off the diversion.

"Ennnnnn!" he rasped, in what sounded like an exhalation of desperate pain.

His attacker had forced him off the chair now and onto his knees, so that he bore the full weight of his brutal killer on his shoulders. Somehow he had to find the strength to cry out once more.

"Ayyyy!" he shouted, though the sound that emerged was more like a whisper.

Out of frustration, perhaps, the attacker now took his hands off his prey's neck and punched him instead, hard in the jaw. Even so, he did not flinch, instead seizing on the chance to cry out, "*Seeeeeeeee!*"

This continued for perhaps ten more seconds, even if it felt like the longest and most terrifying hour of his life. Somehow he found the energy to force his executioner to interrupt the job of asphyxiation — even, at one point, directing a fist into the man's balls — and to do it often enough that eventually he had cried out five times.

It was then his strength left him. He could flail no more at the dead-eyed, grey-faced man in the cheap suit who was squeezing the life out of him. At last he surrendered, allowing him to kill him — as he had known he would.

He ended up on the floor of his own study, curled up and lifeless.

There was a noise outside in the hall. The attacker, unnerved by the sound of neighbours returning to the next-door apartment, moved swiftly — tearing off the top, scribbled sheet of the notepad on the desk and then using the device he had been given to wipe the computer's hard drive.

The knock at the door interrupted his effort to frisk the man he had just killed.

"Hello? Is everything all right in there?" The knocking continued and was getting louder.

The killer held his breath, hoping whoever was there would go away. Then he heard another voice say, "I think we should break it down."

Hastily, he scanned the apartment for the fire escape, eventually finding it in the kitchen where a door led out onto a tiny balcony and, from there, to the narrow, wrought-iron staircase that zig-zagged its way down the exterior of the building. He fled, taking the stairs two at a time until he had reached ground level.

Calmly, he walked from there to his car.

Five floors up, his victim's body lay discarded, the dead man's fingers gnarled around his cellphone as if gripping the hand of a loved one for the last moment of his life.

CHAPTER
FIFTY-FOUR

Coeur d'Alene, Idaho, Sunday March 26, 22.55 PST
To her great relief the cab driver was still outside. He had waited nearly two hours, with only a single Christian radio station and the car heater for company. But he had waited. He had not been driven off the road, his brakes had not been sabotaged. He was still there.

Maggie asked how long it would take to drive to Boise. He gave a snort of disbelieving, mirthless laughter. "Can you show me your money?" He wanted to see the cash before he agreed to go any further. "Lotta crazy people in this state," he said by way of apology.

Maggie took pleasure in pulling out five hundred-dollar bills and agreeing on that as the rate for the evening's work.

"Now can I ask a question?" she asked.

"You got it," he said, his spirits duly lifted.

"If we end up driving through the night, would you mind if we didn't speak for most of it?"

He smiled and turned the ignition key.

The darkness of the Idaho sky and the emptiness of the roads suited her perfectly. It reminded her of those countless night flights she had endured during the campaign, staring into the black nothingness. It was where she had done some of her best thinking.

For a brief, blissful second she had believed she had finally unravelled the knot bequeathed by Vic Forbes. When Anne Everett admitted that her dead daughter had carried a torch for the current president of the United States, Maggie had almost pictured it, a series of strange symbols suddenly turning into regular words — the code breaking.

The young, handsome Baker — Aberdeen favourite son and recent graduate of Harvard — had taken the adoring prom queen a couple of years his junior to bed in a downtown hotel, and there, somehow, she had died. It was a nuclear scandal that had just been sitting there all these years, waiting to be exploded by Vic Forbes, who — alone in the world, it seemed — knew of it and was ready to use it. But this theory had been shattered in less time than it took to think of it. That photograph of a young, eager Baker with Senator Corbyn taken on the other side of the country on the same day as the fire was definitive. If Forbes had ever gone public, Baker would have been able to rebut him instantly, simply by producing that photograph. The perfect alibi.

Could Forbes have made such an elementary blunder? Could he really have invested so much of his life in — and constructed his entire blanket around — a provably false accusation?

But that was not all that nagged at Maggie. She sat back in the car, letting the headrest take the strain on her still aching neck, as she thought back to the public library. Why on earth was that single page missing from the archive? Just one: page five. No others. Who had removed it?

The answer was clear: it had to be the same man who had turned up at the home of Anne and Randall Everett the morning after their daughter's death — breaking the news to them, for heaven's sake — waving an improbable amount of cash in their faces and buying their silence, in perpetuity. Why would anyone do that? If it wasn't Baker who had left Pamela Everett to die, who was it? And who was this other boy, for whose reputation a man had been prepared to pay tens, perhaps hundreds, of thousands of dollars and take the trouble of destroying part of a newspaper archive, in order to keep his secret from ever being known?

Maggie could feel her ribs hurting, as well as her head. She desperately needed to talk this through with someone. She looked at her phone. Unregistered, pay-as-you-go, it should be safe. But she didn't want to risk it. She leaned forward, lightly tapping the shoulder of the driver.

"There's an extra hundred for you if you let me use your cellphone."

He handed it to her, placing a theatrical finger across his lips. I'm sticking to our deal: no chat.

For at least the third time, she dialled Nick du Caines's home number, the only one of his she remembered. Voicemail, yet again. Where the hell was he? Shacked up in a love-drugs-and-booze-fest with some intern from ABC and screening calls? Probably.

She checked her watch. Midnight in Idaho, 8a.m. in London. Worth a shot.

She used the browser of her BlackBerry to find the London number of Nick's forever-ailing Sunday newspaper, dialled it on the driver's phone — hoping he wouldn't notice — and asked for the foreign desk.

A secretary answered. "Unusual call," Maggie began in her politest voice, explaining that she was a regular Washington contact of Nick du Caines and she had been trying to get in touch, though she had unfortunately mislaid his mobile number. She had a story that she was sure he would be interested in. Was there any chance they might help?

"I think you'd better speak to the foreign editor," the woman said, an edge in her voice that Maggie didn't like.

There was a delay until a man — early forties, plummy — came on the line.

"I understand you're a friend of Nick's?"

"That's right."

"I'm afraid I have some rather bad news. We've only just heard. Nick is dead."

CHAPTER
FIFTY-FIVE

Boise, Idaho, Monday March 27, 04.13 PST
Maggie spent the rest of the night alternating between two different kinds of pain. The shock of Nick's death was beyond tears: she was numbed to the bone. She was empty; hollowed out. She sat in the cab like a husk, hardly able even to breathe, trying hard not to think. But her body seemed determined to force reality upon her. Emerging from the taxi as it pulled into Boise Airport in the early hours of the morning, she felt how the ache in her ribs had settled and deepened.

The foreign editor had told her there had been a break-in at Nick's apartment, and that there had been signs of a struggle. His body had been badly beaten and "bore all the hallmarks of death by strangulation". Police were interviewing neighbours, taking prints. But so far there were no witnesses.

Of course there would be no witnesses, Maggie thought. The people who had killed Nick were like the people who had killed Stuart. They were pros: they would leave no trace.

With hours to wait before the first morning flight out, she knew she should try to sleep. She tried curling up on a hard plastic airport chair but — no matter how exhausted she was — real sleep would not come.

She dozed off a couple of times, only to be woken once by the cold spreading across her skin, undefeated even by the swaddling of her coat, and the second time by the clear realization that a man — his face hidden — was standing over her, wearing the satisfied smile of a pursuer who has finally cornered his prey. She woke from the dream and sat bolt upright, clutching at her bag as if it were a weapon and getting ready to run, heart hammering against her sore ribs.

And at once the other source of pain returned. *Nick is dead.* The words she had heard down the telephone played as if on a loop in her head.

Now the guilt came like a rush. It was all her fault. She had offered his drunken, debauched, lecherous and brilliant head up to them. It was just as Liz said. The woman down the street in Dublin wasn't getting strangled in the dead of night, because she had no knowledge that was connected with this goddamned mess. And neither had Nick du Caines — until Maggie had dragged him into it. And now he was dead.

Was she carrying some kind of curse, one that ensured all those she touched turned to stone? She thought of Stuart lying dead, his huge, bloated body beached in Rock Creek Park, bleeding from the wrists, and now Nick, strangled and battered and left for dead in his apartment in New York. All because of her.

Bile rose, acrid in her throat. Grabbing her bag, she dashed for the ladies' bathroom and there heaved her guts up into a toilet bowl, gripping the edges convulsively, retching and retching till her guts felt as empty as her heart.

She wadded up some toilet paper, wiped her mouth and chin, flushed and went out to wash her hands. The huge overlit mirror was unforgiving in its judgment. Dark circles under bloodshot eyes, the newly-dyed hair brassy under the neon: she looked like the guilty fugitive she felt. For a moment she was gripped by the urgent desire to run away, to get on a plane and go somewhere, anywhere, far away from here — where she could do no more damage. She needed to talk to no one, in case she passed on whatever fatal virus she carried. She had become toxic, radiating death.

The idea lingered with her for a while. She pictured herself on some speck of an island in the South Pacific, holed up in a house that no one knew existed. And then she thought of the men whose hands had choked the life out of Nick and who had shoved those tablets into Stuart's mouth and anger rose to replace the guilt. There were people out there who murdered to prevent the truth being told and their killing would stop only when someone made them stop. She had to find them and hunt them down. She had to make them pay for what they had done.

She squared her shoulders. It was time to stop feeling guilty for the crimes of others. She would defend herself, and she would drag the truth out into the daylight. She started walking around again, pacing and thinking, scrutinizing everyone she passed. Are you a part of this? Are you? After some minutes she noticed a man, apparently immersed in the *Idaho Statesman*, standing by the Departures sign, and wondered how long he had been there.

Think, she told herself. She had asked Nick to look into a single, specific aspect of the Forbes story: was there any evidence to link Forbes's former employers, the CIA, with his death? She hadn't considered that a life-threatening question to ask, not when Nick had won himself a shelf-full of trophies investigating CIA conduct in the war on terror. He had exposed the Agency's working methods — and he had lived both to tell the tale and to drink his prize money.

Yet this latest investigation was clearly different. Whatever he had found had struck a CIA nerve that was too raw to be tolerated. CIA agents had been caught bundling men convicted of no crime into chartered aircraft and sending them to faraway corners of the globe where they could be tortured with impunity — and yet worldwide exposure of that truth had not driven the Agency to take Nick du Caines's life. Someone, somewhere, clearly regarded a revelation of CIA involvement in the murder of Vic Forbes as more serious and more damaging even than the rendition story — and were ready to prevent it by killing again.

Shortly after four-thirty in the morning, she felt the vibration of a text arriving on her BlackBerry. It was from her sister:

Call me urgently. Something strange is happening. Liz.

She was half-way through dialling the Dublin number when another message arrived, this time from Sanchez.

The police want to see you. Now. Take the next plane to New York.

CHAPTER
FIFTY-SIX

New York, JFK Airport, Monday March 27, 14.41
They met her off the plane, a detective in plain clothes with two uniformed officers hanging close by. They led her away from the other passengers, towards what they called an "interview suite", in fact a blank room containing a desk and three chairs.

The detective introduced himself as Charles Bridge. In his early forties, African-American and unsmiling, he got straight to business.

"Want to thank you for coming to New York right away. We appreciate that."

Maggie nodded, her heart throbbing. What was this about?

The detective glanced at a piece of paper. "It took us a while to get hold of you, you know."

"Yes?" Maggie said, reluctant to offer anything more.

Still examining the piece of paper, he said, "Yep. A long time. Tried your cell, that just rang out. No response on email. Seemed like you'd just disappeared."

"My phone was stolen. Along with my wallet and computer. In Washington State."

"That right?" Bridge looked at the paper again then back up at Maggie. "Do you know why we wanted to see you, Miss Costello?"

"I know that my friend Nick du Caines is dead."

"That's right. Why else? If you had to guess."

Maggie thought of the drink she'd had with him last Thursday. If she mentioned it, she would have to say what they discussed. "I'm not sure."

"Because, Miss Costello, the last call Mr du Caines made was to you. To your number."

"To me?"

"That's right. To your home number."

"When?"

"His phone says he placed the call at three minutes past eleven last night. Your answering machine confirms that. And, based on what the neighbours have told us, about the noises coming from Mr du Caines's apartment, we think that's the time of death."

"Did you just say my answering machine confirms that? How do you know that?"

"We've got the machine, Miss Costello."

"You've what? How?"

"We tried to contact you by all available means, calling your home number, your cellphone. We contacted your employer —" he glanced back down at his sheet of paper "— excuse me, your former employers at the White House, and they had no idea how to reach you. We had no choice but to obtain a warrant and make an entry into your apartment and impound the machine."

"You broke into my apartment?"

"Our colleagues in Washington made an entry on our behalf, yes."

"Jesus Christ!" Maggie's mind was racing as she thought of what was there, what might have been seen. Had she left anything out that might point to the Forbes business? "And did you find anything, on my machine, I mean?"

"We'll come to that, Miss Costello. Right now, I'm just puzzled why a man who is being beaten and strangled, who would have known he was at the end of his life, would call your number in his death throes. We've heard the message. He doesn't even try to speak to you. Why would anyone do that?"

"What are you suggesting, Detective?"

"I'm not suggesting anything. I'm just wondering. I mean, he didn't dial your cellphone, did he?"

"I told you, my cellphone was stolen. That number didn't work any more."

"But he calls your home number. Almost like that was the only way he could lead us to you."

"Lead you to me? I don't understand."

"Nothing to understand right now, Miss Costello."

"I don't like your tone, Detective." Maggie could feel her face growing flushed. "I don't like what you're insinuating. Nick du Caines was a very dear friend of mine. And I was on the other side of the country when he died. I've just flown in from bloody Idaho."

"You need to keep calm, Miss Costello. I'm not insinuating anything. I'm just asking some questions."

"I want to hear this message."

"Well, I'm not sure —"

"It's my property. It was on my machine, he left it for me."

"This is evidence in the case now, Miss Costello, I can't —"

"That answering machine is my legal property. And right now I am a witness, no more. If you want to arrest me, go ahead. Until you do, I have the right to hear what's on that tape."

The detective pulled out his phone and retreated to the corner of the room to make a call. He was talking in a low voice, apparently to a superior. He returned to his chair looking glum. "Apparently, the advice is that we should play the message to you. See if you can shed any light on it."

He produced a laptop computer, pressed a few keys and then clicked on an audio file. From the machine's small speakers, Maggie now heard a beep, followed by a distant sound of objects clattering off a desk.

Then she heard Nick, bellowing in pain. He must have been winded by an almighty punch: *Ennnnn!*

It was terrible to listen to, the horror of it real and direct. Even distorted by transmission to her answering machine and from there to the audio file, she could hear the fleshy thud of blows to Nick's body followed by exhalations of pain: *Ayyy!*

To think she had brought this on him. It was as if she were there, watching as Nick gasped and kicked out, the breath of life squeezed out of him.

It lasted another full, murderous minute, until an electronic voice announced: *You have ten more seconds to complete your message.* There was a last gasp from Nick — *Phwaw!* — and finally it was over.

Maggie's head was dipped low as she stared at the floor. The detective spoke again.

"It's harrowing to hear. I know that. But why would he do it? Like I said before, he doesn't do anything except leave a recording of his own death. There's no message to you."

A small spark suddenly broke through Maggie's grief. "Can you play it again, please?"

"Why?"

"I'm not sure. Just play it again."

"Did you hear something?"

"Maybe."

Reluctantly, he clicked on the file a second time, watching Maggie closely throughout as she listened. Ninety seconds later, he raised his eyebrows. "So?"

"I'm sorry, Detective. I was wrong." She had to look away from him as she lied, repeating what she had heard in her mind, just to be sure.

"Any idea why he would call you at such a time?"

"Look, Mr Bridge. This is awkward. I had a drink with Nick last Thursday. He was an old friend but he always wanted it to be something more. He said some things to me last week." She looked up briefly at the detective, so that their eyes met. "Romantic things. I wonder if Nick was just trying to say goodbye."

The detective held her gaze and Maggie willed herself to meet it without flinching or flushing. Then, apparently satisfied, he nodded to the uniformed men that the interview was over, packed his computer away

421

and showed Maggie to the door — after he had taken her new cellphone number. "We'll be in touch again if we need any more from you, Miss Costello."

Released back onto the airport concourse, Maggie tried to walk away as nonchalantly as possible, in case the cops were watching her. She forced herself to be patient, to take the elevator to another floor before whipping out her computer and acting on the information Nick du Caines had passed to her as his last, dying act.

CHAPTER
FIFTY-SEVEN

New York, Monday March 27, 15.35
She said the sequence over to herself once more, repeating it as she had heard it. There was no doubting it. It was NICK4.

Sitting at the gate for a flight to Albuquerque, she checked again that neither Detective Bridge nor any of his men — nor anyone else for that matter — were around. No one that she could see. She would stay here, surrounded by people. It was broad daylight; there were crowds. Surely that would make her safe.

She had been recalling the lecture her sister had given her about storing documents online, rather than on disks or memory sticks that could get lost down the back of the sofa or soaked in coffee. And then she had remembered how even Nick du Caines, in his little masterclass on journalism, had confessed that he had screwed up so often, he now wrote everything online, storing it up there "in the ether".

She played back in her head the sounds she had heard, forcing away the vile images they conjured, as her friend was horribly murdered. Concentrate, Maggie, she told herself fiercely. You have to do this for Nick: he died trying to make contact with you. Be strong and bloody well think it through. There was a message within that message: of that she was now sure. At first she had thought they were no more than desperate howls of pain. But Bridge had been right. There was a reason why Nick, while fighting for his life, had fumbled for his phone and dialled her number. He had to be communicating something. And when Bridge had played the recording for the second time, she had heard it. Each apparent sound of pain Nick had made had been different to the one before. That cry — *Ennnn!* — was not just an expression of terrible agony, of a man winded by a punch, though it might well be that as well. It was also the letter N. *Ayyy* was awful to hear but translated into the letter "I". On it had gone until that final desperate noise — *Phwaw*: clearly the number four. She marvelled at the strength and ingenuity of such a feat and, not for the first time that day, felt glad to have known Nick du Caines.

She flipped open her computer, watching as it latched on to the airport's wifi signal. A few keystrokes and she was there, at the Googledocs website. She logged in, typing Nick's name carefully and without spaces: nickducaines. Then the password, constructed from each letter and digit he had cried out: Nick4.

Incorrect name and password.

She tried again, this time spelling Nick's name in capital letters. Now a new error message appeared.

Incorrect password, insufficient characters.

424

Damn. Nick's effort, valiant though it had been, had been in vain. He had not lasted long enough to convey the last few letters.

She stared at the screen. *Nick4*. What could that mean? What might 4 refer to? Guessing, she typed in Nick4duC.

Incorrect password. You are approaching the maximum number of failed attempts. One more attempt allowed.

She looked around, checking the faces of those nearby: a mother with children, a student listening with eyes closed to an iPod.

Think.

Then she looked at it again — Nick4 — and a teenage memory returned. They had all done it, carving it on park benches and on school desks. She had done it herself once: Maggie4Liam. Was it possible that Nick du Caines had been that soft-hearted? Somehow she wouldn't have put it past him. She entered the password field and typed Nick4Maggie.

She was about to press enter on this, her last attempt when something stopped her. She could hear Nick's voice, on the phone or across the table in the bar. *Now listen, Mags, when are you finally going to start moving those luscious lips of yours into the shape of a story for my newspaper?*

Mags.

Carefully, so as not to hit enter by accident, she retyped so that the new password read simply Nick4Mags.

425

Without fuss, as if it had been waiting for her, the page transformed itself, offering a list of documents. She was in. Poor, sweet Nick, sending her an adolescent valentine even in his last moments. She had never once taken his interest in her seriously.

At a glance, she could see all his most recent stories, sorted by date. And there at the top, a document entitled *New Orleans*. She clicked it open, expecting a long, detailed memo, explaining all his findings. Instead there was a single line. Daniel Judd, aviation expert — followed by a phone number.

Maggie pulled out her phone and dialled. After two rings, a voice answered: male, cautious.

"I'm a friend of Nick du Caines," she began. "He left a message on my machine just before he died. I think he —"

"Died? Nick?"

"I'm sorry, that was very insensitive of me. I thought you might have known. Did you know him well?"

"Who is this? What happened to Nick?"

Maggie explained the circumstances that had led to her call. There was a long silence and for a panicked moment she thought the man had hung up, but then he said, "How can I trust you? How do I know you didn't kill Nick and now you're after me?"

Maggie was flummoxed. "I don't know. All I can tell you is that Nick went to very great lengths to let me know how to reach you. He used his dying breaths to leave a message on my answering machine. It was —"

426

"All right, get off this line. Call me on a payphone in thirty minutes. Number is —" There was a shuffling of paper, then he rattled off a number at her.

"Hold on, hold on." Maggie scrabbled one-handed in her bag for a pen. "Say that again —"

"You have thirty minutes. Go buy unregistered, pay-as-you-go phones, as many as you can afford. Call me from one of those. After that, throw it away. Never use any of them twice. And don't give the number to anyone." He repeated the number of the payphone, so quickly she barely had time to scribble it down, and hung up.

Maggie did what she was told, rushing to a cellphone store in Terminal 3. She bought five phones with her now-dwindling cash supply and punched in the payphone number Judd had given her.

He picked up — and spoke — on the second ring. "You say he left my number on your answering machine?"

"No. Nick was smarter than that. A password, then a document."

"No one else has seen it?" The voice sounded harried, feverish.

Maggie looked at the screen, noticing the saved date for the New Orleans document was 10.54p.m. the previous evening — a few minutes before Nick had been fighting for his life — and that, according to its "properties", it appeared not to have been opened again till now. "I don't think so." She needed to get him to talk, before his nerves overcame him. "Listen, Mr —"

"No names on the phone!"

"Of course, sorry. Listen, it was me who put, er, our mutual friend on to the, um, issue that I think he was discussing with you. I was the one who mentioned it to him. I think he wanted me to know whatever it was you told him."

"I'm gonna do this real quick and I'm only gonna say it once. Are we clear?"

"We're clear."

"After we're done, you destroy the phone. Clear?"

"Sure. I understand your anxiety, Mr —"

"No names! You're damned right I'm anxious. This is some serious shit you're wading into here, Missy, I can tell you." She heard the sound of traffic rushing past.

"I know that."

"Right then. Once only. At midnight-thirty local time on March 22, a jet departed from Lakefront Airport, New Orleans, Louisiana, carrying seven passengers. The number of the aircraft was November-four-eight-zero-eight-Papa. That aircraft is registered to one Premier Air Executive Services, an air operator based in Maryland. Its prior history indicates use by the Company."

As Maggie suspected, the CIA.

Judd wasn't done. "That was its *prior* use. Two years ago it shifted ownership. It is now entirely at the service of a single client."

"What kind of client?"

"One time. I will not repeat this, you understand? Premier runs private jets exclusively for AitkenBruce."

428

Maggie couldn't repress her surprise. "AitkenBruce? The bank?"

But Judd was in no mood for discussion. He had one more fact to convey. "Today Premier submitted another flight plan. They have a Gulfstream 550 jet departing Teterboro, New Jersey for Washington Reagan at nineteen hundred hours. Looking back through the flight history, there's only one person who makes that journey on that aircraft. And that's the chairman of the bank."

CHAPTER
FIFTY-EIGHT

New York, JFK Airport, Monday March 27, 16.25
Maggie's thoughts whirled. A bank? What on earth could any of this have to do with a bank? And AitkenBruce specifically. It made no sense. Forbes had no connection with finance in any form. What possible —

The phone she had bought in Aberdeen vibrated, making her jump.

Restricted.

But no one knew this number. And why would they call the second she had finished speaking to Judd? Had someone been listening in, waiting to pounce?

She picked up the device as if it were coated in poison, pressing the green button to answer the call, but saying nothing. And then she heard that voice.

"Maggie? Is that you?"

Uri.

Panic flooded through her. She spoke fast, thinking of Stuart and Nick and the curse that seemed to leave all those she touched dead. "Don't call this number again. Give me a number where I can call you."

Her abruptness shocked him; a sudden wariness in his voice, he replied, "I'm in an edit suite. The number is, hang on, what is the number here?" There was a second voice, barely audible. *Hurry.* Eventually, Uri gave her the number; Maggie scribbled it down, then ordered him to hang up.

She binned the phone she'd used to call Judd, though the waste of a perfectly good phone went against her entire upbringing, picked another and called Uri back.

"Maggie, what the fuck is going on?"

"It's a long —"

"Don't tell me: 'It's a long story.'"

"Seriously, Uri. Anyone who talks to me is in danger. Grave danger."

"Come on, Maggie, that's a bit melodramatic. There's —"

"Remember my friend Nick? He was killed last night."

There was a beat of silence. "Jesus. I'm sorry, Maggie."

"I so want to talk, Uri. Just to have a chance to talk. For as long as we like."

"Where are you?"

She hesitated. She knew it made no sense to say it out loud. But it was a virgin phone; it should be safe. "I'm at JFK."

"I'm coming. Right now."

She tried to argue, insisting it was too far, there was no time, but he bulldozed through her resistance the way she allowed him and no one else to do. By the time she had told him exactly where she was sitting, he was already in a cab.

Her pulse was throbbing now, with a new, gentler kind of fear. How long since she had seen Uri? Not since the inauguration; more than two months. She looked at her reflection in the window: she hardly recognized herself. And there was so much they hadn't said.

She turned back to the computer, still open at Nick's Googledocs account. Focus, she told herself. Focus. There was only one thing she was meant to think about now. She went to the search field and typed "AitkenBruce".

She had heard of the bank, of course; everyone had. It was famous for its squillionaire traders and executives, rewarding themselves with telephone number salaries and even fatter bonuses. But how it could be caught up in all this, she couldn't imagine.

Google led her to AitkenBruce's own website. It was full of corporate puff: pictures of smiling employees — most of whom seemed to be either young, female or black, projecting an image of perfectly inclusive diversity — and blurbs about the generous philanthropic activity the "AitkenBruce family" was engaged in around the globe. She clicked out of it almost immediately.

A fresh search revealed a long piece in the *Sunday Times* magazine, headlined: "The True Masters of the Universe: Inside the World's Richest Bank".

She scanned the first few paragraphs, which revealed an institution with more cash in its coffers than many governments, one whose assets topped a trillion dollars and whose top brass routinely went on to take up posts in the commanding heights of the world's economies. At any one time, the ranks of the AitkenBruce old boys' association would include either a US Treasury Secretary, German finance minister or head of the European Central Bank — and sometimes all three at once.

Now there was a chunk of more familiar stuff about mind-boggling pay. "Last year, Chairman and Chief Executive Roger Waugh took home a staggering $73m, to add to the $600m he already owns in AitkenBruce stock," the magazine reported, before detailing the yachts moored in Monaco and apartments overlooking Central Park, the private islands in Dubai and country estates in Oxfordshire, owned by the bank's senior management.

The article explained that men this rich used their money in part to insulate themselves from those who were poorer than they were, which essentially meant everyone. "Forcefielding", they called it: never flying commercial, but only by private jet; never stepping in a taxi, still less public transport, but seeing the world only through the tinted windows of a Lincoln Town Car.

Maggie scrolled down, looking for anything which might connect AitkenBruce to Forbes, let alone explain why a Company jet might have been despatched to New Orleans to assist in his murder. Had Forbes, in some earlier incarnation perhaps, been a corporate whistleblower? Or had he been blackmailing the bank as well as the President?

She lingered over the section which detailed how AitkenBruce made its vast fortune. For one thing, these bankers worked all hours, never taking holidays, often staying in the office so late there would be no time to go home before morning. For another, AitkenBruce didn't waste its time with the little guy: its customers were governments, from Europe to the Persian Gulf, multinational mega-corporations and only the very richest individuals — a reclusive billionaire stashing his fortune in some Caribbean hideaway, a Saudi sheikh or even the reviled rules of an unstable rogue state.

But knowledge was its secret weapon. If an investor was thinking about getting into, say, timber, AitkenBruce could help because it counted the world's biggest timber companies among its corporate clients. In addition, major investors in the same field were probably also paying the bank for its advice, so the bank knew what they were up to, too. AitkenBruce had every angle covered, which could only help when the bank came to decide how to invest its own money. The article quoted an unnamed critic saying that investing in a world that included AitkenBruce was like gambling in a casino where the house knows every hand at the table: you might pick up a few dollars, but the house wins every time.

She scrolled past the section detailing the stellar career of the bank's alumni, stopping at a photograph of Waugh, the boss. He was fiftyish, bald and nothing to look at. If the caption had read "Accountant living in New Jersey", it would have been utterly plausible. And yet here was the top man. If anyone knew what connected AitkenBruce to Forbes, it surely would be him.

She skipped back a few paragraphs. "No one doubts the extraordinary access and influence of an institution like AitkenBruce. Its links to the White House are solid —" Maggie glanced at the date: the story had been written nearly a year before Stephen Baker had been elected. "And the bank will be watching the coming presidential contest closely. Once again, the moneymen are covering all their bases. Quarterly figures published by the Federal Election Commission confirm that Waugh and his fellow honchos at AitkenBruce gave hefty donations to both Democrats and Republicans."

Maggie looked away from the computer towards the mid-afternoon passengers, some flicking through magazines, others mutely watching CNN on the airport screens. Then she moved her cursor to the Search field and typed "Stephen Baker + Roger Waugh".

To her surprise, the first entry was billed as a "News" result, posted a matter of hours ago. It took her to a page on politico.com listing the President's appointments for the next day. There at 9a.m. was "President Baker meets representatives of America's financial community", listing the personnel involved.

So that was why Waugh was travelling to Washington tonight. He was going to meet the President.

And yet Waugh was somehow tangled up with the death of Forbes and maybe everything else that had happened in this crazy week. A sudden alarm drove through her like a surge of electricity. It would be madness to let Waugh come within a hundred yards of the Oval Office before the President understood what the hell was going on. And that meant Maggie had to find out.

She opened up a new tab and checked out Teterboro Airport, reading that it was a tiny "relief" airport in New Jersey, but very popular with "private and corporate aircraft" because it was just twelve miles from midtown Manhattan. Slightly farther from JFK, but she could make it if she got going right away.

Just then there was a tap on her shoulder.

She froze. And then she heard his voice.

"I nearly didn't recognize you. What's with the haircut?"

She hadn't planned it; she'd had no idea how this moment would feel. But the sight of him now, in his trademark dark jeans and white shirt, his full head of lustrous, almost-black hair, made her stand up and close her arms around him.

They stood like that, saying nothing, holding each other like any other couple having an airport goodbye, for a minute or longer. It had been so long since she had felt the warmth of another human being, so long since she had felt his touch. She wanted to breathe in the smell of him, the scent that instantly transported her back to the thousand different moments of love they had shared.

It was Maggie who eventually broke the embrace, stepping back to take a good look at him. "This is so crazy. Now they can see you."

"I can take care of myself, Maggie. It's you we need to worry about."

She smiled, childishly pleased that he hadn't let go of her hand. "So what couldn't wait that you had to rush over here like a *manyak*?"

"I told you, Maggie, that word doesn't mean what you think it means. But your Hebrew accent is getting better. I'm impressed." He smiled. "It's better than your haircut anyway."

"Uri."

He sat on the stool next to hers, so that they were both facing the observation window. "You know the Baker film I'm making? I've come across something — I don't know — odd."

"What kind of odd?"

"Maggie, do you know how Stephen Baker became Governor?"

"Uri, I'd love to get into this, but I'm really under the —"

"Just listen, Maggie. How Baker became Governor. Do you know?"

"I know he won big."

"Very big. Massive, in fact. Ran against a total nobody who hadn't lived in the state for twenty years."

"OK."

"You know why? Because the Republican opponent he was meant to face imploded three months before election day. During the campaign his divorce papers suddenly surfaced; showed he had a thing about watching his wife have sex with other men. He would hide in a closet, filming it with a video camera."

437

"I really don't see —"

"But that's not all. Baker was never even expected to *be* the Democratic candidate. Everyone thought he'd lose the primary. He was up against a really popular mayor of Seattle. Except someone produced a tape of the mayor talking on the phone, saying there were too many 'chinks and spics' in the city. Baker just glided to the nomination."

"Where's this going, Uri?"

"I don't know. It just seems that — until all this impeachment stuff — somebody up there really liked Stephen Baker. Liked him a lot."

There was a time when that would have been enough to make Maggie tell Uri to piss off. When they were going out, Baker had been a constant source of tension: Uri pointing out flaws in his speeches, little missteps in his tactics, Maggie always getting defensive. It seemed ridiculous now, but Maggie had long suspected that Uri had become jealous of this other man in her life — and took every opportunity to do him down.

Now, though, she was ready to hear anything that might help explain the bizarre and lethal chain of events that had unfolded this last week. Not that she could yet work out how this fitted in. "Uri, I have to leave here any minute now. If I need to reach you, where will you be?"

"In the edit suite. I can't get any work done at home at the moment. My sister's visiting from Tel Aviv — she's decided her mission in life is to clean every surface of my apartment."

438

A different cog in Maggie's mind started turning. "Your sister?" So that had been the woman Maggie had heard in the background on that call to the New York apartment. Not a new lover after all. She felt a knot deep inside her — one she had only been dimly aware of until this moment — begin to loosen and unravel.

"Are you sure I can't come with you, wherever you're going? I might even be useful. I have some experience you know." He did a little mime suggesting a man of action.

"I know, Uri. And I'm really grateful. But I've drawn too many people into this mess already."

She could see that he wanted to insist, but stopped himself, aware that he was in no position to do so. "OK. But take care of yourself, Maggie." They were standing now, close together, with the same hesitation they felt when they would part at Penn Station on a Sunday night before she headed down to Washington. "I mean it. Do it for me, if not for you." He leaned forward and kissed the top of her head. Then he turned and walked away. She watched for several long seconds, wondering if he would turn around. But he didn't.

An announcement came over the tannoy, prompting her to look at her watch: she really would have to leave right now if she was to get to Teterboro in time. But she had the guilty, nagging sensation of something she was meant to do, some task left incomplete. She was about to switch off the computer when it came to her: Liz.

Her sister had sent that text hours ago: Call me urgently. Something strange is happening, when Maggie had still been at the airport in Idaho. But then, straight afterwards, there had been that message from Sanchez about the police and she had put everything else out of her mind.

She picked out one of the unused, disposable phones and dialled Liz's number.

"Christ, thank God Almighty."

"Liz, what is it?"

"Jesus, when I hadn't heard from you, I thought maybe —"

"I'm OK. Liz, calm down." She could hear her sister's breaths coming quickly, as if she were about to cry.

"You may be able to handle all this, Maggie, but I'm not sure we can. Not if something happened to you. Ma and me —"

"You haven't told her anything!"

"Course I haven't." A loud sniff. "But Jesus, Maggie, you had me worried." Now the contagion seemed to have spread, as the phone was filled by the noise of a child sobbing. "Oh, it's OK, Calum pet. Mummy's OK." There was rustling and more sniffing. "There you go, love. Oh look, Peppa Pig's on."

"Liz, I can call another time."

"No! You've got to see this."

"See what?"

"Get your computer out, get online."

"Hang on. I haven't any time, I've —"

"This won't take a second."

"Liz, this better be . . ." She opened the laptop and waited as it came back to life. "All right, it's on."

"OK, go to the Freenet page where . . . You know what, forget it. I've still got remote access, I'll do it."

Maggie watched as the cursor moved, apparently by magic, around her screen. From the internet browser it directed itself to the Freenet and from there to the eerie, unsmiling portrait that constituted victorforbes.gov. Maggie could see that Liz was typing in the password — the twelve letters of "Stephen Baker" rendered as asterisks — that transformed that image into the page that glistened with just a single date. March 15, a quarter-century ago.

Now, though, only a vestige of the original image was visible. It appeared to be slowly fading away on the screen, as square by square it was replaced by another.

On an electronic post-it which Liz had somehow thrown up on the screen, the cursor began typing. Look very carefully.

Before her eyes, a photograph was materializing. It was old, grainy and black-and-white but it looked vaguely familiar.

As the pixels filled out, each one becoming more defined, Maggie saw what she was looking at. It was a newspaper shot of the Meredith Hotel, the night it all but burned to the ground. And there in the foreground were the guests, milling around on the street in a state of semi-dress, most in pyjamas or bathrobes.

Another message from Liz: Do you see who I see?

Maggie looked closely at the picture whose resolution was improving with each second. A cluster of three people were in sharpest focus, their faces wearing the panicked expressions of those caught up in a disaster. And now, with a shudder, she recognized him.

There, hugging himself against the cold night, watching the Meredith Hotel burn down was the man whose face Maggie, along with the entire American people and now the world, had come to know. Younger, unlined but undeniably the same person.

She was looking at Stephen Baker.

CHAPTER
FIFTY-NINE

From TPM Muckraker posted at 16.45, Monday March 27:

> You've gotta love this. With the exquisite timing of the damned, one of the President's key tormentors has just suffered what you might call an ethics malfunction. Sen. Rusty Wilson was all set to play the role of Grand Inquisitor alongside Rick Franklin had the impeachment proceedings against President Baker moved from the House to the Senate. Something tells us Republicans will be revising those plans now.
>
> For Sen. Wilson has just been on the sharp end of a rather unfortunate leak: to wit, the transcripts of every text and email exchange, and every phone conversation, between himself and a thirty-seven-year-old pharmaceutical industry lobbyist from his state who, as luck would have it, is a chesty blonde among whose qualifications for such a policy-intensive job include past service as a waitress at Hooters. The transcripts reveal the senator as a breathy and demanding lover, one prepared to see the sick people of his state pay over-the-odds for prescription drugs, if that would ensure the continuing loyalty of his young mistress.

Maybe this is why they call Republicans the Grand Old Party. Or should that be HOP? Because they certainly seem to be having a Helluva Party.

Be interesting to see if Baker's persecutors on House Judiciary feel as eager as they were twelve hours ago to keep up their moralistic crusade against the President. Or maybe they should check their scripture. Can TPM Muckraker recommend Matthew 7:3? "And why behold you the mote that is in your brother's eye, but consider not the beam that is in your own eye?"

Too early to say Baker's out of the woods, but folks in the White House may be breathing a little easier just now . . .

CHAPTER
SIXTY

Teterboro Airport, New Jersey, Monday March 27, 18.42

For the best part of forty minutes Maggie had sat on the edge of the rear passenger seat, willing the cab driver — turbaned and listening to the BBC World Service — to go faster. He had given her a series of disapproving looks, as if her angst were so much cigarette smoke fugging up his cab. Taking out her compact, she could see why. She looked appalling, like some kind of strung-out addict, pale and drawn and raw around the eyes; hardly a suitable guise for the next stage in her plan. She repaired as much of the damage as she was able to, brushing the unfamiliar hairstyle into some kind of order, applying dabs of concealer, mascara, a touch of lipstick. All it succeeded in doing was papering over the cracks, but it was the best she could manage.

For the rest of the journey she had alternated glances over her shoulder, checking to see if they were being followed, with long spells spent staring at the photograph which she had kept up on her now-offline computer screen. She tried to look at it from different angles, to see if there was any way that the lean, handsome young man in the picture was not Stephen Baker.

She had tried and she had failed.

Could it have been doctored? You could do anything these days on Photoshop. But even as she grasped at that straw, she knew that Forbes would not have gone to such lengths to protect a bogus photograph. This was his "blanket", the insurance policy designed to protect his life. The photo must be real.

And yet, she had seen the picture cherished for so long by Anne Everett, the clipping from *The Daily World* showing young Baker in Washington, DC, on the other side of the continent, on the very same day as the hotel fire. It made no sense.

Eventually the cab passed a sign for the General Aviation building and Maggie jumped out, thrusting a wad of bills into the driver's hand. She looked at her watch: the plane was due to take off in fourteen minutes.

She did her best to straighten herself out and to walk tall. She needed to look like the kind of woman who knew her way around a private airfield for the highest-paying corporate customer.

She strode up to the reception desk. "I'm afraid this is very urgent. I'm here for the AitkenBruce flight to Washington that leaves in a few minutes? I have some important documents to deliver to them."

"Are they flying out of nineteen or twenty-four today?"

"You know, they didn't say. Could you check for me?"

The woman tapped away at her computer. "It's runway nineteen. I'll let them know you're here."

Maggie turned around and headed for the door, the voice of the receptionist calling after her: "Miss! Excuse me! Someone's coming to meet you here. You're not to go out there. Miss!"

As she walked headlong into the wind, vicious in this flat expanse of asphalt, it was a struggle to maintain her confident, head-up-shoulders-back stride. Eventually she broke into a jog. She passed a sign for Runway 1 and, a full five minutes later, Runway 6. It was no good. There was just too much ground to cover. Her sides heaved: her battered ribs complained. She looked at her watch. Six minutes to take-off. She was never going to make it. But she had to: she was perhaps the only obstacle standing between Roger Waugh and Stephen Baker; the only one who could unravel the mystery that tied them together. Taking a deep breath, she drove herself into a faster jog, cursing all the damage that cigarettes and her own bloody-minded refusal ever to visit a gym had done to her poor lungs.

Finally, she saw a marker indicating that she was at Runway 19. Three minutes to take-off. She stood where she was, near three parked, golfcart-style airport buggies, and looked straight ahead.

Before her, separated by a grass strip perhaps seventy yards wide, was the sleek body of a Gulfstream jet. The top half was painted white, with a long curve of black just below the seven passenger portholes. At the rear, flanking the tail, were the mighty jet engines, already revving up. The noise was so loud she could feel it vibrating through her breastbone.

Parked just alongside the open cabin door and the descended staircase was a vehicle no less elegant, a black Lincoln Town Car. That surely confirmed she had come to the right place. She was now in no doubt that that plane belonged to AitkenBruce and that inside that car sat its chairman and chief executive, Roger Waugh.

What was she to do now? Should she just stride up to the car, waving a sheaf of fictitious papers? Even if that worked, then what? She had come this far and yet now, so close, she was uncertain.

Unbidden, a question popped into her mind: What would Stuart say? She was just forming an answer when she felt the sudden and tight grip of a hand on each of her upper arms. A half-second later, there was a hand over her mouth and then — darkness.

CHAPTER
SIXTY-ONE

Teterboro Airport, New Jersey, Monday March 27, 19.01

"Now tell me this isn't the way to travel." The accent was New York, the manner self-satisfied. He spoke again, rapidly, as if he had forgotten something. "Forgive me. Where are my manners? Guys, you can take all that stuff off now."

As the black hood was lifted off her face, light seemed to flood into her eyes. She heard a muffled sound of protest: her own. Now one of the two bodyguards who had dragged her onboard the plane sharply pulled back the strip of duct tape that had sealed her mouth, so that her first audible sound was a howl. It was mixed with a gasp of relief, for now she was able to gobble whole greedy gulps of air — rather than relying on tiny sniffs of the stale oxygen inside that hood.

"Nice to see you, Miss Costello. Welcome aboard. We'll be taking off any moment. I don't need to tell you to fasten your seatbelt."

At that, Maggie tried to move only to realize that she was tied to the armrests at the side of her chair, her elbows and wrists pinned so flat it was if she were a

449

nervous flier tightly clinging to the furniture. Her legs would not move either: they were tied to each other.

She could feel the plane straightening on the runway. Now it began picking up speed, the noise increasing. It was taking off. "Where the hell do you think you're taking me? This is kidnapping. What the fuck do you think you're doing?"

"Come on, Maggie. Let's not get off on the wrong foot." He looked down at her shackled leg. "No pun intended."

Maggie stared at this man directly opposite her, his face corresponding with the picture she had looked up of Roger Waugh. He was bald, with small, mischievous eyes wearing, to her surprise, a rumpled suit and a tie of drab blue. If you didn't know it already, you would never guess that this was the boss of the largest banking group in the world.

The interior of this jet would have given a clue, though. She was facing Waugh, nestled in a wide seat clad entirely in soft, cream leather. Between them was a table, in smooth, polished oak. They appeared to be the only two passengers, save for two middle-aged men with meaty necks in crisp suits: the security detail. The same men, she assumed, who had grabbed her from the tarmac outside.

"You've got a funny idea of kidnapping, Maggie. There's a full bar on this plane, with a selection of Château Mouton Rothschild which you can drink from Baccarat crystal glasses. The carpets alone cost more than your apartment. And if you fancy a snooze — or, rather, if I fancy a snooze — I can go into the cabin where there's a double bed and rest my head on any one of four pillows which — you're gonna love this, Maggie — are made entirely from Hermès scarves."

"I couldn't give a shite how rich you are: you've kidnapped me." Maggie heard the Irish in her accent, a sure sign she was under stress.

"I like to think of it as a meeting. You clearly didn't come to that armpit in New Jersey to admire the scenery: you wanted to see me."

Maggie's brain was spinning. Perhaps it was lack of oxygen; or the sheer shock of the situation. She needed to get a grip. "How do you know what I wanted? How the hell do you know who I am?"

His eyes were disturbingly piercing, though you didn't notice that at first glance. They seemed to bore right into her. "Oh come on, Maggie. You don't get to be me if you don't know what's going on. We've been following you, every step of the way. New Orleans, Aberdeen, Coeur d'Alene, JFK this afternoon. Don't disappoint me: you knew we were there, right?"

Maggie thought of the man across the street from the Midnight Lounge; the headlights in the distance on the way to see Anne Everett. She hadn't been paranoid: her instincts had been right all along.

"So why didn't you just kill me, like you killed Stuart Goldstein and Nick du Caines? It's not like you didn't try."

"An act of over-zealousness. Call it irrational exuberance." He quirked a smile, as if they were co-conspirators sharing a joke. "I'm afraid I was feeling a little pressure from colleagues. And though I detest

451

failure, there was an upside in this case. It meant I could think again, revisit the issue, if you like. I came to see you're of much greater use to us alive."

His smile widened, as if he expected her to be playfully intrigued by this remark.

But Maggie refused to play along. Turning her head from that penetrating gaze, she looked out of the porthole, trying to make her brain work. Who were these "colleagues"? And in what way could he possibly think she was of use to them? Unable to process it all, she asked simply, "Where are we going?"

"We'll come to that. Now why don't you ask me what you wanted to ask? What you came all this way to ask." He settled back in his seat, smiling out of his bald, vole-like head as if he were getting ready to start an amusing parlour game.

At that moment, a woman appeared — early thirties, absurdly pretty — with two flutes of champagne. She nodded sweetly at Waugh as she placed his glass on the table before him, then did the same for Maggie, apparently oblivious to the fact that this particular passenger was in shackles, and then discreetly withdrew.

Maggie clutched at a thought. "People will have seen, you know. What just happened there. Grabbing me — the gag, the hood."

"Oh, I wouldn't worry about that. You know the one thing these private aviation guys learned doing all the rendition work? You'd be amazed what you can get away with in broad daylight. That little corner of the airfield is more or less reserved for us. Not a soul around. And those that are there are paid too well to

452

look too closely." He sipped his champagne. "Mmm. That's very good. You really ought to — oh, there I go again. Sorry, you can't. Silly me. Would you like me to help you?"

Maggie glared at him.

"Please yourself. I always find a meeting goes so much better with champagne. So, to business. We've had to take your phone. Or rather, phones. So many of them, Maggie! One could almost become suspicious of what you were up to. But no phones. We can't risk a recording of this conversation. And Harry and Jack here say they've frisked you thoroughly and you're not wired. Which is good. So let's get to the heart of the matter. I gather you've spoken to Mrs Everett. So now you know almost everything."

Maggie stared back at him. "I know that she has kept a terrible secret for a very, very long time. That someone — probably you — paid her a lot of money to keep quiet about what happened to her daughter. But I don't think she has any idea why."

Waugh looked downward, brushing a speck of dirt off his creased trousers. Maggie decided the costume was deliberate, a way for this billionaire banker not to appear ostentatious when in public: crumpled suits when visible, Baccarat crystal when out of sight.

"I agree with you about that. I don't think she has any idea." He looked up again, the diamond-bright eyes drilling into her. "Which is as it should be."

"Now why is that?" Maggie was thinking of the photograph, unveiled a pixel at a time at Vic Forbes's website.

Waugh put his champagne glass to one side, a signal that the conversation was about to become more serious. "Let me ask you a question, Miss Costello. You're a clever woman. You served on the National Security Council of the President until last week. I am a humble bean-counter, but you have a grasp of politics. So tell me this. Have you never thought about how the great political leaders made it to the top?"

"I'm not in the mood for a political science seminar."

"Have you never noticed how smooth their path was? How the luck always seemed to go their way?"

Maggie thought suddenly of her conversation with Uri.

Waugh was warming to his theme. "Take Kennedy. He won in 1960 by a whisker. Nearly seventy million votes cast, and the handsome, smart JFK edges it by a hundred thousand votes — which just happen to turn up late in the day in Chicago. Could so easily have gone the other way. But no. Kennedy got the break.

"Or Reagan. Remember 1980? Carter sweating night after night to get those hostages out of Iran. Didn't do him any good. Lost the election because the ayatollahs just wouldn't let go. And then, just minutes after Reagan takes the oath, hey presto, the Iranians release every last one of them. Made him look like a hero.

"Or Florida in 2000? Bush loses the popular vote but somehow ends up getting two terms in the White House. All thanks to a few recounts that got stopped in the nick of time and a ruling of the Supreme Court that came down to the decision of a single judge. Gore was

454

a decent man, I suppose, but for some reason fate just didn't smile on him."

"What's your point?"

"I want you to tell me, Maggie. I want you to work it out all by yourself. You're the smart one. And it's not just America, you know. In Britain, that nice, smiling guy with the teeth, remember him? He was prime minister for ten years — all because his party leader had a heart that gave out at the crucial moment. Are you really telling me you never thought about those things? You really thought it was all just a series of lucky accidents?"

Maggie's head was throbbing. She told herself it was the shock, the shoving and gagging at the hands of Waugh's meatheads, or perhaps the bruises and smashed ribs from the car crash in Aberdeen or maybe simple sheer exhaustion. But she feared it was something else: the anticipation of a truth she had glimpsed some time ago, but did not want to see.

"There are no accidents, Maggie. There is no luck. There was a pattern to all those events. There always has been and there always will be."

Waugh looked out of the window, his earlier smile gone, and suddenly the affable vole was gone too, replaced by a reptilian predator. Maggie shivered. This was a dangerous topic, and, for her, probably lethal. She had seen what happened to anyone who knew too much.

"Why are you telling me all this?"

He turned back to face her. "Oh, we always tell them in the end. We always find a way to let them know. That's all part of the process."

"Who's *them*?"

"Those we choose."

"Choose?"

"Maggie, you're being very slow. Come on, you have a reputation to live up to. Yes, *choose*. We spotted Stephen at high school. We have our people everywhere, you know, in high schools, in colleges, keeping an eye out for the smart ones, the charismatic ones, the future stars. We started getting word of young Mr Baker: the captain of the debate team and all that. We sent someone in to take a closer look. They saw it straight away: so handsome, so clever. And that back story. The son of a logger! He sounded like Abraham Lincoln."

"At school? You're a banker and you were aware of Stephen Baker when he was at *school*? What the hell is this?"

"Oh, it wasn't me then, Maggie. It was my predecessors at AitkenBruce, just like their predecessors before them, going back a long, long time, back to the days of McKinley and Taft and all the others you've hardly ever heard of. And it's not just AitkenBruce either. We work together, all the big banks. We realized decades ago that more unites us than divides us. We have the same interests.

"And it's not just America any more, like it was in the early days. It's a global economy now, money floating across borders like clouds in the sky. So we work with our colleagues in London and Frankfurt and Paris. And in Asia too: can't move without Tokyo or Beijing. And the Middle East of course: too much oil —

too much money — there to ignore those places, even if the regimes are a little, shall we say, unsavoury. This is a global enterprise. It has to be."

"And what exactly is this enterprise?" Maggie could feel her legs going numb; she was desperate to stretch.

"Talent-spotting. We're the best talent spotters in the business. Always have been. The original Aitken made his name that way, more than a century ago. That's what we do — what we've always done. And we did it with Baker. We spotted him at high school and we watched him. Kept an eye on him. By the time he was at Harvard, we had made our decision."

"What decision?"

"That he was to be it. Our chosen one."

CHAPTER
SIXTY-TWO

US air space, Monday March 27, 19.21
"Let me correct that. He was *one* of our chosen ones. There are always several. Dozens of them in fact, in each generation. To allow for all eventualities: hedging, if you like. But of that cohort, Baker was our preferred one. If all went to plan, he was the one we wanted in the White House. And, guess what? Despite a couple of hitches along the way, all went to plan."

Waugh smiled, then took another sip of champagne.

Maggie felt her throat turning to dust. So Baker was a hired gun, bought and paid for by the most venal institutions imaginable, the world's biggest banks. The disappointment — in him, in the system, in her own poor judgment — seemed to be choking her from within. So much for all that grand talk of ethics and ideals, of changing the world. Baker was as rotten as all the rest of them, and he had played her. They all had played her, for the fool she was.

Disappointment gave way to a rising resentment, an anger she now attempted to channel. "So it was you who got those opponents out of the way, in the governor's race?"

Waugh put his glass down. "Well, yes and no, Maggie. Yes in the sense that it was us who released the relevant information at the right time. And no, in that it was not me or any of my colleagues who forced the Republican nominee for Governor of the State of Washington to film his wife having sex with other men. He did that all by himself. Same goes for the Mayor of Seattle: no one forced him to use disparaging terms for the city's Hispanic-American and Chinese-American communities." He smirked again, this time in mockery of politically correct convention. "We very rarely force anybody to do anything. That's the joy of politics. It's a human business. There's human error. That's the joy of it, but it can also be a huge pain in the ass. And that's what we try to protect our clients from: unpredictability. To take the unpredictability out of politics. So that they — and we — can look to the horizon and say, whatever I have now I'm going to keep. In fact, I'm going to have more."

Maggie didn't want to hear his philosophizing. She just wanted to have the facts straight in her mind; she needed something firm to hold on to. "And Chester's love-child: was that you too?"

"Well, it was his rather than mine, but yes."

"That revelation changed the presidential election. Chester never stood a chance after that."

"That's true."

"You did all this for Baker?"

"Yes."

"But why? Why would you work so hard to get Stephen Baker elected? He doesn't even *agree* with you. He wants to take on the banks."

"That, Maggie, only makes him all the more credible. For the day he gets out his pen and vetoes the banking bill that threatens to cripple my business. That threatens to deny me and my colleagues the money that is rightfully ours."

A small light dawned in the darkness. Was it possible that Stephen Baker did not *know* he had been chosen, that his path had been smoothed all these years? Maybe it was *him* who had been played all along. Maggie shook her head, confused. "He'd never do it. Why would Baker veto a bill he believes in?"

"Ms Costello, when are you going to get *smart*? This conversation is proving to be a major disappointment. I have junior analysts of the beer industry who are sharper than you are. Come on. How could I know with absolute certainty that he would veto that bill? Because one day, we'd knock on his door and tell him what we have on him. Lay it all out. Show and tell, like at elementary school.

"We'd show him the photos of the Meredith Hotel, burnt to a crisp. Remind him we knew he was there. Maybe we wouldn't even have to do that. We'd probably just have to say a single word." His voice dipped and he let out a breathy whisper, as if he were naming a sexy fragrance in a perfume ad: "Pamela."

"But there's a photo of him in *The Daily World*, shaking hands with a senator in Washington. It was taken on the same day." Maggie could hear the desperation in her own voice.

"Senator Corbyn was always a good friend to our industry. A most co-operative friend. If we asked him to

460

shake hands with a bright young man from his home state, why would he refuse? And as for the date, well, who can blame the editors of The Daily World if they accepted the information they were given? They didn't have the advantage we had: a copy of the photograph duly date-stamped, proving that that meeting between the Senator and the future President actually took place on March 17. Two days *after* the fire at the Meredith Hotel." Waugh paused for effect, to let this sink in, infuriatingly self-satisfied.

"So we'd show him what we have and we'd give him a choice: of course we would. Veto the bill — or we reveal that you left a young girl to die. Simple. That's how we do it. Don't tell me you never wondered why politicians always break their promises, Maggie. Well, now you know."

Maggie felt as if she had been punched, hard, in the stomach. She had clung to that photo of the young Stephen Baker shaking hands with the veteran senator just as tightly as Anne Everett had. They had both desperately wanted it to be true. But now she could not escape what Waugh had told her.

Of course she had believed in Baker more than any other politician she had ever known. So had everyone else. But that wasn't the part of her that ached now. She had believed in Baker more than any *man* she had ever known, with perhaps two exceptions. She had been ready to turn her life upside down for him, because she truly thought he was different: that he was that rarest of people, a good man who would use his talents to make the world better and safer. Surrounded by a morass of lies and deceit, he had seemed . . . solid. Like a foundation you could build on.

Instead he was no better than Kennedy's kid brother, the man who let a girl drown just so he could save himself.

The funny thing was, she wasn't angry with Stephen Baker, not really. She was livid with someone else. Not Stuart Goldstein for insisting that Baker was "the real deal". Not Nick, who had told her she'd be insane not to work for the coolest president of their lifetimes. She was furious with herself, for allowing herself to believe. She had let down her guard — hard-won, over long years — and this was her just reward.

But she was determined that Waugh should see nothing of the turmoil she was feeling. Let him think she had long known the truth about Baker and Pamela. "So Vic Forbes was working for you," she said finally. "That blackmail message was really from you."

He smacked his palms on the solid oak table so hard that the crystal glasses wobbled. "Christ, no! You think we operate the way that prick did? Give us some credit, please. We get a meeting in the Oval Office. We're photographed going in. 'Today the President hosted leaders from the finance industry', all that garbage."

Like the meeting you have scheduled tomorrow, Maggie thought but did not say.

"We go in through the front door. What Forbes did was cheap and nasty." Waugh looked affronted.

"So he didn't work for you?"

"Forbes? As it happens, he *did* work for us. Once. A long time ago. As I understand it, he did some of the very early groundwork on Baker, gathering material in Aberdeen. He gave us the tip-off about the hotel fire, stalking Baker there probably. Jerking off outside the room as Baker got it on with Pamela, for all I know. And he told us about the shrink, which enabled us to destroy all the files and billing records so that they never came to light."

"How did you do that?" Maggie asked, astonished at the sheer reach and depth of this effort.

"A break-in at the doctor's office. No big deal. So Forbes gave us some early help. I'm told there was deep personal animus between him and Baker, which always comes in useful. Meant he was motivated to do the work.

"But after that, no. He joined the CIA, went to Honduras or some other shithole. He was off our radar. We kept tabs on him, of course, but they grew looser. Other people took over the file. And he seemed to have moved on. And then, last week, he pops up all over the TV making those wild accusations."

"Not on your orders?"

"Are you crazy? He was ruining everything! The guy had gone rogue, doing his own thing. I don't know why. Maybe he was trying to get Baker to pay — waiting till he was settled into The Oval Office, reckoning he'd get maximum payout from a sitting president — though that seems nuts. Maybe it was just plain jealousy. He did hate the guy's guts. Everything he wasn't, all that.

"Anyway, we didn't care what was in his mind. We just knew he had to be stopped. He was threatening to throw away our greatest asset before we'd had a chance to use it. All those decades of work would have been for nothing. We'd have been powerless to control Baker."

Maggie was thinking hard, despite the ache in her ribs growing ever more intense. The pain was becoming unbearable. She desperately needed to move. For a moment she considered asking him to loosen the restraints, but couldn't bring herself to do it. She didn't want to owe him even that. She shifted the inch or two her shackles allowed. "You say he'd only worked for you in the early days, in Aberdeen. So how come he knew about the Iranian donation?"

"Well, that was confirmation he was off the reservation. Because that was expressly nothing to do with us. Even *we* didn't know about that. Our information suggests that was an initiative out of Tehran, the mullahs wanting to embarrass Baker. You gotta remember, Maggie, there's a helluva lot of people around the world who don't like the idea of Stephen Baker as President. He's too different."

"So how did Forbes know?"

"Not sure. But, like I said, the guy was an obsessive. Not impossible that he went through every donation Baker received, then traced them. He was crazy enough."

"So you got him out of the way. Sent some bait into that strip club, led him away and that was that."

Waugh said nothing.

Maggie pressed on. "And you did all that to save Stephen Baker?"

"I wouldn't put it quite like that. We needed to keep him in post. So that he would veto the bill."

"Why didn't you save yourself the bother, and just let Chester win?"

"Could have done that. Trouble was, our main asset there was the love-child. We weren't confident that that was sufficiently proprietary — that it was going to remain exclusive. Too many moving parts, too many people sniffing around. Rumours had been circulating for years. With Baker, the Pamela information was hermetically-sealed. No one knew."

"Except Forbes."

"Right."

"So you sent a team into New Orleans, brought them out by private jet. You're like your very own CIA."

Waugh pretended to look offended again. "I like to think our quality control is rather superior to theirs."

"It wasn't such a smart plan, though, was it?" Maggie persisted, beating back the discomfort. "You bumped off Forbes and the next minute, the whole blogosphere's lighting up with claims that Baker's Tony Soprano."

"Call it the law of unintended consequences."

"He's facing impeachment!"

"I think you'll find things are back on track now."

"You mean, the —" She shook her head, too numbed to complete the sentence. So even this latest boost to Baker, the story of the Republican senator and the pneumatic lobbyist, had come from Waugh and his pals. They were behind everything. Maybe even that demo on Sunday, that had seemed to come out of nowhere. At that, Maggie's fatigue and pain was replaced by a sudden onrush of anger. "So why Stuart? And why Nick? Why did you have to kill them?"

"Now, now, Maggie. Don't play the hysterical woman. You can do better than that. With Stuart, we were left with no choice. Not after that phone call you had with him."

"Me? What phone call?"

"The one where Goldstein — you know, 'the man the President listens to more than any other' — threatened to urge Baker to resign. 'Better to leave with some dignity,' he said. No, no, no. We could not have that. Not until the banking bill was dead and buried."

"So you killed him?"

"The coroner's report says he took his own life."

A nauseating wave of guilt passed over her, as she imagined, yet again, Stuart lying dead in Rock Creek Park. She had been ready to believe he had taken his own life — just as this fucker, Waugh, had wanted her to. She flexed her muscles against the restraints, but the plastic ties cut into her flesh, allowing her no movement. Waugh was right to have bound her: if she could, she would have smashed her fist right into his face. How would that be for "playing the hysterical woman"?

"As for Nick," he continued. "I'm afraid that was your fault. You involved him. He found out about this —" he gestured at the smooth, noiseless interior of the jet "— and New Orleans. The line that led you to us. We couldn't risk him publishing that in a newspaper. No way."

"So why not me?"

"Excuse me?"

"I asked you before and you didn't answer me. Why not kill me? I know that you wanted to because, like I said, you tried."

Waugh gave her the hint of a smile. It was chilling. "I repeat, we've come to realize, Maggie my dear, that you're more useful to us alive than dead. At least for the time being."

"How's that?"

"Because you're going to work for us. Negotiate the deal. Isn't that your forte? Maggie Costello the great negotiator? Besides, we know you're close to Baker; you're one of the few people he trusts. All that 'integrity' you both share." He released a smile, short and nasty. "In ten minutes this plane will land in Washington, DC — and you're going to see the President."

CHAPTER
SIXTY-THREE

Washington, DC, Monday March 27, 20.16
The car hummed along sleekly, gliding down George Washington Memorial Parkway with its view of the Potomac, now glittering in the moonlight. They had taken away her phone, so she couldn't call ahead. She would have to turn up at the visitors' entrance to the White House and explain herself.

As they had untied her, she had considered delivering a delayed, but richly-deserved response to her imprisonment, hoiking up a big ball of spit and launching it into Waugh's face, but had baulked at the futility of it. Whatever small satisfaction it would have provided, the meatheads would have paid her back with interest.

Besides, Waugh had not let her go without a warning. Standing on the tarmac in the corner of Reagan National Airport that was reserved for private jets, waiting to step into one of the two glistening limos that had pulled up just a few yards from the aircraft, he said, "Maggie, I haven't been chairman of our little fraternity for very long. There are some of my colleagues — in Frankfurt or London or Dubai — who will say I should have been firmer with you some time ago. But I'm trusting you to live up to your reputation: to achieve better terms than I could. That's why I told you everything. So that Baker doesn't nurture any delusions about defying our will. I trust you to convey what I have said so that he understands he has no choice in this matter.

"And if there are any heroics, he will pay and you will pay. Severely. And so will those you love." He had fixed her then with those chilly eyes, holding the look for two, three, four seconds. "I don't think you doubt that we can do it. So God speed — and don't disappoint me." With that, he stepped into the Lincoln and drove away, leaving her with just one of the bodyguards for company. She cast a quick, sideways glance at the man. Could she outrun him? He was muscle-bound, meaty; she had broken ribs and was utterly out of condition. He'd catch her in no time. She was going to have to be cleverer than that, and bide her time.

The guard then looked left and right before speaking into his lapel: "The Principal has departed. Repeat, the Principal has departed."

That tiny moment stayed with Maggie as they took the 14th Street exit off I-395 and headed into downtown Washington. *The Principal.* Roger Waugh had his own secret service detail as well as his own version of Air Force One on which she had just taken an involuntary ride. This man for whom no one had ever voted and whom hardly anyone had ever seen, conducted himself as if he were the true power in the land, with the elected President of the United States a mere puppet whose strings occasionally became tangled and needed straightening out.

The dread thought weighing on Maggie as she saw the familiar landmarks emerge from the dusk was that when it came to the true balance of power in this country and the world, Waugh had spoken the truth.

She yawned, long and hard. She wanted desperately to fall into a deep sleep, one that might clear her head, allowing her to make a fresh start on this strange, awful riddle, to find time to think, talk to Uri and make a plan.

Uri.

Waugh had been explicit, leaving his warning hanging so that there could be no doubt. *You will pay*, he had said, *and so will those you love*. They had been at JFK: they must have seen her with Uri. The thought of that chilled her.

They had not hesitated to kill Stuart and Nick, when faced with the mere prospect of a disruption to their plans. How much more determined would they be faced with total exposure? And yet she was able to hold that threat over them: they had handed her that weapon. But that was what so few people understood about information. It was indeed a weapon — a sword whose blade was double-edged.

They were here now. The bodyguard nodded at her, nudging her to get out and complete the task she had been set by his boss "the Principal".

She got out at 15th and Hamilton Place and looked upward, seeing the two red lights at the pinnacle of the Washington Monument, blinking in the moonlight. She

470

remembered looking upward at that cool, solid needle after completing her very first day's work at the White House. She had allowed herself to wonder if they were about to make history, if one day there might even be a Baker Monument in this town. She shook her head in disbelief that that was little more than two months ago.

She approached the White House security station, the low-ceilinged cabin wide enough to accommodate two scanning machines and an airport-style arch, through which all visitors had to pass. A guard, young and with a soldier's buzzcut, beckoned her to open the glass door and enter. She began her explanation, that she was Maggie Costello, former official of the White House and that Doug Sanchez was expecting her. They scanned their list of scheduled appointments and shook their heads. Reluctantly, feeling like a traitor who had slipped into her former comrades' barracks only to poison them in their sleep, she told the guard on duty to call Sanchez's office.

While she waited she tried to digest all she had heard in that short, vile flight. The scale and comprehensiveness of their operation was breathtaking. They had thought of everything, not just paying hush money to Pamela Everett's grief-stricken parents, but getting a United States senator to pose with young Baker so that he would have a perfect alibi, printed and published in the local newspaper. They had taken the time to remove the relevant page of *The Daily World* from the archive in Aberdeen, such was their determination to leave no trace.

A moment she had forgotten floated back into her mind: Principal Schilling telling her that he had sent the Baker file to his presidential library, but had noticed that it was "unusually thin". Now she knew why.

"Maggie! Is that you?" It was Sanchez, looking as if he had lost ten pounds in weight and had had only ten hours of sleep in the several days since she had last seen him. He moved past the security equipment and, having approached warily, now opened his arms for a hug. Maggie let him hold her, hating herself for what she was about to do. She could feel her eyes tingling: she was just so exhausted.

"So what's this, you go off the grid in the Pacific North-West and change your whole look?" Sanchez said, as he walked her into the lobby, then turned left towards the Press Secretary's office.

Maggie kept her head down as she walked, hoping not to make eye contact with anyone she knew, hoping she wouldn't have to talk to, or explain herself, to anyone. She wouldn't know where to begin. Inevitably she glimpsed the one person she least wanted to see: the silver-haired Chief of Staff, Magnus Longley, slipping out of one corridor and into another, a portfolio tucked under his arm. She shuddered at the sight of him. He spotted her too. Taking a second to confirm that, despite her new look, it was indeed her, he shot her a glare that clearly said, "What are you doing here? I thought I fired you."

"So what the hell happened, Maggie?" Sanchez, drawing back her attention.

472

"It's such a long story, Doug. And the only person I can tell it to right now is the President. I'm sorry."

He gave her a long, compassionate look which left her feeling more guilty than ever. Then he nodded, suggested Maggie take a seat in his office and embarked on the short stroll down the corridor to the President's personal secretary.

Maggie looked at the TV, tuned to MSNBC. She had been here only a few days ago, but now it felt like a different lifetime. The juvenile egghead from the New Republic was on:

". . . I think the word of the hour is 'exit strategy'. I've been talking to House whips and they say the numbers are just not there on Judiciary for the Republicans to move forward with this thing. Democrats are closing ranks behind the President and those two crucial waverers are no longer wavering. So, as I say, I think the pressure is now on the Republicans to find a way out of this without losing too much face."

The interviewer was nodding: "And what's turned things around for the President?"

"Well, the implosion of Senator Wilson is certainly a factor . . ."

Maggie sighed, knowing that everyone in this building would be jubilant at that news, believing it to be a rare stroke of good fortune. Believing that Baker's lucky streak had at last been restored.

But all she could think of was Waugh's smirking face.

Sanchez appeared in the doorway. "He's ready for you now."

CHAPTER
SIXTY-FOUR

Washington, DC, Tuesday March 28, 10.58
Somehow, despite herself, Maggie had had a decent night's sleep. Baker had only given her one assignment and that she had promptly delegated to Uri. He had agreed to do it on the strict understanding that she went straight home to bed.

Her meeting with Baker had been awkward, no doubt about it. Trapped behind his desk in the Oval, he had blanched when she finally uttered Pamela Everett's name, the blood seeming to drain out of his face as she watched. He had shaken his head, murmuring that this was what he had feared — what he had always feared. He began to explain, to tell Maggie what had happened that night and then he had stopped himself. "This is something Kim deserves to hear first."

He glanced up at Maggie and she could see from his eyes alone that condemnation from her was unnecessary, no matter how much she wanted to express it: he was judging himself harshly enough.

He had then picked up the telephone on his desk and asked that all his meetings be cancelled until further notice, all calls held unless it was a matter of national emergency.

He had sat and listened in growing disbelief as she told him what Waugh had told her: that he, Stephen Baker, had been spotted as a teenager, marked out for great things — that he had been their chosen one. She explained how Waugh and his predecessors had smoothed Baker's path, removing the obstacles in his way one by one. Growing ever more pale, he said quietly, more to himself than to her, "My whole career has been a sham."

Then she spelled out Waugh's ultimatum: veto the banking bill or he would tell all. It pained her to have to say it, to be acting — even against her will — as the agent of those men. But she regarded it as her duty and, through a feat of determination, forced herself to assess and walk through each option that faced him. She wanted to put aside the shock of the moment and speak practically. She wanted, in other words, to do what Stuart had trained her to do.

He nodded and probed at the right places, responding as she sought to approach the problem from all angles, answering when she asked what level of support the banking legislation commanded in Congress, giving a view on how public opinion might respond. He even allowed her to present possible compromises that might be offered to the other side which, years of service as a negotiator had taught her, could always be found if the will was there.

He listened to it all but Maggie knew he was indulging her. His heart was not in it; his heart was not even in the room. At the end of the meeting, he simply nodded and said he had a decision to make.

They parted with a handshake, the President thanking Maggie for her "remarkable" service. His last words to her were, "I know I've let you down. But I will find a way to make this right."

And now Sanchez was on the phone, telling Maggie to switch on the TV.

"Which channel?"

"Any of them."

The President was about to make a live address to the nation, carried on all stations. A pit began to grow in Maggie's stomach. They had discussed so many options, she realized she didn't know which one he was going to choose. Would he fold, announcing a delay in the banking legislation, a move that would at least buy some time to take Waugh on? Would he perhaps opt for the other, riskier scenario she had put forward: that he veto the bill as Waugh had requested, only then to embark on a covert effort to find the congressional votes needed to override his veto and pass the bill into law anyway?

If he did that, defying the blackmail of AitkenBruce and the others, she would have to admire his courage, but it would spell disaster for her — and for Uri. And, given the tentacles of these people, maybe even for Liz and Calum and her mother, too. *You will pay and so will those you love.*

Yet she knew it was wrong to think of her own safety, her own needs, when something so much larger was at stake. Sure, if Baker caved she and Uri and her family would be off the hook, but what would that mean for the country? Waugh would have neutered Baker, he would have destroyed him. Everything he had planned to do — for America and beyond — would be in ruins.

What was he going to do? She realized she had no idea — and the knot was hardening in her stomach.

And suddenly, there he was, at his desk, the stars and stripes behind him.

"My fellow Americans. You have all been through quite a week. I apologize for my part in those events. I promised to bring a spirit of calm to Washington, to lower the temperature of our politics, and these last seven or eight days have been anything but calm." He flashed that Klieg-light smile of his and Maggie felt her heart contract.

"Last night I finally discovered the true explanation for a chain of events that began with the shocking and hurtful revelations made by the late Mr Vic Forbes about my personal past and my political funding arrangements. These events went on to include unfounded rumours linking me to his death; calls for my impeachment and the apparent suicide of my own closest advisor and best friend, the much-cherished Stuart Goldstein." He looked down at the table, seemed to gird himself, and carried on.

"The details of all this and much else will come out in due course, and there will be consequences for those involved. But let me speak about something for which I alone am responsible.

"As you know, I spent my late teenage years in a small town called Aberdeen, Washington. It was a place where even if everyone didn't know your name, they all knew your business." He smiled a rueful smile. "People there worked hard, with their hands, and were as honest as the day was long.

"I went off to college but I always came back for the vacations. I'd get a job, usually in the lumber yards, to pay my way. And it was during one of those vacations that I met a girl by the name of Pamela Everett. She was very sweet, she was very beautiful and if you could ever persuade her to sing for you, you'd swear you'd been given a little glimpse of heaven. And though we were too young to get married or engaged, I loved her very much and she knew it. We would stay up till late, imagining our future together.

"Well, one night we were in a hotel together, asleep in each other's arms. In the early hours, I suddenly woke up to see smoke seeping under the door of our room. I could feel the heat and I could smell the flames. It was a terrible, terrifying smell that I have never forgotten. I shook Pamela — but I did not stay long enough to see if she was fully awake. In the panic of that moment, I rushed out and saved myself. And though I told the firefighters she was there, I did not go back to save her. In the end, it was too late and Pamela Everett died that night.

"What happened was the mistake of a frightened young man and not a day goes by when I do not think of it. I should have been honest about this terrible truth a long, long time ago — but I never said a word about it. Not even to those closest to me.

"I'm telling you this now not because I'm seeking your forgiveness. What I did was so wrong, I don't think I deserve that — not for a long time. I'm telling you

478

because I have discovered that a handful of men — men who hide in the shadows, trying to influence the fate of our republic without ever exposing themselves to the daylight — have known about that grave mistake of mine for many years. And now they are using it to blackmail me."

Maggie gasped with disbelief. They hadn't discussed *this*.

"They want me to abandon a key part of my programme — a programme you, the American people, voted for in your tens of millions last fall — in return for their silence. They believed that faced with that choice, I would save my own hide rather than do what's right for this country I love.

"Well, these men — who spend their lives calculating profit and loss, nickels and dimes — do not understand that you cannot put a price on the workings of the human heart or the human conscience. They calculated wrong. I know I did a dreadful thing and I intend to pay for my actions. That is why I shall resign the presidency effective at noon tomorrow. Vice President Williams will be sworn in as President at that hour in this office.

"I know you will show him the kindness and grace you showed me. And I hope that good fortune — *true* good fortune — shines upon him.

"May God bless his presidency. May God bless you. And may God bless the United States of America — and the precious, fragile world we all share."

CHAPTER
SIXTY-FIVE

Washington, DC, Tuesday March 28, 11.07

Maggie sat, her palms flat against both sides of her face, shaking her head over and over. She wanted the correspondent gabbing on the TV to shut up, but she couldn't move. She was frozen, not so much by shock as disappointment. In truth, it was more than that: it was a feeling she had had at the hands of two other men over the course of her life. It was heartbreak.

So that explained the assignment Baker had given her. He had asked her to draft a short summary of Bradford Williams's career, as personal as she could make it: "triumphs and tragedies", he had said. Exhausted, she had asked Uri to do it for her, to apply to Williams's life the same laser focus he had brought to bear on Baker during the research for his film. Knowing how close to collapse Maggie was, he had worked on it all night.

She had feared this was the reason Baker had asked for such a paper; of course she had. But that made it no less awful to hear out loud. He had resigned. He had sacrificed everything he had worked for his entire life.

480

And then, a guiltier thought. Baker had defied AitkenBruce — and that meant she would pay. She and those she loved.

Twenty minutes later the phone rang. A female voice, level and calm: "Please hold for the President."

There was a click, then another and then: "Maggie, I'm sorry."

"So am I, Mr President. And there are lots of people who feel the way I do right now, all over the world. Was there no other way?"

"I thought about it, Maggie, I really did. I talked about it with Kim. But I couldn't see it. Remember, no one is indispensable, Maggie. Not even me."

"But what about everything we believed in? Everything we worked for?"

"Williams believes in all that, too. Truly he does. He's a good man, Maggie. The work will go on." There was a pause. "He and I are already collaborating on the first order of business."

"What's that, sir?"

"A file detailing the evidence that links AitkenBruce and the other banks to the deaths of Forbes, Stuart and Nick du Caines — and maybe many other deaths too. Lawyers at the Department of Justice and the FBI are already on the case. They're talking to Interpol."

"I'm glad to hear that, sir." Panic was flooding through her: she fought it down. Mastering herself, she let the silence linger and then asked, "What will you do now?"

"I don't know, Maggie. I need to think a while. But I do have one immediate plan."

"Yes?"

"I'm going to fly straight from here tomorrow to Idaho and see Anne Everett. Apologize to her in person. The first of many conversations, I suspect." He cleared his throat. "I've also been thinking about you, Maggie. How to protect you. We need to give you what Forbes gave himself."

"A blanket, sir."

"That's right. A blanket."

"You should have one yourself."

"I'll have the Secret Service looking after me and my family for the rest of our lives, Maggie. But I think I may have found a way for you to have some peace of mind."

"How?"

"One of the advantages of being President is that I have access to the database of the National Security Agency. Ever since 9/11 they've had satellites watching all our airports in real time. 'Eyes in the sky' they call them. Record everything. You just have to know where to look and you can magnify the image, hundreds of times over. They can zoom in on a baggage-handler having a smoke and tell you what paper he was reading."

"I don't see how —"

"It means, Maggie, we have footage from both Teterboro and Reagan National airports which clearly shows you being assaulted and then bundled into an aircraft registered with AitkenBruce on which Roger Waugh was the listed passenger. That footage will now be lodged with Agent Zoe Galfano and her colleagues in the Secret Service. If anything happens to you, Waugh personally — not just his bank — will be the prime suspect."

"Thank you, Mr President." She didn't feel that she could voice her worry that that might not be enough. Hadn't Waugh told her that he had only recently become the leader of his fellow bankers? Even if he was incapacitated surely there were others who would come after her. And Uri. And Liz — and Calum. She shuddered.

"It's me who needs to thank you, Maggie. For everything. I know you risked your life for me these last few days. You put yourself in harm's way, facing men prepared to kill — and you did that for me. I will never forget that, Maggie. Just like I will never forget your passion, your devotion to those who have no other voice but yours. You are truly a remarkable woman, Maggie Costello. And I hope one day to find a way to repay you."

"I don't know what to say, Mr President."

"I also need to thank you for something more immediate — that paper you sent over this morning. On Vice President Williams. Very helpful."

"Was it, sir?"

"Oh, yes. It confirmed what I had suspected, which made me feel all the more comfortable handing over to him."

"And what had you suspected, Mr President?"

"Well, you saw what kind of career he's had, Maggie. Tried and failed to get into Congress three times. Was forty-two years old before he got elected to anything."

"I see."

"No one smoothed Bradford Williams's path, did they? He got there all by himself. It means nobody will have a hold over him. Except the voters, of course."

Maggie smiled. "I think you're right, sir."

"And do you know why that is, Maggie? Because I have a theory."

"What's that, sir?"

"Our friends the bankers didn't bet on Bradford Williams, did they? They didn't spot his talent. And I suspect that was for one very simple reason. They never believed a black man could become President."

CHAPTER
SIXTY-SIX

Wire story from the Associated Press, posted on March 28, 11.45 EDT:

Police in at least four cities across the globe have launched raids against the headquarters of some of the world's biggest banks, in what appears to be internationally co-ordinated action triggered by outgoing President Stephen Baker's stunning resignation announcement.

The key target of the arrests is AitkenBruce bank, which posted $12bn in net profits last year. Its premises in London, New York, Frankfurt and Dubai were raided within minutes of each other, as international law enforcement officers immediately impounded computerized records, ordering what a spokesman called a "total lockdown" so that crucial evidence could not be destroyed.

Update posted at 12.01:

Federal agents have arrested Roger Waugh, the Chairman and Chief Executive of AitkenBruce, at his $35m Long Island home. In front of waiting photographers, Mr Waugh was led out in handcuffs and leg-irons — a signal, according to an FBI source who spoke to the AP on condition of anonymity, that prosecutors plan to level "the gravest charges" against the banking giant and its boss . . .

CHAPTER
SIXTY-SEVEN

One week later

"Ladies and gentlemen, the President of the United States!"

Maggie watched closely to see which senators and congressmen were clamouring to shake the new President's hand and which were withholding their affection. When Baker had done a televised address to a joint session of Congress, the Democrats had all been desperate to touch him, hoping some of his stardust might fall onto their shoulders. But the Republicans had held back.

Now both sides were eager, applauding wildly, stretching to get within back-slapping distance of Bradford Williams as he waded through the thicket of people jamming the entrance to the chamber. Democrats were determined to use the occasion to shore up the new man; the Republicans, Maggie suspected, were keen to demonstrate their colour-blind comfort with an African-American as president.

It took four minutes for all four hundred and thirty-five representatives and one hundred senators, along with the nine justices of the Supreme Court as well as the Joint Chiefs of Staff, in their starched uniforms, to still their applause. When they did, Williams began.

"My fellow Americans — all I have I would have given gladly not to be standing here today. The departure of Stephen Baker was a deep blow to our nation, one that seemed to shake the foundations of our entire system. It will take us a long time to recover. It won't be easy. In fact, it will be hard. For me as well as for you. But together I believe we can do it."

Another round of applause. Maggie noticed that Williams's forehead was already glistening.

"It was a shock not only because this nation had put its trust in Stephen Baker and given him a mandate to govern just a few short months ago. It was a shock because of what we had discovered. That there had been a conspiracy to deny the American people their right to be a free and sovereign people, a conspiracy to hold to ransom the man this nation had chosen as its president. Tonight I am here to tell you and those behind that conspiracy, wherever they may be: this will not stand."

A thunderclap of applause. Maggie sat forward.

"Tomorrow I shall put a bill before you that will regulate those banks who have not only grown too big to fail but too big — period. I plan to curb their reckless dicing and slicing of our money. No longer will our nation's economy be used as a casino. It's too important for that."

By now he was drowned out by waves of applause. But he rode right over them. "I plan to cap their pay, so that it reflects the real world the rest of us live in — so

488

that those who work hard can get on, but those who lie, steal and cheat are no longer rewarded for their efforts."

Maggie watched all but a handful of diehards applauding. The politicians knew how such a populist message would be playing with their constituents back home: they'd be fried alive if they dared to disagree with what Williams had just said.

He talked for a while about education and the environment, with a short passage on social security. He seemed to be getting into his stride. And then he turned to international affairs.

"I cannot promise to be the same as my predecessor. We are different men. But Stephen Baker was full of great plans and some of those now fall to me. One in particular I want to mention tonight.

"A slaughter has been underway for too long far away from here in Sudan, a terrible war against women and children and men who want only to live in peace. No, I'm not going to threaten to invade that or any other country we don't like. Such heavy-handed interventions do not work. But nor am I going to suggest we stand by and do nothing.

"Which is why tonight I am ordering the Department of Defense to prepare the despatch of three hundred of our best-equipped helicopters to the African Union. They will be the eyes watching over that troubled land. If the killing continues, those killers should tremble — because they will be watched."

Maggie shook her head in delighted incredulity. She had assumed that the Darfur plan she had discussed with Baker had been buried the instant he resigned. It was a pet project of his and hers; there were no votes in it. And yet he had clearly handed their plan to his successor. Baker must have told Williams it was a priority too, or it would never have been included in an occasion as important as this one. And then she remembered Baker's parting words to her: *I hope one day to find a way to repay you.*

CHAPTER
SIXTY-EIGHT

Washington, DC, three months later
Maggie surveyed the crowd in the Dubliner bar, trying to work out who worked for whom, which group were Republicans and which were Democrats, who worked for the administration and who on the Hill. Within a minute she had given up. The men in their buttoned-down shirts, chinos and blue jackets, the women in their regulation Ann Taylor suits — they all looked the same. And not one of them would know a real Irish pub if they walked headlong into it.

She knocked back the dregs of whisky in her glass and contemplated ordering another. Uri had texted to say he was running late, so there was no point in watching the door. But still she kept glancing up, hoping to see him come in. She pictured him, his skin warm after a day in the June sunshine. He would be in a good mood: the distributors had just told him his documentary — *The Life, Times and Curiously Short Presidency of Stephen Baker* — had been picked for the Toronto Film Festival.

But still she could not help feeling a little on edge. Why had Uri suggested meeting here, rather than at the apartment? You only selected a neutral venue if you thought negotiations were going to be tense and complicated, she had learned that long ago. So what choppy waters did Uri want to negotiate?

She raised the glass to her lips again, even though she knew there was nothing left in it. It was true that the last few weeks had not been great. After those lunatic final days of March, they had decided to get away, to go on holiday together. They plumped for the volcanic, Aegean islands of Santorini.

Some absurd cloak-and-dagger arrangements had followed, ensuring that their destination remained secret. At the insistence of Zoe Galfano, the Secret Service agent tasked with what was officially called "aftercare", the US consul in the region had been notified and a "discreet" security presence arranged. When Maggie had objected, protesting that Roger Waugh and his pals were now behind bars, Zoe had shaken her head and said plainly that former President Baker had been adamant: Maggie Costello had earned the protection of the US Government.

She would like to be able to blame the guards for what followed, but it was hardly their fault. They had indeed been discreet: close enough to deter anyone planning mischief, distant enough that no regular person would even spot that they were there. What happened was nothing to do with them.

It had started off well enough, Maggie relishing the chance to catch up on sleep, food and . . . Uri. They would wake up late, she waving Uri off as he went for a run on the black sand, and then they would eat an unhurried breakfast together. They would make slow,

492

tentative love in the afternoon — slightly unsure of each other after their time apart — then walk and talk until sunset before eating late. She would look at Uri, still handsome enough to make other women turn their heads, whether he was splashing in the sea or dozing in the hammock, and marvel at her luck. After a few days of the quiet and peace, though, she had found herself itching to pick up the BlackBerry. At first Uri merely rolled his eyes.

"What are you doing?"

"Nothing."

"A special kind of nothing that requires a hand-held device."

"*The New York Times* is running a series on Williams's first hundred days."

"And you want to read it. Even though you're on vacation."

"It's nothing to do with you, Uri, so why should it bother you?"

"It doesn't bother me. I just don't know why you can't lie on a beach and relax like a normal person."

"I don't like being in the sun, that's why. I'm Irish. I burn."

"But you're in the shade."

"That's so I won't burn."

Those clouds would pass eventually, but as the week wore on they came more often.

"What about a swim?" Uri might suggest.

"I've already had one."

"But that was yesterday."

"I think you'll find it was today."

"It was definitely yesterday."

"I'm amazed you can tell: one day is the same as the bloody next."

"We've only been here five days, Maggie! Why don't you read?"

"I don't want to read. I don't want to swim. I don't want to jog and I don't want to get sunburn. I want to *do* something."

She smiled about it now, recalling that Liz had always said her definition of hell would be a two-week holiday alone with her sister. She had been impossible, no doubt about it. Irritable, scratchy and bored.

Since then, Uri had been working flat-out finishing the film. She had spent some time with him in New York, and he had come down to DC for a few last-minute interviews. And now it was completed, he had needed to be in Washington for a dinner with PBS executives to discuss transmission dates. He had suggested they meet for a drink straight afterwards.

She was about to go to the bathroom to sort out her hair, now grown back to its familiar colour and length, when she saw him walk in. Those eyes — at once those of a strong, brave man and a haunted boy — melted her the way they always had. He sat down next to her at the corner table she had been zealously keeping as her own since she had arrived nearly twenty minutes earlier. But when she tried to kiss him on the lips, he offered her his cheek. That alone gave her a small shiver of anxiety.

"So, well done on Toronto!"

"Thanks."

494

"This film is going to be massive, Uri, I'm sure of it."

"Thanks."

"Who knows, it might go down in history as the one successful achievement of the Baker presidency."

"Don't forget 'Action for Sudan'. The helicopters."

"That's true."

"Your legacy, Maggie."

She nodded, felt a fleeting stab of guilt at what she hadn't told him, then ordered drinks. Another whisky for her, a beer for him.

He took a swig straight from the bottle, then said, "Maggie, we should talk."

"That sounds ominous."

"Hear me out."

"That sounds even worse."

"Just listen. Remember that night on the beach in Santorini, when we'd finally settled in and we went for a walk by the sea? There was a full moon."

"Of course I remember." She felt her throat turn dry.

"I had a whole speech prepared that night. I was going to tell you that I couldn't bear being apart — which I couldn't — and that we're meant to be together. I was going to say that life is so short and so precious, and in life we all have to choose. At some point we just have to choose."

Maggie nodded but said nothing.

"I'd made my choice. I was going to say, 'I want you, Maggie. You're the one I choose.'"

She reached for his hand, but he moved it away.

"That's what I was going to say. I had it all planned out."

"And what happened?" Her own voice sounded distant to her. She sensed what was coming.

"You know what happened. You were itching to get away from the moment we got there."

"I don't think that's fair."

"You're always so restless, Maggie. You start a job at the White House — a good job — and then, before you know it, you're jetting around the country, dodging killers in New Orleans and the north-west and —"

"That was an insane, crazy week, Uri."

"It's always insane and crazy with you, Maggie. Something always happens. When we met in Jerusalem you were fleeing for your life. And then suddenly, here, you were doing the same thing all over again."

"Come on, that's just a coincidence. When —"

"Is it though, Maggie? Really? Because I'm not sure I believe in coincidences any more."

"What's that supposed to mean?"

"It means that it can't just be fate or bad luck or coincidence that always leaves you dead-centre in the middle of a shit-storm."

"So what do you think it is, Professor Guttman?"

"I think you like it."

"Have you been talking to my sister?"

"I mean it, Maggie. I think on some level you enjoy it. You *need* it."

"Oh, for God's sake —"

"It keeps happening. You try to come back, settle into a normal life, have a job that would have you sitting at a desk and keeping regular hours and then something always goes wrong."

"I was fired, Uri!"

"For calling the Defense Secretary an asshole! Who writes that on an email, unless they want to sabotage everything they've got? And it worked too. The next minute — boom — you're off nearly getting killed."

"Someone was out to destroy the President! And in case you didn't notice, Uri, they succeeded." Her voice was getting louder: people were staring.

"I'm not saying it's not a good cause, Maggie. I'm just asking why it always has to be you."

"A good cause? A good *cause*?" Now her blood was rising. "Do you not know the first thing about me?"

"I know what you once told me."

"And what was that, Dr Freud?"

Plenty of others would have risen to her sarcasm, but Uri kept his voice low and even. "You said that even though the place was a dump, and there were people dying all around you, and you went to sleep to the sound of sniper fire, you were never happier than when you were in Africa."

"That was bloody years ago. I was young."

"I saw it myself, Maggie. In Jerusalem. You were that close to death every day and you know what? You were loving it. You even said it. 'I've never felt more alive.'"

It was true. Maggie remembered it. Quieter now, she said, "So what are you saying?"

"I'm saying I want you, Maggie. But I also want a life. To live in one place. To have children."

"But I want that too!" She was looking at him now, her eyes reddening. "I really do."

"Maggie, I'm not sure you know *what* you want. But *I* know you'll always want something else more. To save the world — or at least not stay in one place long enough to get bored. It's happened too many times."

The urge to fight back was draining away. She couldn't say anything to change his mind, just as she could never say anything to persuade Liz. Which was because, although she had tried so hard for so long not to admit it, she knew there was an element of truth in what they were saying. Even at the worst moments, whether driven off the road in Aberdeen or coming face to face with Roger Waugh, she had felt the adrenalin thumping around her system. She was doing what she was good at and she was doing it for a good reason. What Uri said was true: she had felt alive.

She looked at him, his eyes dark and intense, his face unmoving. He had tried hard to be with her and she had wanted so much to be with him. They had tried to make it work in several cities and several different ways, full-time and part-time, working and on vacation — and they had driven into the same roadblock every time. It was just as Liz had told her in one of their countless blow-outs, though Liz had been more savage than Uri would ever be. "An adrenalin junkie with a Messiah complex", that was Liz's latest formulation to describe her sister. Maggie had slammed the phone down, telling Liz she could fuck right off, but the line had stuck. Partly because it was such a good soundbite, and partly because it sounded like a judge handing down a life sentence.

498

She could feel the tears building up, but she desperately didn't want to cry: not here. Looking away, she scanned the faces around her and a sudden loathing welled up inside — for the bar, its occupants, for Washington. She couldn't bear to stay in this city a day longer. She had been deceiving herself as much as Uri pretending that she could make it work here.

For a brief moment she remembered the call she had received — but not mentioned to Uri — from President Williams's Chief of Staff, offering her the job of co-ordinator of the Action for Sudan plan. She could accept it on one condition: that she be on the ground, in Africa.

She had been pushing the thought of that offer away, as if it were a guilty treat she was not meant to open. She could see that now. Perhaps they were right about her, Liz and Uri; maybe they knew her better than she knew herself.

She turned to him, forcing the tears back inside. "You know what, Uri? I *do* need to know that what I'm doing matters. And yes, I *do* go out of my mind if I get within a hundred yards of clocking into a bloody office. And let's say you're right and I do get off on the thrill of danger. Let's say all that's true. Is it such a crime, Uri? Really? Is it such a crime to have seen such terrible things in such terrible places that I want to use every ounce of energy I've got to make things better? You can call it a Messiah complex if you want to —"

"I never said anything about —"

"— but this is who I am. And I'm sick of apologizing for it. To you, to my sister, to Magnus fucking Longley.

499

I don't want to be on the couch, I don't want to be analysed. I've learned how to cope with danger, I've learned how to solve problems that apparently freak out everyone around me, and I'm good at it."

He moved to speak but she held up her hand. "I can't be like these people, Uri." She gestured at the lobbyists, lawyers and legislative aides in their Banana Republic uniforms. "I can't keep pedaling away on my little hamster's wheel, chasing the next promotion, never breaking the rules, never thinking of anywhere else in the entire world except this tiny little city."

She looked into his eyes. "You know," she said. "I wanted to be with you, I really did. But I can't be someone else, Uri. It's taken me a long time to see it, but this is who I am. I'm sorry."

She leaned across the table to kiss him long and hard on the lips. And then she stood up, quickly gathered her things and strode towards the door before the tears could fall.

EPILOGUE

That same night . . .
Senator Rick Franklin of South Carolina put aside the memo he had just received, detailing the results of a poll commissioned by CPAC, the Conservative Political Action Conference, which asked likely Republican voters how they rated a series of leading party figures. To his team's delight, he had come in second, just behind the party's rock star former vice presidential candidate who always topped these surveys, if only on the grounds of instant name recognition.

He knew how this had happened. Even if most of the country had been distraught at Stephen Baker's removal from office — prompting vigil-like scenes at the White House, as thousands of supporters gathered outside, holding candles and singing old protest songs — among the hardcore American right it was a day of celebration and Rick Franklin was rapidly hailed as its hero. He was the man whose persistence had driven Baker from office. *The Weekly Standard*, the pundits on Fox, the *Wall Street Journal* op-ed page — they were all as one, anointing Senator Franklin as the frontrunner for the Republican nomination to take on the unelected President Bradford Williams in the election that was now little more than three years away.

His supporters were ecstatic; so was his wife. Only he felt a knot of anxiety at all this presidential talk.

He had seen Baker having to confess to those misjudgments from his past. They had broken him. And wasn't he, Rick Franklin — family man, poster boy of the Christian right — just as vulnerable? His affair with Cindy had gone on for nearly two years; there was nothing they hadn't tried, some of it illegal in several states. He would be destroyed.

It was a good thing she was away for the week, at that conference in Colorado. She would enjoy herself and, when she was back, he would tell her it had to end. She would understand that it was for the best. His mind was made up.

Perhaps twenty minutes later, there was a call from Charleston.

"Senator, it's Brian." One of his lowlier aides, sounding anxious, his voice wobbling as if he were a high school girl at prizegiving.

"What is it, Brian? Come on, spit it out."

"It's Cindy, sir. We've just had a call from —"

"What's happened?"

"She's dead, sir. In a skiing accident."

Franklin felt his heart thumping. Was he about to have a heart-attack? He put down the receiver slowly and carefully and took several deep breaths. He told himself this pain in his chest was grief and, in part, it was. He'd been very fond of Cindy: she was a lovely girl, with a body shaped by the Lord's own hand . . .

But there was more to that tension in his chest than sorrow. A thought was brewing. Was this Providence stepping into the affairs of men, acting to remove the last serious obstacle between him and the White House? Could this have been the work of the same beneficent God who had lent a helping hand at so many other awkward times in his career?

Rick Franklin spent the afternoon making dutiful calls, to Cindy's parents and to his staffers, offering to deliver a eulogy at the memorial service. But in between, he stole another look at that memo and those poll numbers.

They really were very encouraging.

In amongst all the calls was one he hadn't expected. It came from that veteran creature of Washington, Magnus Longley, the man who'd served as Baker's Chief of Staff and been around longer than the Lincoln Memorial.

"To what do I owe this pleasure, Mr Longley?"

"Senator, I just heard about the loss of your very talented Head of Legislative Affairs."

"You are on the ball, Mr Longley: that hasn't even been announced yet, just immediate family and friends."

"I believe I was among the first to know." A long pause. He cleared his throat. "Anyway, my condolences. I was hoping that we might have a conversation."

"Of course. Yes. I —"

"Let me begin by saying — and this may surprise you — that my colleagues and I hold you in the highest possible regard, Senator Franklin.

"We always have."

ACKNOWLEDGEMENTS

Once again I have been assisted by friends generous enough to share their wisdom with me. Richard Adams, John Arlidge, Andy Beckett, Laura Blumenfeld, Jay Carney, Steve Coombe, Tom Cordiner and Monique El-Faizy all deserve to be singled out.

For the fifth book in a row, Jonathan Cummings proved himself an indefatigable sleuth for the elusive fact: working with him is only ever a pleasure. At HarperCollins Jane Johnson — ably backed once again by Sarah Hodgson — was tireless, even keeping the same lunatic hours as I did as she guided this book towards its birth. She was not just meticulous, but sensitive and shrewd. I consider myself lucky to have her as my editor. A word too about Jonny Geller: he's often referred to these days as a "super-agent". What fewer people know is that he is a super friend, a constant source of advice, encouragement and understanding.

Finally, my wife Sarah, along with my sons, Jacob and Sam, had their patience tested by this book, as so often before. It kept me from them for more hours than any of us would have wanted. But Sarah was never anything other than full of love, offering just the right word of support at just the right moment. Every day I feel glad that I chose her — and that she chose me.

Jonathan Freedland, March 2010